SHINE LIKE SILVER

ALICIA HUNTER PACE

carina
press

carina press®

Recycling programs
for this product may
not exist in your area.

ISBN-13: 978-1-335-42486-0

Shine Like Silver

Copyright © 2022 by Jean Hovey and Stephanie Jones

For questions and comments about the quality of this book, please contact us at CustomerService@Harlequin.com.

Carina Press
22 Adelaide St. West, 41st Floor
Toronto, Ontario M5H 4E3, Canada
www.CarinaPress.com

Printed in U.S.A.

For my own HEA hero, Dale. SLJ

For Milla Kennamer Averett,
who talks to me about my characters
like they are real. JPH

SHINE LIKE SILVER

Chapter One

Though Ava Grace Fairchild worried about little, she wondered about a great many things.

Was there a scientific explanation for ghost activity? What happened to the Lost Colony of Roanoke? How many National Championships would Nick Saban win at the University of Alabama before retiring or dropping dead on the football field?

She never wondered, however, how her life would turn out; it was as predestined as Presbyterian salvation. Lately, she *had* begun to wonder exactly when the rest of her life was going to start. In fact, the wondering might have slipped into the worrying category when she wasn't looking.

But the wondering—and the worrying—was over.

The dress Ava Grace had chosen to wear for the occasion of her engagement was pale silvery blue and sparkled like a star in the winter sky. The matching silver and crystal stilettos elevated her already tall frame to regal. She looked in the mirror and felt like Cinderella. Finally, finally her prince had come and she was going to the ball. Everything was perfect.

Almost.

The shoes were one half size too small. She winced as her toes pinched, but she didn't complain. That was something Ava Grace never did. She'd learned her mother's rule early. *"Nobody wants to hear you complain, Ava Grace. It's better to use your words to compliment people."*

Instead, she sat down at her dressing table and removed from the drawer a book with *Gratitude Journal* printed in silver on the dark blue leather cover.

She'd filled up three such books in as many years. As always, there would be a brand-new one under the Christmas tree in two days, pristine and ready for January first.

But then a knock came at her bedroom door. Hastily, she shoved the book back inside the drawer under her well-worn copy of *Anthology of Romantic Poetry*. Before Ava Grace had a chance to open the door, Emma Frances Fairchild glided in, ever tasteful in dove gray beaded silk.

"Hello, Madam Mayor." Ava Grace stood up and turned toward her mother.

"I'm not the mayor tonight. I'm just a mother hosting a party where her daughter is getting engaged."

"You're always the mayor." *You were the mayor even before you were elected. You were the mayor when you were five years old.* But Ava Grace wouldn't dare say that last part; it was too close to snark, the first cousin of complaining.

Emma Frances smiled and ran her hand over Ava Grace's hip. "I don't know when I have ever seen you look so beautiful. What a perfect fit. Hyacinth is a wonder."

The dress was severely straight and fell right above her knees, with a modest slit on each side to allow for walking. Her mother was right about the fit—thanks to the expert tailoring skills of Hyacinth Dawson, who owned Trousseau Bridal. Ava Grace had put as much time and emotion into the selection of this dress as other women put into picking their wedding dresses.

After all, that was a dress she would *not* be choosing. That choice had been made by her great-grandmother fifty years ago. The proof hung on the library wall of Fairvale Manor—portraits of the three generations of brides who had worn the dress that Ava Grace secretly thought of as the Ancient and Honorable.

She would be the fourth to wear it—unless the thing was dry rotted. That was a cheery thought.

"I have something for you." Emma Frances opened a small leather jewelry case. "Would you like to wear this?" She held up a delicate sapphire and diamond choker that had been in the family forever.

"I've always loved that." Ava Grace took the necklace and fastened it around her neck.

"Perfect." Emma Frances adjusted the middle stone. "You know your father. He wanted you to wear Great-Aunt Corinne's sapphire necklace, but I vetoed that. It's too heavy. Anyway, you are so beautiful you don't need something so ornate."

"Thank you, Mama."

Emma Frances gave Ava Grace a conspiratorial smile. "I have it on good authority from Celeste Landry that Skip took his grandmother's ring—the sapphire and diamond one that she always wore on her right hand—in for cleaning."

A wave of pleasure washed over Ava Grace. Any ring would have been fine, but she'd been hoping for that one—hoping, and waiting, for four years. Longer really. For most of her life, but in earnest for four years. It had long been a foregone conclusion that she and Skip—James Patton Landry IV—would get married, that he would propose publicly at the Laurel Springs Christmas Gala. Landry men had been popping the question there since the inception of the party in 1945 when the war was over and Fairvale Manor was brand-new.

Ava Grace sometimes got the idea that her friends Hyacinth and Evans thought she was being ramrodded by her parents into some kind of archaic arranged marriage, but it wasn't true. She *wanted* this—the marriage, the home, the children. True, it was what her parents expected, just as they had expected her brother, Emerson, to go into the family business, but so what? Emerson was happy and so would she be. She considered herself extremely fortunate that their expectations and her desires coincided.

Ava Grace had never doubted that this day would come. Along with their other best friend, Brad, Skip had been a constant in her life from the time they were babies. They'd learned to dance together at junior cotillion and they'd had their first real date when they were fifteen; neither of them had ever dated anyone else. He'd seen her through high school proms, college sorority formals, and her debutante ball. There was no way he would ever let her down in this dance called life.

Still, it had been a long and, in many ways, humiliating four years. She had expected to get a Landry family heirloom ring the December before she and Skip graduated from college—she from Belmont, he from the University of Alabama. He would go to work in his family's investment banking business; they would get married and continue to live in the Birmingham suburb of Laurel Springs Village, a twenty-minute drive from his downtown office.

She'd chosen a dress that year, too, but he hadn't proposed. She didn't question him because one didn't, but he gave her a sideways explanation anyway. After graduation, he was going to work in the Charleston office for "a year or so" before returning to Alabama to "get on with their lives." He thought—and his parents agreed—it would be valuable to learn the ropes somewhere other than the Birmingham office, where his grandfather was still king and his father crown prince.

Fine. It made sense and they were still young. So, Ava Grace spent that next year doing volunteer work, going to the beach and on ski trips with her sorority sisters, and waiting for the next Christmas Gala.

She bought a dress in Vail that Thanksgiving.

Only Skip didn't propose that year either, and people began to whisper. Skip had transferred to the Atlanta office "for a different kind of managerial experience" and offered no explanation, but his intentions seemed to remain the same. He visited, sent flowers on a regular basis, and spoke of *"once we are married"*—though it never seemed to occur to him that she could move to Atlanta, or for that matter, visit him there. In fact, every time she suggested she drive over, he responded by saying, *"I'll come home. It'll be easier."*

She couldn't continue on like life was one big spring

break but, though she had studied interior design at Belmont and passed the ASID exam, she had no desire to pursue design as a career. So, she went to work in her family's long-established accounting firm…where she proved her incompetence every day that God sent. Ava Grace had been blessed with many skills, but a head for numbers was not among them.

She didn't buy a special dress for the gala last year. There was no need. That weekend Skip went to Vegas for a pledge brother's bachelor party, but promised he'd see her at Christmas. She'd fleetingly wondered if he might break with the Landry public proposal tradition, but that was about as likely to happen as she was to buy a wedding dress off the rack at Dresses by the Pound.

Meanwhile, Birmingham was getting a pro hockey franchise and Claire Watkins, an old money heiress and smart businesswoman in her own right, was on a mission to make Laurel Springs an appealing place for members of the Yellowhammers organization to live and spend their money. When she'd approached Ava Grace about partnering to open an antiques and gift shop, Ava Grace jumped at the chance. She wasn't sure if she really wanted to do that, but anything was better than being the boss's inept daughter at Fairchild and Fairchild Accounting.

So now, along with Hyacinth and Evans Pemberton Champagne, who owned a gourmet pie shop, Ava Grace was one of "Claire's Girls."

And she was about to be Skip's fiancée, probably within the next two hours. Skip had come home for good two days ago and would finally be starting work in the Birmingham office at the first of the year.

"I guess it's time to get the wedding dress out of storage and see about alterations," Emma Frances mused.

"And here I just got dressed," Ava Grace said.

"I didn't mean *right* now, Ava Grace. After Christmas."

Ava Grace sighed inwardly. Did her mother really think she was that dumb, that she hadn't been joking? Though to be fair, she didn't let many of the jokes that showed up in her head come out of her mouth. Besides, it had been a trying few years for Emma Frances, too. Tonight she was a perfect swirl of relieved and anxious.

"Ava Grace, Buck and I have been talking. We think after the wedding you and Skip should move in here."

What! Stay in this mausoleum? No. Wearing an old wedding dress was one thing. This was another. Her sole reason for majoring in interior design at Belmont had been so she could decorate her own home—much as her sole reason for minoring in literature had been because she loved it. She wanted a light airy space with an unexpected mix of modern, traditional, and antique furnishings—and a nursery as soon as.

And there was that other thing. From Evans's and Hyacinth's veiled comments, accompanied by blushes and giggles, Ava Grace had begun to suspect that there was a lot more to sex than she and Skip had experienced—but no wonder. They'd never had sex until college and, since that time, they'd only had a few days together, here and there. About the time they'd get used to each other again, they had to go their separate ways. She reasoned they needed extended, uninterrupted time together when they could be spontaneous to achieve what Evans and

Hyacinth had. And it would be better accomplished in a place that was not her childhood home.

"Think of the money you'd save," Emma Frances went on. "We were going to turn Fairvale over to you and go live in the windmill house eventually anyway, like Buck's parents did for us. In fact, as soon as the wedding is over, we'll start doing a little renovating and be out of your hair in a year."

"Mama, I don't think—"

"Now, Ava Grace." Emma Frances waved her silent. "Your brother is never going to live here. He's settled in at the Savannah office and now with the baby on the way and Sharon's parents over there, they aren't budging. So, why shouldn't you? Of course, I'd still want to hold the Christmas Gala here and the spring garden tour. Maybe a few parties and fundraisers now and again, but it would be your house."

Sure it would—right up until the time I wanted to move a Lladro figurine or change a paint color. She wasn't going to argue with her mother tonight of all nights, but she wasn't going to agree either.

After a moment of silence, Emma Frances said, "Well. There's time enough for that. We'll talk to Skip about it. Later. But here's something else to think about—closing your shop."

"What?" Merry hell, had she heard that right?

"Why not? You don't care about it anyway. It was something to do while…while…you waited."

That might have been true at first, and she wasn't doing as well financially as Evans or Hyacinth, but close Heirloom? Sales had improved. More and more lately, she'd been successful with matching the right item with the right person—something Claire insisted was a rare talent that Ava Grace only needed to develop. It was surprisingly satisfying. Also, she loved learning from Claire, and she loved the camaraderie and friendship that she had developed with Evans and Hyacinth.

They were her first truly close girlfriends. Sure, she'd had classmates and sorority sisters who she was fond of, but nothing really deep had ever developed. Skip's sister, Adele, was a good friend, but she was older, already married eight years with two children. Brad and Skip had always been her best friends and she wouldn't change that for the world, but it was nice having girlfriends to laugh, shop, and have lunch with. Without the Claire's Girls connection, she wasn't sure that would endure.

Her mother went on. "Getting rid of Heirloom would free you up to plan the wedding, and you know there will be lots of parties. Plus there's the flower guild at church, symphony board, and your Junior League work to keep you busy. I wouldn't be surprised to see you elected president of League in a couple of years. From my year in that position, you know how much time that takes. And——" Emma Frances smiled and let her eyes sparkle "——babies won't be far off."

Of course she wanted babies—without question. But the thought of closing her beautiful little shop sent a spike through her gut. Couldn't she have both? At least until the children got old enough to have busy schedules? Others did it. Though her mother was probably right—that it would be too much. On the other hand, Claire had such faith in her. When Hyacinth had admitted what a disaster she'd been at Fairchild and Fairchild, Claire had insisted it didn't matter, that she would learn to be as good with a balance sheet as she was at displaying merchandise. And she had learned, though probably not enough.

One thing for sure—she couldn't debate this with her mother when she didn't even know what she thought.

So she did what she always did in such occurrences: she changed the subject.

"Shouldn't we be getting downstairs?" Ava Grace asked.

"No," Emma Frances said firmly. "*I* should be getting downstairs. I want you to make an entrance. Fifteen minutes. Then come down and join us all in the receiving line."

At last, something she could easily accommodate.

"All right. I'll see you then." She touched the sapphire that sat at the base of her throat—the one that perfectly complemented her dress and would match the ring Skip would put on her finger. "Thank you for this, Mama."

Emma Frances stroked her daughter's cheek. "I'm so proud of you, my precious good girl." And she was gone.

Ava Grace stood still and let out the five sighs she'd been holding inside. Then she went back to sit at her dressing table again, opened the drawer, and took out her journal and a gleaming fountain pen. With one bold stroke, she made a thick black line across the page's header. No one suspected that she always struck through the word *gratitude* on the top of each page and wrote in *grievance*.

She didn't feel guilty about what she wrote there.

It was how she kept the things rambling around in her head from coming out of her mouth, or—even worse—from telling the world via social media, as most seemed inclined to do. While Ava Grace wasted as much time as the next person perusing the sites, she wasn't inclined to share even the most benign things about herself.

She had some time on her hands—fifteen minutes to be exact—so she leafed through her journal and read some of her recorded grievances over the past year—though some were not so much grievances as annoyances. No matter. She wasn't allowed those either.

People who go to Las Vegas instead of getting engaged.

People who talk to other people in the room when on the phone with me.

People who go on Facebook and write letters to dead people, especially if the dearly departed in question never had a Facebook page.

People who tell me to keep my fork for dessert instead of giving me a clean one.

She laughed out loud. Petty? Sure. Judgmental? Fair enough. Fun? Without question. Necessary to keep her head from exploding and spewing a river of lava all over whoever was handy? All the yeses in the world. *Oui. Da. Si. Ja.*

The year was almost over and there weren't many pages left. She'd promised herself she would keep her journal for the New Year for its intended purpose, striving to be the same person on the inside that she projected to the world: sunny, kind, and one hundred percent positive.

But for now she still had a few things left to say.

She picked up the pen and wrote:

People who plan my whole life out without consulting me and expect me to wear a dress that three other brides have sweated in and shoes that cut off the feeling in my toes.

Then she hid her book in the back of the drawer again and went downstairs to get engaged.

Finally.

Chapter Two

Luka Zadorov did not want to be at this party, yet here he was.

Not only had the Yellowhammer organization required him to attend, he'd had to pay five hundred dollars for the privilege. True, that was for two tickets, but what good was a second one when he had no one to invite? All his teammates had also been required to buy tickets and he hardly knew anyone else in this godforsaken backwater.

Thankfully, his agent was working on getting him out of here. At twenty-eight, he was playing on borrowed time. *If* he didn't get hurt, *if* his game didn't go to shit, *if* his luck held out, he had maybe five good years left, and he wasn't going to spend them in Alabama. Hockey was his life and he had never played where the sport did not get the respect it was due—not Russia, where he'd gone to hockey school and played when he was young, not Minnesota, where he'd begun his professional career at age nineteen, and certainly not Boston, where he'd spent the past five years being an integral part of a revered and successful team with history and tradition.

And in the blink of an eye, for the need of a goalie, Boston had traded him. This, he understood. It was part of the game, though he had never thought it would be him. You could be on the ice practicing and, an hour later, packing to leave for another team in another city.

But where had they sent him? Birmingham, Alabama, to a brand-new team where no professional hockey had ever been played. It was true the team was doing well enough to bring out a respectable number of fans—though he would bet half of them were not native to the South and the other half were just looking for something to do. He liked his teammates fine. Most of them, anyway. As for the head coach, Luka liked and respected fellow Russian, Olympian great, and former Nashville Sound player Nickolai Glazov.

But none of that made up for living in this godforsaken land of football. That's all they cared about here, and not even professional football. *College* football. *Roll Tide*. Sometimes, *War Eagle*, but mostly *Roll Tide*. That's all they said all day long instead of *hello*, instead of *goodbye*, instead of *how are you*. Women probably screamed it during sex, though he unfortunately had not had occasion to find out.

All those were excellent reasons for needing out of here, but the biggest was he had no intention of staying where Boston had sent him. He had given his all to them and had expected to retire there. In his head, he knew the trade was just hockey; in his heart, he had been betrayed. He had been up front with his new coach about how he felt. Unlike his previous coach, Glaz hadn't been delighted at the prospect of losing Luka, but had said he wouldn't hold him back.

"You're scowling," said Logan Jensen, who suddenly appeared at his elbow. He and Luka had known each other in Minnesota when Logan had played at university and Luka had been with the Walleyes. Getting to play together was one of the only good things about the Yellowhammers.

"*Nyet.* Is my natural expression."

Logan laughed. "This is quite the house, isn't it?"

Luka looked around. "A palace. It seems if they cared so much for history, they would sell it and give the money."

"What are you talking about? You can't give money to history."

"They say that's what the ticket money is for."

"Oh. Wasn't that the historical society?"

"I don't know. I don't care. I paid the five hundred dollars and I came. That has to be enough."

"Why don't we get some food?" Logan said. "Maybe it'll put you in a better mood."

"There is no food."

"Sure there is. They said the food and drinks were on the third story in the ballroom."

"Robbie McTavish says there's only dessert—pie, cake, cookies. Let's leave. We can get real food—beer and a steak."

"Maybe in a little while. I like pie, cake, and cookies. Don't you want to recoup some of what you spent to come here?" Logan moved toward the stairs. When Luka turned to follow him, he caught sight of Ava Grace Fairchild again. She'd been in the line of people who said hello when he came in the door. Now she was talking to one of the waiters and a blond man who looked a little too perfect to be real.

The blond must be the man she was getting engaged to. Too bad. She was as hot as they came with long legs, a body that could keep a man up nights, and silvery gray eyes unlike any he'd ever seen before. Her thick chestnut hair, which fell in waves to her shoulders, deserved a crown.

He'd first taken notice of her at another party he'd been required to attend back in October. After seeing her around here and there, he'd decided to go into her little shop and ask her out. Thankfully, before he had the chance, he overheard a conversation between her and a woman who seemed to be this future fiancé's sister. They spoke of how the men in this family always proposed to their women in front of everyone at this Christmas Gala party and the ring this man would give to Ava Grace. So Luka had bought an antique brooch for his mother and left the shop.

It was of no consequence. He wouldn't be in town too much longer anyway. He'd dismissed the incident—and Ava Grace—from his thoughts until now.

Public proposals—that was something he'd never understand. He'd seen his share of them broadcasted on Jumbotrons and always wondered what would happen if the woman said no. He supposed the men who did that were very sure of the answer, but hadn't he been sure when he'd asked Tatiana? Sometimes *sure* meant foolish.

Maybe there would be a *no* tonight, though he doubted it. Ava Grace knew it was coming and she was here. But she didn't look happy. In fact, she looked to be in pain as she shifted her weight back and forth from one foot to the other. Maybe she wasn't happy—but at least she knew what was going to happen to her for the rest of her life, which was more than he could say.

The great after hockey question: Coach? No. Sports announcer? Hell no. Lazy ass with too much money? Unappealing, but maybe the only option.

"Hey, are you coming?" Logan called over his shoulder.

"*Da.* Sure."

He glanced at Ava Grace again and accidentally caught her eye. She gave him a million-watt smile and a little wave.

He hoped blondie knew what he was getting.

"Do y'all want a drink?" Brad asked.

"No, thanks." Brad dressed as a waiter with a tray of drinks felt wrong to Ava Grace. "I wish you had only been a guest tonight."

Brad's mother had been the Fairvale estate manager for more than thirty years, and Brad had grown up on the property, as much her brother as Emerson. Brad didn't normally work here, of course. He was Hyacinth's right-hand man at Trousseau, but Carolyn Thomas wasn't one bit reluctant to call her son into service when there was an event going on at Fairvale.

"You know my mother. Nobody tells her no. How about you, Skip?" He held out the tray. "Cranberry martini? Or I know where Mr. Buck keeps the good bourbon. I can sneak you some."

"I'm good." Skip looked like a Ralph Lauren ad—golden hair styled to look like he'd just run his hands through it, perfect James Bond style tuxedo. Everyone said they would have beautiful babies. Looking at him, she could believe it.

But something was off with him tonight. He seemed nervous, though maybe that was to be expected. He was about to propose in front of two hundred people. Or maybe his stress came from all the pretending. Ava Grace sure felt it.

They all knew he was going to propose. He knew that she knew—yet they had to act like it was a huge surprise.

Brad was not his usual self either. He seemed almost sad. An outsider wouldn't have noticed, but he was working a little too hard to put on an exuberant face. Maybe that was to be expected, too. Growing up, the three of them had been so close—spending every possible minute together, especially in the summer, swimming, roaming the grounds, playing tennis, and watching movies. Though they'd known this day was coming, Brad probably felt left behind now that she and Skip were finally beginning their life together. They had found love and, though Brad had been in a couple of relationships, nothing had stuck. Suddenly, she desperately wanted another taste of those childhood/school days times.

"Hey," she said. "Let's order a pizza tomorrow night, the three of us, and watch—"

"*Wedding Crashers*!" they all said together. The tension broke and they laughed.

Skip shook his head and smiled. "How many times did we watch that movie?"

Before anyone could answer, the sound of silver tinkling bells rang throughout the rooms. "Attention!" a voice called out. "You're all invited upstairs for a toast. Please make your way to the ballroom."

This was how the Christmas Gala always opened— a welcome from Ava Grace's parents, the presentation to the charity of the year, and a toast to the holiday before the band struck up and the dancing started. But this year it would be different. Skip would propose; she would say yes, and the toast would be for them.

"Are you ready to go up, gorgeous?" Skip's edginess seemed to have evaporated. He winked at her and slipped an arm around her waist. She longed to include Brad in this moment, but she couldn't. She had to pretend like she didn't know what was about to happen.

Skip took Ava Grace's arm and led her up the stairs to the beginning of the rest of her life.

"What kind of pie is this?" Luka asked.

Having had their fill of socializing, Luka and Logan had found a secluded spot behind the portable stage where the band's equipment was set up. The rope barrier had been easy to move, so they figured it had to be only a suggestion that this area was off-limits.

"Lemon chess pie is what the little sign said. Never heard of it," Logan answered. "Are you packed?"

"Yes." Logan had invited Luka home for Christmas and they were flying out tomorrow afternoon. If not for this party, they could have left today after practice. Still, though the time there would be short, it would be nice to be in hockey country again, nice to see Logan's family.

Logan took another bite of the pie. "This is really good. Must be a Southern thing."

"Don't eat all that," Luka said. Besides the pie, Logan had a slice of cake and four cookies on his plate. "Remember, we're getting real food."

"I'm going to put the cookies in my pocket for Alexander. What do you say we get out of Laurel Springs to eat? Go to downtown, Birmingham. I've got a babysitter until midnight."

"Do we have time?" It would be great to eat somewhere different. The team hangout, Hammer Time, had good food, but he was tired of it.

"Sure, if we leave soon. It's only twenty minutes down there."

"As far as I'm concerned, we can go right now," Luka said, looking for a place to set down his pie.

"Wait," Logan said. "We can't. The Fairchilds are taking the stage."

Luka looked around the row of large speakers that obscured them from the rest of the room. They were lining up like toy soldiers. Ava Grace looked as good from behind as from the front. Maybe better.

"So?" Luka said.

"We're not supposed to be back here. Everyone's looking. If Glaz sees us come from behind this stage, he'll skate us until we puke. They're probably going to make some kind of talk. When they're done, people will scatter. We can leave then."

Except for the skating until he puked, Luka didn't care about any of that, but knowing Glaz's stance on the team following rules that hadn't even been written yet, he settled back into the metal folding chair to bide his time.

Microphones squealed and the crowd quieted. Logan started eating cake that was a color of red never found in nature.

"Red velvet," Logan leaned in and whispered, pointing at the cake. "You want a bite?"

"*Nyet.* You shouldn't eat that either. You will pee red tomorrow."

"I probably will anyway. I got hit in the kidney today at practice."

"Information I did not need."

"Quiet."

Luka didn't point out that Logan had started it with the cake talk.

Ava Grace's father had begun to speak. "Good evening, everyone. My family and I would like to welcome you all to the seventy-sixth annual Christmas Gala." He went on to introduce his wife, Ava Grace, a son, and a pregnant daughter-in-law, whose names Luka didn't pay attention to. Maybe he was done.

But no. He suspected that Ava Grace's father was the kind of man who liked the feel of a microphone in his hand.

"As most of you know, the first Christmas Gala was held at Fairvale in 1945 to celebrate the end of World War II. The tradition of the dessert buffet started two years later with the end of sugar rationing."

So that's why there was no real food. It looked like he wouldn't be going downtown to get any either because this man was just getting started.

"It was in 1950 that my great-grandparents decided

to make the Christmas Gala more than a party. They charged twenty dollars admission that year, with proceeds going to benefit the newly built library that still serves our community today."

Even twenty dollars was a little steep for a plate of sugar, but at least there were things to buy for a library. He still didn't see why history needed money.

"This year, we're proud to say that the Laurel Springs Historical Society is the recipient of the proceeds. I'm going to let my wife tell you more about that. You know her as your mayor."

What? More Fairchilds were going to speak? Perhaps Ava Grace, the son, and daughter-in-law had things to say as well. Perhaps they would still be here when the baby was born and it, too, would have a speech to deliver.

Luka finished his pie. Might as well. He'd have plenty of time to be hungry again before he got to eat—*if* he got to eat.

Ava Grace's back was beginning to hurt from standing still in such high heels. As for her toes—they were so numb she wasn't sure if she had any anymore. Daddy hadn't talked as long as usual, but Mama had taken her time presenting the check to the president of the Historical Society and urging people to remember to visit the silent auction tent outside. Now Miss Evelyn was droning on about the projects the historical society had done in the past year and how they planned to use this windfall.

Ava Grace tuned her out and took stock of the room. Skip and his family stood a few steps from the stage.

Skip's sister, Adele, caught her eye and mouthed what Ava Grace thought was "sister." Claire was in the corner with the other Yellowhammer owners. When Ava Grace found Evans, who was standing with her husband, Jake, and the Glazovs, their eyes met and Evans gave her an excited smile. Brad, along with some of the other waiters, was filling trays of champagne flutes. Carolyn was nearby with her clipboard, wearing a headset and the understated black cocktail dress she always wore to Fairvale events. Ava Grace couldn't find Hyacinth in the crowd, but surely she was here somewhere. She was in charge of the silent auction, but she would have stolen away to see Ava Grace get her ring.

Most of the others in the room wore expressions of impatience with a little boredom mixed in. She felt that herself. She wondered if they were impatient to see if it would finally happen or if—yet again—it wouldn't.

But they were about to find out. Miss Evelyn had uttered her final thank-you and Daddy had the mic again.

"I know y'all are ready to get on with the dancing and socializing, but if you'll indulge my family for a few more minutes, Skip Landry has a word to say."

And the crowd went wild, clapping and cheering. Relief seemed to wash over the room and joy bubbled up in Ava Grace. They were happy for her—happy for them!

Skip stepped onto the stage and took her hand. He looked deep in her eyes and smiled the smile he'd been smiling for her since they were in play school at Laurel Springs Country Day. Here, in the crowded room, it was a supremely intimate moment—and a loving one.

"Thank you, Buck," Skip said as he took the microphone. When had he dropped the "Mr." when addressing her father? She supposed she should try to be less formal with his parents now, too. She could try it out tomorrow night when she had Christmas Eve with them.

"Wow. What a welcome," Skip said. "Most of you have known Ava Grace and me all our lives." More applause. Skip dropped her hand, put the mic under his arm, and turned and applauded in her direction.

Ava Grace had never had a moment like this, never felt so adored, so special. Suddenly, she couldn't wait for the wedding. She didn't even care if she'd be wearing someone else's sweaty old dress. And she would never, ever write another grievance. Anyone as lucky as she was had nothing to complain about.

When Skip began to speak again, the crowd went silent. "Over the years, many of you have told me I'm a lucky man." His tone was almost reverent. "Believe me, no one knows that better than I do." When his voice cracked, Ava Grace's eyes filled. He was actually choked up. This was the world's most perfect proposal, so worth waiting for. Skip went on. "There's never been a moment of my life when this woman wasn't part of my forever. That is literally true since she's older than I am." He paused for everyone to laugh. "Don't hate me for telling your age, honey. It's only four and a half months more." He turned back to the audience. "I know you have all been waiting for this for a long time. So have I. And to that end…"

He slipped the mic in his breast pocket, went down on one knee in front of her, pulled a timeworn leather ring box from his pocket, and opened it to reveal the sapphire and diamond ring that she knew so well. He took her hand in his and waited for the applause to die down.

It was almost here. Soon, very soon, the ring would be on her finger and Skip would sweep her into his arms, kiss her, and waltz her across the floor the way they'd been taught in eighth-grade dancing class. The life she had always wanted was finally beginning.

"Ava Grace, there's nothing I can say that could begin to express my love, respect, and appreciation for you. I have tried to become the man you deserve but, somewhere along the way, I realized that could never be, so I just have to be thankful that you're willing to take me as I am. You're my best friend. You always have been. And now, I ask you to do me the honor of becoming my—"

And he stopped. She understood why. His speech had been rehearsed, which in no way made it any less sincere. But he had probably practiced many times. His nerves had gotten the better of him and he'd gotten lost. He was wondering what he had already said and what came next.

She wanted to prompt him. Wife, *Skip! The word you're looking for is* wife!

"Hey, Skippah!" came a voice from the crowd. That would be one of his fraternity brothers. They were the only ones who called him Skipper. "Wife! Get on with it—that or let me have her."

Uneasy laughter came from the crowd and Skip gave her a miserable look. Was something wrong? No, there couldn't be. He was only rattled because he thought he'd bungled the whole thing. This would make it more special and funny in the telling for the next fifty years.

But he stood up, removed the mic from his pocket and turned it off. Then, he hung his head and closed the ring box. "I can't do it," he whispered.

The air in her lungs froze, leaving her chilled and unable to breathe.

"I'm sorry." He was speaking, not to the room, but to her—though no doubt they could hear. They could have heard a feather drift, the crowd had gone so silent. "I am so, so, so sorry, Ava Grace. I love you so much. But I can't."

With that, he turned as if to leave, but she caught his arm.

She had never once expressed to him her anxiety over waiting for this, never asked him for explanations, but that day was done.

"Explain yourself," she whispered. There was vehemence in her whisper, but whispering was necessary if she didn't want this to be a public conversation.

Skip looked around. "Not the time and place, Ava Grace."

He might be right, but no way was she letting him walk out that door with no clue where he was going, or if he would ever come back to explain himself.

"It's exactly the time and place. Give me a reason and give it now."

He looked panicked. "Then come away with me…"

"No. Right now. Right here." She pointed to the floor. She'd been living on his terms long enough and—dammit—she was going to have her way about this one thing.

"Everyone is watching."

"No shit, Sherlock, and whose fault is that?"

He nodded. "All right." He pulled her nearer the back of the stage, away from the bright lights and away from her family, who looked like an exhibit at Madame Tussauds. "I didn't want to tell you like this. I didn't want to tell you at all. I wanted...wanted to do what we planned. But I can't." He swallowed hard and shook his head, looking as inconsolable as a man could. "I'm gay, Ava Grace."

Chapter Three

Well.

That explained a few things.

Skip gave her one more tortured look and left the stage.

She didn't try to stop him.

How many pages did she have left in that grievance journal? Funny what a person pondered at a time like this—as if there had ever been a moment like this in the history of her world.

Then the pondering was over. The room exploded into chaos, and there was no more time for it.

Ava Grace bowed her head and closed her eyes, but only for a second. As much as she wanted to, she couldn't check out. When she looked up again, her brother was staring at her with one part compassion and two parts fury. It was the fury that concerned her. She'd seen that look before and what followed never came to anything good.

"Emerson," she called, but it was too late. He had already jumped off the stage and was hot on Skip's heels.

"Skip!" Emerson exploded. "Stop right there! We are going to have a conversation!"

Emma Frances looked from Ava Grace to Emerson, wild-eyed, and then turned to her husband. "Buck! Do something. This is bad enough without Emerson shouting the house down!"

Damn, damn, damn.

"Mama," Ava Grace said through gritted teeth. "Go with Daddy. Let Skip go."

"Darling!" Emma Frances reached out to her. "What about you?"

"What *about* me? Go, Mama. I'm all right." She wasn't, but there was no help for that.

Sharon had started to cry, but what was new? It was her hobby, especially now that she was pregnant.

Ava Grace quickly inventoried the room. Skip's mother had collapsed against her husband, who looked like he didn't know whether to shit or go blind. Adele was headed straight for Ava Grace, her arms open, her expression horrified. Brad was rushing toward her, too. And there was Evans, running as fast as her shoes would allow, shoving people out of her way, left and right, like some kind of kung fu princess superhero.

They would want to hug her. They would want to say—well, she didn't know what, but whatever it was she didn't want to hear it, couldn't hear it. She needed to process this, if that were remotely possible.

What to do, what to do?

Then she felt two hands close around her waist from behind. Hyacinth? No. The hands were too big. Ava Grace whirled around—and looked up into huge stormy brown eyes.

"Luka Zadorov...?" How had he gotten behind her?

"Do you want me to take you home?" he asked.

"I am home! I live here." Of course, he would assume a woman her age wouldn't still be sleeping in her childhood bed. Who did that? A woman who was too dense to see what was right in front of her, a woman who *waited* for what wasn't coming.

"Do you want me to take you somewhere else, then?"

"There *is* nowhere else."

"There is always somewhere else." His voice was quiet—rational and steady in a situation that was anything but. "I can take you there."

"Ava Grace!" It was a chorus of voices—Brad's, Adele's, and Evans's—and they were close.

Ava Grace only hesitated a second. "Merry hell, yes! Get me out of here."

He jumped off the side of the stage, lifted her down as if she were a rag doll, and ran toward the back of the room, half dragging, half carrying her.

"Way out?" he said.

"Behind there." She pointed to the curtain on the back wall that hid the opening to the old servants' passage.

Instead of pushing it aside, the hulking hockey player, her very unexpected white knight, ripped it down.

He knew it! Public engagements *could* go wrong—though Luka hadn't imagined one could go this bad.

And now he had the casualty of that bad plan in his charge.

He still wasn't sure what had come over him, but Ava Grace had stood there ramrod straight and taken it when a lesser woman would have run, fainted, or burst into tears. He knew something about that from the last time he saw Tatiana—though that had only been private humiliation while Ava Grace's had been public.

"Thank you!" Ava Grace said breathlessly when they reached the bottom of the final flight of stairs.

He opened the door to the outside. "Was nothing." They stepped outside and he looked around trying to orient himself. "Where is large tent? That is where I park."

"This way." She headed left.

When she stepped into the grass, her heel sunk into the ground, causing her to stumble. Luka considered picking her up, but took her arm instead.

"Here, I will help you. We should go through tent. Is shorter distance."

Ava Grace shook her head. "No. There may be people inside at the silent auction. I can't see people."

They took the long way around and he guided her to where he'd parked his Harley-Davidson.

"What?" She looked at his motorcycle with horror. "You don't have a car?"

"*Da.* I have car. But I have this, as well. I did not know I would be giving a ride."

She looked back at the bike and screwed up her pretty face.

"I am safe with motorcycle," he assured her. "I have never crashed."

"It's not that." She pulled at the bottom of her skirt, testing it, it seemed.

Oh. The dress was tight. It was a dress for taking little steps, getting engaged, and slow dancing—not for climbing on a bike.

"Do you have car?" he asked.

She spread her hands to show that they were empty and looked toward the house. "No key."

He fished his phone out of his pocket. "I will call Uber."

She straightened her spine and set her jaw. "No. I can do this."

And with that, she kicked off her shoes, ripped her dress from hem to hip, and climbed on the back of the bike.

His mouth went dry. His eyes wouldn't look away.

What a woman. What a leg. She tried to cover herself, but with little success. Except for a thin strip of blue lace with a little bow below her hip, she was basically naked from the waist down.

He wished for more light.

He wished he could untie the bow.

He wished he wasn't a horn dog with no control over his thoughts.

He tossed her his helmet. "For your head."

"What about your head?"

"I told you, I never crash. Besides, my head is used to getting banged about."

Mounting the bike was awkward with Ava Grace already on, but he managed without kicking her. She'd been kicked enough tonight.

He revved the engine. She wrapped her arms around his waist and they roared off into the darkness.

He felt a smile creep onto his face. He couldn't remember the last time that had happened.

Chapter Four

As they flew through the cold night past houses decked out for Christmas, the lights laughed at Ava Grace with every twinkle.

If she had wondered at all where Luka was taking her, she would have assumed to his place. It didn't matter. Hell was better than home right now. She'd figure out what to do next when she got there.

That might take a while, though. How did you figure an alternate path for a twenty-six-year-old one? One by one her dreams exploded—the independence from her parents, the new modern house mixed with the old things she had been collecting, and the babies—oh, God, the babies.

Luka slowed and turned into the Laurel Springs Inn.

Well, of course. It was the obvious solution. And not a bad one—or it wouldn't have been if she had a credit card, a phone, and wasn't half naked. Actually, the credit card probably wouldn't be much of a problem. The people here knew her. She'd never stayed here, of course, but she'd been eating at the historic inn at least once a week all her life. As for the phone—she didn't want to call anyone anyway and if she did, there would be a landline in the room.

Navigating the lobby with her fanny hanging out of her barely there thong was a bigger problem—but she would do what she had to. After all, it would come in a very distant second on the list of the most humiliating moments of her life.

She expected Luka to drop her off under the front canopy, but he went around back and pulled into a parking place. Now to get off this thing.

"A moment, *dorogaya*." Luka cut the engine. "Is best to dismount while I am still on bike to keep it stable." He fiddled with a few things. "Is safe now."

Getting off wasn't the most graceful thing she'd done all day, but not the least either.

Once on her feet—*bare* feet—she tried to pull her dress together, but it had been tight and there wasn't enough material.

"I can't thank you enough, Luka. It was…a lot. Goodnight." She removed the helmet and held it out to him.

He swung his tall frame off the motorcycle in one fluid, athletic move and took the helmet—but instead of putting it on, he hung it on the handlebars.

"A lot. Yes. Too much, I think. Though why a man would do such a thing I can't think." He got a faraway look in his eyes, then shook his head, removed his suit jacket, and held it toward her. "Come. Put this on. I should have given to you before, but—as you say—it was a lot."

She could have cried. The jacket came well below her hips. "You're the best person on this planet." Her feet might be bare and she might not have any money, but no one was going to see her butt—and on a night like tonight, that was a priceless blessing. She buttoned the jacket. "I'll take good care of it and get it back to you. Goodnight."

He looked confused. "*Nyet.* We go inside. You are cold. This way. I have back-door access."

"You do? How?"

"This is where I stay." He removed a key card from his pocket and led her to the door a short distance away.

"All the time?" she asked once they were inside. The inn was nice—posh even, included on all the lists of best boutique hotels in the South. Hockey players made a lot of money, but this must be costing him a fortune.

"*Da.*" He looked around like he was casing the joint. "My time here is short. My agent is exploring other options for me." He met her eyes. "I am on second floor. The stairs are here, but if you prefer elevator—"

"No." She moved quickly toward the staircase. Jacket or no jacket, being spared the lobby was yet another gift.

She owed this man big-time.

The brass plate on the door read *Bryant Suite.* Ava Grace had never been inside, but she knew the story. Alabama's legendary football coach had stayed here when recruiting in the Birmingham vicinity. It was no surprise the living area was decorated in black and white houndstooth with crimson accents. Nice. Tasteful. It could have so easily been overdone with bad art depicting Bryant–Denny Stadium and the man himself.

She stopped to inspect a lampshade. Ecru silk. So many people ruined the look of a perfectly fine lamp with a shoddy shade. She was a snob about lampshades and only sold silk ones at Heirloom.

And now her mother wanted her to sell Heirloom.

The universe quaked around her. No. That was in a different world, where she was going to have a wedding to plan and parties given in her honor. Her head began to spin and she grasped the edge of the table. What the hell was wrong with her, standing here thinking about houndstooth, lampshades, and a dead football coach when her whole world had been blown to bits?

In that moment, the cold caught up with her and she began to shiver. Luka had said outside that she was cold, but she hadn't felt it then.

"Here." Luka appeared beside her and took her by the shoulders. "Come and sit." He led her to the sofa and disappeared into what she presumed to be the bedroom. When he returned, he covered her with a soft gray blanket. "Was cold on motorcycle."

"You must be cold, too." The sapphire and diamond choker was biting into her neck and she considered removing it, but remembered her mother's mantra: *"The quickest way to lose your jewelry is to take it off."*

"*Nyet*. Not so much." He tucked the blanket around her shoulders. "I am Russian. I live my last five years in Boston. Before that, Minnesota. This is nothing."

He stood in front of her now. She'd met him several times, but had never really taken stock. His looks were very different from Skip's, who was practically Nordic. Luka's thick dark hair fell in layers, and she got the feeling the slightly shaggy look was intentional. His face was all smooth planes, high cheekbones, with large brown eyes and a full, sensuous mouth, the lower lip slightly plumper than the top—not that she was any authority on sensuality.

Luka loosened his tie, removed his cufflinks, and rolled up his shirtsleeves with smooth, efficient moves. Everything about him shouted capable and that was very appealing.

Please, God, don't let him start asking me questions because I don't have any answers.

And he didn't. Instead, he told her things.

"I will go downstairs now and secure a room for you. I will bring you a drink to warm you and ease your shock. I will also get some food and maybe you will eat something."

His words were a lifeline. They meant she didn't have to think of options or make decisions. Even in her state, she knew those were the very things that contributed to where she'd landed tonight and that needed to change, but it couldn't be right now. For now, there was a plan and she hadn't had to make it.

"Lie down if you like," Luka said. "I shouldn't be long."

She didn't lie down, but settled into the large downy crimson sofa pillow and took a deep breath. A good smell invaded her senses—maple, cedar, and a layer of something she couldn't identify. Maybe balsam. It was a comforting, safe scent. Then she realized it was coming from Luka's jacket that she still wore. She remembered now catching the scent as they sped down the highway away from pandemonium. She didn't want to think about that; she didn't want to think about anything. She let herself sink deeper into the pillow, buried her nose in the lapel of Luka's jacket, and put her mind on cruise control.

Luka had failed at his mission.

The drinks had been easy—hot cider and brandy, though he would probably do no more than sip his. As for the food, he'd ordered a hamburger for himself and asked for a selection of food he thought a woman like Ava Grace would like—some tiny sandwiches, a bit of fancy cheese and fruit, and some of the scones they ordinarily served only at breakfast. He'd tipped more than the meals cost since Ava Grace's food wasn't on the menu.

The stumbling block had been the thing he needed most—a room for her. He needed her out of his. There were no rooms to be had, though, because of the people who had come from out of town for that party from hell. He considered knocking on doors and offering bribes until someone agreed to vacate, but figured they were all still at the gala, eating cake and reliving the drama.

There wasn't much chance she would want to go back home tonight, and who could blame her? He supposed he could take the sofa and let her sleep in his bed.

Sleep in his bed. Ebat! The image of that, even without him beside her, was not what he should be thinking of.

He would go to Logan's for the night after she settled in. That was the best solution. After she had her drink and some food, he would give her one of his shirts to sleep in and...damn. He wanted her in his shirt. He wanted her in his bed.

Yes. Logan's was the best plan. She was too tempting and he had never taken advantage of a woman in his life.

Sure, he'd gotten around when he was younger. After Tatiana, he'd landed in Minnesota with a nineteen-year-old libido and a broken heart ripe for the puck bunny trail, and he'd gone down that trail for a long time. But it had gotten old, and by the time he'd landed in Boston he was done with it. He'd dated some, of course—a couple of models, a ballet dancer, and a couple of women who were famous for being famous. Nothing had stuck more than a month or two until Marla. He'd been with her for over a year, though they'd never lived together. She was his investment banker and he liked her. Both of them seemed to want the same thing, which was nothing more. They might have stayed together, at least until he'd been traded, if her biological clock hadn't had a talk with her head. She'd been very forthright about it as soon as she knew her mind. She not only wanted a baby, she was determined to have one. She liked him; they got along. And she was basically giving him the right of first refusal.

He had refused. There'd been no hard feelings. She still managed his finances and she had a husband and one-year-old. After that, he'd dated here and there again. Pleasant times, good sex, but nothing that had rocked his world.

But *this*—Ava Grace. He couldn't explain it, but he didn't need to.

All he needed to do was provide her with a drink, some food, and a bed, and leave her to sleep. Maybe take her home in the morning, depending on what she wanted.

He stood outside the door of his suite and took a few deep breaths. He had to get in there before her drink got cold and her little sandwiches got stale—and before he thought of her in his shirt in his bed.

Too late.

Stop it! he commanded himself. *Even if she wasn't hurt and confused, she's not for you. Like Tatiana, she's way, way out of your league.*

That settled things down.

Chapter Five

Ava Grace wasn't sure how much time had passed when Luka maneuvered his way in the door, carrying a tray full of food and drinks.

"You should have knocked," she said. "I would have opened the door for you."

"No need. I earn my living balanced on blades. I can handle tray. Should I put it here?" He nodded to the coffee table in front of her. "Or the dining table?"

"Here, please." If she never had to move again it would be too soon.

"Bad news. There were no vacancies, but after we eat, I will go to stay the night with Logan and you may stay here."

"I'm sorry to put you out. Maybe I could…" *Could what?* Go home? Call Evans, Hyacinth, or Brad? Or even better, call Skip? Those were all the people she had run away from.

"I don't mind. He has an extra bed and we are good friends." He placed the tray and came to sit on the sofa beside her. "For you." He held out a mug. When she took it, his hand landed on top of hers and he left it there for a moment. "Your hand is still cold, but this will warm you—hot cider with brandy. I asked them to go light on the brandy."

"Good idea." She sipped. It was delicious and comforting. "I've been enough trouble tonight without being drunk on top of everything else. And I'm a cheap drunk."

"Perhaps you do not hold your liquor well, but there's nothing cheap about you."

"Thank you for not denying that I've been trouble. I couldn't trust you if you did that."

He shrugged. "Only a small bit of trouble and I offered my assistance." He held out a plate with tea sandwiches, cheese, grapes, strawberries, and a scone, not unlike a Regency duchess's repast at afternoon tea. "You may not feel like eating, but maybe a small bite?"

She almost waved him off. After all, it was expected that someone who'd been the costar of such a real live horror movie wouldn't want food. Luka didn't expect her to eat; he'd said as much—and he didn't even know the whole story. She wondered idly if anyone else did.

Then it hit her. Brad knew. That accounted for his unease earlier. If she knew him—and she did—he would have tried to talk Skip out of going forward with the plan to propose tonight, but Skip must have insisted on powering through. She understood Brad's loyalty to Skip, but what about his loyalty to her? Shouldn't he have told her?

"Would you like me to take this away?" Luka held out the plate.

But she was hungry and well past tired of doing what was expected.

She took the food. "I'm starving. I may eat it all—unless you want some?"

His mouth twitched in what might pass for a smile. "*Nyet*. I'm starving, too, but I have this." He picked up a burger, took a bite, and a bit of ketchup landed in the corner of his mouth. She had the strongest desire to wipe it away, but she wasn't fast enough.

His tongue darted out and licked it away. Her stomach turned over.

She ate a sandwich and then another. For a while, they ate silently, but it wasn't awkward. He wasn't expecting her to make witty, interesting conversation; he wasn't expecting anything—and that was nice. She watched him eat, his jaw moving as he chewed. Appealing. He must have felt her eyes on him because he looked up.

"Are your sandwiches good?"

"Yes. Chicken salad, pimento cheese, and smoked salmon." She knew the inn's dinner menu by heart and tea sandwiches were not offered. He must have asked for them specially. "Thank you for getting them for me."

"You're welcome. If I had known you were so hungry, I could have gotten you something heartier. I still can."

"The kitchen is probably closed by now." As soon as she said it, she realized how ridiculous that was. No closed kitchen would stop this man. "But no matter. This is great. Perfect."

He held out his plate to her. "Would you like some of my French fries?"

She almost said no, but why? Truth was, she *did* want the fries and he *had* offered—just as he'd offered to get her out of hell earlier. She was in the habit of giving more thought to what was expected of her than what she wanted, but why shouldn't she have what she wanted?

"Only if you'll share the cheese and scone," she said.

"I'll have some cheese, but no scone. I had pie at your party." He raked half of his fries onto her plate and took a slice of Gouda and a chunk of saga blue. "We can get more food if we want it—anything you like."

She ate a bit of brie. "A consolation prize for not getting engaged?"

He produced that almost-smile again. "Sure. Why not? Not as good as getting engaged, I suppose, but is something."

She sighed. "I don't know. In this particular case, I think I'm better off with the grapes."

"This particular case?" Luka took another bite of his burger.

She hesitated. Skip's news wasn't hers to tell, but on the other hand, Luka ought to have an explanation for his trouble. Besides, it wasn't as if Luka was part of Skip's life or ever would be.

"Please don't repeat this, but it would seem that Skip is gay. He told me when I took him aside and demanded to know why he was walking out on me."

"I see." Luka nodded and ate a fry.

"You don't seem surprised."

He shrugged. "There had to be a good reason for a man to abandon a woman such as you."

That gave her ego a lift—brought it to only a mile below sea level.

"But still no reason to handle it as he did," Luka continued.

"Ah, well. Things happen," she said flippantly. She wasn't ready to think about Skip right now. Eventually, she would have to, but eventually wasn't tonight. She popped a grape in her mouth and held one out to Luka.

They locked eyes. Instead of taking the grape with his hand, he leaned forward and captured it with his mouth. Her fingers landed on his lips and she felt them move as he ate the fruit.

Something stirred in her. She wanted him. Oh, she wasn't stupid; she knew exactly what was going on. She'd fallen off a cliff, he'd caught her, and she wanted to cling to him, to escape. A little voice inside her told her to jerk her hand back, look away, and pretend she'd never had that thought. But the big voice inside her said she should do what she wanted. It didn't have to be complicated. He'd said he wasn't going to be in town much longer.

His eyes still held hers, but she broke the gaze and looked him up and down.

He wanted her, too—or at least wanted sex and that was good enough for her. She knew this not because she was savvy or empathic.

The proof was in the bulge in his pants.

She ripped the sapphire choker from her neck and tossed it on the table. "Don't go to Logan's tonight."

"What?"

"Stay with me."

How much could one man be expected to endure—the long looks, hands touching around her mug, her fingers on his lips? And the bow on her underpants—couldn't forget that.

And now this—an outright invitation.

He closed his eyes. "I can't."

"Can't you?" He'd not heard that tone in her voice before and it commanded that he open his eyes and look at her.

"I'm not that kind of man."

"What kind are you?"

"I often wonder that myself, but I'll tell you who I'm not—one who takes advantage of a woman who is…" *Weak* was the wrong word, but he couldn't find the right one. Despite his accent, his English was near perfect. Ava Grace had robbed him of his words. "…vulnerable." He finally stumbled onto it.

"*Advantage?* Really? Seems like I was the one who did the propositioning. And I have to say, that makes you pretty special, because that's not something I've ever done before. I'm not usually one to speak my mind or put myself out there."

"Which is why I must say no. That's not who you are. You were rejected tonight—"

"Thanks for the reminder, but I got that. And don't tell me who I am. I've had a gut load of that."

Where had she found that sassy mouth? Or had she had it all along, but never opened it—at least in his limited contact with her? Damn, it made him want her all the more. His head pounded, his heart pounded—his feet ought to be pounding their way out of here.

"You owe me nothing," he said.

"I do, though not this. Nobody ever owes anybody sex. But I've had a rough night. I was thinking more in terms of what I want."

He took a deep breath. "It would be wrong of me. You're hurt, and are reacting to pain."

"Even if all that were true, do you think being with you would be the worst thing that happened to me tonight?"

"*Da.* I do. Being taken advantage of is…" What was this woman doing to him? Again, he couldn't find word. *Predosuditel'nyy.* "Bad," he substituted, but *bad* wasn't good enough. "Of the devil, even worse."

Her silver gray eyes caught fire. "You listen to me, Luka. People have been telling me what to do, what is expected of me all my life—what I want, or ought to want. So far tonight, you have treated me with respect, as an equal."

"You *are* equal—better than equal. You deserve respect."

"Then don't ruin it now by telling me what I want. I'm a grown woman with a made-up mind and it's time I let people know that, starting with you." She shrugged. "Now, if you don't want me…that's a different matter."

That was his undoing. "Not *want* you?" He grabbed her shoulders. "All I've done is want you. *Proklyatiye!* Has nothing to do with what I want. I *want* to finish ripping that dress off you and look and touch every part of you."

She threw the blanket off her, stood up, and let his jacket drop to the floor. His head spun. She held her arms out, palms up, as if to welcome him in an embrace.

"Then do it." The commanding, the sass was gone from her voice. Now her tone was beseeching. "There's not enough of it left to save."

With that, he found out what a man's—or at least

this man's—limit was. He jumped over the coffee table to get to her and did as she asked.

Angely na nebesakh. She stood regal in the blue sparkling underpants that were no more than ribbons and a playing card. She was so beautiful in the matching transparent bra that he was torn between wanting to rip it off and kiss her through it.

It made no difference to him that she'd worn those things for another man, the man she thought would become her husband. She was his now, at least for tonight. He wanted to fall down and worship her. It was killing him not to touch her, but he couldn't yet.

"If we do this," he said slowly because he knew his accent was growing thicker as his passion grew, "you must understand that once will not be enough for me. I must have you many times before morning."

She opened her eyes wide, suddenly looking as innocent as an angel. "I've heard that's possible, but I have no proof."

"You'll have your proof, *dorogaya.* You'll have it all night long."

And with that, he did something he'd never done with another woman: he threw her over his shoulder and carried her to the bed.

Chapter Six

She was airborne and Luka was on the move—aggressively so.

He'd proven himself to be capable, but who knew he was so strong? He had to be. He was holding her over his shoulder with one hand while he ripped the duvet from the bed with the other—and, at five foot ten, she was no slip of a girl.

When he laid her down on the soft sheets, his actions shifted to tender. His eyes, inches from hers, were soft, his lips parted.

She had to kiss him. She would have grabbed his lapels if he'd had any. As it was, the collar of his shirt would have to do. She was pretty sure she heard it rip. By the time his mouth met hers, it was open and ready for action. That was when she stopped being the boss of the kiss and he took over, all soft lips, exploring tongue, with the perfect amount of wet. She opened her mouth wider, welcoming him, but he wanted another kind of welcome.

He parted her legs and settled there, never breaking the kiss.

She was overwhelmed with the feelings coursing

through her, putting her in sensory overload, yet it wasn't enough.

When they came up for air, she blurted her thoughts. "It's never been like this."

Luka rose to stand over her and unbuttoned his shirt. "I would guess not. You are the most beautiful woman I have ever seen—a goddess. You deserve everything. I will give you everything."

And he dropped his pants. Not only appealing. Impressive—*damned* impressive.

"Well, well, well. You have *a lot* to give."

And he came to her. His hands were magic, his mouth a miracle. She had expected a fast coupling, but he had other thoughts. He was slow and so very, very thorough—kissing, sucking, and exploring every part of her, guiding her hands to explore him.

Somewhere along the way, she had a revelation—he was *enjoying* her, relishing every second. It was a heady feeling. He moaned to show his pleasure and whispered sweet things as he drove her to places she'd never been.

"It's lovely, but it must go," he said as he tossed her bra aside. "And this, as well."

He reached for her thong, but didn't slide it off right away. In fact, he was uncharacteristically fumbling a bit, pulling at the elastic below her hip. She raised her head to get a better look.

"These pants—they are confusing," he said.

"In what way?"

"The bow." He pulled at the elastic again. "I have wanted to untie it ever since you climbed on motorcycle."

She willed herself not to laugh. "It doesn't untie. It's decoration."

He let out a frustrated cry and ripped them right off. "*Krastoka*, you need no decoration."

And with that, he buried his face where her thong had been and she shattered into a million pieces.

That was only the first time. So many times—with his hands, with his mouth, and finally inside her— he brought her almost to the point of no return, then down again, until she begged for more, then begged him to stop.

"Too much for you, *dorogaya*?" He stroked her hip and kissed her brow.

"Overload. I can't take any more—not right now."

He chuckled. "Then I have succeeded. Was good for you?"

"No. It sucked."

"That too, you say?" He got out of bed.

"Where are you going?"

"Not far." He retrieved something from his dresser drawer and climbed in beside her again. "Here is this. I do not want you to grow cold." He slipped a T-shirt over her head. It had his smell.

There was something about that sweet gesture and his repeated attempts to make sure she was warm; it did something to her. Though she didn't see it coming, didn't feel it coming, she collapsed on his chest and began to cry.

"Ah, there it is. I've been waiting for this." He put his arms around her and stroked her hair.

Luka let her cry for a while. He'd distracted her for a long time—and admittedly, very well—but it wasn't going to last forever. Too bad. She had been eager to please and never had he been so pleased.

"It's been hard day," he prompted her. Maybe she needed to talk.

"Hard and good and confusing," she said.

"I know the hard. I know the good. The confusing? I don't know. What has confused you?"

"How could I not have known? I must be a complete moron." Her words were rich with tears. "I knew things weren't all that great in the bedroom, but I thought it would get better once we were married, living together...had more time. But this..." She stroked his cheek. "We needed no time."

"Time would never have fixed it. None of it was your fault, Ava Grace. It could not be."

"I tried so hard. So did he, but sometimes it didn't work at all. Other times, it was adequate. Or I thought so at the time."

"No surprise." Though he didn't want to hear the answer, he asked, "Were you very much in love with him?"

She hesitated. "Of course, I loved him. I still do. You heard him. We were children together. We never dated anyone else—or *I* haven't. Unless... Is this a date?"

He laughed a bit and brought her hand to his lips. "*Da.* I think so. Do you want it to be?"

"Yes. I want to have dated somebody else." She had stopped crying.

Somebody else. Not him particularly, but that was fine. "Then you have."

"I guess I knew our love was not like what others

had. It was—" She stopped short. "You don't want to hear all this. And it's not like me to spew my emotions."

Luka propped himself on his elbow. "I do not mind, and maybe you need to—as you say—spew. Maybe you need to tell someone how you feel."

She nodded. "Our love was quiet and companionable, not passionate and...volatile, where you laugh one minute and cry the next. Skip never once made me cry—at least until tonight. I thought that was a good thing, but maybe I was wrong."

He hesitated before speaking. Who was he to school Ava Grace on love? But he spoke anyway. "I think that is difference in loving and being in love."

She sniffed. "Maybe you're right. Sometimes you have to get over being in love when it doesn't work out."

"That is God's truth." She was wiser than she knew.

"But how do you get over loving? Plain loving, not being in love?"

"Why do you have to?"

"Isn't it obvious?"

"*Nyet.* Is obvious you won't marry him, but you don't have to stop caring for him. Maybe you need some time to breathe; maybe not. You don't have to throw him out of your life—not if you do not want to."

"You know what Lord Byron said about friendship," she said.

He laughed a bit. "No, *dorogaya*. That, I do not know." Why would he? Such babble had no place on the ice.

"I'm paraphrasing. Friendship may grow into love, but love never settles into friendship."

What? "Maybe this Lord Bryon is wrong. Even if

he is not, were you ever really in love? Either of you? Perhaps you can salvage this friendship you once had."

"You're very sympathetic toward him."

"You think that? *Nyet.* I think he behaved like an ass. But he's not part of my life. I don't have to think well of him. Is not as if he is my teammate."

"He played football in high school, you know. Quarterback."

"Bah. Football. I should have known."

"You find him distasteful because he played football?" There was a bit of amusement in her voice. That was good.

"Is a good reason, though not so much as for his bad timing and embarrassing you."

"I know he didn't always realize he was gay," Ava Grace said. "I think when he figured it out, he thought he was in too deep."

"Is understandable that he didn't always know, but he clearly knew before tonight. He's an ass for not ending it with you privately."

"Hard to argue that. I'm so dumbstruck, I don't even know if I'm mad."

"You don't have to know. When you do know, you can change your mind. You can change it over and over again—mad one day, sweet the next, then back to mad. Don't let anybody tell you is not your right." He ran his hand up the back of the T-shirt she wore—his T-shirt—to rub her back in little circles.

"Thank you for that."

"Was nothing."

"Was everything. I have to give myself permission to be Ava Grace."

"That makes no sense."

"It does to me. Luka? Have you ever been in love?"

He wound one of her curls around his finger. "Yes, but not for a very long time."

"It didn't end well, I take it?"

"*Nyet.* Else I wouldn't be here with you." He kissed her and moved his hand to her luscious little breast, hoping to distract her from this conversation.

It worked. She shifted and ran her hand up his thigh and beyond. He reached to remove the T-shirt.

"No. Leave it on. I like wearing your shirt and I don't need anything else. I'm ready for you now."

If he hadn't been ready for her anyway, that would have put him over the edge. He reached for another condom.

Honestly, he had more sympathy for Skip than he'd let on. He could see how it would be easy to get in too deep with Ava Grace.

Not that he was in danger of it—well, except in one way.

She raised her hips to help him accomplish that.

But then again, maybe there was no such thing as too deep.

Chapter Seven

When Ava Grace woke, she thought it was the morning of the gala and that her blue silver dress was ready and waiting.

Then she remembered. That dress was lying in tatters on the floor—like all her future plans. Her heart raced. She didn't do things like this. What had she been thinking?

And yet, she didn't have any regrets. The night with Luka had been a revelation. Sex could be good every time and orgasms did not have to be hard-fought. Beyond that, it *had* been a sweet time. He'd held her all night, even after they were too drained to have sex again.

But he wasn't holding her now. She turned and opened her eyes, only to find an empty space beside her. Where was he? She sat up and listened—no sound of the shower or movement in the next room. He was gone and it wasn't only the silence that told her so. She could feel it; there was no life at all in the spaces around her.

Did the Yellowhammers practice on Sunday mornings? Was it still morning? Yes, but it was going fast. The clock said 10:22. Her parents must be frantic.

Then it hit her. It wasn't just Sunday; it was Christmas Eve. She groaned aloud. It had never occurred to her that Luka wouldn't be her way home.

Maybe she should call someone else to come get her. Even if Luka had only gone out for coffee or a newspaper, she'd been enough trouble to him.

Besides, she needed someone to bring her some clothes.

Evans would do it without question—if she and Jake had not already left for the Delta for the holiday. Even if they hadn't, she didn't want Jake to know she'd spent the night with his teammate. Hyacinth was a better choice. She reached for the landline on her bedside table, but realized to her horror that she didn't know Hyacinth's number. There had never been a need; it was programmed into her cell. She didn't know anyone's number except the Heirloom and home landlines. Heirloom was closed and she'd rather walk home naked than call her parents—which, come to think of it, she'd have to do if she walked anywhere.

There was nothing to do but wait. Luka had to return sometime.

Or did he? This had been a onetime incident and they didn't owe each other anything.

He'd said he wouldn't be with the Yellowhammers much longer. Maybe the trade had come through. Since becoming a hockey fan, she'd been doing some reading. Sometimes players had to leave within hours of being traded. But on Christmas Eve? Seemed unlikely. Maybe he'd gone somewhere for Christmas.

Surely, he wouldn't have left without waking her. On the other hand, what did she know about him? He'd been amazing last night—in more ways than three—but how was she to know how he'd act after a one-night stand? Or was it a hookup? Was there a difference? She'd never needed to know.

She sat up and looked around. His phone charger was on the bedside table, but that didn't mean anything. People left chargers all the time, especially if they were in a hurry.

Her gut said he wouldn't have abandoned her, but maybe he had. Not that she was his responsibility, but he had been so caring last night. What to do, what to do?

She never had to figure that out. Relief rained down on her when she heard the door open.

Seconds later, he filled the doorway. "Sorry I was gone so long. Not enough checkers for such a big store. So many people who waited until last minute to buy things for Christmas." He crossed the room and put a bag in her lap. "I guessed at the sizes."

When she opened the bag, she almost cried. A Paris original couldn't have been more welcome than the sweatpants, socks, white granny panties, and knockoff Converse sneakers.

"Thank you," she whispered.

He held up the panties. "I tried to get such as you had before I destroyed them, but it became too confusing. I will give you a clean T-shirt and sweatshirt." He moved to the dresser, opened a drawer, and removed the garments. "There are clean towels in the bathroom."

He left the room and closed the door behind him.

The encounter had been so fast that she'd had no time to discern if it had been awkward. Did he have regrets? Probably not. This kind of thing was almost certainly old hat to him. It didn't matter anyway. He'd be gone soon.

Oh, well. No matter. Last night had been fun, but there wasn't going to be a repeat. Her out-of-character behavior was understandable considering, but this was a new day, and Ava Grace didn't do out of character. She found her bra under the bed before heading to the shower.

Nothing like being fourteen years old in a twenty-eight-year-old body.

When Luka had entered the bedroom, he'd almost kissed Ava Grace, but had hesitated and questioned his inclination like a fourteen-year-old would. It had been that long since he'd given such a gesture any thought. If he wanted to kiss a woman, and she seemed inclined, he did; if not, he didn't. It was that simple—but nothing was simple about this morning after. There was no question of what he'd wanted. He'd longed to crawl back in bed with her and re-create everything they'd done last night, only more and better—if that were possible.

But he had been unsure of what she wanted. Usually, he never gave it much consideration, trusting that the woman would rebuff him if they weren't on the same page. That seldom happened, but when it did, he politely walked away and never thought of it again. But if Ava Grace rejected him, he was afraid he would give it a great many thoughts.

When he heard the shower turn off, Luka put the pod

in the coffee machine and pushed the button. He hoped she didn't mind the little pots of creamer, provided by the hotel, that wasn't really cream. If she used cream. Not since his puck bunny days had he not known how a woman he slept with took her coffee. But he didn't know if Ava Grace drank coffee at all.

The machine spewed and hissed the last drop into the insulated disposable cup. It was ready if she wanted it, though it might be cold by the time she emerged. He'd assumed she'd be out soon after finishing her shower, but—again—how was he to know? She didn't have makeup, but there was hair and she had a lot of it.

The coffee cup was still hot in his hand when she came through the bedroom door wearing the clothes he'd provided for her.

"I'm sorry the pants are too short," he said.

"Don't be," she said. "You'll never know how much I appreciate it."

What was *it*? The clothes? The rescue? The orgasms? He'd been too busy to count how many she'd had.

She lifted her red-sneaker-clad foot and moved it in a circle. "These are the best shoes I've ever had. I'm never taking them off. I might sleep in them."

That image—Ava Grace naked in his bed except for the shoes he'd bought for her—moved through him like water through a sieve. He almost crushed the cup in his hand. If she'd been glamorous last night, she was cute and sexy today in the too-short sweatpants and the Yellowhammers sweatshirt that came halfway to her knees. It was a Sunday kind of look, made for cuddling and napping on a couch, with a hockey game on the television and a midafternoon lunch. But by midafternoon today, he'd be on a plane with Logan and Alex and she'd be back to her life.

He held the cup out to her. "Do you want coffee?"

"You're a prince." Not the best choice of words to describe him. She took the cup and sipped.

"There's sugar and such by the coffee machine."

She shook her head and sipped again. "I take it black."

So noted. If there was a next time. And perhaps there would be. It wasn't as if she was going to reconcile with Skip.

"Would you like some breakfast? We could go down to dining room, or I could have something brought up."

"No, thank you. My parents will be worried. I need to go home, if you don't mind taking me."

"I don't mind at all."

He minded very much.

Outside, Luka helped Ava Grace into his Range Rover. "I thought we'd be going on your motorcycle."

He'd told her last night he had a car. He supposed it was understandable she didn't remember. What else had she forgotten?

He slid under the wheel. "This vehicle is good on the ice and snow. Not true of the Harley."

"You won't get much of that here," she said. "What little we get never lasts long."

"I am hoping to be where a snow-worthy vehicle is needed soon."

"You like snow that much?"

"No. Snow, I can take or leave, but with snow comes ice—real winters. With real winters comes hockey and the love of it. Here, people do not love hockey. They worship football—college football. I want to be back in a real hockey city—where you can taste the competition in the air, where men will fight in a bar for the love of the game."

"That happens here, too. But—as you say—it's over football."

"Do you buy into this football lunacy?"

She shrugged. "It's a way of life here, like hockey is a way of life up North. Both my parents went to the University of Alabama." She swallowed and looked at the floorboard. "Skip, too."

"But not you?"

"No. I went to Belmont—a small private school in Nashville."

Probably expensive and elite, like her. Strange that she and Skip had not gone to the same university. Perhaps if they had, she would have discovered the state of things and last night wouldn't have happened. But if that hadn't happened, he and Ava Grace wouldn't have happened and that would have been a shame.

"This Belmont—is that the team you care for?"

She laughed. "No. They don't have a football team. If they did, it wouldn't be elite Southeastern Conference. No, it's Roll Tide all the way for me."

"Roll Tide! You ruin a perfectly good day with those words. I grow tired of them. At least it will end soon after this National Championship game everyone is speaking of."

"Don't count on it. The season may be on hold, but it's never really over. I'm surprised you're willing to stay in that suite."

That made no sense. "The rooms where I live? Why?"

She laughed. "You don't know? The *Bryant* suite—named for Coach Bear Bryant. He's a legend. He wore a houndstooth fedora. That's why the room is decorated like it is."

He groaned. "Those little checkers?"

"Checks. Yes. I thought you knew."

"No. See? Is everywhere. I cannot escape. No one cares about hockey."

"I do," she said.

That was a surprise. "You go to Yellowhammer games? You understand the rules?"

"I do go. I have season tickets. I'm understanding more and more as time goes on."

"You go to *all* the games?"

"Home games. I did miss a few when Alabama was playing."

"See there? You choose football first."

"Not all football. Just my team. And that's not fair. There's only one football game a week per team. There are lots of hockey games."

"My point. There are eighty-two hockey games a season, not counting playoffs. And we must perform on skates. Yet, football gets all the respect."

"Not all," she said.

"No?"

"Lots of people love baseball, too."

In spite of himself, he laughed. She was making jokes. That meant she felt better. Maybe it was partly because of him.

"Do you know when you're leaving town?" she asked.

"No. The trade deadline is the last Monday in February. It can happen after that, but guys traded after the deadline cannot participate in the playoffs. There will be none of that for me. I will be wanted for the playoffs."

"Oh."

There was surprise in her voice—maybe because he was leaving too soon, or not soon enough. Not a question he wanted—or needed—an answer for. Because, after all, he was leaving. He had a couple offers on the back burner, but was waiting for better.

"So it's a sure thing you're going?"

He hesitated. "Almost. I was honest with Coach Glazov and he was honest with me. He would like me to stay and will not trade me without my knowledge. I could be forced to stay, but he will not do that. My agent is looking out for opportunities. When an acceptable one comes my way, he will arrange it."

"Why do you want to leave? Do you dislike your team?" Ava Grace asked.

"No. Most are good guys. Some annoy me, but that is true of every team. Logan is my best friend and I like Coach Glazov. He is a Russian and an Olympic gold winner—like me, though not same Olympics."

She was quiet for a minute. "I assume you like the practice facility and the arena downtown. Everyone says they are some of the best."

"*Da*. Is true, though, for me, ice is ice. Some quibble about good ice and bad ice, but I adapt. Nice workout room."

"So you're saying what you hate is the South and Laurel Springs."

"*Nyet*. Not exactly. Is not what I'm used to. I feel... wrong. Like I'm not home."

"I'm sorry." She sounded like she really was—sad. He'd said too much. At least he'd stopped before he'd said hockey was his life—his only life. "This makes me wonder why you came here to begin with."

"I had no choice. I was traded. It's the way of the game. This, I understand, but we don't always like things we understand. Above all else, I do not like being in a place I was forced to be. I want to choose."

"I understand about wanting to choose. I'm sorry that you don't like it here. There really is a lot to love."

He had insulted her home and he regretted that. "I like this barbecue you have," he offered. "And grits. The inn serves them at breakfast. With cheese."

"Both very fine things. Hampton's has the best barbecue. It's a hole in the wall out in the sticks, but everybody goes there. You should go, if you haven't. Get the pork."

He had not been there and he didn't know where the sticks were. Maybe he would ask if she would like to go there with him, show him the way to these sticks.

"Would you like—" he began as he turned down the long tree-lined driveway that led to her house.

"Wait. Stop here," Ava Grace interrupted him.

"Stop?" He didn't understand, but he hit the brakes anyway.

"I'll walk the rest of the way."

He started to protest, but changed his mind. It was clear. She would rather walk what had to be a half kilometer in the cold than be seen with him by her family. If she wouldn't let him drive her to the door, she would certainly not want to go to the sticks with him where "everyone" went to eat pork.

She unbuckled her seat belt, but he made no move to get her door. Too risky being seen by people who mattered to her. Bitterness flooded his mouth.

Ava Grace opened her door and turned toward him. "I can't—"

"Thank me enough. I know. So you have said. Good luck, Ava Grace." He let his eyes bore into hers and willed them to be cold. She sat still for a few beats.

"Goodbye," she said softly.

After having been with Ava Grace, Luka saw her home at the end of the driveway in a different light. Fairvale, they called it. It was not just a large house where a party had been held, but a great, shining fortress. Ava Grace carried herself toward her fiefdom, tall and proud, eyes straight ahead. The absence of royalty in this country didn't stop Ava Grace from being a princess of her own little corner of the world—like Tatiana.

After one final glance, he pulled away.

Tatiana hadn't been a princess, not literally, but close enough. Luka had known that her family lived in genteel poverty and were proud that they descended from nobility, but he hadn't known how proud. After all, the exalted classes were a thing of the past in Russia.

They had met at his teammate's birthday party, and he had fallen hard and fast. It was as if she broke something inside him that allowed insecurities and fears to flee and good things to seep in.

She had seemed to return his feelings. Looking

back, he realized it was significant that she had always wanted to meet him somewhere, only allowing him to come to her house a few times in the eight months they were together.

But he hadn't thought much of it at the time. He'd been cocky, a top pro hockey draft prospect with a shiny Olympic gold medal. He'd thought money was a great equalizer and if he had enough, he could have any-thing—even Tatiana. When the contract came through with a signing bonus for more than he'd ever dreamed possible, he'd bought Tatiana a big, Western-style di-amond engagement ring. After all, they were going West, where she would never live in poverty—genteel or otherwise—again.

But Tatiana had not cared about any of that. She wasn't unkind, but she was matter of fact. She liked him and it had been fun, but they were of different classes. She thought he understood that. No matter how much money he made or how many Olympics he played in, he was still the son of the owners of a neighborhood restaurant that served good, but common, hearty, tra-ditional Russian food. She was nobility, and meant for something else. As far as leaving Russia—unthinkable.

In a mad fit of passion, he'd thrown the ring in the river. He could afford it; the Walleyes had wanted him badly.

That had been a long time ago and it had been his last fit of passion—until last night.

And last night had just walked away from him.

No matter. Even if he wasn't leaving, Ava Grace wouldn't want him. She would want someone from her own world, like Skip, only straight—straight, willing, and able was essential for Ava Grace. He'd learned that much last night and he suspected she had, as well.

The sooner he left, the better. If Tatiana had broken something loose in him, Ava Grace could do more. There was something beyond broken: destroyed. She could destroy him. It would feel good as it was happening, but what would be left once she walked away—as Tatiana had done?

He turned back toward the inn and stepped on the gas. He was hungry. After he ate, he'd give Kurt a call and see how the trade search was going.

Chapter Eight

The rental company was breaking down the silent auction tent.

Ava Grace searched the area to make sure her mother wasn't out trying to supervise. She loved to do that—supervise things she knew nothing about. All Ava Grace needed was for Mama to see her walking down the driveway. She hadn't thought about how she would explain returning on foot. Explaining her disappearance and absence was going to be bad enough without throwing how she'd spent the night with Luka into the equation.

Her parents were going to be nine parts worried and one part angry—not that she blamed them. She would have felt the same if they'd done something similar. But so far, so good. There was no evidence of Emma Frances. Ava Grace could carry through with her plan to say she'd gotten a ride and gone to the inn. She didn't have to mention that the ride had been on the back of a Harley-Davidson motorcycle and she hadn't been alone.

But she was alone now. She'd never felt so alone, and it wasn't only losing Skip. There was a void where Luka had been, and their parting had been strained and awkward. She couldn't sort that out any more than she could sort out how she felt about Skip and his place in her life, if there was one. But there was no time for that now. She had more immediate problems—like what she'd say if they wanted to know how she'd gotten home.

Maybe with everything else going on it wouldn't come up. If it did, she'd make up something. She hated to lie, but sometimes it was the only option for people who didn't have the guts to say, *It's none of your business.* These were desperate times.

She cut around the house and went in the kitchen door. Maybe she could snag another cup of coffee before facing the music.

She stopped short. Music was waiting for her. Her father was sitting at the table calmly drinking coffee and reading the paper.

There was no surprise in his face when he looked up—no panic either.

"Sister, there you are," he said as if she were returning after an hour of shopping. He got up, crossed the room, and hugged her. "I sure do hate this happened to you."

"Where is everybody?" she asked.

"The staff is off. Emerson and Sharon left this morning. They had to get back for Christmas with Sharon's folks. Your mama has gone to church."

"Church?" How did you go off to church after such a debacle, without knowing where your daughter was?

"She had to go teach your Sunday school class."

Right. She and Molly Abbott taught the preschool class, but Molly was opening the toy store today for last-minute shoppers. Ava Grace would have been on her own, so she should have been grateful to her mother. But she wasn't feeling grateful at this particular moment. Leave it to Emma Frances to do what was expected, no matter what. Perhaps Ava Grace had overestimated her importance in their lives.

She headed for the coffeepot. "Glad to see I didn't worry y'all." A bit of sarcasm crept into her voice.

Either Buck didn't notice or he was cutting her some slack. He took her arm and steered her to the table. "Sit down here." He poured a cup of coffee and set it in front of her. "We were worried about how you're feeling, but we knew you were safe."

"You did?"

"Do you think I wouldn't have been tearing this town apart if I hadn't been sure of that? We figured out you left with Hyacinth. She's the most levelheaded young lady ever born. We knew she'd take care of you."

Ava Grace had been about to sip her coffee, but set the mug down again. They knew *Hyacinth* would take care of her—not that she could take care of herself.

"Hmm. How did you know I was with Hyacinth?" The more correct question would have been, *Why did you* think *I was with Hyacinth?*

"She went missing about the same time you did. Her car was still here, but we figured she got blocked in and called an Uber. She's not the kind to stand around wringing her hands."

Like me? Clearly, her father admired Hyacinth for being all the things they'd raised her not to be. Ava Grace was torn between using her energy to be offended and wondering what had happened to Hyacinth. She'd been seeing Robbie McTavish, but they'd had a messy breakup. Maybe they had made up. Or maybe she'd had enough of the party. Either way, Hyacinth was fine, or they would have heard about it.

"So." She took a drink of her coffee. "I assume Emerson didn't make a scene with Skip."

A storm cloud moved over Buck's face. "No, but I doubt they'll be taking any fishing trips together anytime soon. I wish I had turned Emerson loose on him."

"You don't mean that."

Buck ran his hand over his face. "No. I don't, but I'm plenty mad."

"I suppose I am, too, but do you think it would have been better if he'd married me—given that he didn't want to?"

Buck frowned and sipped his coffee. "Sister, I know now that it was more than he didn't want to. He couldn't."

Her head snapped up. "You know? That he's gay?"

Buck nodded. "Jim and Constance paid us a visit early this morning. Skip came out to them last night and they figured we had a right to know why their son jilted our daughter with half the town laying witness. Said he told you right before he made his exit last night—and that it wasn't a secret, that they could tell anybody they saw fit."

Oddly, Ava Grace felt some of her burden lift. At least she didn't have to worry about whether or not to tell her parents news that wasn't hers to tell.

"Constance said she planned to tell her Sunday school class this morning," Buck went on. "Knowing that bunch, it's a good bet everybody in town will know before sundown. She said it would save people asking you and Skip a lot of questions. I guess I'm glad if it saves you some discomfort, but I say let him fend for himself."

"Don't be too hard on him," Ava Grace surprised herself by saying. "I'm sure he's had a tough time."

"Why the hell not? I understand why he did it, but it's all beside the point. This isn't about the *why*, it's the *how*. And the *when*."

That was basically what Luka had said.

"I would have preferred an alternate method, for sure, but I think he was trying to please everybody right up until the end. I know something about that. You probably do, too." Here she was, the great defender of Skip. At least some things were falling into place about how she felt.

"I guess I do. And I'll tell you this, getting folks to simmer down last night after the debacle was no easy job. You were smart to beat feet out of there with Hyacinth."

If she responded to that without telling him she hadn't been with Hyacinth, she was going to end up deep in the Land of Liar, Liar Pants on Fire—at least by omission.

"I'm sure plenty of people were reveling in it all."

"No one who cares about you." Buck put his hand over Ava Grace's. "I wish Skip could have worked all this out sooner so you both could have gotten on with your lives."

That niggled at her a bit.

"Daddy, when you said I could have gotten on with my life—you meant find someone else to marry?"

"That and…other things."

She didn't ask what those other things were, because she knew there weren't any, unless it was having babies. It wasn't fair that she was affronted, when those were the very things she'd wanted herself.

"But that's all a done deal. How are you?"

Good question. "I'm okay, considering that nothing I thought was going to happen is, but what of it? I can plan a new life." And it was time she did, starting with where she was going to live. "Daddy, I've been thinking." And she had, for all of two seconds. "I'm going to move down to the windmill house."

He looked more surprised than he had when Skip jilted her. "The windmill house? Here on the grounds?"

"Do you know of any others?"

"No, but I don't know why you would want to do that."

"I need some space." Trite, but true.

"From your mother and me? You can't be serious. After all that's happened. You're tired. You couldn't have slept well."

Not true. She'd slept fine and frequently—just not for very long at a time.

"Why don't you go crawl in your bed and get some rest? When you wake up, Emma Frances will be home. We'll get some lunch—not here. Downtown Birmingham, so you don't have to see anyone you don't want to. Maybe we could go out to the Summit, do a little shopping. We can be back in plenty of time for Christmas Eve at Deborah and Randal's."

These *were* desperate times. Buck hated shopping, but that was his solution when things were rough— *get some rest, have some food, buy something pretty.*

This might have annoyed her as little as five minutes ago, but he was doing the best he could. They'd all been thrown for a loop. As far as him assuming she was going to her aunt and uncle's for Christmas Eve now that she wouldn't be with Skip—she wouldn't take that up now, but she wasn't going. Escaping Christmas Day at Fairvale was impossible, but she was not doing Christmas Eve.

"Might be fun—out in the Christmas Eve crowd." No doubt, Buck was trying to convince himself.

She got up and kissed his cheek. "I love you, Daddy."

"I love you, too, baby girl."

"But I'm going to move down to the windmill today."

"Ah, sister." He stood up. "If you have to do this thing, wait until after Christmas. You wouldn't even have a tree down there."

As if she wanted a tree. "No. It has to be now."

He sighed. "Well. It ought to be clean. The Brazzeltons stayed there last night after the party. Let me round up somebody to change the sheets."

"You are not going to bother Carolyn or any of the staff on Sunday, and Christmas Eve, at that. I'm perfectly capable of changing sheets."

He looked miserable. "At least let me help you."

"Give me an hour. Then you can help me take my things down."

And she went upstairs to pack, wondering what Luka was doing.

"There." Emma Frances straightened the cornflower blue checked shams and smoothed the floral comforter. "If you're determined to sleep down here tonight, you've got fresh bedding." She said it like Ava Grace was only planning on staying in the windmill house temporarily. "But you'll come up early, won't you? To do stockings and have breakfast?"

The house wasn't a real windmill and never had been, but apparently converted windmills were common in New England. Thirty years ago, Grandmother Fairchild had become enchanted with them on a leaf peeping tour and had had this one built.

Emma Frances looked around the bedroom. "I couldn't sleep in here. I'd be afraid all these botanicals would come to life and choke me to death." Emma Frances had returned home from church as Ava Grace and Buck were loading Ava Grace's things into Buck's pickup truck. Ava Grace had been forced to have basically the same conversation she'd had with Buck all over again. "It looks like your grandmother went into a Laura Ashley store and said, 'I'll take it.'"

"It could be worse," Ava Grace said. "She could have built this place in the '70s. Then it would be all harvest gold, avocado green, and fake Colonial furniture."

Truthfully, Ava Grace didn't mind the shabby chic retro, with the wicker tables, overstuffed furniture, and fussy mixed florals and patterns. Dated, sure, but the furnishings were top quality and showed very little wear. Besides, décor was not at the top of the list of her worries.

"You've got to be hungry." Emma Frances smoothed Ava Grace's hair off her face. "I know you don't want to go downtown, but tell you what—let's go to the inn and have a little combo late lunch/early dinner in about an hour. By then, the after-church crowd will be long gone. Call Hyacinth and ask her to join us. I want to thank her for getting you out of that ghastly situation last night."

Well, Mama, you'd be thanking the wrong person, but you'd be going to the right place to find him. Running into Luka was the only thing that was appealing about a trip to the inn—not that she was going. All she needed on top of everything else was for him to think she was stalking him.

"Come to think of it, ask Hyacinth to join us for Christmas Eve at Deborah's."

Now was the time. "I'm not going to Aunt Deborah's."

"What? It's planned, Ava Grace—has been for months."

"It's not planned for me. I'm not expected. I was going to the Landrys'. Remember?"

"Hard to forget." Emma Frances closed her eyes—something she always did when she was trying to compose herself. "And you don't have to be expected. It's family."

"I'm not going. I don't have it in me. I want to stay here."

"You can't be alone on Christmas Eve."

Why were people always saying that? Alone wasn't the worst thing that could happen.

Buck came in the door. "I've got your TV all hooked up."

"Buck," Emma Frances said. "We've decided to go to the inn to get something to eat. Ava Grace, we'll leave you to change your clothes and call Hyacinth. When we get back, we can all have a glass of wine and relax a bit before we need to be at Deborah and Randal's. Hyacinth, too, of course. I'm sure I have something in my gift closet y'all can wrap up for Dirty Santa."

What? No. The only thing that was going to happen on that list was the call to Hyacinth.

"Wait," Ava Grace said. "No. I don't want lunch. I need to settle in and unwind. It's been a lot."

Emma Frances and Buck frowned.

"I need some rest." That ought to get them.

"All right," Emma Frances said. "But what will you eat?"

"Mama, I would throw up if I had to eat." That was the truth.

"All right." Emma Frances frowned some more. "Then call Hyacinth to come over for a glass of wine so we can all go to Christmas Eve together. I'll put together a charcuterie board and we'll cut the coconut cake."

Merry hell, the world had ended. Emma Frances was going to cut the special Christmas cake before The Day.

"Will you do that?" Emma Frances persisted.

Ava Grace took a deep breath. "I've got just about one Christmas celebration in me. You choose. Tonight, at Aunt Deborah's, or tomorrow with y'all at home. I'm not going to do both."

This was a crapshoot. Emma Frances wasn't above choosing tonight and then badgering her about Christmas Day in the morning.

But Buck to the rescue. "Of course, we want you tomorrow, sister. You stay here and rest."

Relief. Apparently she could get what she wanted by standing her ground. "Y'all go have a nice lunch," Ava

Grace urged. "I'm not the only one this happened to. Y'all need a break, too. Go downtown to Sideboard." They loved Sideboard.

"We'll bring you something," Buck said.

"No, Daddy, don't," Ava Grace said. "It would be a waste."

"There are still some snacks from the Brazzeltons staying here," Emma Frances said. "Some cheese, fruit, and such. Wine—at least a couple of bottles."

All this talk of wine. You'd think they were a bunch of winos. "I'll be fine, Mama."

They moved toward the door. "Remember, sister," Buck said. "We're right up the hill. And if you change your mind about tonight—"

"I know, Daddy. Thanks for everything."

Once they were gone, Ava Grace sunk down into one of the rose striped club chairs. It was like sitting in a cloud. Maybe those 1990s designers were onto something. She could have easily drifted off to sleep, but she had a story to get straight.

Her phone had been ringing when she had gone to her room earlier to pack and she'd turned it off without checking to see who was calling. Now she scrolled through the missed calls—her brother, Brad, Claire, Jen from Heirloom, Molly Abbott from church, two from Adele, and three from Evans. Nothing from Hyacinth—which was strange.

And nothing from Luka. He didn't have her number, but that wouldn't stop him if he wanted to talk to her. She shook her head, hoping to clear it. Crazy thoughts. She was too freshly dumped to be thinking about another man.

But not to sleep with him, a tiny voice whispered.

No time for this. For all Ava Grace knew, Emma Frances was banging on Hyacinth's door and hauling her to Sideboard for the Christmas Eve prix fixe lunch special.

She was getting ready to leave a message when a sleepy-sounding Hyacinth answered the phone after five rings.

"I am so sorry, Ava Grace," Hyacinth said in a whispery voice.

"I know. Did I wake you?" Ava Grace had never known Hyacinth to nap. The only thing that was more unlikely was her sleeping this late. "Are you sick?"

"No." Hyacinth yawned and Ava Grace could tell she was moving around. "Just a minute." Still whispering. "There." A door closed and Hyacinth spoke in a normal tone. "I am so, so sorry I missed it. Tell me everything. Was it the sapphire ring? I hope you took lots of pictures."

She didn't know! "You didn't miss anything. Or maybe you did—the spectacle of the decade. There is no ring. Skip changed his mind at the last minute."

Hyacinth took a sharp intake of breath. "What? No! That bastard. Tell me."

She could not tell the story. She'd lived it and she would probably have to talk about it eventually, but not yet.

"First, where did you go, Hyacinth?"

"I, uh. Robbie came into the auction tent where I was…"

"And you made up." It made sense now. She'd still been in bed with Robbie. They'd probably been making love and napping ever since leaving the gala last night and Hyacinth had gone to another room to keep from waking him.

"Yes. We did. Everything is fine now." Hyacinth sounded happy.

"So I guess I'm not mad at him anymore?"

"I'd appreciate it if you wouldn't be. Besides, sounds like you've got bigger fish to fry. Enough about me. What about you?"

"I'm okay. But, listen, Hyacinth. I…left. After it happened. You were gone, so everyone thinks I left with you. I've let them think it. I need you to back me up."

"Yes. Sure. But, Ava Grace, after *what* happened? I have to know. And where did you go?" Hyacinth cursed under her breath. "Hold on. It's Evans beeping in. She's called five times."

"I bet she has. This is what I need you to do. Call her back. She can tell you the whole story. I can't talk about it right now. She's been calling me, too. She's probably going to want the two of you to come over here. But don't. Please."

"She's on her way to the Delta," Hyacinth said.

"Right. Yes."

"So it would be me, alone. I ought to come."

"Yes. You should. Tomorrow for Christmas lunch, like we planned. And you can bring Robbie. But I do not want to talk about it then either. I'll meet you and Evans for lunch on Monday. Is that the day after Christmas?" Now she didn't even know what day it was.

"Tuesday. Christmas is tomorrow, Monday." Hyacinth always knew what day it was, what time it was, the weather report, and if Mercury was in retrograde.

"Okay. Lunch Tuesday. I'll be ready to talk then."

Hyacinth was silent for a moment. "All right." She had that steely sound to her voice she always had when she was about to get her way. "But not lunch. I won't wait that long. Breakfast. They start serving at the inn at seven in the morning. Be there."

"Seven? You know that won't work for Evans. She's always deep into making pies by then."

"She'll make an exception. It's breakfast or I'm coming there right now—and I might call Evans and tell her she has to turn around and come back."

"All right." What were the chances of running into Luka at that hour? Slim. Nobody except Evans and farmers were out and about then—and, if Hyacinth was to be believed, people who served breakfast at the Laurel Springs Inn.

When she ended the call, Ava Grace realized she was alone for the first time since before the gala, alone with her thoughts and feelings.

Then, like a bolt, it hit her. For the first time, she was living alone. She'd had roommates at Belmont and, after, she'd never considered moving out of Fairvale because she'd been waiting—waiting for something that wasn't going to happen after all.

So here she was in her first home—circa 1992, and not at all what she had imagined. No light airy spaces with unexpected mixes of modern, traditional, and antique furnishings.

No nursery.

No bedroom where she and Skip would finally, finally get it right and make a baby to go in that nursery.

Of course, she knew now that they would have never gotten it right and she understood why.

It was so, so unfair.

Suddenly, it sounded like machine guns unloaded on the windows.

Ava Grace ran and looked out. An ice storm! What next? Locusts? She should have asked Hyacinth for a weather report. No matter. It wouldn't last long. At least she had wine and a generator if the power went out.

Every muscle, every joint in Ava Grace's body ached. She sunk down lower in the cloud chair, rested her head on an eyelet ruffled pillow, and pulled a yellow and blue cabbage rose throw over herself.

She ought to read some John Milton. Maybe she would've if she hadn't left all her books except for the grievance journal in her old room. Not that she liked John Milton. Who did? After he went blind, his own daughters hid from him so they wouldn't have to take dictation. So no, she didn't want to read John Milton. He was like bad medicine and she needed reminding that there were worse situations than hers, what with hell, the devil, and Adam and Eve's bad decisions.

But so what? She didn't care that other people had it worse.

She had never been much of a crier but, with the sleet violently pelting against the windows, the tears came for the second time in less than twenty-four hours. Right before she drifted off to sleep, Ava Grace wondered for the first time where Luka was spending Christmas.

Chapter Nine

Luka entered his suite to find it clean and empty. It was no emptier than usual, of course, but Ava Grace had taken up a lot of space and he felt the vacant places profoundly.

He sat down in his favorite chair—the large one facing the television—but he didn't reach for the remote. Instead, he unpacked the fast-food breakfast he'd picked up—sausage and eggs on English muffins, oblong slabs of hash brown potatoes, and a cinnamon roll. This proved he was not upset. Upset people didn't eat such as this.

Sure, he'd been a bit disgruntled earlier, but he was over it. Ava Grace had needed a distraction and he had provided it. Certainly it was no sacrifice. It was a good night—but it was over.

He knew he ought to go work out after eating, but to hell with it. He almost always did what he ought to do, but he was giving himself a break today.

He'd decided not to call his agent, after all. Kurt would call when he had news. Besides, the man should be left alone on Christmas Eve to spend time with his wife and children. Unlike Luka, in this suite named for a football coach, Kurt would not be in an empty space.

He was opening his second breakfast sandwich when the knock came at the door.

His heart skipped a beat and then sped up. He knew it wasn't Ava Grace, but it didn't.

It was only when he opened the door and felt disappointment at finding Logan there that Luka knew he hadn't known it either, not for sure.

Damn that woman, anyway.

"Where is the little Viking?" Luka used the boy's nickname.

"Cookie decorating party." Logan stepped inside. "I have to pick him up in an hour. I thought we might get in a quick workout, before our plane leaves."

"*Nyet.* It is starting to sleet." He went back to his breakfast, so Logan would get the message he wasn't going.

"It's not sleeting inside the gym." But Logan went to sit on the couch across from him—in the place where Ava Grace had sat last night. "That was some scene at that gala, huh? What happened to you? One minute we were planning to go downtown for food. Then I looked around, and you were gone."

"I left."

"You don't say. I thought you were still there. You loved that party so much."

Logan put his feet on the coffee table. "I went looking for you. I figured with all that was going on, Claire and Glaz wouldn't know—or probably care—if we left. When I gave you a jingle, you didn't pick up."

"I guess my phone was off."

Logan let out a heavy sigh. "That poor girl."

"Da," Luka spoke without thinking. "Was hard for her."

"Oh, really?" Logan sat up straight and a knowing look moved into his face. "You left with her, didn't you?"

Luka shrugged. He'd never lied to Logan and he wasn't going to start now. "She left with me. Was a bad situation. I offered to get her out of it. She was grateful."

"Rescued her, did you? I never figured you for a knight in shining hockey gear." Logan let his eyes dart around the room and settled them on Luka's food. "You're just now eating breakfast. You brought her back here. She stayed the night with you."

"That's none of your business."

"Which answers my question."

"You didn't ask questions. You stated facts, as you perceive them, that may or may not be true."

"I knew you had your eye on her—before you knew she was spoken for, I mean. Good on you. Seize the opportunity."

Anger rose in Luka and he had to remind himself that Logan was his best friend. "It wasn't like that. I would not take advantage of a woman."

"I wasn't talking about sex, Luka. I meant an opportunity for a relationship. Maybe it would make you give up this crazy idea of leaving the team. I need you to stay here and help me raise Alex."

"You make too much of things. You need no help with your son." Luka wasn't convinced that was true, but he wasn't the one to help Logan raise his child.

"Anyway, I will not see Ava Grace again. She has many issues to deal with."

"Maybe you could help her deal with them."

"I'm leaving this town. Remember?"

"Yeah, yeah, I know. You hate football. You must be where there is snow and hockey is king." Logan did a poor job of imitating his accent.

"You could come with me."

Logan laughed. "I'm not moving Alex again until I have to. Maybe Ava Grace would go with you."

"Unlikely." He didn't like how much the idea appealed to him. No. He would not see her again; he would avoid her at all costs.

"She left with you last night."

"Was different. She was in distress." And he hadn't been trying to take the princess from land that she ruled.

Logan frowned and shifted. "There's something…" He ran his hand under him and, to Luka's horror, came up with the blue and diamond necklace Ava Grace had been wearing last night. "What do we have here? It was between the couch cushions."

Hell. No point in pretending he didn't know who it belonged to. Besides, maybe Logan could be of some use.

"Will you return it to her for me?"

"No."

"You would if you were a true friend."

Logan rose and placed the necklace on the table. "I *am* a true friend and I'm not returning it for you. I have to go get the little Viking."

Then, their phones chimed simultaneously.

Logan reached for his. Luka reached for his cinnamon roll.

"Damn it all to hell!" Logan exploded. "It isn't only sleet. It's a fucking ice storm. They've canceled our flight!"

"Snow?" Luka asked. "I thought there was no winter weather in Alabama."

Logan fiddled with his phone. "According to the Weather Channel, no snow, just ice." He sighed and looked at the ceiling. "I had all Alex's Santa presents shipped to my parents. Damn, just damn!" He headed to the door. "I have to figure something out."

What a day this was shaping up to be. There would be none of Mrs. Jensen's ham and Swedish meatballs, no playing in the snow with Alex, no being in hockey country even for a brief time—though he wouldn't miss the lutefisk. At least the inn had a Christmas buffet.

His eyes fell on Ava Grace's necklace and he briefly wondered if it was costume jewelry and he could get away with forgetting about it. Not a chance. He had to return it—and see Ava Grace one more time.

As Logan had said, *Damn, just damn.*

Shit! Ava Grace sat bolt upright. She had forgotten the doorbell sounded like a foghorn. That had to go.

It was probably her mother, come to try to make her go to Aunt Deborah's—if they weren't already there. She had no idea how long she'd slept, but it was dark outside. She stomped to the door, determined to tell Emma Frances that, once and for all, she was not in the mood for eggnog and carols.

But when she threw open the door, it wasn't Emma

Frances. It was someone much worse, and something she was in even less of a mood for.

"Skip." The frozen rain was coming down hard and the awning over the small stoop wasn't much protection. She let him stand there. She didn't know how she felt, but she knew it did her some good to see him getting pelted.

He looked at her beseechingly. Strange. She'd never seen that look from him before. Apparently there was nothing he'd ever wanted from her that much. What did he want now?

"You look like hell," she said. And he did—bloodshot eyes, uncombed hair, and beard stubble had never been a good look for him. It usually wasn't for blonds.

"I feel like hell."

Lighting cut across the sky, bright and close, followed by thunder loud enough to shake the teeth of the dead. She didn't know winter storms came with lightning, but she could add that to a long list. Maybe she'd repurpose her gratitude journal for *Stuff Ava Grace Doesn't Know Jack Shit About* instead of grievances. Another bolt lit up the sky.

Enough. She wanted Skip wet and cold, not struck dead by lightning.

She moved aside, but he stood still. "Well. Come on in here."

He stepped inside and shed his coat. *Mighty sure I'm going to let you stay, aren't you, mister?*

But she took his coat and hung it on one of the white distressed wrought iron hooks beside the door.

"You look like you've been crying," Skip said. "You've never been one to cry."

"Yeah, well." She massaged the back of her neck. "I've never been one to get dumped in front of the entire town either."

His face crumpled. Good. If he'd looked like hell before, now he looked like the deepest, hottest part of it.

"Sorry." She really wasn't, but that was a line for the grievance journal, not one to be spoken out loud by good girls.

"That's rich. You saying you're sorry to me."

"Sit down."

She went back to the cloud chair and he pushed aside five floral pillows to make room for himself on the pink plaid sofa.

"How did you know where to find me?" Moving to the windmill house wasn't exactly Ava Grace–typical behavior.

"Carolyn told Brad you'd moved down here. He said you weren't answering the phone and I ought to leave you alone."

"Well, Brad always was the wise one. I'm just guessing here, but I'd bet my sparkly hell shoes that you told him you were gay and he advised you to break things off with me before the gala."

"Don't be mad at Brad," Skip said.

"I'm not. I'm mad at you."

"I don't expect you to forgive me, but I had to say I'm sorry."

"I don't forgive you for being gay because there's nothing to forgive, but, damn, Skip. In front of all those people? For God's sake. You're a smart man. What were you thinking?"

He shook his head. "I'm sorry—sorrier than you'll

ever know. I was in denial for so long. I didn't want to let you down—or our families. The whole town. They'd been waiting for it for years. So had you."

"I assume you didn't come to the gala still in denial and had your epiphany right there in the ballroom."

He shook his head. "After a time, I convinced myself I was bisexual and there was no reason it couldn't work with you and me—that I would be faithful. Then, I knew I wasn't bisexual, but I was going to marry you anyway. I love you. I was going to make it work for you, and I didn't care about how I felt. But then, when it was time, I faced what Brad had been trying to tell me. I'd be giving you half a life."

"Oh, come on, Skip. Don't pretend it's all about me. I get it. I do. You are who you are. But did you have to humiliate me in public? Even if you thought you could go through with it right up until the last second—and I guess you did think that—couldn't you have just proposed and then told me privately afterward?"

"Would you really have wanted that? Would it have been better to put that ring on your finger and then later say, 'Oh, by the way…'"

There was some truth to that. She sighed and closed her eyes. "No. I guess not."

"I wish I could make it up to you. I wanted to bring you that ring. I know you love it. But Adele wouldn't let me. She said that was the worst thing I could do."

Ava Grace barked out a mean little laugh. "Giving me that ring, worse than last night? Not hardly, but plenty bad. You're lucky you have Adele to save you from yourself."

He shook his head. "I don't think she's nearly as interested in saving me as she is in saving you."

"She'll come around. She's your sister. She loves you."

"You're probably right. I don't think your brother loves me, though."

"No. Probably not."

Skip shrugged. "I think our fishing trips are a thing of the past anyway. He can't stand someone who can out-fish him."

They were quiet for a bit, the pelting of the ice the only sound.

"If it matters," Skip said, "it's not like there's anyone else."

"Spare me." Sitting in a room and having a conversation with him was one thing—hearing about his dating life, even if it was lack thereof, was a big hell no.

"So do I walk out of here now? Promise that you never have to see me again?"

Memories of all their summer days came rushing back—the friendship, the fun, the comradery. What was it Luka had said? *"You don't have to throw him out of your life—not if you don't want to."*

"I can't think straight, Skip. My whole life just blew up. I love you, though I don't like you very much right now. I think we'll be okay eventually, but right now I need to be mad."

He nodded. "That's more than I deserve." He was quiet for a moment. "Brad's going skiing with a group of friends. He says I ought to go—get out of town until after the holidays. I told him no, but maybe it's a good idea. But I'll stay and let you shun me in public if you want."

Relief settled over her at the thought of not running into him on the street. "Yes, do that. Go. I told you Brad was the wise one."

He nodded. "If that's really what you want." He stood. "I guess I'll go."

"Going to the Landry family Christmas Eve?" She walked him to the door and handed him his coat.

He shuddered. "No. I think we've all had enough of each other for a few weeks."

She wasn't sure why she allowed him to hug her, but she learned something. It was the first time there was no reservation or awkwardness in his embrace.

If not for last night with Luka, she wouldn't have known the difference.

Chapter Ten

Christmas was in the books, the ice storm a memory.

As always, Fairvale had been filled with no less than forty assorted friends and relatives. It wasn't as ghastly as it could have been. Although she'd gotten her share of sympathetic looks, no one had directly mentioned the spectacle. True to her word, Hyacinth had pretended like nothing had happened and she and Robbie had been a nice distraction.

Ava Grace had received a new gratitude/grievance journal, an Italian leather purse, the usual assorted sweaters and socks, and an exquisite pair of vintage pearl and diamond earrings that she suspected had been chosen for her wedding day. They were too fancy for everyday wear but she loved them and found that she didn't care—which is why she had them on right now, on a Tuesday morning at 7:14 a.m. standing in the door of the Laurel Springs Inn dining room.

She peered through the door.

Who were all these people out eating breakfast when they ought to be sleeping?

Crack of dawn at the Laurel Springs Inn was a whole different world. Besides the people Ava Grace didn't know, there was a tableful of bankers, a men's prayer group from First Methodist, a birthday celebration with the entire staff from the jewelry store, and architect Cassandra Hargrove making a presentation to a client.

Astounding.

All of it, with the possible exception of the Methodists, seemed to be work related. Even the birthday party was probably about workplace morale. One thing for certain: a daybreak birthday party, no matter how well intended, would not have the desired effect on Ava Grace's morale—quite the opposite.

Heirloom didn't open until ten o'clock, so she never got up before eight thirty.

Hyacinth and Evans would be at the table by the French doors. They knew that was her favorite table and would make sure she had what she wanted—at least for a week or two—no matter who they had to kill to get it.

Most of the people in this room had been at the gala. The rest would have heard about it and word had gotten around about Skip's reason for jilting her. They were going to look at her. Who could blame them? She was the closest thing to a train wreck available at the moment.

She took a deep breath, held her head high, and stepped into the room.

If Belinda hadn't appeared with Luka's food at that precise moment, she would not have blocked the view of the little table in the corner where he always sat, and Ava Grace might have seen him.

But as it was, when Ava Grace made her entrance, Belinda was asking if his eggs were all right and promising to return with more coffee. Though she didn't see him, Luka had a good view of Ava Grace over the waitress's shoulder.

He briefly wondered if she was here looking for him—or more likely her necklace—but dismissed the idea. He'd seen Hyacinth and Evans come in earlier and disappear around the corner. They'd had their heads together whispering and hadn't noticed him either. He might have realized that Ava Grace was meeting them if he hadn't assumed she would be lying low. Not that she had any reason to, but considering how humiliated she'd felt, it was a good assumption.

Dressed in a gray plaid wool skirt and pink sweater with little beads around the neck, Ava Grace owned the room. No high heels today. Not flat shoes, but little black ones with a short square heel. She hid it well, but he could tell by the way her hands were clenched that she was apprehensive.

Heads turned her way. Maybe they would have even without the recent spectacular event. She had a head-turning way about her. But tension filled the air. Some looked at their hands, others stared at Ava Grace.

Luka's first instinct was to run to her, throw an arm around her, and rush her away, like a bodyguard helping a movie star escape the paparazzi.

But she didn't need him; she didn't need anyone. She unclenched her hands and, with quiet dignity, began to glide through the room—smiling, waving, mouthing hellos, and stopping to speak to one woman for a moment. When she approached one particular table of men, they put their Bibles aside, stood, and buttoned their blazers—all in unison.

She murmured greetings and patted an elderly man on the arm, yet never slowed her steps. But she wasn't hurrying either; she was moving at her own pace, in her own way, in her own time.

What a woman. Not his—she never would be—but she was a pleasure to behold. He watched her disappear around the same corner Hyacinth and Evans had, then quickly ate his breakfast and left.

He hadn't figured out how to get the necklace back to her yet, but when he saw her again it would be planned, and on his terms.

It had to be, else he might do something foolish. She could, indeed, destroy him—in that good way—and he wanted to let her.

"Sorry I'm late." Hyacinth and Evans were sitting across from each other at a square four-top table, leaving the chair for her that faced the French doors, with her back to the other diners. There was already a plate with a slice of quiche, some fruit, and a compote dish of yogurt at her place. "It was the best I could do."

Despite not being a morning person, Ava Grace had tried really hard to be on time, but going through boxes and bags to find what she needed to put herself together had been a challenge. She would definitely unpack tonight.

"It doesn't matter," Hyacinth said—which was a lie. Punctuality was at the top of Hyacinth's list of things that mattered, along with being prepared, and having an alternate plan, in case the primary one didn't work.

Evans reached across and squeezed her hand. Ava Grace was surprised there hadn't been any hugging.

Evans was an eager hugger and Hyacinth a reluctantly willing one, with Ava Grace somewhere in between. They were probably afraid if they hugged her, she would fall apart. That wasn't anywhere close to happening, but she didn't want it to look as if she needed consoling in front of this Laurel Springs breakfast crowd.

Ava Grace withdrew her hand from Evans's and folded her napkin onto her lap. "I had no idea there was such an opportunity for early morning socializing. I bet things are really popping at the Waffle House."

Hyacinth and Evans exchanged knowing looks. Unless she missed her guess, they thought she was in denial—though what she might be denying, she had no clue. Skip was gay and that was hard to deny. Not that she wanted to.

"Evans told me what happened," Hyacinth said.

Good. Hyacinth was a great fan of economy in all things—money, time, words. She wouldn't make Ava Grace repeat it.

"How *are* you?" Evans asked.

"Much better than two days ago." She took a sip of her coffee. "I've seen Skip." Evans gasped audibly and Hyacinth clinched her jaw. "We talked. He's had a hard time."

"*He's* had a hard time?" Evans exploded. "I was there, Ava Grace. I saw a hard time and it wasn't Skip Landry who was having it."

"No kidding," Hyacinth said with a sneer. Ava Grace loved her for that sneer.

"I appreciate you both for that. I do. But this is for the best."

"You said a mouthful," Hyacinth said. "I have a

whole list of bad things I want to do to him. It's not because he's gay, it's—"

"How he handled it," Ava Grace finished the sentence. "That's what everyone says—my parents, my brother, Adele, Brad, and me. Even Skip."

And Luka. She looked at the ceiling. He was probably up there in the Bryant suite, still dead to the world—if he was still in town, or back from wherever he'd spent Christmas. She hadn't heard a word from him so she had no idea where he was. Not that it was her business.

"I'm glad everyone recognizes that," Hyacinth said. "Too bad Skip didn't recognize a few things earlier."

Right. There was a conversation going on here that she needed to participate in instead of speculating on Luka's whereabouts. She'd done a lot of thinking over the past few days and come to some conclusions. She usually kept her conclusions to herself, but there was something in the way that they were looking at her— Evans, like she wanted to tuck her into bed and bring her cocoa laced with brandy, and Hyacinth, like she was about to start a street fight on Ava Grace's behalf—that made her inclined to share her thoughts with them.

"I wasn't in love with him. I love him. I always have, always will. But I didn't know there was a difference. When it all went down, I found that I was upset about losing the life we'd planned—the house, the entertaining, the trips, the Christmas mornings, the birthdays, the babies." Especially the babies. "But when I was considering the loss, I didn't think very much about Skip."

Evans frowned. "It sounds like you've got this all tied up with a pretty bow—that you have let Skip off scot-free with your blessing."

Ava Grace laughed. "Does it? I assure you, not by a long shot. I'm still mad and beyond hurt that he did that to me. But I'll get over it. Eventually. Skip, Brad, and I were three parts of one before anyone ever made any lifetime promises, and that's not something that easily goes away. I just need some time—maybe *a lot* of time."

"That's a relief," Evans said. "I thought there for a minute you were fooling yourself."

"I've been fooling myself all my life. I'm going to do my best to be done with that," Ava Grace said.

"I hear he's gone skiing. Can we at least roll his yard while he's gone?" Hyacinth asked.

"Sure," Ava Grace said. "Have at it. But remember he doesn't have a place of his own. You'd be rolling Constance Landry's yard and she doesn't take kindly to a mess."

Hyacinth pursed her lips and squinted her eyes. "I'm a patient woman. I'll put that plan on hold for now, but he's got to move out sometime."

"Do what you've got to do," Ava Grace said, "but we've talked enough about me. Hyacinth, tell me what happened with you and Robbie."

Hyacinth smiled a dopey little smile that wasn't like her at all. "As you know, we had a falling-out. We weren't happy. We saw each other and talked. Now we're happy."

Economy of words. No more details would be forthcoming, so there was no need to try to get them.

Evans laughed a little. "Isn't that the way it always goes? That's what happened with Jake and me, too—in a nutshell."

"I talked to Brad before they left for Aspen," Hyacinth said. "He's only letting Skip go on that trip to get him out of town so you can have some breathing room. I doubt if it's going to be an easy trip for Skip."

"Brad won't stay mad long," Ava Grace said. "Like I said, we all go back too far. I don't take any pleasure in him giving Skip a hard time."

"You're a better woman than I am," Evans said.

"Nobody is a better woman than you are," Ava Grace said. "But can we please not talk about Skip anymore? I'm Skipped out. Let's talk about Christmas, dogs, aliens from outer space—anything."

"Sure," Hyacinth said. "I have one more question. Where did you disappear to after it happened?"

Oh, hell. She should have anticipated this. What to say, what to say? Should she lie? Say she caught a ride to the inn? Or tell the truth? Hyacinth and Evans were her friends. They loved her; they wouldn't judge her for hooking up with Luka, especially under the circumstances.

But she didn't want to tell them. It was private.

Hyacinth leaned forward and widened her eyes, waiting.

"Yes," Evans said. "Who were you with?"

Nothing to do but tell the truth—or was there?

The little cartoon light bulb bloomed above her head. She didn't *have* to tell them anything. They loved her and they wouldn't stop loving her. After all, she hadn't stopped loving Skip or, for that matter, Brad. She hadn't thought about it overmuch, but Brad had known about Skip and hadn't warned her. She didn't have to be the good, perfect girl, who always gave an answer and tried to please everyone. She didn't have to spill everything and then write in her grievance journal, "Friends who ask personal questions that you don't want to answer."

"Ava Grace," Hyacinth said, "tell us."

"No." She spooned fruit into her yogurt. "I'm not going to talk about that."

Hyacinth and Evans exchanged baffled expressions. And no wonder. She'd never denied them information or anything else before. The silence was deafening, but Ava Grace held her ground.

That felt...different—and good. Empowering.

"Well..." Evans said. "If you change your mind and want to talk..."

"I know where to find you. Now, what did everyone get for Christmas?"

Chapter Eleven

When Hyacinth and Evans went to their respective shops, Ava Grace decided to go to Heirloom since she was already out. It was slightly before 8:30 a.m. when she unlocked the door with hands shaking from the cold. She'd left home without a coat or gloves, telling herself her twin sweater set, wool skirt, and tights would be enough. But might as well face it: winter had come to the South. It might not be Luka's kind of winter, but it was as much as Ava Grace wanted to endure.

She had to search to find where she'd texted herself the code for the security system. There was a reason for that. Unlike Hyacinth and Evans, who were always the first ones to arrive at work, Ava Grace left opening to her employees, Piper and Jen, who were both just shy of twenty-two. They had always made coffee, vacuumed, swept the front sidewalk, and opened the register by the time Ava Grace arrived.

For the first time, she wondered what they thought of that.

Once inside, she locked the door behind her and turned on the lights.

Heirloom was a different shop today.

Oh, it looked the same as the last time she was here, with the case of sparkling sterling silver, vintage jewelry display, and selection of fine, carefully selected furniture and accessories—some antique, some modern. The Christmas decorations contributed to the whole jewel box effect of the shop. But she was looking at it through different eyes today.

She might have balked at her mother's suggestion of selling Heirloom right now, but she had never imagined she would keep it forever. It had always been a stopgap, a hobby—something to do while she waited for two o'clock feedings, kindergarten pageants, girl scouts, Little League, prom dress shopping, and college applications.

But now, the waiting was over and Heirloom was her future. She wandered over to the mahogany Regency Chippendale dining table, set with vintage Johnson Brothers Merry Christmas china and emerald Bubble Foot glassware. The base for the centerpiece was a cranberry glass epergne, filled with holly, paperwhites, and antique blown glass ornaments. She loved this part of the job—the collecting things and making beautiful presentations—and she loved the juxtaposition of the funky red lacquer chairs she'd partnered with the traditional look.

Where she fell down was the actual selling.

Claire insisted Heirloom was doing well considering the short time she'd been in business and the specialty high-end goods she carried. But Ava Grace wasn't so sure; she simply lost interest when it came to moving the merchandise and went on to something that intrigued her, like acquiring nineteenth century Paris salon paintings or Victorian music boxes. She bought what she wanted for the shop and paid Jen's and Piper's fulltime salaries, often using dividends from her trust fund, with no thought to what the shop had earned. She might not have the best head for commerce, but she knew that was a recipe for a failed business.

She'd told herself she wanted to sell more, but did she really? Or had she just been creating a beautiful little world in which to bide her time while she waited?

She should have been elated last month when she'd sold the 1896 Gorham sterling punch bowl to a couple of snowbirds on their way to Florida. She'd made a huge profit and Claire had been so impressed, but instead of being happy, Ava Grace had felt loss. It had been displayed in a place of honor on an English sideboard and she missed seeing it, missed polishing it.

Obviously, that had to change—at least it was obvious to her. She might not know what was going to happen, but she knew what was not. She wasn't going on a hunt for a man to cut and paste into Skip's vacant spot in her fantasy future. She knew her strengths—she was a good decorator with excellent taste and an outstanding eye for quality. She had good contacts and could often get into estate sales ahead of time. That was more than a lot of people had.

She would figure it out, but for now she was going to clean the floor—as soon as she discerned how the vacuum went together, which proved to be harder than she had thought.

But she conquered it and was returning the demon machine from hell to the storeroom when the back door opened.

Jen came in and gave a little yelp.

"What?" Ava Grace said.

"Oh." Jen passed her hand over her face. "You're here. And you vacuumed?"

Ava Grace couldn't blame her for being surprised on either count.

"Yeah. It took me a bit to make sense of the attachments, but I did."

"I tried to call you," Jen said.

"I know. I saw. I haven't gotten around to returning all the calls yet."

"How are you?"

If only she had her grievance journal. *People who won't stop asking me how I am.* That wasn't fair, of course. What were people supposed to say? *How's that public humiliation going? Did you kill Skip?* Too bad there couldn't be a great gathering when something like this happened, sort of like a wake. Everyone could come and file past the wronged party and state their condolences. Then it would be over. But there was no such thing and she had to answer Jen.

"I'm fine." Was that what people wanted to hear or did they want gory details? Hard to know, but Ava Grace knew what she wanted—the elephant out of the room—and that answer did it. "Did you have a good Christmas?"

"Yes. I hope yours was, too," Jen said.

"It was nice." Not a lie. It had been nice—but not a place she had wanted to be.

"Piper worked Saturday and comes in at noon today." Thank goodness Jen had changed the subject.

"I know," Ava Grace lied, but vowed to herself it

would be last time she lied about not knowing her staff's schedule. "I'll go set up the register."

Jen reached for the broom. "I'll make coffee and then sweep the leaves on the sidewalk."

"Great."

But when she turned to go, Ava Grace caught sight of the corner where she had set aside things for her erstwhile future life—the rosewood writing desk, the Art Deco silver coffee service, and the mid-century burl wood liquor cabinet with brass inlay that she'd thought would be perfect for Skip's home office. Besides that, there was all manner of dishes, crystal, obscure silver serving pieces, framed artwork, and knickknacks.

And then there was the hand-carved cherry cradle, assembled entirely with pegs. It didn't meet today's safety standards, but it would have been so precious with stuffed bears and dolls peeping over the side. She gave it a little rock.

"Wait, Jen." Ava Grace walked over and picked up the pair of silver berry spoons with gold wash. "After we get these last few chores done, let's price these things and put them out."

"Are you sure?" Jen frowned.

"The small things. I'll have to figure out where to put the desk and cabinet. Do you think your little brother can get a friend to come move them for us? Maybe tomorrow? I'll pay them, of course." Brad and her daddy usually did that, but Brad was gone to Aspen and she had to stop calling her daddy every time she needed something.

"It would have to be after basketball practice, but sure. I can arrange that." Jen rifled around until she found the silver polish. "I'll get that silver polished as soon as I sweep." She paused.

"Thank you."

"Ava Grace?"

"Yes?"

"What about this?" She laid her hand on the cherrywood silver chest that had been pushed to the back of the shelf.

It was the service for twelve that Skip had surprised her with for Christmas last year—vintage English King by Tiffany. She'd stored it here with the other things she'd collected and included it on the shop's insurance. She'd found it at an estate sale and fallen in love with it. It was a ridiculous, frivolous purchase—not that she thought silver flatware was frivolous, as many did these days. But they hadn't needed it. She had her maternal grandmother's Francis I coming when she married and Skip had inherited Chantilly from his great-aunt. When she'd showed the English King to Skip, she'd never intended him to buy it, never suspected that he would. But there it had been under the Christmas tree.

She'd thought it the most romantic gesture she'd ever seen, but not because it was so frightfully expensive. He'd wanted to please her. Though looking back, maybe it had been, in part, a consolation prize for the engagement ring she hadn't gotten last year. She'd never know. She doubted if Skip knew himself. Should she offer it back to him? Sell it and give him the money? No. That would be almost as bad as him trying to give her his grandmother's ring. But what the hell was she going to do with it? Take it to the windmill house and eat canned soup with the spoons? She could. After all, there were cream *and* broth soup spoons.

"Let's leave it for now, Jen," she said. "Let's take care of the other things first." She needed to change lanes—fast. "But something else—you have such pretty handwriting. Can you make a sign that says, 'Christmas Items, Half Price' and put it on the front door?" She should have planned on this beforehand, but better late than never.

They were small steps, but Ava Grace felt a little better with each one.

When she was setting up the register, she remembered something Claire had suggested, but Ava Grace had resisted, saying she didn't have time—when the truth was she simply hadn't wanted to do it.

Before she could change her mind, she picked up the phone and called Stanton Signs.

"Mr. Stanton? This is Ava Grace Fairchild over at Heirloom Antiques and Gifts. Yes, my mama and daddy are fine. If you remember, you painted the name of my shop and the hours on the glass door last year. I'd like something added, in the same font and burnished gold paint. 'Ava Grace Fairchild, Proprietor. ASID Certified Interior Designer. Free Consultations.' I'll email it to you so you'll have the correct spelling. Yes. This afternoon would be perfect. Thank you. Tell Sarabeth I said hello."

She'd need new business cards, too. But first she was going to memorize Jen's and Piper's schedules.

Luka had heard of people who went to sleep with a dilemma and woke with a solution. That had never happened to him, but he understood it because it was that way with him and the ice—on with a problem, off with an answer.

It had happened again today. He knew what he was going to do about Ava Grace's necklace.

"Not a bad practice." Logan sat down in his stall beside Luka's and started to unlace his skates.

"Productive," Luka agreed. In more ways than one.

"You seem almost happy."

"Do I?" Luka took a long drink of Gatorade. "Am the same as always."

It was determination that Logan was seeing in him. It couldn't be happiness that he was going to see Ava Grace, though he *was* about to see her. He had decided to go to her place of business as soon as he left here. He would ask what she wanted to do about the necklace and offer her options—one that would involve another encounter with her and one that would not. It would be her choice and then it would be finished. Probably. If she chose to see him again to receive the necklace, it could be simply that or perhaps more.

"Here comes Wings." Logan interrupted his thoughts. "Don't kill him, please. We need him tomorrow night."

Luka looked up. Sure enough, the arrogant, wet-behind-the-ears puppy was waddling toward him, still in his cumbersome goalie pads.

"I seldom kill people, even those who annoy me to the degree of Dietrich Wingo."

"Good practice, guys," Wingo said. "Zov, your slap shot was looking a little rusty—but it was close to perfect today."

There were too many things to be angry about to count, but foremost was the nickname. Luka hated nicknames and was proud he had survived so many years in the league without acquiring one. Now, this self-absorbed little prick had gifted him with one—and worse, his teammates and the people of Twitter had picked up on it.

Wingo stood there for a moment. When Luka said nothing, Wingo said, "Keep it up," and moved on.

"Thanks, Wings," Logan called after him.

"Don't encourage him." Luka finished removing his skates, stood up, and shucked his jersey.

"You're too hard on him," Logan said.

"And you are going soft on him? He annoys you, too, with his conceit and big mouth."

"True. He annoys me, but I don't have contempt for him."

All Luka needed was a lecture from Logan. "There was nothing wrong with my slap shot."

"Is that so? I could have sworn you were bitching about it just the other day."

Next time he would be silent on matters that concerned him. "Still. Who is he to comment on the play of his superiors? A rookie."

"I don't disagree, but he's young, Luka, and in a unique circumstance. Not many rookies come out of the gate as a first line star. Remember, he sees everything on the ice from the net and he's trying to be a leader. He could dial it back a notch, but I give him points for effort."

"There are no points for effort in hockey. The puck

goes in the net, or it doesn't." Luka wiped down his skates and put them on the drying apparatus in his stall.

"True. And Wings's save percentage so far this season is .923."

"I have not doubted his prowess on the ice. It's his attitude."

"Maybe you could help him improve it." Half naked, Logan leaned on his stall.

"*Da.* I've considered doing that in some back ally."

Logan burst out laughing. "You have not. You talk big, but you are no more going to beat him up than you are me."

"You're not safe from me, and are getting more unsafe by the second. I think I have been exceptionally benevolent toward him considering the degree of his cockiness."

"Luka, you stabbed the back of his hand with a fork."

"Was an instant reaction! He put his hand in my plate. I might have stabbed you if you had tried to eat food from my plate."

Logan's expression went to serious. "You do know he only wants your approval, don't you? He looks up to you."

"I cannot matter to him. I am—"

"Yeah, yeah, I know. Leaving. As soon as you can manage it. Not interested in staying here and helping raise Wingo and the little Viking." Logan's phone rang then. "Hello?"

It was good that Logan got a call. Luka was tired of this conversation. He was ready to shower and resolve this necklace issue. Once it was out of his possession maybe he could stop thinking about Ava Grace.

Luka finished undressing, but wrapped a towel around his waist before removing his compression shorts. He wasn't one to strut around the locker room totally naked—unlike most. Wingo, Miklos Novak, and Christophe Bachet were the worst offenders, swaggering around like they were proud of their bodies. Ava Grace was the last person who'd seen him naked. His body wasn't as pretty as hers, but he hadn't been ashamed of it either.

"Hey, Luka." Logan still held his phone. "Can you help me out?"

"Possibly." So long as is it didn't interfere with his visit to Heirloom.

"Claire has set me up to go read to a third grade class at the elementary school. Mrs. Houston just lost a filling and needs to go the dentist. Can you watch Alexander?"

"Now?"

"Yes, now. When did you think? Next week? The woman's in pain. Or you could go read to the class for me."

No way he was doing that. "I'll take Alex."

Logan nodded. "Thanks. Mrs. Houston?" Logan spoke into his phone again. "Bring him by the iceplex on your way to the dentist. Luka Zadorov will be waiting for you. Yes. He's the one they call Zov."

Damn, just damn, for so many reasons.

Luka hurried to the shower. Little Vikings waited for no one.

Chapter Twelve

"Go to lunch, Jen," Ava Grace said as soon as Piper came in.

"Me?" Jen looked up from where she was polishing the silver serving pieces Ava Grace had so carefully selected for her new home—among them the Old Colonial sardine fork, Repousse grape shears, and Chrysanthemum punch ladle.

She would have never used those things anyway. Who went around serving sardines? But she'd loved the look of them, the mix of the patterns, loved imagining a woman from days gone by bringing out her sterling shears to serve grapes from a big cluster. Now she was pricing them for someone else to buy.

"You always go to lunch at noon," Jen said.

"I'm not going to lunch today," she said. "I had a big breakfast." Actually, any breakfast at all was big for her. That was why she'd always been so eager to get out the door at noon. Now that she thought about it, it had been inconsiderate to insist on going at noon, when the others had arrived at work at least an hour earlier than she had.

"Thanks," Jen said, removing her polishing gloves. "I *am* hungry."

Ava Grace picked up the sterling silver nut picks and laughed. *Nut picks*, really? What had she been thinking? Actually, she knew. She'd been thinking they were vintage Tiffany and—if she remembered correctly— she'd gotten them at an estate sale for a song. She typed in *nut picks* and hit enter. At least she'd kept meticulous records. Yes, not only a song, a very sweet song. Now she'd price them for what they were worth. People said her generation didn't want nice things, or old things, anymore, but there were some who did—like herself.

The front door bell jingled. Maybe it would be that one person in the market for Tiffany nut picks, circa 1872.

"Hello," she called out. "Can I help…" Her voice trailed off.

Luka.

And he had a baby with him—a toddler, really. Her heart went into high gear. Luka had a child? How could he? He lived in a hotel room! Or maybe he had a wife, too—one who had refused to move to Alabama, but she had come for Christmas. Oh, damn, damn, damn. A one-night stand was one thing, adultery quite another. He'd said he'd only been in love once a long time ago. But it didn't take love to make a baby. Maybe he wasn't married, but he had his child for the holiday.

"Hello, Ava Grace." He knelt and unzipped the boy's coat and pulled the knit hat off his head. "It's gotten cold out. Not *real* cold, but cold enough."

The child's poker-straight hair was so blond it was almost transparent, his eyes blue like sapphires—a huge

contrast to Luka's dark curls and deep brown eyes. But
that didn't mean the boy didn't take after his mother.

"Who do we have here?" She was surprised her voice
sounded so normal.

Luka picked up the boy and stepped up to the counter. "This is Alexander, the son of Logan Jensen."

Relief washed over her. Right. Yes. His best friend.
No wife. No adultery.

"Logan was scheduled for volunteer duties and the
nanny had dental emergency." Luka smiled that rare,
fleeting smile. "So today I am nanny for a little while."

"Hello, Alexander," Ava Grace said.

"I'm free!" the boy called out cheerfully.

"You're free? In that case, I'll take you. I would be
glad to pay money for you."

Luka shook his head. "He means he is three, but is
not true. He is two."

"Down!" Alexander grabbed a handful of Luka's
hair. "Down, Luka!"

"Nyet!" Luka captured the boy's hand. "Do not pull
my hair. I will put you down, but you must not touch
the pretty things. Do you understand?"

Alexander nodded. *"Da."* The boy knew the Russian
word for *yes.* Luka must spend a lot of time with him.

"All right. No touching." But he still didn't put him
down. "Do you promise?"

"Yes. Santa came! Alex a good boy."

"That remains to be seen," Luka muttered, but he set
the boy on his feet. "Do you have rope, Ava Grace?"

"Rope? No. I don't think…" He came here for rope?
"The hardware store is right down the street."

"Was kidding. I do not think Logan would be delighted if I tied Alex up." She noticed Luka held tight to the boy's overall strap. "So many things to break." He looked toward the shelves of crystal.

"They're only things, but it would be awful if he got hurt. I should get some toys—to distract the children who come in." Why had she not thought of that before? Children who came into Heirloom invariably made their adults nervous. A distraction would help.

"I will be fast," Luka said. "So we can leave your pretty shop intact."

Fast. Yes, he was here for a reason, and not to see her—or even to ask how she was. He looked so, so tempting with his damp hair and cheeks ruddy from the cold and exercise. He must have come straight from practice. He had a bit of five-o'clock shadow—the best kind, not an intentional fashion statement, but the kind that had appeared because of the testosterone that raged through him. He stood close enough that she could smell his maple cedar scent, causing her mouth to water at the memory of his taste.

"You left your necklace in my rooms." His words called her back to the present.

"I did?" Though it made no sense, her hand flew to her neck. "I haven't missed it." And she was lucky Emma Frances hadn't.

"It appeared to be quite valuable. I thought of bringing it, but I did not want to walk around with it in my pocket, where it might be lost. I left it in the safe in my rooms. I can bring it here, if you like. Or I can have the concierge lock it in the inn safe and you can pick it up there."

For reasons she couldn't figure, his eyes seemed to challenge her.

"Luka!" Alexander's little voice tore through the air. "Let go!"

"Alex," Luka said quietly, but firmly. "Do not jerk away from me. There are many pretty things here and they must not be broken."

"What's that?" Alex jerked as hard as he could and pointed to the maple cradle that Ava Grace had just priced and put on display. "Want to see!"

Luka took a deep breath and said to Ava Grace, "Excuse me. He is at stage where he must know what things are." He walked with Alex to the cradle. "See?" Luka rocked the cradle. "Is a baby bed. You rock the baby." He took Alex's hand and laid it on the cradle. "You can do it, but slowly, gently. This is not so easy to demolish."

A warm, sweet feeling washed over Ava Grace.

"Rock baby?" Alex said.

"Yes. You put baby in here." He patted the inside of the cradle.

"Baby sleep?" Alex said.

"Yes."

Alex proceeded to try to climb inside.

"No, no." Luka caught him, firm, but so, so kind. "This is for *little* baby. Alex is a big boy, with a big boy bed."

Alex laughed and nodded. Then he did something that would have melted the hardest heart ever forged. One by one he pulled small toys from his pocket—a car, a ball, a stuffed lion, a dinosaur—and kissed each before laying them in the cradle. Then he gave it a little rock. "I need for my baby."

Luka laughed and hugged the child. "You need? For the doll baby Santa brought to you? Seems like you need everything these days and so soon after Santa, too." He looked at the price, flinched a bit, and then shrugged. "If we buy this, will you be a very good boy and eat your green beans when we go for lunch?"

"Alex eat mac and cheese."

"*Da.* But will Alex eat green beans, too?"

"*Da!*"

Luka looked back at Ava Grace. "I guess we need to buy this cradle. Alex got doll for Christmas."

Surprisingly, a jolt of joy went through her. She had thought she would be sad to see the cradle meant for her child's room sold, but how could she not take delight in this? It had been meant as a safe haven for beloved toys and now it would be.

Luka left Alex to rock the cradle and approached the counter again.

Ava Grace began to write up the sale. "How was your Christmas?"

"Unremarkable. I was to go to Minnesota with Logan, but the ice storm grounded the flight. Is no matter. We will celebrate with the Jensens when we play the Walleyes in February—if I am still here in February."

"Any progress there?" she asked.

He removed his wallet from his pocket. "*Nyet.* But the world stops for Christmas, even without grounded flight. Was your holiday very bad?"

"I got through it. Glad it's over."

There was a long beat of silence. In the background Alexander sang, "Twinkle, twinkle, little car…"

"So about the necklace?" His bottom lip was chapped and peeling. He licked it.

Her brain began to race at warp speed, her heart not far behind. Did she dare say what she wanted? She had earlier to Evans and Hyacinth and the world hadn't spun off its axis.

"Actually, would you mind bringing it to me? Tonight? At my house. In fact, come for dinner. I'll make chicken and dumplings."

"To your house?" Luka asked. That had not been one of the choices.

She had seemed fine, even happy, but now the light faded from her silver eyes. "I shouldn't have asked that of you. It's too much trouble. It's fine. I'll pick the choker up from the inn."

"*Nyet.* Not trouble. I am…surprised that you invited me to your home." Maybe he'd been wrong when he'd dropped her at home on Christmas Eve, overly sensitive. If she was inviting him to her house, she couldn't be ashamed of him. Perhaps she hadn't wanted to explain having been with any man. That was fair.

"Why not?" She blessed him with a smile. "You invited me to yours."

Her cheeks colored to match her pink sweater. She was remembering what had passed between them—and she knew he was thinking of it, too. Her eyes said she hoped it would happen again. It would be his greatest pleasure to arrange that—though it probably could not be tonight at her family's home.

"*Da*. I will come to your home tonight to bring your necklace and eat this meal you will make."

"Wonderful. Seven o'clock?" She picked up a business card from beside the cash register, turned it over, and wrote something. "My cell number." She handed it to him. "And I've moved to a guesthouse on the property. When you come in the gates, drive around the main house, past the pool and the tennis court. There's a little grove of trees and it's right past there. There will be a gazebo on the right and the house on the left. You can't miss it. It looks like a windmill."

So she *wasn't* inviting him to her family home.

His first inclination was to tell her he'd changed his mind, that she could pick up the necklace herself.

But, then, why do that?

She wasn't Tatiana; he didn't want to marry her, so why should he care if she didn't want to be seen with him? So what if she just wanted a distraction? Wasn't that what he wanted? Being Ava Grace's distraction wouldn't be a hard job, and going to this house that looked like a windmill had its advantages. She lived there alone.

Their eyes locked and sweet, hot recollections of their night together flew between them on the wings of anticipation. Her lips parted. Not much, but enough that his eyes were drawn there and the memory of the taste of her kiss flooded his mouth. Perhaps if he leaned in, she would as well, and the memory would be reality. He inclined his face toward hers and, after the barest hesitation, she bent forward. Only inches to go…

"Luka!" The little Viking tugged on his jacket and the moment was lost. "Alex hungry!"

They sighed and laughed a bit in perfect unison. That wasn't the first time he'd felt perfect unison with her.

"Lu-*ka*! Mac and cheese!"

"Da, detka malchik." He picked the boy up and sat him on the counter. "We will get some food. But first, I must pay for your cradle."

He removed his card from his wallet. Ridiculous purchase. He didn't usually do ridiculous things.

Or at least he didn't used to.

His fingers brushed Ava Grace's when he put the card in her hand. There was electricity there, to be sure.

Electricity that promised pleasure.

Chapter Thirteen

Ava Grace tried to roll out the dough on the counter, but it stuck to the rolling pin—again. Why, oh, why had she told Luka she would make chicken and dumplings? She couldn't make chicken and dumplings; she couldn't make anything except deviled eggs.

She'd opened her mouth and it had come out. So many times she'd heard her mother confer with Dorothea about the menus for the week and remembered her saying they should have a "simple meal" on particular nights because she had a council meeting, Buck was out of town, Emerson had a game, or Ava Grace had dance. The choices for those simple meals were things like jambalaya, beef stew, chicken pot pie, chili—and chicken and dumplings.

Ava Grace realized now that when Emma Frances had said *simple meal*, she meant simple and fast to eat, not simple to make.

She had panicked the minute Luka left Heirloom and immediately looked up a recipe on the internet, telling herself the whole time that it couldn't be that hard. After all, it didn't have a lot of ingredients like the other things on the simple list.

She had eaten the dish hundreds of times. It was basically chunks of chicken and strips of dough in a thick sauce. But there had been so many steps—boiling chicken with celery and onion, deboning the chicken and boiling the bones and skin until the broth was rich. And that was only the beginning.

Then you had to mix up dough from flour, baking powder, salt, shortening, and milk, and roll it out with a rolling pin! There were basic pots and pans at the windmill house, but she was pretty sure there was no rolling pin. Once you did all that, you were to cut strips of dough and drop them, one by one, into the boiling broth. Don't overcrowd, the recipe cautioned. Don't over stir, or the dumplings will disintegrate. Couldn't have that. Then it wouldn't be chicken and dumplings. It would be chicken and…disintegration.

Hell, damn, and all the other bad words.

She'd thought of calling Dorothea; she would have come to the rescue. Anyone at Fairvale would. But what was the point of moving to the windmill house if she wasn't going to work things out for herself? So, she'd done the only reasonable thing she could.

She'd called the Laurel Springs Country Club and begged Chef Isaac to make it for her. "I'd do it for you, baby," he said. "You know I would. But I've got two private parties going on here tonight, plus the regular dinner to get out. Can it wait until tomorrow?"

It could not. "Well, listen," he said. "Buy yourself some of those cartons of broth and boil your chicken in that instead of water. Your dumplings are only as good as the broth and double broth makes the best. Enrich it with some butter. And don't fool with baking powder and plain flour. Get self-rising flour—White Lily. It's all I use."

So she'd gone to the Piggly Wiggly and bought all that, plus a rolling pin, and here she was—with dough stuck to her new rolling pin. Plus, the chicken was still boiling in the broth, though it had probably been done a long time ago. Could you overboil chicken? She turned the heat off, but the deboning, the chopping, the discarding of the vegetables, and the straining of the broth would have to wait until she conquered this dough. There would be no further boiling of the bones and skins. It was too much.

Calm. She would be calm. She closed her eyes and took a deep breath. Then she scraped the dough off the counter and off the rolling pin. Now that she was calm, she'd start again. That would help. She'd seen Evans roll out pie crusts a thousand times and she made it look so easy.

But it wasn't easy. It was hard, the hardest thing she'd ever done, and she wasn't really doing it. Evans ought to be charging a hundred dollars for her pies and Ava Grace would tell her so tomorrow.

She plopped the ball of dough on the counter. Maybe it would help if she patted it out a little before going in with the rolling pin from hell. The recipe didn't say to do that, but recipes clearly expected you to know some things and maybe that was one of them.

Then the foghorn blasted, causing her to jump and drop the rolling pin on her shoeless foot.

Noooo. It could not be seven o'clock already! Forgetting about her dough encrusted hands, she grabbed her phone. Seven—on the dot.

She still had to shower, dress, and do her makeup—not to mention make the meal—but there was nothing to do but let him in. It took a bit to turn the doorknob because of her sticky hands.

And there he was—looking better than any man had a right to. Freshly shaved, wearing faded jeans, a black turtleneck, and a taupe corduroy blazer. A lot of men couldn't carry that off, but he could.

And here she was, still in the skirt, sweater, and tights she'd worn all day, covered in flour. And her foot hurt where the rolling pin had attacked it.

Surprise crossed his face. Of course it did, but if he was surprised to find her in this state, she was astounded.

"Hello, Luka." She stood aside. "Won't you come in?" Maybe if she ignored the state of things he would, too.

"It smells good," he said, and she supposed it did. Too bad that boiling chicken was making an empty promise.

He held out a bottle of wine. "I brought chardonnay—to go with chicken."

"Thank you so much." She took the wine—and got dough all over the bottle.

Ava Grace was a complete mess of flour and dough. Her face was shiny and her hair damp. Luka had not guessed that he would know her long enough to see her in such a shape—even if he would know her a hundred years.

Clearly, she was having trouble with the meal, and it took him about fifteen seconds to deduct that she had never cooked this dish before—or maybe any dish. He was reasonably sure that she didn't know she had dough in her hair and on her face.

And, yet, she stood there, regal, like she was totally unaware that anything was amiss.

She studied the wine label. "Nasty Pirate, 2018. Nice."

She knew wine; he'd counted on that. All he knew was this one had cost seventy-eight dollars. He was a vodka and beer man.

"In spite of the name?"

She smiled as if little bits of raw dough were not falling from her fingers onto the floor. He wasn't a man given easily to laughter, at least not the kind bubbling up inside him. But he didn't dare; she would think he was laughing at her expense, when he really, for reasons he didn't particularly understand, found the whole situation enchanting.

She came across with a dazzling smile. "You have to wonder how they come up with these vineyard names, don't you?"

Truthfully, he did not—though he did wonder when she was going to have a meltdown and admit there was no dinner.

Apparently no time soon. "I'm never really certain if I should offer to take a man's blazer in a casual situation." She laughed. "Is it a jacket to combat the cold? Or is it part of the outfit? So you choose. I'll be happy to hang it up for you."

Not likely. Laurel Springs Dry Cleaners had proven to be competent so far, but they had to have their limits.

"I will wear it for now." He looked around the room.

Might as well join in and pretend everything was ordinary. "I like your little house—the pretty soft colors
and the fat, puffy furniture. It looks comfortable and
cozy. Not like the dead football coach suite."

She pushed her hair off her sweaty face, leaving
more sticky residue behind. "Really? It's a little out of
date, but it *is* comfortable."

"You are concerned about something being out of
date, when you sell antiques? Things don't stop being
pretty because they are old."

"You make a very good point."

"That reminds me." He took the necklace from his
pocket. "I think this is very old, but beautiful."

She stretched out her hand to take it, then drew it
back, and looked at him sheepishly. "Why don't you
put it there on the wicker table at the end of the sofa?"

It seemed the thought of dirtying the jewels was
too much for her. She was nearing the end of pretending that nothing was amiss. Too bad. He had been enjoying it.

After placing the necklace on the table, he looked
back at her.

"I suppose you are wondering why I am covered in
flour and dumpling dough."

"I hadn't noticed." He felt that laugh coming, but
bit it back again.

"That's what I was hoping, but we all know how
good I am at self-deception."

"I think you are having some trouble with the meal
you are preparing."

"Yes. There seems to be something wrong with my
rolling pin."

He nodded and willed his face to be serious. "A defective rolling pin can make things difficult for the best cook."

"Well." She tilted her head toward him. "I am not the *best* cook—that is to say, not a cook at all, except for deviled eggs. I can make those. But you have been so nice to me. I wanted to make a meal for you. I don't think I chose the smartest way to show my appreciation."

In that moment, he didn't question her motives. Somehow, he knew she meant it. She was only thinking in the short term, but so was he. She wanted him here and that was enough for him.

What *he* wanted was to whisk her away to a bath, order her some food, feed it to her in bed, and make love to her.

But that wasn't the right answer.

He removed his jacket, folded it over the back of a chair, and pushed his sleeves up.

"Let's see if I can fix that rolling pin. Where's the kitchen?"

Her eyes went wide. "You can cook?"

"A bit," he said.

She looked apprehensive. "The kitchen is somewhat of a mess."

He suspected *somewhat* didn't begin to cover it.

"Kitchens are workrooms. They are meant to be messy. Take me there."

It was a pretty little room, blue and white, made all the whiter with the spilled flour and splattered dough. Somehow she'd also soiled the ruffly checked curtains, though the matching cushions on the chairs that surrounded the round white table seemed to have been spared. There was a Scrabble game set up on that table, but with only one rack of tiles. Interesting. That was his favorite game, though he played online. She must play alone, as well, but with a board.

"I should clean up." When she moved toward the counter, he noticed she was limping.

"Are you injured?"

She made a face. "Just a bruise, I think. The rolling pin hit me on the foot."

"On its own?" He stepped up to the counter, turned on the water, and began to fill the sink. "Or did you drop it."

"I dropped it," she said sheepishly.

"You should rest your foot. This is really a one-person kitchen." Though it might not be even that. It wasn't particularly small, but there was so much stuff it was doubtful that much cooking had ever gone on there. The whole point of the room seemed to be the glass front cabinets, pottery dishes, and counters covered with glass jars of pasta, crocks filled with matching utensils, and wooden dough bowls. The most puzzling thing was the mortar and pestle collection. There had to be at least a dozen made of different materials, from tiny to huge. There was no reason anyone needed more than one. He wanted to find a garbage bag and chuck it all.

"Why don't you wash your hands and sit down? I'll clean up after I cook." Though there would have to be some cleaning before he could begin. How had one person managed this?

She hesitated.

"Really. I want to. You've worked hard and you have

a hurt foot." He took the bottle of wine from her. "I'll pour you a glass of this while you clean your hands."

She surrendered. "There's a corkscrew in the drawer next to the sink."

Their fingers brushed when he handed her the wine. She looked up at him from where she sat at the round table. She'd felt the jolt, too, though she tried to hide it by looking away and sipping her wine.

"This is good—but I probably shouldn't have it. I'm already sleepy. I got up at the crack of dawn to meet Hyacinth and Evans for breakfast. They go to work early."

"You don't go to your shop early?"

She hesitated. "I didn't used to. I think I do now."

What a strange thing to say, but he didn't ask what she meant. He had cleaning to do. The dough had to go. He knew his definition of *dumpling* was probably entirely different from Ava Grace's, but he'd thought he might be able to salvage her dough. Impossible. He scraped the sticky mess off the counter into the side of the sink with the garbage disposal, ran water in her mixing bowl, and washed the defective rolling pin. The boiled chicken on the stove looked okay. He could use the broth. The filling for *pelmeni* was made with raw, ground meat, but he could improvise by mincing the cooked chicken and mixing it with some onion.

"Your chicken looks good." It was the only compliment he could think of.

"Does it? The chef at the country club gave me some tips. Maybe now I can make deviled eggs and boiled chicken. That's almost a whole meal."

"With a salad." Luka poured fresh flour into the clean bowl. "You can make salad."

"Yes, I can." She sounded happy. "I can buy those mixed organic greens. They are the best. You only need to add tomato and cucumber."

"You consulted with a chef?"

She sighed. "Turns out making chicken and dumplings is more complicated than I thought. I was going to buy some—though I wouldn't have lied and said I made it. Too bad for us, Chef Isaac didn't have time, but he coached me a little." She sipped her wine. "Though not enough, I guess."

"Do you have eggs?" he asked.

"Eggs? Yes. I didn't know dumplings had eggs. Maybe that's where I went wrong."

"The dumplings I know have eggs." He went to the refrigerator, found the carton, and cracked three into the bowl.

"You can crack an egg with one hand?" She sounded more impressed than she should have, but he'd take it.

"Yes. I've never given it any thought."

"Where did you learn to cook?" she asked.

"My parents." He added water and salt to the mixture. "My family has restaurant. There are many fancy restaurants in Moscow—opulent, like the home of your parents. Our restaurant is more like your little house—cozy, warm. A place you would go to on a cold winter night with friends and family for a good, hearty meal. It is a happy place, with many regular customers."

"It sounds wonderful. What's it called?"

"Zadorov's. Not very original, no?"

She came to stand beside him. "Did you cook there?"

He laughed. "*Nyet.* My younger brother does. His wife makes the desserts. My older sister does whatever needs doing. She is good at everything. I washed dishes and cleared tables. But I picked up a few cooking skills." He floured the countertop and turned the dough out.

"You put flour on the counter. Should I have done that?"

"*Da.* Keeps the dough from sticking. On the rolling pin, as well."

She drained her glass and set it down. "I guess it was me who was defective—not the rolling pin."

"No, *printsessa*, not defective. You just hadn't learned yet. Now you know. Would you like more wine?" He formed the dough into a smooth ball.

"No. Please, is there something I can do to help? My foot doesn't hurt anymore."

He opened his mouth to decline, but changed his mind. "Do you know how to knead dough?"

Chapter Fourteen

Luka had looked delicious when he came in the door. He was all the more so now that she was a little tipsy. She never had eaten lunch today and she'd drank the wine too fast.

"Do I know how to knead dough? I think you know the answer to that. I didn't even know to flour the rolling pin. But I could learn."

He locked eyes with her. She'd always fancied blue eyes over brown and now she wondered why. Luka's drew her in like no eyes ever had.

"Here. Come." He took her elbow and moved her to stand at the counter with her back to his front. "Put your hands on the dough like so, on either side of the ball." He put his arms around her from behind and covered her hands with his. "We want the dough to be smooth and elastic. Pull it toward you with your fingers, and push it away with heels of your hands."

It was the most tactile experience of her life: warm, dreamy, almost floating. Maybe not almost floating, but *truly* floating—against him, with him, his arms around her and his hands on hers. Gradually she became aware that their bodies moved together in perfect rhythm.

"Push, pull. Fold it over itself. Pick it up and turn it over. Push, pull." His breath was warm against her ear as he spoke and the cadence of his words soothing. "Yes. That's good. You're a quick learner."

If he thought she had the hang of it, would he back away and leave her to do it on her own? She didn't want that.

But he showed no sign of it. "Sometimes, if I am angry, I like to give it a punch, as if it is an opponent who high sticked my teammate." He curled his fingers over hers until her fist was nestled in his. Then he gave the dough a playful punch with both their hands.

"Are you angry now?" she asked. "Maybe because I promised you dinner that I didn't produce?"

He laughed, warm and sweet. "*Nyet, dorogaya.* I am often angry, but I am finding I am not now." He unfurled his fist and they began kneading again.

"What does *dorogaya* mean?" He leaned closer next to her. Merry hell. He was hard against her bottom and making no attempt to hide it. She trembled inside and worked very hard indeed to conceal it.

"It means *sweetheart.*" He pressed his cheek against her temple. *Push, pull, work the dough.*

"Do I? Have a sweet heart?" Right now it was more of a thunder heart.

"I am unsure. You have not shown it to me." He bent and opened his mouth against her neck. "But you have a sweet neck." He raised a hand to cup one breast and then the other. "And sweet breasts. Those, you have shown me. And now I have marked them with flour. Perhaps I must buy you new sweater."

He dropped his mouth to her neck again, this time lightly biting and sucking.

"I think the sweater was ruined anyway." She turned in his arms and said something she might have never said if not for the wine. "But even if it wasn't, entirely worth it."

His breath caught. "I want you very much."

"Even in my nasty, disgusting state?"

He brought his mouth to hers and kissed her briefly three times, once in each corner and then on her bottom lip. "Not nasty and never disgusting. That would be me after I skate. Perhaps a bit soiled." He opened his mouth and kissed her long and deep, their tongues mingling—so sweet, so miraculously slow.

It was the *slow* that reached the deepest part of her.

At last, he lifted his mouth. They were both breathless. "We will take care of the soiled." He must have had some kind of toilet homing device because he led her to the bathroom without asking for directions.

"Good." He nodded with approval. "You have large tub. With feet. Interesting."

"Claw-foot tub. Farmhouse cottage, circa 1992," she muttered as he turned on the water.

While the tub filled, he slowly, slowly undressed her, kissing and stroking as he went, murmuring soft words in Russian, then—when she stood before him naked—in English. "So, so beautiful."

Never had the word *beautiful* meant so much. She'd heard it all her life and her mirror told her she was fortunate, but what she saw in his eyes made her feel it to her core.

"Lift your foot." He ran his hand over the top and wiggled her toes. "*Da.* As you said. Just a bruise."

"You're a medical expert?"

"*Da.* From observation. I have been examined many times."

"Have you ever been hurt?"

"Here." He took her hand and helped her into the warm water. "Of course. Hockey is a rough sport. But never badly. Cuts, bruises, a broken finger once. Only one concussion."

When he stripped his own clothes off, Ava Grace thought he would join her in the tub, but he didn't. Instead, he knelt beside it and gently washed her face. "Do you know you have dry dough on your face?"

"No!" Her hands flew to her cheeks. "Why didn't you tell me?"

"Because." He slipped an arm under her neck and dipped her back to wet her hair. "You are so perfect it gave me pleasure to see you a bit—disheveled. Is that the word? Is sweet."

"No one has ever washed my hair before," she whispered. "Unless they were paid to."

"I have to. There is dough."

She groaned. "Where else?" He reached for the bottle of shampoo and began to soap her hair.

"Hmm. I don't know, but we must make sure. Lay back and enjoy. Close your eyes."

"And miss the sight of you? I don't think so. You have the most beautiful body I've ever seen." She wouldn't have described his face as beautiful. No. His features were too strong for that. With his chiseled cheekbones, cleft chin, and full mouth, it was beyond that. Perfection.

He rinsed her hair, reached for her lemon verbena soap, and sniffed it. "I am thinking you have seen not so many bodies."

She searched for a snappy comeback but, by then, he was soaping her breasts and she forgot everything else except his hands slowly, slowly circling, lifting and squeezing—until he gave her something else to remember when his soapy hands slid lower.

She fell apart.

When her quakes subsided, he stood and took her hand and lifted her to her feet.

"Come. Is not possible for me to wait longer."

But despite his words, he took his time, drying every part of her with a big fluffy towel before leading her to the bed. There, he gave her time and slowly woke the desire in her again before sheathing himself deep inside her. Even then—though he trembled with desire—he took his time, remaining perfectly still, allowing her to enjoy the fullness of him. Only when she lifted her pelvis did he begin to move, thrusting, circling, then circling in the other direction.

How had she lived without this? How would she?

They moved together, so perfectly, so in unison, so slowly until it was impossible not to quicken the pace.

Finally, they cried out together at the same instant.

When he started to withdraw, she couldn't bear to let him go.

"No. Not yet." She wrapped her arms and legs around him. "Stay."

He hesitated and kissed her temple. "You're very tired, *dorogaya*. Sleep a little."

And she did.

By the time Ava Grace entered the kitchen wearing yoga pants and an oversize T-shirt, the *pelmeni* were done, the workspace clean, and Luka was sitting at the table with a glass of wine.

His breath caught. She had been glamorous at the gala, classy in her work clothes, endearingly messy tonight, and—always—beyond beautiful naked in his arms. But there was something about her with damp hair, no makeup, and barefoot.

And then—only then—did he realize the T-shirt she wore was his, the one he'd given her the morning after the gala. For very little, he could fall at her feet and worship. A disconcerting thought, surely one born of good sex. The line of a country song he'd heard came to him. Something about how she destroyed him in a T-shirt. Luka understood that kind of destroy—good, but terrifying.

She smiled and she blushed; she, too, was thinking of the good sex.

"Sorry. I don't know how long I slept."

He rose. "Not so very long." He wasn't altogether sure exactly how long she'd slept because he'd fallen asleep, too, while still deep inside her. It was a very pleasant way to fall asleep—and wake up. "Would you like some food?"

"I'm starving. And it smells so good. I'll move the Scrabble game so we can eat at the table."

He crossed to the stove and picked up one of the

bowls he'd set next to the pot. "I think you will like it. *Pelmeni* is a dumpling filled with chicken."

"It sounds wonderful. Hey! You finished my game. And you bingoed twice."

"I am good at Scrabble. I learned to play to help my English."

"You used Russian words. No fair."

He dipped *pelmeni* into the bowls. "You are one to talk. I know you cheat. The Scrabble dictionary is still open to the word *faqir*."

"Not cheating. I give myself permission to use the dictionary when I play alone. It's like hockey practice. I'm improving my game."

"And I give myself permission to use Russian." He carried the bowls to the table. "*Pelmeni* is traditionally served with sour cream, but you don't have any. No matter. Is also good with butter, which you do have."

"Really?" She paused with the boxed game in her hand. "Would you like sour cream? I'm sure there's some at my parents' house. We could walk up there and get it."

She was offering to take him there?

"I don't care about sour cream," she went on. "But I wouldn't mind a little walk if you want some. I probably ought to check in with them anyway. I have avoided them today."

"I don't care about sour cream either." And he didn't care about meeting her parents—but he cared very much that she was willing to take him there.

"If you're sure." She set the game on the counter and filled their wineglasses.

He placed the bowls on the table and considered very carefully before he spoke again.

"You say you go to the Yellowhammer games. Will you go tomorrow night?"

"Yes. Definitely. I'm having drinks with Hyacinth, Evans, and Claire after work and we're going to drive downtown to the arena together in Claire's car. That way Hyacinth and Evans can ride back to Laurel Springs with Robbie and Jake."

"Perhaps. Maybe—" he fetched the cutlery he'd found earlier and brought it to the table "—you would like to ride back with me? Perhaps go to Hammer Time for food. Most of the team goes."

She looked surprised, but pleased. "Yes. Evans and Hyacinth say Hammer Time is a good time after the games." A bit of a storm cloud moved into her face. "I've never been with them. Seems like I was always in a hurry to get home and talk to Skip."

He crossed the room and pushed her hair off her face. "But no more?"

"No more. Not to say I'll never speak to him again as long as I live. We have spoken—cleared the air to some extent. I'm not ready to talk to him again yet, but we're still friends. Thank you for encouraging me to consider it. It was good to realize I had a choice."

"There are always choices. How do you feel?"

She bit her bottom lip and considered. "Good. After I got over the shock of it all, relieved, if that makes any sense."

"I think it makes perfect sense to be relieved not to marry someone you should not."

"I always knew things weren't right, but I thought time would take care of it."

"Time takes care of many things, but not that."

"Like time will take care of getting you out of Alabama?" He searched her face for a clue to how she felt about the thought of him leaving, but found nothing.

"*Da.* But not only time. I must play my best hockey ever, trust my agent, and be patient."

"Does patience come easily to you?"

"No. Patience isn't easy for anyone, I think. But I am finding the wait a bit easier for some reason." He gave her a look that he hoped left no doubt that she was that reason.

She rewarded him with a smile. "So about tomorrow night… Should I dress for the motorcycle?"

He laughed at the thought that he'd allow her to ride the Harley for such a distance in cold weather.

"No. I think the Range Rover. Come. The food will get cold." He waited until she was seated to take his chair.

She put a bite of food in her mouth, closed her eyes, and moaned. "Luka, this is so good. You should become a chef when you retire from hockey."

"*Nyet.* I like to cook, but only when I feel like it. Is not my passion. That is necessary to be successful, especially when the work is so hard."

She stopped with her spoon in midair. "I don't know what it feels like to be passionate."

"I disagree."

She rolled her eyes and took another bite of food. "I mean about work. How do you get there? Was hockey always your passion?"

He considered. "*Da*, to a degree. But success feeds passion."

"Do you think you can work to become passionate about something? Or does it have to come natural?"

"I hope that you can. I am almost twenty-nine. I play a young man's sport. Soon, I will be old—but only in the eyes of hockey. I will have to find something else, and I don't know what that is." His words surprised him; he'd never shared that with anyone.

She frowned. "What do you think you'd like to do?"

Damn. He should have known she would try to solve the problem that he'd been pondering for many months in the next five minutes. She was a fixer, one who wanted to make people happy, but he didn't want to think about it.

He lightened the mood. "I was thinking of becoming a professional Scrabble player."

She narrowed her eyes and sipped her wine. "Yeah? You can't beat me."

"Ridiculous! I can. I'll even let you use the dictionary."

"I guess we need to find out, don't we? After we eat? No dictionary and no Russian words."

"Sure. If you're brave enough."

Was there such thing as strip Scrabble? If not, maybe he could invent it.

Chapter Fifteen

Ava Grace rang the bell of Claire's mint-condition mid-century modern house. There was movement behind the column of small diamond-shaped windows, and the burnt orange door opened.

"Come in out of the cold." Claire stepped aside to admit Ava Grace. She was dressed for the game in Yellowhammer colors, but no hockey jersey for Claire. She wore black pants and a gold blouse with a silver belt made of interlocking leaves. You had to look closely to see the small jeweled Yellowhammer logo on the collar of her blouse, but her fandom wouldn't be lost on anyone. Claire was the kind of woman people tended to look at closely.

Claire's silver, pink, and turquoise Christmas decorations still glowed—as did the fat, retro blue lights that lined the roofline and windows outside. It all matched the style of her home perfectly.

When Claire's grandparents built the house in 1954, it was considered a modern showplace. Claire was committed to keeping the house in perfectly preserved condition, from the sleek, functional furniture to the geometric wallpaper and original-to-the-house appliances. Mid-century modern was not a style that appealed to Ava Grace very much, but she could appreciate its artistry.

Ava Grace removed her gloves and handed Claire her coat. "Thank you for letting me come over early, before Hyacinth and Evans."

"I'm glad you did." After hanging Ava Grace's coat, she closed the closet. "I've been concerned about you. I tried to call before I left for Merritt on Christmas Eve."

"I saw." Ava Grace followed Claire into the living room and they sat on the lemon yellow sofa with the built-in end tables. "My not answering wasn't personal. I wasn't answering for anyone." Partly because she'd still been in Luka's bed.

"Entirely understandable." Claire filled a glass from a pitcher on the kidney-shaped coffee table and handed it to Ava Grace. "It's a Queen Bee—bourbon, sherry, honey, a little lemon. I have some hot hors d'oeuvre in the oven. I thought to bring them out when the others arrive, unless you'd like something now."

"No, thank you. I'm not hungry." Ava Grace took a sip of her drink. "Delicious. Tastes potent."

"Which is why I'm not having any," Claire said. "I'm driving."

Ava Grace took a deep breath. "I hope you don't mind, but I won't be returning to Laurel Springs with you tonight. Luka Zadorov asked me to ride back with him and go to Hammer Time."

Claire raised her eyebrows. "I don't mind." She didn't comment further. Ava Grace hadn't expected her to. Besides, what was there to say? She was the injured party. People might be surprised, but no one was going to judge her for moving on so soon after Skip—if moving on was what she'd done. "Luka is very talented," Claire said. "I wish he were more committed to the Yellowhammers. He's been up-front about his plans. We don't like it, but we won't stop him."

Ava Grace nodded to acknowledge that Claire had spoken, but she didn't respond otherwise. She didn't have an answer and it was nothing to do with her. Instead, she asked the obligatory seasonal question. "Did you have a good Christmas? I hope so."

Claire nodded. "I did. I stayed with Uncle Tiptoe and Aunt Carol Jane. It was a full house. I suppose it's too much to hope that yours was very festive."

"It's over. That's the best thing I have to say." She hadn't come here to talk about the debacle, but she would have to give Claire a report before moving on. "I'm fine. It was a shock; that goes without saying. But it's over now and things will get better for all of us. Skip has always been part of my life and he always will be, though I need a break from him. We're going to find a different way to be—eventually."

"That's good to hear," Claire said. "I've watched the three of you grow up. It's hard to think of one of you without the other two. I've always admired how you step up and do what you have to, Ava Grace."

Perfect segue to what she *did* come here to talk about. "That's a lovely compliment, Claire, though a bit generous. I haven't always stepped up. But I'm ready to."

Claire nodded and Ava Grace got the distinct feeling Claire knew exactly what she was talking about. "Go on."

"We both know I've not been all in with Heirloom. I've made it more of a hobby—my own little playground. My mother suggested closing when we thought I would be getting married—said I didn't like it anyway. That wasn't true. I do like it, but I haven't been committed."

Claire sipped her water. "You're going a little hard on yourself."

"Maybe. Sometimes I key into customers and am able to find exactly the right things for them. That's a good feeling."

"That's your talent. I've told you that all along."

Ava Grace nodded. "I believe that, but I stumble onto those situations. I don't make them happen. In the back of my mind, Heirloom was always temporary. I know I must have been a disappointment to you."

Claire shook her head. "No, you have not been a disappointment to me. I knew your strengths and weaknesses from the beginning, and your strengths are stronger than you think—your weaknesses not as deep. I knew you viewed Heirloom as temporary, but I was always confident that you would come into your own and that would change."

Ava Grace laughed and took a long drink. "It's going to have to. I might have landed here kicking and screaming, but Heirloom is my future."

A ghost of a smile crossed Claire's face. "I knew this day would come. It would have come even if your private life had gone as you originally planned."

Ava Grace wasn't so sure about that, but maybe it was true. Claire was almost always right. Anyway, it didn't matter.

She took a deep breath. "I've already made some changes and I wanted to get some advice about other things I can do."

"What have you done?"

"First, I am not going to leave opening and setup to Piper and Jen anymore. I'm going to behave professionally and get to work early, instead of when it's nearly time to open."

Claire nodded. "Taking charge is important."

"I'm offering design consultation, like you advised me to do a year ago. I've already had it painted on the door and ordered new business cards." Claire looked surprised. That didn't happen often. "I'm going to make a concerted effort to move merchandise, rather than putting my energy into buying up French hand-painted oyster plates and abstract art because they caught my fancy. And I'm going to stop using my personal money to buy merchandise—unless it would really be a good business decision." Though she might have to dip into it to pay Piper and Jen. It had probably been a mistake to hire them full-time, but it was done now and they'd earned their place. She wasn't going to reward their hard work and loyalty by cutting their hours.

Claire leaned toward her and smiled. "Those are all smart decisions, Ava Grace. I'm proud of you."

"But there's something missing. I feel like I've landed on little pieces of the puzzle, but not the whole picture. Does that make sense?"

"More than you know. You've found the part of the business that really speaks to your heart—gives you real satisfaction."

"My passion?" She parroted Luka.

"Yes. A perfect way to put it. Too many people go into business thinking the profits are the goal. Most of them fail. The passion has to come first. The money will follow."

"You say I've found mine?"

"You said it yourself—putting the right person with the right piece of merchandise."

"I don't feel passionate about it."

Claire squinted and let out a deep breath. "No. You haven't experienced it often enough to achieve true satisfaction. You have to look at the broader picture, find the avenue—the philosophy—to get there consistently."

That was no help. "What do you think that could be?"

"I don't know, but you'll find it now that you're looking for it."

Clearly Ava Grace's confusion showed on her face.

"Let me explain. As you know, my first business was a bookstore in downtown Birmingham."

"The first of many," Ava Grace said. And not just her first bookstore—her first business. Claire had her finger in countless pies and everything she touched turned to gold.

"When I opened my first bookstore, I was about your age. I wanted a warm, cozy atmosphere where people would come and stay for hours to read. Some said that providing an inviting place for customers to sit would cause them to read without buying. I didn't believe that. People who read buy books. And I was right. I provided upholstered chairs with ottomans, study tables with good lighting, and soft music. I was almost there, but not quite. I was missing a piece, but I couldn't find it.

The store was comfortable and almost welcoming, but not a hundred percent. I wanted it to be a place where people longed to be, that they could sink into and relish. Then one day, someone came in with a cup of coffee. One of my clerks pointed out the no food or drink sign, and it clicked into place. Is there anything more comforting than a warm drink, a cookie, and a good book?

"It was the missing element. I put in a coffee shop. Now coffee shops in bookstores are common, but they weren't back then. It was expensive to implement, but I did it and book sales went up. Hardly any were ruined with spilled coffee. A sizable part of the revenue from my stores comes from the coffee shops. In a time when bookstores are struggling, mine are not because we give our customers a feeling of home every day and in every way."

It was becoming clearer—at least where other people were concerned—but she wasn't sure it would ever pertain to her. "Like Evans puts her heart and soul into her crusts to make superior pies and Hyacinth will go to any length to make sure her brides feel special."

"Exactly."

"So I just wait for an epiphany to find my vehicle?"

Claire shrugged. "Yes. I wager you won't have to wait too long. Meanwhile, there's something more concrete you can work on."

Ava Grace sighed. "I know. My web presence." This wasn't the first time this had come up. "A Facebook page isn't enough."

"And you haven't updated that in three weeks. Do you go online at all?"

"Oh, all the time. Like most everyone else, I spend

way too much time on social media. I read several blogs every day and follow a lot of decorating Instagrams. I just never post." Lately, she'd also been reading *The Face Off Grapevine*, a pro hockey gossip blog, but she wasn't going to mention that. "And I know I need a website. I've looked at a lot of examples. I even know what I want. I keep intending to figure out how to do it—and then I get distracted by an estate sale."

"You don't have to do it yourself. Your time is better spent at estate sales. Hiring someone to build a website would be money well spent—certainly more so than a dozen oyster plates. I can put you in touch with someone."

"Yes. Send me the name." This was progress, whereas she had her doubts about the whole abstract looking-for-a-vehicle concept.

"Both Jen and Piper are active on social media. While you need to make an effort to interact with people yourself, it doesn't all have to be on you. You could ask them to take that up for Heirloom. I bet they'd love it—especially if you offered an incentive, like a hundred dollars each month to the one whose posts get the most activity."

So simple, yet so effective. "You're a genius. Why can't I think of things like that?"

"You will eventually. Meanwhile, I'm your mentor."

The doorbell rang and Claire rose. "That will be Evans and Hyacinth. But, Ava Grace?"

"Yes?"

"Have a good time at Hammer Time tonight, but careful about rebound."

Rebound with Luka? Is that what this was?

* * *

Luka ushered Ava Grace through Hammer Time.

It was more crowded than usual, probably because the week between Christmas and New Year's was like one interminable weekend. He supposed a lot of people took off work that week—not that he'd know anything about that. Hockey players didn't take off work because it was a holiday. Practice yesterday, game tomorrow, early practice Friday, and leaving afterward for three cities in three days.

And then there was the game tonight—and what a game it had been. They'd lost to Nashville, 5-2, and Glaz was not amused. Luka didn't blame him; he wasn't amused either, especially with his own performance. He hadn't stunk up the ice that bad in a long time. Worse, Ava Grace had been there to witness it.

It had been a mistake to ask her here tonight. He wasn't fit company. Coming back from the arena downtown, traffic had been heavy, so conversation had been light. She probably thought he was pouting because of the loss. Maybe he was. He hated to lose under ordinary circumstances, and these were not ordinary circumstances.

Kurt had called. Ian Lassiter, of the Pittsburgh Locomotives, was out for the season with a knee injury and the team was looking for a center. Pittsburgh was one of the best hockey cities in North America and Luka's former teammate and friend Andrei Petrov played for them. If traded to Pittsburgh, Andrei and his wife, Ellie, would welcome Luka into their home until he could make other arrangements. There would be no squatting in a hotel suite—especially one named for a college football person.

So he was hopeful—or he had been before the game. Given his performance tonight, he'd be lucky to be allowed into the minor league.

None of this was Ava Grace's fault. He had asked her here and he would carry through—but he would not be going home with her.

Hockey players—maybe all athletes—were notorious for wanting sex after a game. Luka was no different, but only when it had been a good night. Unlike his teammates, past and present, he didn't want comfort after a bad night, whether the bad came from a sore shoulder or bruised pride. Comfort was only temporary solace; it meant nothing. He needed to be alone—and he would be later. For now, he would act better than he felt.

"Is Hammer Time always this crowded after games?" Ava Grace asked as they moved through the building.

"Perhaps not so much as tonight, but there have been more people since these college football games have ended."

She cut her eyes at him. "There's one more. Alabama plays Clemson for the National Championship in twelve days."

"You will go to this game?"

She shook her head. "I had planned to, but I changed my mind. It's in California and I don't want to be away from Heirloom. I told my daddy to sell my ticket."

He took some satisfaction in that. "You will come to the Yellowhammer game instead? Is not so far as California." Maybe he'd play better.

"You don't have a game that night. You're fresh off

the road from the weekend. You play at home the next night—Tuesday. Florida."

"You know my schedule better than I do." He guided her toward the glass French doors that led to the private room reserved for the team after games.

"I have good reason," she said. "You may not be here by then, but I will."

There was a lot he didn't like about that, starting with how she would continue to go to the Yellowhammer games once he was no longer a Yellowhammer. At best, that made no sense. At worst, it made him a selfish bastard. What did he expect? For her to fly in for the games wherever he ended up? Or move there? She was as likely to leave Laurel Springs as Tatiana had been to leave Moscow. Perhaps she would visit him— but that was crazy thinking, and to what end? He discarded the thought. She was a princess and he was a pauper—well, not a pauper, but beneath her.

"We will have to wait and see," he said. "Who knows how long I'll be here?" He caught sight of Sparks and Robbie already seated with Evans and Hyacinth at the end of the table. "Do your friends know you will be here tonight? That you were coming with me?"

"Yes. I told them." As he reached to open the door, she stopped him. "What's with these jerseys on the wall? Where's yours?"

Damn. *That.* "Mine is not on the wall. Claire chooses when a jersey goes on the wall. She says it must be earned. For now, there is only Robbie's, Able Killen's, and Wingo's."

He told himself he didn't care, and he didn't. It was silly, like affixing a foil star to a child's spelling paper.

Grown men should not need such accolades. Their paychecks were reward enough. No other team he'd ever played for had lived and died by having jerseys hung on the wall of a mediocre sports bar. Still, it was embarrassing to admit to Ava Grace that he had not been chosen for the "honor."

She studied the wall and when she turned to meet his eyes, her face was stony. "I don't know what Claire's criterion is, but it's not fair."

"Is fair if tonight was any indication."

"It's not," Ava Grace said with conviction. "You had a terrible night tonight. It's true." At least she wasn't shining sun rays up his jersey. "But you weren't the only one and there have been games when you've outplayed everyone on this team. You're better than Robbie and Able. You've scored the winning goal twice this season and had three hat tricks."

She knew what a hat trick was?

She went on, "I don't know if you're better than Dietrich. I don't know how to compare a center and a goalie; I don't know if you can. But I know this…" To his surprise, she went on to cite statistics—points, goals, assists, penalty minutes—not only from this season but from teams and seasons past.

She had it right, too. "I had no idea you knew so much about hockey," he said.

"You can thank your good friend college football. It made me a sports fan. The leap wasn't that hard. Besides, it's easy to find online. Let's go. I'm hungry."

She strolled through the French doors straight for the chair beside Evans like she owned not only the room, but every room. Made sense, since she was the most beautiful woman in every room.

Maybe he would rethink his need to be alone tonight. He didn't require her comfort. Turns out, she'd already given him that—but her company would be a fine thing.

Chapter Sixteen

"May we sit here?" Ava Grace asked.

"Of course." Evans moved her purse. "You don't have to ask."

"You never can tell." Ava Grace unbuttoned her coat. "You know how people are about their pew at church. I thought y'all might have something similar going on here."

"Even if we did," Robbie said, "it would not affect you. You just walked in here with the most feared man on the team." He slipped an arm around Hyacinth.

"*Nyet.* That is you, Scotty." Luka used Robbie's nickname. "Everyone fears you will bend over while wearing your kilt and we will see things we do not wish to see." Luka took Ava Grace's coat and pulled a chair out for her. "I will hang this up so these philistines do not soil it with barbecue sauce and beer."

When he was out of earshot, Evans whispered to Ava Grace, "He sniffed your coat. I bet he sniffs your hair."

"Stop it, Evans." When she'd told Evans and Hyacinth she would be coming here with Luka tonight, she had expected the third degree, but they had only exchanged knowing looks and said she deserved to have some fun. Maybe being publicly humiliated by your gay boyfriend had at least one perk. The eggshell-walking wouldn't last forever, but she'd take it while she could get it.

Luka slid into the chair beside Ava Grace. "Much of the team is missing tonight." The long table was more than half empty and there was no one at any of the satellite tables for four. "The room is usually full."

Able Killen and his girlfriend sat at the other end of the table with the one they called Magic Man and the model-perfect Frenchman, whose name Ava Grace couldn't remember. They all waved and called to Luka, who returned the greeting.

"Can you blame them?" Jake asked. "They've gone home to lick their wounds after the ass-whipping we took and the ass-chewing we got from Glaz."

"I feel it," Robbie said. "Losing is bad enough. Losing to your former team is hell, even if you left on good terms."

"*Da.* Worse when the terms were not so good," Luka said. "I hope I do not have to find out when we go to Boston at end of the week."

Right—the team that had taken his choice away and sent him to football country; he would be out for revenge for sure.

"We've got your back, man," Robbie said. "We'll beat them."

Luka filled her glass, and then his from the water pitcher on the table. "I did not have yours tonight when we played your former team."

"It happens," Jake said. He opened his menu. "I think I'll have pizza."

Everyone laughed except Ava Grace, the joke lost on her.

"He has pizza every time. Is always his after-game meal," Luka said to Ava Grace.

Robbie reached for his menu. "And—this is going to be a surprise—I'm having two cheeseburgers and double fries."

"What's your go-to, Luka?" Ava Grace asked.

"I have no regular meal. I am not superstitious as these two are. They are wet behind the ears. They will learn."

"It's not superstition," Robbie said. "It's a ritual."

"Is same thing." Luka studied his menu.

"Anyway," Robbie said. "We're only three years younger than you."

"In years, yes. In pro hockey world, no. You are college boys. I went to the Walleyes straight from juniors at nineteen."

"My parents wanted me to get a degree so I'd have something to fall back on," Jake said.

"Yes?" Luka looked interested. "What is your fall-back?"

Jake laughed. "No idea. I majored in business administration, but I can't see it. Maybe I'll live off my wife when I get too old to play."

"So being a college boy did not help you. Did it help you, Scotty?"

"Nah," Robbie said around a yawn. "Maybe I'll go work for Hyacinth at Trousseau."

This time Ava Grace was able to join in the laughter because she knew how unlikely that was to happen.

"Don't hold your breath." But Hyacinth gave him a dazzling smile.

"Jake, maybe Robbie can teach you to decorate cakes," Evans said. "Y'all can open a cake shop."

"Careful what you wish for," Jake said. "People might like cake better than pie. The competition would be stiff."

"From you two?" Evans said. "Is this the face of someone who's worried?"

"How about you, Luka?" Robbie asked. "Since you're so old, what are your plans?"

Ava Grace stiffened. Watching Luka's easy comradery with his teammates was so nice, but had Robbie brought up a sticky subject that would end it?

Luka pointed to his menu. "My immediate plan is to eat this pasta with shrimp and crab. For future, who knows? Not me. But then, I was not college boy. Maybe I go to college." He cut his eyes at Ava Grace. "Maybe I go to Belmont, like Ava Grace, where there is no football team."

It pleased her more than it should have that he remembered what she had said.

"Take your order?" The waitress appeared at the end of the table beside Jake. "The special tonight is butter garlic basted ribeye with rosemary potatoes, and the soup is chicken and dumplings."

This time it was Ava Grace and Luka who laughed, when the others had no idea what was funny.

It felt good to laugh.

Luka wasn't given to laughter and certainly hadn't expected it to flow out of him like toothpaste from a tube, tonight of all nights. He found he did not dislike being here with his teammates as much as he had thought he would. The loss and his performance still weighed on him, but it wasn't as heavy.

He put a bite of delicious pasta in his mouth and stroked Ava Grace's knee under the table. She turned and smiled at him, and he was considering sliding his hand up a little higher when everything went bad.

"I'm here! Finally!" the most annoying voice in the universe rang out.

Sparks and Scotty groaned in stereo, which didn't begin to describe how Luka felt.

"And was such a pleasant meal," Luka muttered. Wingo was alone, which was unusual. He'd probably picked up a puck bunny from the autograph line and taken care of business in the parking lot before coming here.

"What's that you say, Zov?" He came to loom over Luka.

He would remain calm. He would not let him know that it bothered him to be called by that ridiculous nickname.

Luka laid his fork down. He'd already stabbed him once and he didn't want to give in to the temptation a second time. But the knife was so handy... Never mind that it was a butter knife. It would hurt, probably more than a sharp one.

"I say, it was pleasant time until you came along."

"You don't mean it. You know you love me." Wingo reached out toward Luka. He loved to try to ruffle Luka's hair.

Luka picked up the butter knife. "I swear, Wings, if you touch my hair, I will gut you right here."

"It's hard to resist. It's so silky. But you won't stab me. You've been threatening me with bodily harm all season. You need me in the net too bad…" His voice trailed off. "Whoa! What have we here?" He homed in on Ava Grace. "A.G.! You finally came. That Skip needs to be run out of the country and I'm the very one to do it for him."

Luka went completely numb, head to toe, and before he could find the feeling again, Ava Grace smiled up at the asshole. "Hello, Dietrich. That's not necessary. I hope your sister liked her Christmas gifts."

"Absolutely. Loved them. Especially that fancy comb and brush. I'm coming to you for all my presents from here on out. You're the best present picker."

"Glad I could help."

"Plus, I get to look at you while you pick. That's life changing." Wings looked from Ava Grace to Luka and back again. "Say, Zov? Suppose you slide down one so I can sit by my personal shopper, A.G.?"

Time stopped. The earth shook. Trumpets blew. This had to be the end of time.

Luka looked around him. Sparks, Scotty, Hyacinth, and Evans were statues, and not of people who had posed to be pretty. They were more like those dead Pompeii people who looked like they knew something bad was about to happen.

But no. He would remain calm; he would not let this kid push him over the edge.

"No," he said simply and took another bite of his pasta. "Go sit somewhere else."

"Ohhhh! I get it. Ava Grace, don't tell me you came here with him. He's not nearly good enough for you. I would have brought you."

And Dietrich Wingo laid a hand on Ava Grace's shoulder.

Luka's heart pounded and, for the first time, he understood the meaning of seeing red. He was no stranger to anger, but this was something new.

He was jealous; insanely, without reason, jealous.

It wasn't that he thought anything had happened between Ava Grace and this ridiculous man-child, or that it ever would. As for her encouraging him—unthinkable. She had too much sense. So why the jealousy? As his reasons became clearer, the anger and jealousy were replaced with fear.

He didn't want anyone, let alone Dietrich Wingo, looking at Ava Grace, talking to her, thinking about her, and *especially* not touching her. That wasn't realistic or rational, yet he couldn't make the feeling go away.

But he could make Wingo go away.

He took another bite of his food and took his time about chewing it before he spoke. "Go away, Wings," he said with no inflection. "Go find a chair with Killjoy and Magic Man." *And get your fucking hand off Ava Grace!*

Wings looked up and down the table, held up his index finger, and nodded. Luka did not understand that gesture, nor did he care. He only knew Wings was walking away and that was enough.

Luka resumed eating.

"Holy family and all the wise men," Robbie said under his breath.

Luka looked up. No. It could not be. Wings had gone around the table, past the others, and come back down the other side.

"There!" He let himself down in the chair beside Hyacinth and across from Ava Grace. And if that wasn't bad enough the waitress appeared and set a plate in front of him.

"There you go, Mr. Wingo," she said. "We saw you come in and knew this is what you'd want. Broiled salmon, no butter, steamed kale, and a half serving of wild rice. Did you want a beer tonight?"

"Thank you for looking out for me, Stacy. No beer. I'm having water tonight."

"Happy to do it." She looked around. "Can I get anything for anyone else?"

"May I get a knife?" Luka asked. "A sharp one?"

"No!" Jake said.

Stacy looked from Luka to Jake, confused.

"He's kidding, Stacy," Jake said.

"I say let him have it," Robbie said.

A bit of panic crossed Stacy's face.

"I apologize, Stacy," Luka said. "I was kidding. I'm fine with my present cutlery." He felt bad for confusing the girl. He'd make it up with her tip.

"All right…" She made a quick exit.

Wingo's eyes zeroed in on Ava Grace. "They know what I eat here. My body is my temple. I don't put anything bad in it. I only allow myself a beer as a reward when we win." He looked at Luka's mug, pointedly.

"Not me," Robbie said. "I have an ale, win or lose, play or not." He took a long drink.

"Me, too," Jake chimed in. They were trying to defuse the situation. "I eat a whole pizza, the greasier the better. My body is Evie's temple."

Wingo was oblivious, as usual. "So, Zov, where's your little brother tonight?"

Wingo knew Luka did not like for him to refer to Logan as his brother, but he would not bite, would not make a scene in front of Ava Grace no matter how much he wanted to. "I think he is still sleeping. Is early in Moscow."

"I meant your Yellowhammer little brother."

And yet, he couldn't let it pass completely. He'd be polite. He wouldn't raise his voice, but he had to speak. "I tell you before. Logan is my friend. Not my brother. You choose friends, not brothers. Friends care for you, because they want to, not because they have to. I wonder if you understand that."

Wingo shoveled salmon into his mouth. "I hear he got himself a girl over Christmas."

"Don't trust all you hear." What Wingo said was true, but not Luka's news to tell—and definitely not Wingo's.

"Yep. Molly, from the toy store. I saw them leaving the game together, with Logan's kid. They looked very cozy."

"Really?" Ava Grace said. "That's great."

"I'm so glad," Evans chimed in. "Molly's a sweetheart. She's had a hard time since her fiancé died a few years ago. She could use some happy."

"Oh!" Hyacinth rubbed her hands together. "Wouldn't she be a beauty in candlelight?"

These people were insane—talking like this relationship was a guarantee. Logan seemed to like her and Luka hoped it worked out, but it had been a short time.

A short time—like Ava Grace and him. And what kind of relationship were they in, anyway? Was it even a relationship? Would they see each other again? He never knew day-to-day. Would she think it was strange if he called her while he was on the road this weekend? Not that he couldn't get through three days without talking to her. Of course not.

He turned to look at Ava Grace, searching for a clue. That's when he saw it—Wingo's hand creeping slowly, slowly across the table, his eyes on Ava Grace's fried shrimp.

Enough! He could stand no more!

"Dietrich Wingo!" Luka slammed his hand on the table. "You will not put your hand in Ava Grace's plate! You will not mention what happened at the gala. You will stop pretending like you never eat unhealthy food! You will stop saying your body is your temple. You will stop gossiping about my best friend!"

Wingo grinned. "How about saving ninety-three percent of the shots on goal? Should I stop that, too?"

Visions of murder danced in Luka's head. *Nyet*, maybe not murder, but maiming. Defiantly maiming. All he had was a fork and a butter knife, but they would do.

Ava Grace chose that moment to touch her napkin to her lips and stand.

"Luka?" She laid a hand on his arm as though nothing had happened. "I really hate to ask you to cut your evening short, but I need to be at work early. Would you mind very much taking me home?"

Great. Now he had embarrassed her, maybe scared her. She would never want to see him again.

"*Da*. Of course," he said quietly. He threw some bills on the table. "I'll get your coat."

They were silent until they were in the parking lot beside his car. "I am sorry, Ava Grace. My temper... Was inexcusable to embarrass you."

"Nonsense." She slipped an arm around his waist. "He's not a bad person, but he's insufferable. I suspect he'll grow out of it, but for now, he's way too big for his britches."

A warm cloud settled on him. He didn't understand that phrase—too big for his britches—but liked the sound of it. "Logan says I am too hard on him, that he looks up to me."

"I'm sure that's true. Logan knows him better than I do. But regardless of Dietrich's motivation, he's very good at pushing your buttons. Nobody ought to have to tolerate that."

A truth slapped him in the face. He knew she could have defended Wingo—probably with legitimate points. But she understood he needed to hear that his reaction was valid. This must be what it felt like to have someone who would always be on your side.

"So." He pushed her hair off her face. "Must you really go home? And if so, must it be alone? Or perhaps you could go to my home, such as it is."

She hesitated. "Are you sure? It's been a hard night. I wouldn't be offended or feel slighted if you wanted to be alone to 'lick your wounds'—as Jake said."

His stomach turned over. Did she understand *everything*? T-shirt or not, she destroyed him.

"Nyet, dorogaya." He crushed her to him. "I'd rather have you lick my wounds."

"That can be arranged." She laughed, sweet and easy, always so sweet and easy.

He opened her car door and took her hand to help her in—but once she was seated, he didn't let go. "Ava Grace, it has been a short time. I know you are still finding your way; my time here is limited. But for now, we are here and I like being with you. I don't like every time I see you to wonder if I will not see you again."

"I don't like wondering that either," she whispered.

"Then we will wonder no more." He felt happy, and a laugh bubbled up inside him. "Except one thing."

"What?"

"We did not decide. Your place or mine?"

Chapter Seventeen

Three Weeks Later

Ava Grace scrolled through Heirloom's various social media accounts. The girls were doing a great job. Jen had insisted that more than two posts a day would be counterproductive and had made a schedule so they alternated morning and evening posts. Piper's posts were more interesting, but Jen's were more informative.

Piper looked over her shoulder. "Did you see my picture of the Edwardian writing desk? And how I tricked it out with some books, stationery, and an oil lamp?"

"I did." Ava Grace laid her phone aside. "I especially liked that giant stuffed panda you put in the chair."

"Wasn't he great? I brought him from home. I wanted a top hat for him, but I couldn't find one."

"He was eye-catching enough. Someone has already called to ask about the desk."

Piper widened her eyes. "Really? If they buy it do I get extra points?"

"No. That wasn't part of the deal."

"I don't need them anyway," Piper said. "I have one

hundred ninety-three more social media interactions than Jen. I'm totally going to win that hundred dollars."

"You think?" Ava Grace looked up from the Valentine's tablescape she was working on and couldn't help but smile. If Jen was meticulous and a self-starter, Piper was a creative free spirit. She needed to be given direction, but she put her whole heart into everything. "What are you going to spend it on?"

"A tattoo. I can't wait."

"What kind of tattoo? And where?"

"A wind rose. A little one." She made a circle with her thumb and index finger. "On my ankle bone. It was either that or a high heel shoe."

Ava Grace burst out laughing.

"Yeah, that's what I thought," Piper said. "It would be hilarious, but I don't think a tattoo ought to be funny. It ought to mean something since it's going to be with you, like, forever."

"And what would the wind rose mean to you?" Ava Grace began to place the cranberry goblets on the table.

"I've actually given it a lot of thought," Piper said seriously. "I want it to remind me that I shouldn't be afraid to walk away from home, and that I'll never get so lost I can't come back."

"Why, Piper. That's very profound."

Piper squealed a little—it was *a little* because Ava Grace had broken her from squealing a lot. "I have the best idea! Come with me. I know the best place to go. My cousin got a picture of her dog on her arm. Not what I would do, but it looks exactly like him—the dog, I mean. This guy is great. You should totally get a tattoo."

"Maybe I would," Ava Grace said, "but I don't have

a dog." She could just about imagine her mother's re-action if she got a tattoo of any kind. They'd have to call the undertaker for sure.

"Nooo." Piper gave Ava Grace's shoulder a friendly little shove. "Not a dog. Not a wind rose either, because you're *never* leaving home. Something special for you."

"Why do you think I'm never leaving? I could. We could get matching wind roses." Not that she would get a tattoo—ever. And, to be honest, she was about as likely to leave Laurel Springs, but she didn't like being so predictable.

"Oh, you. I would totally get a matching tattoo with you but, like I said, you don't need a wind rose. You wouldn't leave Laurel Springs. Not that I think you should. You know—you fit here. It's like Laurel Springs is your favorite cousin, or something. You always know what's going on with everybody, always want to help people. It wouldn't be right without you. If you left, I think everything would kind of freeze in place, you know. What do you call it? When time stands still?" Piper struck a pose, with her mouth open and her hands in midair.

"Temporal stasis?" Ava Grace opened the box of antique Valentines and spread them on the corner of the table. "I can promise you Laurel Springs wouldn't miss a beat without me."

"Ah, but do you really *know* that? It could be like that castle in the fairy tale. You know."

"No. I don't know, Piper. Most fairy tales have a castle. You have to tell me more." Maybe she should lay a valentine on each salad plate. Not bad. Not really what she was looking for, but it would do.

"There were fairies. And a spindle."

"'Briar Rose'?"

"I've got it! You should get a laurel wreath." Apparently they'd moved on from fairy tales. That often happened with Piper. "It's classy, like you. And you *are* Laurel Springs. Plus, it symbolizes victory."

"You're good for my ego, Piper, but I haven't won anything."

"Sure you have. You win every day, just by being Ava Grace." She tapped her fingers against her cheek. "Now, where should we put it? Hm. If it were me, I'd get it on my wrist, but that's not you. You're private. Mysterious. I'd say on the back of your neck. Or your hip. That way, only somebody you allowed *very* close to you would see it."

Luka would be surprised. She could imagine him lifting her hair to kiss the back of her neck and finding it, or—even better—slipping her panties off and seeing it on her hip. Would he be intrigued or appalled? He didn't have any tattoos, so maybe he didn't like them. On the other hand, what did it matter?

Her gut clenched. It was mid-January—six weeks, give or take, from the trade deadline. He was still confident that a good deal would come through. Meanwhile, the Yellowhammers were doing well and were playoff bound. She and Luka had fallen into a pattern. They ate dinner together every night—often with him cooking. They played Scrabble, watched movies, or sat quietly together reading and surfing the web. As for the sex—better and better. The only nights they'd spent apart were when he was on the road.

She didn't like those nights.

"Look, Ava Grace," Piper said excitedly and stuck her phone in Ava Grace's face. "Laurel wreath tattoos. Who knew there would be so many? This is the one I would pick for you—delicate, in pale green. Colored ones cost more, but I think a laurel wreath has to be green, don't you?"

"Oh, yes. Definitely."

"I'm going to text it to you, so you'll have it when we go." She fiddled with her phone and Ava Grace's chimed. "We're ready—as soon as I win the hundred dollars. Or you don't have to wait. You could go whenever you want. I'll totally go with you."

"I'll think about it," Ava Grace said. *And I'm thinking absolutely not.*

"Just say the word. Hey! Can we go to the Purple Onion when we go downtown? To celebrate our tattoos? I love that falafel." Piper didn't wait for an answer. She looked at the table and zoned out. "Hey! You know what I'd do with those old valentines?"

"Let's try to remember to use the words *vintage* and *antique*, Piper."

"Sorry. But here's what I'd do: make a centerpiece. Clip the valentines to two of those silver trees you had in the window at Christmas. The smallest ones. Put that white swan planter in the middle. Fill it with chocolate kisses and tie a red bow around its neck. Then put the trees on either side."

And this was why Ava Grace put up with Piper's incessant chatter and surfing from topic to topic without taking a breath. "That's a great idea, Piper."

"Somebody might buy the whole setup, swan and all.

Though I don't see why anyone would want old valentines that were sent to somebody else."

"*Vintage*, Piper. And sometimes you want things just because they are."

"Me? I would want a new valentine—one of those that plays music when you open it."

"Then I hope you get it. Will you go get the trees out of the storeroom?"

Ava Grace wondered if she'd get a valentine. Sure, her daddy would buy her a Whitman's Sampler—and then proceed to eat it. Her mother would buy her some perfume. Realistically, she couldn't expect Luka to still be here, but it would be nice to spend a holiday together before he left.

Luka had been on the road with the team over New Year's, so she'd spent New Year's Eve with Hyacinth and Evans, and New Year's Day with her family.

Luka's impending leaving aside, the New Year had been mostly good. She had only written two things in her grievance journal: One, *When a hockey player gets a special parking place at Hammer Time because he's first star, but still doesn't get his jersey on the wall*, and two, *When Jake Champagne and Logan Jensen get their jerseys on the wall, leaving only one first-liner who hasn't*.

She still didn't understand that, but it wasn't like she could take it up with Claire. Luka tried to act like he didn't care, but she didn't believe it. There was nothing she could do except file it under things she couldn't do anything about.

Her parents knew about Luka, though she hadn't told them, mostly because she didn't know what to say. *No,*

I don't see any future here. It started out as a one-night stand, morphed into a fling, and it might be friends with benefits now. Yeah. That would have gone over well. She was only glad that when they'd strolled down to the windmill house with a pot of chili, she and Luka were playing Scrabble instead of in bed. They had visited for a while and the next day Emma Frances's questions had been minimal—at least for Emma Frances. Buck had said nothing. He seemed to not know what to do with her these days.

January was a notoriously slow month for retail in general, but Heirloom had done better than expected so far. Ava Grace had done two home consultations that resulted in selling some artwork and a rug. Due to the new website and the girls' social media efforts, there had been a lot more foot traffic, which was nice, though most didn't buy anything.

As far as that elusive key that Claire spoke of—it hadn't shown up and Ava Grace didn't expect it to. And that was all right. She was proud of the job she was doing now and that was going to be enough. Not everybody was meant to be Midas.

"Here are the trees." Piper interrupted her thoughts.

"Great," Ava Grace said. "Will you set them up? I need to go to lunch. I'll get the chocolates for the swan while I'm out."

"Sure," Piper said. "But isn't it early for lunch?"

"I'm meeting someone, and he needs to go at eleven."

"Ahhh." Piper winked. "The hunk? He must have practice."

"Actually, it's Brad. He has an appointment with a bride." He'd been back from Aspen for almost two

weeks and, though they had texted a few times, she'd
been avoiding him. It wasn't that she didn't want to see
him—she did. What she didn't want was to talk about
Skip, which was going to be inevitable.

Hammer Time. It was becoming a home away from
home for Ava Grace.

Brad stood when she approached. He took her coat
and hung it on the hook on the booth.

"Finally." He hugged her. "I don't think we've gone
this long without seeing each other except when you
were away at school."

"You may be right," she said as if she hadn't already
known that. She slid into the seat across from his.

"I ordered for us," Brad said. "Chef's salad with
extra avocado and a skewer of grilled shrimp on the
side for you. Blue cheese dressing."

She laughed. "I'm predictable. How was Aspen?"

"Good, mostly. The skiing was great. I brought you
something." He set a large shoebox on the table.

"Thank you, Brad. I have a Christmas gift for you. I
should have brought it." It was still at her parents' house
somewhere, along with the other gifts she'd never delivered. She should do that.

"Christmas was…a challenge this year. Anyway,
that's not a Christmas present. It's a bring back present. Open it."

Ava Grace dreaded it. Brad was notorious for giving her over-the-top, ostentatious gifts: gaudy earrings,
sweaters with sequins, and—once—a custom bobble-
head that was supposed to look like her.

She put on her game face, but her expression quickly changed to delighted surprise once she opened the box.

Knee high cowboy boots—or was it cowgirl boots? Either way, they were lovely and beautifully made. Soft, buttery off-white leather, with silver stitching and rhinestones. A few more spangles and a bit more stitching and it would have been too much, but they were perfectly exquisite.

"Brad, thank you. They are absolutely beautiful. I didn't know I wanted Western boots until now."

"I hope they fit."

She checked the size. "They should be perfect." Now she had to figure out what to wear with them. They'd be nice and warm for hockey games.

The waitress appeared with their food and Ava Grace put the boots away to make room for her salad.

"So how are you?" Brad asked once they were alone again. "Everyone I ask says, 'She's fine,' but are you?"

"It's been tough, but I'm better. Moving on."

He grinned and took a bite of his burger. "I hear you're keeping company with Luka Zadorov."

"Don't talk with your mouth full."

He swallowed. "Don't give me etiquette lessons to avoid the subject."

"What if I am? Seeing Luka, I mean," she said decisively as she removed the shrimp from the skewer and sprinkled them over her salad. "I wish they'd take the tails off shrimp."

"Hey, hey!" Brad put his hands up. "Good on you. Surely you don't think I'm sitting here judging you. You were the wronged party."

She sighed. "Do we have to talk about this?"

"Absolutely," he said.

"Then let's start with this. Why didn't you tell me? If you'd told me, you could have saved me the humiliation."

"You are not going to lay this on me, Ava Grace. Yes, Skip confided in me. But it wasn't mine to tell. I kept thinking he would come to his senses and do the right thing—which I guess he did. I didn't think he would do it in public."

There was really nothing to say to that. Since, unlike some people, she didn't talk with her mouth full, she took a bite of her salad.

"For what it's worth," Brad went on. "I would not have let you get married without knowing, whether it was mine to tell or not. Once he got on the stage, I thought maybe he needed to just go ahead and propose like everybody was expecting and then break it off."

"No," she said. "That would have been worse, but I admit, the same thing crossed my mind."

"Don't think I wasn't plenty mad," Brad said. "I took him skiing to give you some space. He had to hear from me on a regular basis what I thought about how he handled things."

"How is he?" she couldn't help asking.

"You could ask him that yourself."

She shook her head. "Not yet. I know we need to find our footing in a different place, but I need some time. It might be a month. It might be ten years. I don't know."

"That's fair," Brad said.

"Fair or not, that's how it is."

"As long as you know you have to forgive him eventually. We all go back too far for you not to." He smiled and dipped a fry in ketchup. "Besides, I miss the three of us and this is all about *me*, after all."

She laughed. "Everything is, darling boy. Can we talk about something else now?"

And they did—how things were going at Heirloom, the guy Brad met in Colorado who, turned out, was from Gulf Shores, and the fussy bride Brad was about to have to deal with.

"Speaking of—" Brad threw some bills on the table "—I need to get back."

"So do I," Ava Grace said. She still needed to buy the chocolate for the tablescape.

He seemed hesitant as he helped her on with her coat.

"What?" she asked.

"What do you mean, 'What?'" he retorted.

"I know you're dying to say something else. Might as well go ahead."

"I shouldn't."

"Do it now. Do it later. You know you will."

He nodded. "It's about the boots. I didn't buy them for you. Skip did."

"Oh, hell!" That explained why they weren't encrusted with blinking lights and flashing purple stars. "You can take them right back to him. I won't be bought." She held the box out.

Brad bored his eyes into hers. "Ava Grace, he didn't want you to know he bought them for you. And are you really going to stand there and tell me that you believe Skip Landry thinks he could buy his way back into your life with anything, much less a pair of *boots*?"

He had her. It was true. "He's trying to ease his

guilt." Why, why, why were they having to do this? It was almost like it was happening again.

"Believe this, if you never believe another thing. Skip will never forgive himself for embarrassing you like he did, even after you have forgiven, forgotten, and laughed about it."

"The day will never come that I will laugh about it." But he had a point about the other things.

"Maybe so, but he bought the boots for no other reason than that he thought they were beautiful and would be beautiful on you. He wanted you to have them because he loves you. That's all. He never wanted you to know I didn't get them for you. But I kept one thing from you that maybe I shouldn't have. I'm going to think long and hard before I do that again. I'm trying to help you get to a better place—because I'm not totally over it either and I probably won't be until you are."

"No pressure there."

Brad shrugged. "Keep the boots. Wear them. Know there was no ulterior motive."

Finally, she nodded. "I should have known you didn't pick them anyway."

"I know! Right? There were these magnificent ones—gold glitter, with fringe and silver buckles. He said they didn't suit you."

She shuddered. "I love you, Brad. *You* suit me."

"Love you, too, sis. And you love Skip. You just aren't feeling it right now. And that's okay."

She glanced at the box she held. She was feeling it a little.

It had been a good practice.

Luka stepped out of the shower and wrapped a towel

around his waist. He was going to make beef Stroganoff for Ava Grace tonight, which required a trip to the market. First, he needed to have some lunch, or he would buy a multitude of junk foods that he shouldn't have, but would eat all the same. Maybe Logan would be available—if he didn't have plans to take lunch to Molly at her toy shop. Luka briefly considered taking lunch to Ava Grace at Heirloom, but discarded the idea.

He had seen her this morning; he would see her tonight; he did *not* need to see her in the middle of the day.

He made a mental list of what he needed for the Stroganoff—mushrooms, noodles, sour cream, beef. Maybe he would go to the hardware store and buy some decent knives. Ava Grace had the worst knives ever made and she didn't care. Why would she? It didn't take much of a knife to spread peanut butter on a piece of bread.

"You look happy—or as happy as you ever do."

He looked around. "Oh. Killjoy. You always look happy, so is hard to tell when you truly are."

"I pretty much always am. What have I got to be unhappy about?"

He didn't know, didn't want to. It was best not to get more involved with these people than he was already.

"Anyway, Glaz wants to see you—as soon as you're dressed."

What was that about? "*Da.* Only Magic Man and Wings would go to Coach's office naked."

Ten minutes later, Luka knocked on the man's door.

"Come in. Ah, Luka," Glaz said when Luka entered—then he shifted into Russian. "Sit down." He opened the small refrigerator behind his desk. "Sports drink or water?"

"Water." It was nice to be able to speak his native tongue. Ava Grace still wouldn't allow him to play Russian words in Scrabble—which was why he had only beaten her three times.

Glaz handed him two bottles, settled into his chair behind his desk, and opened his sports drink. "Excellent skate this morning."

"Thank you. The line works well together."

Glaz nodded. "I like that—that you give credit to your teammates when you are instrumental in their success."

"They are talented. Even our esteemed goalie, who annoys me."

Glaz laughed. "He annoys everyone—especially me, but he will grow. Or someone will kill him. I am hoping for the growth. I notice you have lightened up on him."

"I did not plan it. I guess I got tired of it. Americans have a saying about teaching a pig to sing. Teaching Wings humility is like trying to teach a pig to sing. It only wastes your time and annoys the pig." But it was more than that. After Ava Grace had affirmed his feelings, some, if not all, of his annoyance had lifted.

"You are a good leader, Luka," Glaz said. "I hate to lose you."

Luka looked up, surprised—not that Glaz knew he was looking for a trade. That was no secret, but he hadn't expected him to bring it up.

"Nothing acceptable has come through," Luka said vaguely. There had been interest, but Pittsburgh had been the only team that had all he was looking for. That possibility had died on the vine after that unfortunate game against the Sound.

"But it will. We know that. You are too valuable— you are a value here, as I knew you would be. That is why I insisted on having you for Dustin Carmichael. Boston didn't let you go easily, but they were desperate for a goalie."

"Are you going to try to change my mind?" Luka asked.

"No. I won't fight you, nor will Polo MacNeal or Nathan Ayers." He named the team's principal owner and general manager. "We all understand that an unhappy player will eventually be a liability. I understood why you were unhappy in the beginning. After so much time in Boston, you were sent here—to an untried expansion team, with an untried coach, in a culture that is not like any you've ever experienced."

"It is not you," Luka said. "I respect you."

Glaz nodded. "I know that. Things have changed since you arrived. Now we are headed to playoffs. We may not win the cup, but we will soon. Once you decided to let yourself, you began to enjoy your teammates. Your best friend is here. I know you love his little boy. And now, my Noel tells me, you are keeping company with the lovely Ava Grace Fairchild."

"Is temporary," Luka said. He knew the words were true, but they were like a knife in his gut. When he visualized the future, she kept sneaking into the scenes. "She is getting over hard times. Besides, I don't have enough khaki trousers and navy blue blazers." He'd seen Skip around town a few times. Did the man own any other clothes?

Glaz frowned, puzzled. "I don't know what that means, but there are the other advantages, if you will see them as such. How could things be so bad for you? You had a near perfect game against Ottawa two days ago."

"Does it not bother you that hockey is a second-class citizen here? Or not even second. Maybe fifth."

"No," Glaz said without hesitation. "You cannot change a culture. These people love football. They always will. But I will be a building block in making hockey loved, too. So will this team. We will not change the culture, but we will be part of it. I wish there were better hockey opportunities for children—hockey schools. Camps. Perhaps that will come in time." He looked at his phone and stood up. "I must go. My Noel has a doctor's appointment. Today we find out if the baby is a boy or girl. Maybe. If he isn't shy about showing his genitals—or she."

Not sure why he had been called here, Luka stood. "Good luck with that."

Glaz must have read his thoughts because he said, "I only called you here to say I will support your decision, but I hope you will think of the assets here. I am wondering why you have not been able to be happy—or perhaps you are happier than you think, but refuse to see it. You are a stubborn one—and that is a blessing and a flaw. I should know. I am the same."

There was no point in trying to explain it to Glaz. Hockey was a huge part of his life, but it wasn't all he was. Glaz didn't need a hockey atmosphere to thrive. He would say that Luka was thriving, and to the outside world it looked that way. After the Ottawa game, a commentator had said he was playing the best hockey of his life—in spite of that abysmal showing against the Sound three weeks ago. If that were true, the motivation for his recent performance was to get him to a new team where he understood the culture and felt at home.

He turned to go. "Perhaps you will get good news today? That the baby is a boy? Yes?"

Glaz laughed and shook his head. "It makes no difference. A little brother or sister for Anna Lillian will be equally welcome. You'll understand that in the future."

Luka nodded, but he knew it wasn't true. He didn't expect to have children, so how could he?

Chapter Eighteen

In the break room at Heirloom, Ava Grace made a pot of coffee and set out the remains of the *sharlotka*—apple cake—that Luka had made for dessert last night.

It was cold out—spitting rain, mixed with some sleet. It had been hard to leave Luka in her bed this morning, especially when he'd begged her to stay. But she hadn't failed to arrive at Heirloom before Jen and Piper since she'd turned over a new leaf and she wasn't going to start today. So she'd pulled the blanket tighter over him and said she'd see him after the game tonight.

Jen entered and hung her coat. "Good morning, Ava Grace."

"Good morning. It's cold. Have some coffee."

"Cake!" Piper sailed in wearing patchwork overalls and purple Converse shoes.

"My, aren't you bright?" Jen said as she poured coffee. "Are you going to plow today?"

Piper took the coffee Jen had poured. Jen grimaced a bit, but just reached for another mug.

"At least I'm not trying to be Ava Grace," Piper said.

"What?" Jen looked down at her clothes—gray wool pants, black twin set, pearls, and black flats with bows.

Ava Grace bit her lip to keep from laughing. Had Piper not pointed it out, she wouldn't have noticed that, except for the colors and shoe bows, she and Jen were dressed pretty much alike. Maybe she ought to try to mix it up a little.

"Not that there's anything wrong with being Ava Grace." Piper cut a hunk of cake. "It's just that Talbots and Ann Taylor ain't big enough for all three of us. I made my outfit, if you can believe it—that is, I bought the overalls at Goodwill and added the patches."

"I can believe it," Jen deadpanned.

This banter didn't fool Ava Grace. They liked each other. She'd seen them out together when they didn't have to be.

Piper bit into the cake and moaned. "So good! Ava Grace, did the hunk make this?"

Ava Grace had made the mistake of telling them Luka had made the leftover *piroshki* she'd brought for lunch one day.

"Don't ask Ava Grace about her personal life," Jen admonished.

"I think I want a hockey player, all my own," Piper said. "Ava Grace, can you get me one? Preferably one that looks as good as the hunk and can cook—and in time for Valentine's Day?"

"No, Piper, I don't think I can do that."

Piper sighed and finished her cake. "I guess I'll have to work that out for myself. I'm going to sweep the front sidewalk."

"I'm going to straighten up the displays." Jen picked up her coffee and left.

Ava Grace was only a little bit afraid of how Piper was going to "work that out" for herself.

The cold rain continued to fall, making for a quiet morning. Piper and Jen worked together photographing merchandise and posting the pictures to Heirloom's social medial accounts, while Ava Grace perused estate sale sites for vintage linens. True to her vow, she wasn't looking for dresser scarves and dollies because they'd suddenly caught her fancy. She'd had an inquiry and hadn't had much in the shop.

It was almost lunchtime when the little bell above the door jingled and a woman about Ava Grace's age came in. She closed her Black Watch umbrella and wiped her green duck boots on the mat.

Jen appeared like magic. "Can I take your raincoat?"

The woman pushed her damp blond hair off her face and removed her coat. "I don't think I'll be here long, but I wouldn't want to get your lovely things wet."

Ava Grace had learned a few things since paying more attention to her shop. If this woman didn't think she'd be here long, that meant she was looking for something in particular. Ava Grace closed her laptop and walked toward her, smiling. "I'm Ava Grace Fairchild. Can I help you with something?"

"Celia Tipton." She extended her hand and smiled. "I hope so. I saw a picture posted to your Instagram—a set of silver. Do you still have it?"

"Yes." Ava Grace didn't have to ask which set. She only had one complete set—the English King that had been meant to grace her own table. After much reflection, she'd decided the right thing to do was to frankly discuss with Skip what to do with it. Besides, it was time she saw him if she was ever going to, and this was a good reason. They had met for lunch and while they didn't share a dessert or sing "Kumbaya," it was less awkward than she'd anticipated.

As for the silver, Skip had insisted it was hers to keep, sell, or throw in the river if she wanted to. As much as she loved it, it was meant for another life, and she couldn't see herself using it. Obviously throwing it in the river was not on the table, so she'd polished it and put it out. Only yesterday one of the girls had put up a picture of it.

It was the cradle all over again. She felt nothing but joy at the thought of someone using it and enjoying it—and Celia seemed lovely.

"It's here in the silver case." Ava Grace retrieved her keys from her pocket, stepped behind the glass and wood case, and brought it out. "It's vintage English King by Tiffany, first made in 1885." She unrolled a velvet cloth and spread out a place setting, including a fish fork. "This is an eighty-five-piece service for twelve, including a full suite of serving pieces."

"May I?" Celia inclined her hand toward the cold meat fork.

"Of course." Ava Grace liked her. Most people would have grabbed it without asking. "I love it. It's ornate, but in a very gentle sort of way, don't you think?"

"It's perfect." Celia ran her finger over the shell motif. "I can visualize it."

Yes. Ava Grace would be so happy if this silver found a home with this woman. It was hard to tell what people could afford. Celia might know exactly what a full set of vintage Tiffany would cost and pull her credit card out without blinking. But if that wasn't true, Ava Grace was going to do everything she could to help her have it—even if she had to allow Celia to pay fifty dollars a month for years. That might not be the best business decision but, on the other hand, she had no money in the silver and it was hers to do with as she pleased—and it would please her for this silver to grace Celia's table.

"One of the wonderful things about English King is that it's still being made. This set has many wonderful obscure pieces." She pulled out the tomato server and the jelly spoon and laid them on the velvet. "And there are many fun pieces to be had that you can collect through the years if that's something that interests you—things like crumbers, ice cream spoons, sauce ladles, sugar tongs."

Celia picked up the tomato server. "No, I wouldn't collect any more."

"No? Well, there's certainly enough here to set a large, beautiful table."

Celia looked up, confused. "I don't want it for that. Nobody does that anymore. Who has time for all the polishing? People don't know what to do with things like this anymore." She held up the fish fork.

Ava Grace felt a frown creep over her face. Of course, she knew a lot of people felt that way, but she wouldn't have pegged Celia for one of them—which brought up an interesting point.

"Then why are you interested in it?"

Celia smiled. "I'm going to repurpose it."

Repurpose? How did you repurpose silver flatware?

"See?" Celia fiddled with her phone and held it

where Ava Grace could see it. "It's a huge thing since nobody wants silverware anymore. I'm going to make other things from it and sell it on eBay. Useful things like jewelry, key chains, coat hooks."

Horrified, Ava Grace looked at the pictures before her. Besides what Celia had named, there were drawer pulls, cabinet handles, wind chimes, and even a chandelier—all made from lovely old silver flatware. For a second she thought she was going to be sick.

"Let's get down to business," Celia said. "How much?"

Ava Grace briefly considered quoting her an inflated price, but no. If she was willing to pay the asking price it would be hers to do with as she pleased. Wordlessly, Ava Grace removed the card from the chest with the price and showed it to Celia.

"Holy hell!" Celia burst out. "I can't pay that. I'd never recoup my money."

Relief washed over Ava Grace. "I understand, as I'm sure you understand this is vintage Tiffany." She began to store the pieces back in the chest.

"Wait. Hold on," Celia said. "I do like it. What's the best deal you can make me?"

"That *is* the best deal," Ava Grace said. "I'm sorry." She wasn't, but she was polite.

Celia stood there, looking like she was torn. "It *is* pretty and I could probably get more for my items, given that they'd be Tiffany. What if I took the forks, maybe eight spoons, and five knives? I'd like to make pens from the knives."

Ava Grace took a deep breath to keep from passing out. "I'm sorry. I can't break up the set."

"You might as well," Celia said. "You aren't going to sell that, not to anyone who has any sense and is living in this century."

"That might be true, but there are lots of people walking around with no sense living in the past." *People like me, I guess.*

Celia nodded. "Do you have any other silver? Maybe some odd pieces? Or maybe some silver plate?"

"No. I'm sorry." That was a lie. The were some odd sterling pieces, including the ones she had collected for herself, on the bottom shelf of the case, and a sweet little set of silver plate in the storeroom waiting to be polished. But the odd sterling pieces were waiting for someone who wanted to complete a set, and the silver plate for a young bride who loved fine things but perhaps couldn't afford sterling.

Celia looked at the case and her eyes landed on the punch ladle, sardine fork, and the rest of it. "You just made a very bad business decision."

That might be true, but she'd made a good decision of the heart and that counted for something. "I'll get your coat."

When Celia had gone, Ava Grace staggered back to the checkout counter. Never had she needed to write in her grievance journal more. She stared into space for a full five minutes, random thoughts running through her mind.

Then she remembered a series of memes that had been popular on Facebook a while back. She found a piece of paper and drew a picture of a stick figure standing behind a silver tea service. Then she wrote: *This is Ava Grace. She appreciates having her heirlooms and*

*memories around her. She doesn't let social media tell
her what she likes. She thinks—and decorates—for herself. Ava Grace is her own person. Be like Ava Grace.*

She stood back and looked at it. She didn't want to
write in her grievance journal. She wanted to tell the
world.

That was when she knew she'd found the avenue
to her passion. And she understood her passion better, too. She wasn't meant to serve the world. She was
only meant to put particular things together with particular people. She had a purpose. Merry hell, no. Not
only a purpose. A crusade! And she would fight it with
a damn sterling silver butter knife for a sword, and a
bone china soup tureen lid for a shield!

"Piper!" she called out as loud as she could. "Jen!"
One might have said she bellowed.

They both came running, looks of terror on their
faces. No wonder. They'd never heard her raise her
voice. Hell, she couldn't remember the last time she'd
heard it, not counting when Luka buried his face between her thighs.

"What's wrong?" Jen demanded.

"Can you take a picture of me? And help me make
a meme?"

Chapter Nineteen

Luka and Logan emerged from the locker room together.

"I expected to beat them," Logan said, "but I didn't expect to beat them so bad." Neither had Luka, but the proof was on the scoreboard—5-0. "Good job staying out of the box."

"Can't score in the penalty box." He'd gotten two goals and an assist.

"I'd say you have redeemed yourself for that shit game you played against Nashville," Logan said.

"There is no such thing as redemption. Not in hockey."

Logan's eyes drifted across the way. "Is there such thing as redemption for a bad parent?"

Molly stood leaning against the wall, weighed down by Alex, who was asleep on her shoulder. Things seemed to be going well for the three of them.

"Why do you think you are bad parent?" Luka looked around for Ava Grace, but didn't see her.

Logan quickened his pace. "Some would say keeping a two-year-old out until almost ten thirty is bad parenting."

"Bah. What do we care for these people called *some*? You are pro hockey star. Your son should be in attendance. Even if he does not remember, he will see pictures. He will be proud you wanted him with you."

"I'm not a star," Logan said. "You're a star. You got the parking place tonight." It was true. The first star of the game got a dedicated parking spot at Hammer Time for a week or until there was another first star at a home game. "Surely your jersey will go up on the wall after this."

He ignored the part about the jersey. It didn't matter.

"Too bad I probably won't get to use the parking spot." They were about to be gone for three days, to Canada—a two-game series in Toronto and then a Sunday afternoon game in Winnipeg. He scanned the crowd, but still failed to find Ava Grace.

"You aren't going to Hammer Time tonight?" They had reached Molly. Logan dropped a kiss on her lips and took Alexander from her. It was good to see Logan with a nice woman after the sadness of Carol's death.

"Nyet," Luka said. "Plane leaves early. Hello, Molly." Luka's plan was to get back to Laurel Springs as quickly as possible so he'd have more time with Ava Grace before the road trip, but where was she? Since they'd been seeing each other, she had always met him here outside the locker room where only family, friends, and the press were permitted. He patted Alexander's sleeping head.

"If you wake him, he's going home with you," Logan said.

At least he wouldn't be going home alone. Had Ava Grace failed to come tonight? His heart raced. Had she decided she wanted no more of him? Or worse, was she hurt or ill?

He reached into his pocket for his phone just as she emerged from the ladies' room. He let out the breath he'd been holding and everyone faded to a colorless blur except for her. It was as if there was a spotlight on her. No. That's wasn't right. She was the spotlight, luminous from within.

Tonight she wore black pants and a gold silky blouse with a big fluffy bow that sat on her left shoulder. The wool coat folded over her arm was black with gold trim. Yellowhammer colors. This was the first time she'd worn this combination, and she'd done it for him. Perhaps he should offer her his jersey. That had not occurred to him. He had never given a jersey to a woman, not even Tatiana. Evans and Hyacinth wore the jerseys of their men. Did Ava Grace feel left out? But then, he wasn't her man, at least not for long-term. Some of the words Glaz had spoken to him tried to play in his mind, but he beat them back.

Ava Grace looked around, searching. When her eyes settled on him, her face became radiant—also for him, like the gold and black clothing. She waved and started toward him. He closed the distance between them.

For the first time in public, he folded her against him and kissed her hard. She kissed him back, so he kept kissing her until he came to his senses.

He broke away. "Sorry. That will likely appear on *The Face Off Grapevine*. They have spies everywhere. I was not thinking. I would not wish you embarrassed."

She shrugged. "I wouldn't be. If I minded people knowing I kissed you, I wouldn't kiss you."

This woman would destroy him yet.

He spoke before he thought. "I wish you were coming to Canada with me."

Before he had time to regret his words, she answered, "So do I."

They had a silent, sweet moment. "I thought to avoid Hammer Time tonight and go straight home."

She nodded. "Great idea. There's leftover goulash."

"Good." Though he wasn't concerned about his stomach. Oddly, though he wanted her—he always wanted her—it wasn't sex that dominated his thoughts either. Being with her seemed more important.

"Excuse me? Luka?" There was a microphone in his face. "You were first star tonight—in more ways than one. How are you feeling right now?"

Fuck. He had forgotten they were not alone. He wanted to curse, shove this man away, and run out the door with Ava Grace.

But he couldn't. A good slap shot wasn't enough. A marketable hockey player had to be able to talk to the press—and interact with the fans.

"A moment, *dorogaya*?" he whispered in Ava Grace's ear. "I must speak with this gentleman and sign autographs."

"Take your time." She stepped to the side near the wall. "Go be a legend. I'll wait for you right here—as long as it takes. I'm proud of you."

The bottom dropped out of his stomach.

She was proud of him. *Da*, she would destroy him. Did he have a ghost of a prayer?

Almost as soon as they were in the car Luka's phone rang.

"Do you mind very much if I answer, *dorogaya*?" he asked. "Is my family. They got up early to talk to me."

"Please, go ahead. After all, I have you the rest of the night." He smiled before activating his Bluetooth.

He'd been doing that more lately—smiling. Could it be that there was a deal in the works to get him out of Laurel Springs and that was why he was happier? Too bad she couldn't pick up a clue from the conversation he was having with his family. The mood of the call seemed happy and easy, but she had no idea what they were saying. Perhaps she'd take Russian lessons.

The thought brought her up short. No point in that. She didn't know any other Russians and this one had one foot out the door. She'd do well to remember that.

But she wasn't going to let it kill her mood. He wasn't gone yet and she wasn't going to be sad about it until it was time.

They were barely inside the door of the windmill house when Luka swung Ava Grace into his arms.

"You are very beautiful tonight." He pushed her coat off her shoulders and stroked the sleeve of her blouse. "These colors—Yellowhammer colors. Was it accident or did you wear them for me?"

"I did it for you. I wasn't sure you'd notice."

"Not notice you? Is not possible." His eyes went liquid and there was that smile again. "You destroy me, *dorogaya*. You must know this."

Then he laughed and the whole room was infused with joy. Ava Grace was too much of a realist to think his happiness was because of her, but she would revel in it anyway—even if it was because he'd had a good game, talked to his family, and was about to get out of Laurel Springs for three days.

So she laughed with him. "Destroy you? With a silk shirt? Now, that's valuable information. Maybe I should sell it to those Canadians you're going to keep company with this weekend. I can see *The Face Off Grapevine* now: 'Silk revealed to be Luka Zadorov's kryptonite.'"

He took her coat and hung it on a hook by the door. "Not any old silk. Must be the silk of Ava Grace."

She had a new silk nightgown he hadn't seen. Maybe she should go put it on, though he would probably want to eat first.

"Would you like me to warm some goulash for you?" she asked. "I can have it on the table by the time you change out of your suit and tie."

He considered. "Do you know what would be my perfect night?"

Sure, I do. Food, sex, sleep. They had fallen into a pattern after games. Not a bad way to spend the evening.

"No table. I would like to have some food, while we cuddle under a blanket on your soft sofa, and watch this new Spider-Man movie people are speaking of. I want to be close to you while I eat."

And he claimed *she* would destroy *him*.

"Would you wear my T-shirt?" he asked. "Is a look I like."

She found her voice after a moment. "Silk or T-shirt? Which is it, Zov?"

"Not you, too!" he said with mock horror. "That ridiculous nickname. I will get Wings for that yet."

Later, warm in each other's arms as Spider-Man saved the world again, Luka dropped a kiss on her brow.

"Would be nice if you could go to Canada with me. You could wear the Yellowhammer colors and root for me."

"I hear that, as a rule, players'…" she searched for a word "…companions don't travel to away games unless it's playoffs."

"Is true," he agreed. "Perhaps I pack you in my hockey bag."

"Wouldn't that be a little smelly?"

"Yes." He sighed and kissed her. "Not a good place for Ava Grace."

Then he tucked her head in the curve of his neck and they watched Spider-Man scale a building.

There was nowhere else on earth she wanted to be.

Chapter Twenty

Ava Grace made her way down the street toward Laurel Springs Apothecary, where she was meeting her mother for lunch. She'd been surprised when Emma Frances suggested the Apothecary, given that it wasn't exactly her kind of lunch spot. But it was fine with Ava Grace. They had a great patty melt.

Maybe she'd eat two. She was starving. Lately, she'd been eating breakfast, but she'd missed it this morning. After morning practice, Luka was leaving for three days and she wouldn't see him before he left, so instead of eating, she'd used her breakfast time to give him a proper goodbye. Once she got to Heirloom, there had been no time to run out for something. She was still reeling from the response to the little meme she'd made yesterday. It had attracted more attention than she'd dreamed possible and she couldn't wait to tell Emma Frances. Social media moved at the speed of light.

The Apothecary was alive with teenagers, which was a surprise for midday on a Friday. It had been the high school hangout for years—Ava Grace, Skip, and Brad had spent their share of time here—but not when they were supposed to be at school.

She worked her way through the crowd until she found her mother in a booth right in the middle of it all.

"Looks like you need to call the truant officer, Madam Mayor." Ava Grace removed her coat and took the seat across from her mother.

Emma Frances grimaced. "I forgot today was a teachers' work day. I thought we'd have more privacy here than at the inn or Hammer Time."

Ava Grace's radar went up. They needed privacy? That was no good.

Just then Jacob Winterberry set down two plates in front of them.

"I ordered for us," Emma Frances said. "Chicken salad plates. I hope that's all right."

Ava Grace looked at the food—a scoop of chicken salad that someone had dipped from an industrial size tub, a pear half with cottage cheese, and a stack of crackers. Emma Frances did not know how to order here.

Oh, well. She picked up her fork, but stopped. "Wait, Jacob. I'd like a patty melt with French fries." He looked from her to the plate and back again, obviously unsure of what to do with the food. "It's okay," she assured him. "I'll keep this. I want a patty melt, too."

"Ava Grace, are you going to be able to eat all of that?" her mother asked.

"No, Mama. I appreciate your ordering, but it wasn't what I wanted. I have decided grown-ups don't always have to eat what's put before them." She scraped the cottage cheese off the pear. "I'll eat this pear. It'll make a fine appetizer."

Emma Frances frowned, but let it go. "Of course you should have what you want."

Ava Grace hoped she meant that.

Emma Frances took a bite of the chicken salad. "I'm surprised that I had to arrange a lunch date to talk to my daughter."

"I'm sorry, Mama. I've been busy."

"I'm well aware of that." She began to pick little bits of pickle from the chicken salad and line them up on the edge of her plate.

"I've started doing design consultations."

Emma Frances nodded. "Ruth Ann Carter told me she bought some Chinese vases and you came over and arranged her mantel."

"It was fun." Ava Grace finished the pear off. She'd forgotten how good canned pears were. Why had she let herself become a fresh fruit snob? It had its place, but you never knew if it would be sweet or how long before it would turn to a bruised, mushy mess. But you could depend on a Bartlett pear in heavy syrup. Peaches and pineapple, too.

Emma Frances laid her fork down. "Ava Grace, I have tried to hold my tongue, but it's time we had a talk."

Ava Grace nodded. Might as well go with it. Emma Frances would have her say or die trying.

"I realize what happened with Skip was a terrible shock—and a disappointment. It follows that your behavior would be somewhat…eccentric. Erratic, even." Whoa! Emma Frances could live with eccentric—even admire it on some level—but she did *not* like erratic. "So, as I said, I've remained silent. I let it pass when you moved out of the house, and when you refused to be with us on Christmas Eve."

"Mama, I wasn't refusing to be with you, so much as needing to be alone."

"But you weren't. When we came home, we were going to check on you to make sure the generator was working since the power had gone off. Skip's vehicle was there."

Ava Grace sighed. She had a feeling this was only the beginning.

"At first, I was hopeful."

"Hopeful? What were you hoping?" What kind of fantasy dream was she in? Surely one of Emma Frances's making, because even Ava Grace's subconscious couldn't come up with that.

"I don't know. That it had all been a mistake, I guess. That Skip had gotten cold feet and started imagining things—and later, decided he was wrong."

Merry hell. "Mama, I realize that after all the plans we'd made, what happened was hard on you. I'm going to mark that up to your being in the denial stage of grief and let it go."

She nodded. "I know, Ava Grace. And I love Skip. You know I do. He's practically one of my own. But do you really think it's in your best interest to march into the inn and have lunch with him like you're best friends?"

"We *are* best friends." She squeezed lemon into her tea. "I'm not saying I'm over it, but I intend to get there. So yes, I do think it's in my best interest to ease back into seeing him."

Emma Frances looked as rattled as Ava Grace had ever seen her. "I'm not saying this very well."

"Then say it better."

"I don't mean you shouldn't care about Skip—even see him. But later, after people have had a chance to forget what happened and have stopped talking about it."

Ava Grace laughed and knocked back a drink of her iced tea. "If you think people are going to ever forget that spectacle, you're more optimistic than Tigger and Anne of Green Gables rolled into one. Oh, good. Here's my patty melt. Thank you, Jacob." She shook ketchup onto her fries.

"I've never seen you so flippant, Ava Grace," Emma Frances admonished.

"Would you prefer I throw myself onto the floor, beat my breast, and wail?"

Emma Frances closed her eyes and shook her head. "I know it's been hard, but three people have asked me if you're serious about this hockey player you've taken up with. I don't know what to say."

"Say you don't know." *That's what I'd have to say because I damned sure don't.* "And he's got a name. Luka. You sat at my kitchen table and had a glass of wine with him."

"All right. Luka. I didn't mean to disparage him. He has lovely manners. But it was so fast, Ava Grace!"

"After all that's happened, *that's* what you're worried about." She ate a bit of her sandwich.

"Honestly, if I didn't know better, I'd think you went off with Luka the night of the gala instead of Hyacinth."

Tempting as it was, Ava Grace would not confirm

that. It wouldn't be productive—and it wasn't any of her mother's business.

Emma Frances leaned in. "You may think I don't know what's going on, but I do. I know Luka spends the night with you most of the time, and the nights his car—or that giant motorcycle—isn't at your house all night, I highly suspect you're with him wherever he lives."

"Laurel Springs Inn."

"What?"

"You were wondering where he lives. He lives at the inn."

"I wasn't wondering where he lives. I was saying you've spent every night with him since you took up with him."

"That's not true, Mama." She wiped her mouth and took a sip of tea.

"No?" She looked hopeful.

"No. He has a lot of away games." Too many. Now, for instance. Three days was an eternity.

"Ava Grace! Thank goodness Buck doesn't know. I don't know what he'd say."

Ava Grace put down her glass. "Maybe he would say I'm an adult and should be left alone to make my own choices. And don't be too sure Daddy doesn't know. He doesn't miss much. He just doesn't always feel led to hold forth on everything."

"I'm worried about you, Ava Grace."

"Don't be, Mama. I'm better than I've ever been. I'm learning to live in the present and plan for the future instead of waiting for things to happen to me." Maybe if she'd try to change the subject… "Things are great with Heirloom. I've never given it my all until lately and it's already paying off."

"That's another thing. Ava Grace. I saw that meme you put up—with you standing behind the tea service. It was snarky, high-handed, and unbecoming of you."

Well, hell. She was finally going to get to share her news, but there would be no congratulations coming. It took every bit of willpower she could muster to keep from rolling her eyes.

"I can't believe you let Jen and Piper do that," Emma Frances went on.

"They didn't," she said proudly. "They helped with the technical details, but the concept was all mine. It's gone viral."

"I'm well aware of that." Emma Frances picked up her phone and began to scroll. "It has become inspiration for other such 'art' as well."

"What are you talking about?"

"Here." Emma Frances handed Ava Grace her phone. "This popped up on a Facebook page I follow—'Preservation and Restoration.'"

"Merry hell!" It was a meme, featuring the picture of Ava Grace and Luka kissing outside the locker room. "'This is Ava Grace,'" she read aloud. "'Ava Grace kisses hot Russian players. Be like Ava Grace.'" The caption on the post read, *I know we've all seen the "Be like Ava Grace" meme with the teapot, so I couldn't resist when I saw this picture on a pro hockey gossip site. I think we're going to hear more out of Ava Grace—and I think we're going to like her.* She'd forgotten Luka had said the picture would show up on *The Face Off Grapevine* and she hadn't had a chance to look at it today yet.

She handed the phone back to Emma Frances. "Did you reply and tell them I am your daughter?"

Emma Frances couldn't have looked more shocked if Ava Grace had announced she was having Satan's love child. "No. The damage is done, but you should take that original meme down."

"Mama, I know you understand what viral means. I couldn't take it down, even if I wanted to, which I do not. This is a good thing. You wouldn't believe the comments I've gotten, the sales I've made. Someone called this morning asking if we had a T-shirt that says, 'Be Like Ava Grace.' There's a whole segment of people out there who are tired of gray walls and minimalist furnishings, but they don't want their homes to look like their grandmothers' either. And I'm going to help them." She would spare Emma Frances the plans she and the girls had for more memes, a video blog, and—possibly—a T-shirt. She wasn't so sure about the shirt, but Piper was already drawing designs.

"Success only counts if you have comported yourself like a lady achieving it."

Ava Grace closed her eyes. It would have been so easy to say something sarcastic and storm out—easy, and the easy way out. But she wouldn't. Nor would she cave, change the subject, or remain silent like she had so many times in the past.

She reached across the table, put her hand over her mother's, and drew on every lesson Emma Frances had ever dictated to her.

"Mama, I love you. I also like and admire you, but I'm going to do things my way. The irony is you're strong, dedicated, and willing to do whatever is necessary to be the best mayor you can be. But it seems you wanted to turn me into some kind of stereotypical doll. I went along with it for a long time, probably still would be going along with it if things hadn't gone as they did."

Emma Frances's face softened. "Of course, I want you to be strong, Ava Grace. I wanted you to have an ideal life. I was only trying to make that happen."

Ava Grace withdrew her hand and put half of her sandwich on Emma Frances's plate. Hungry people were grumpier than the well-fed and her mother was not going to eat that chicken salad.

"Eat that. Never order anything else here except milkshakes. They use Blue Bell ice cream and they're to die for." She ate a fry. "My love life is not up for discussion. Now, if you aren't comfortable with my choices, I'll certainly understand if you want me to move out of the windmill house." Maybe she could move into Hyacinth's house. Since getting back together with Robbie, Hyacinth was all but living at his condo.

"No!" Emma Frances looked aghast. "I never meant to imply I was issuing an ultimatum."

Ava Grace nodded. "That's fair." Her mother had never been a "my way or the highway" kind of person. No. Ava Grace was a big part of why their dynamic had developed as it had. Emma Frances might have been given to making strong suggestions, but it was Ava Grace who meekly followed them without question—at least none she asked out loud. "You are a wise woman. I don't want you to stop giving me advice. I'd be a fool not to consider anything you might have to offer and I like to think I'm not a fool—at least not anymore. But I'm done letting anyone tell me what to do. That's long overdue."

Emma Frances looked as though she wanted to say something, but she only nodded and took a bite of the patty melt. "This is good."

"Don't worry too much, Mama. The apple doesn't fall far from the tree and I'm still me. I'm not quitting Junior League and I'm still going to teach Sunday school. I haven't changed. I've grown."

Emma Frances smiled. Was it her imagination or was this a woman-to-woman smile rather than a mother-to-child smile? "I haven't had a milkshake in years. Do you want to split one?"

Not really. Ava Grace wanted one of her own, but every compromise wasn't a sign of weakness and she could share this moment—and this milkshake—with her mother.

"Absolutely. The strawberry is the best."

When they parted, Ava Grace was exhausted and elated at the same time. This must be what it felt like to win a battle, and she *had*, though not so much against her mother as against herself.

Win. She had had a victory. She stopped outside the toy shop and scrolled through her phone. Ah, there it was—the laurel wreath. She'd earned it. Was she out of her mind?

Quick, before she could change her mind, she texted Hyacinth and Evans.

You're going to think I've lost my mind, but I want to get a tattoo and I want y'all to go with me.

Chapter Twenty-One

Luka entered the room where the team's private breakfast was being served. A cheer went up from his teammates. Toronto had been heavily favored last night, but the Yellowhammers had pulled it out in the last seconds of the game, 4-3.

Logan signaled from a table for four in the corner where he was seated with Jake and Robbie. "There's the man." Jake stood up and shook his hand.

"As I said last night, I was in right place at right time." He sat in the chair they'd saved for him. "Robbie, with the assist, deserves more credit." He sipped the juice at his place. "And there were three other goals on the board—and many saves."

"Cut the crap," Logan said. "We're not the press."

"You can repeat the part about how I deserve more credit," Robbie said. "Put it on a shirt and wear it to Hammer Time."

"*Nyet.* You love yourself almost as much as Wings loves himself." A waiter appeared and set a tray of food in front of Luka. He had to hand it to the Yellowhammer staff; he always got his preferred game day breakfast on the road—oatmeal, a bowl of berries, a banana, three

scrambled eggs, two slices of whole grain toast, half
an avocado, and skim milk. He felt a smile creep onto
his face. "That goal *was* pretty sweet." He wondered
if Ava Grace had seen it. She didn't have any hockey
channels, but Robbie and Jake had them all. Maybe she
had watched with Hyacinth and Evans.

"What?" Jake Champagne looked up with an expression of mock horror and halted spreading peanut butter
on his toast. "The great, brooding Luka Zadorov smiles
and admits something went well?"

"And the Southern mama's boy isn't complaining
about the cold?" Luka countered.

"I'm proud to be my mama's boy. Not everyone
can be the progeny of Ole Miss royalty—homecom-
ing queen nineteen-something, I can't remember. That
makes me a prince."

"I hope it goes as well tonight," Robbie said. "I understand our women are getting together to watch the
game at Jake and Evans's condo." That probably meant
Ava Grace, too. He'd call her later and ask.

"I appreciate them inviting Molly," Logan said.

"So how's that going?" Jake asked. Anyone who
thought men didn't gossip had never been around these
men.

Logan nodded. "I really like her. She's great with
Alex."

"From the looks of what I saw on *The Face Off
Grapevine*, things are going right well for someone
else," Jake said.

Fuck. As he had predicted, the picture of him and
Ava Grace kissing had appeared and apparently Jake
had seen it, too. He hadn't really understood the cap-

tion, but quirky phrases were often lost on him. *Does Luka Zadorov want to be like Ava Grace? We don't have an answer for that, but he sure seems to like her.* Now these guys were probably going to give him a ration of shit about his intentions toward Ava Grace.

But maybe not. Robbie only said, "Better be careful, man. Glaz does not like us on *The Face Off Grapevine.*"

"Shut up, Robbie," Jake said. "As usual, you've got it wrong. Glaz threatened to bench us if we made the site with any of the hell-raising like we did when we were with the Sound. Kissing your girl after a game is hardly bench-worthy bad behavior."

His girl? Was that what people thought? Surely they knew that he was only a phase for her.

Robbie had a text come in and he grabbed his phone off the table. "I've been waiting for this." He punched the screen a few times. "Whoa, ho, ho," he chuckled. "Better than I thought."

Everyone was quiet, waiting.

"Well?" Jake said. "Are you going to tell us or not?"

Robbie looked torn. "I shouldn't." He put his phone on the table, facedown.

"But you will," Jake said.

"No?" There was a question mark in Robbie's voice.

"You can do it now or do it later, but you know you're dying to show us whatever it is that came through just now," Jake said.

Robbie looked around the table. "Aye. But I shouldn't—though maybe… I can trust you not to tell." That was a statement. "Because it absolutely must be a secret until Valentine's Day."

"That's three weeks off. You've never kept a secret that long in your life," Jake said. "Give me that phone."

Robbie picked it up and handed it to Jake, who studied the picture for a bit before passing it to Logan. "That's really big."

"And fancy." Logan passed the phone to Luka.

They were right on both counts. It was a ring with an emerald—the biggest one Luka had ever seen, not that he went around looking at a lot of emeralds. It was surrounded by diamonds and purple stones that formed little flowers. There were more diamonds and purple stones set in the band all the way around.

"These are flowers made of diamonds?" Luka said because he had to say something.

Robbie nodded, obviously pleased with himself. "Yes. Regular diamonds and orchid diamonds—very rare. The flowers are hyacinths. It's her engagement ring. I had it made by Neyland Beauford. She just finished it and sent the picture."

"An emerald instead of a diamond?" Logan asked.

"Aye." Robbie widened his eyes. "Hyacinth likes my eyes—really she likes everything about me, but she remarks on my eyes, quite often. Green." He pointed to his right eye in case they had missed the color. "My thought was every time she looks at the ring, she'll think of my eyes."

Jake looked a little befuddled, though Luka didn't know why. It was obvious even to him that Robbie and Hyacinth were headed in this direction.

"So, Robbie, does Hyacinth know about this?" Jake asked. "Did she, maybe, help design the ring?"

"Oh, no!" Robbie waved his hand in front of him.

"Nooooo. Neyland had some input, but the design was mostly me. It's a surprise. But she'll say yes. It not like we don't talk about things—the house we'll buy, the kiddies we'll have. But the ring will be a surprise."

It was good that Robbie hadn't just assumed before buying a ring, like Luka had done with Tatiana. That was a lot of ring to have to throw in the river.

"She'll be surprised, all right," Jake said. "I don't think there's any way she would ever expect a ring of that…caliber."

Luka got it now. *Caliber* wasn't the right word. Luka knew that from Scrabble. But Jake hadn't wanted to use words like *gaudy*, *ostentatious*, or *vulgar display of wealth*. And Jake knew this was probably not going to be to Hyacinth's taste. It sure wouldn't suit Ava Grace—not that he needed to know that. But she would want something understated, quietly elegant—like her.

"This is how I see it," Robbie said. "Being in the wedding dress business, Hyacinth sees lots of engagement rings. When we visit my family this summer, she'll see more, since there will be weddings almost every day at Wyndloch." Robbie's ancestral home was a wedding venue. "No matter how many rings she sees for the rest of her life, I want her to always have the best one." Clearly Robbie equated *best* with *biggest*. "So do you think I did good?"

Something passed between Robbie and Jake then. It was familiar—Luka could almost feel it. Something similar had passed between him and Logan on a few occasions—at Logan's wedding, the night Alex was born, and when he'd flown in the night Carol died. The feeling didn't come often, but it was strong and deep when it did. He was suddenly a little sad that he was leaving Logan and the little Viking. They would always be a big part of his life, but he wouldn't see them every day anymore.

Jake chapped a hand to Robbie's shoulder. "Yeah, Robbie. You did good. You got the best one." Then Jake laughed and took a drink of his milk. "But no way will you wait until Valentine's Day. You'll give it to her the minute you get your hands on it."

Robbie shrugged. "I might—wait, I mean." He didn't look too confident.

So what if she didn't like the ring? Robbie would never know. A woman who talked about a man's eyes would not say such a thing.

"Remember, it's a secret." Robbie laid his phone aside and picked up his oatmeal spoon. "Don't even tell Evie, Molly, or Ava Grace."

They all assured him they would not.

"So is everybody ready for the weather in Winnipeg?" Logan asked. "It's going to be a lot worse there than it is here."

Jake shuddered. "At least we won't be there long. I'm hoping to make a whole Canadian sweep."

"Good chance of it," Logan said. "We've got a pretty good arsenal, and momentum is good."

"I wish we were going to be able to keep this arsenal intact." Robbie's eyes landed on Luka.

Aside from Logan, Luka hadn't discussed his impending move with any of the guys, but they all knew it and he felt he owed them some sort of answer.

He swallowed his last bite of eggs and put his hands on the table. "Is not because of any of you that I must go," he said. "I have some of the best teammates I have ever had." Luka was surprised at the words—true words—that had come out of his mouth. When had that happened? "But it feels wrong here. It's not what I'm used to. The culture is…off." Though really, it didn't feel as off as it once had. At least football season was over. "Maybe not so much wrong, or even off. Just not for me."

More important, he couldn't stay in a place where a woman was destroying him with her every movement, smile, and kind word. He couldn't be there when she was healed and didn't need his comfort anymore, couldn't watch her walk away with a man in a navy blazer with silver buttons engraved with his initials.

And when in the hell had this become about that?

Jake nodded. "Look, man, I get it. I've been there. I loved the Sound, loved my team, but Nashville wasn't the place for me anymore. My ex-wife was remarried and pregnant, plus all over the society page every day for chairing this committee and attending that fundraiser. I didn't want her anymore, but I didn't want to see all that either. And I'd been on a bad path, waking up in beds I barely remembered getting in. I needed to clean up my act and that's hard to do in a place where your bad boy ways are expected and considered entertaining. I know my reasons are not yours, but a man has to do what a man has to do. I just wish you didn't have to do it."

On some level, Luka wished that, too. He got the feeling Jake wished it for more than his slap shot and what it could help the Yellowhammers get.

"Has not happened yet." He dug into his oatmeal. "I

will not take *any* offer. Has to be right. And the right one may not come."

Somehow, that possibility didn't feel as bad as it might have at one time.

"Let me take your coat," Evans said as Ava Grace stepped into the foyer of her condo.

"Sorry I'm late," Ava Grace said, "especially since you and Hyacinth are taking off this afternoon to accommodate me." This was the first time since turning over a new leaf that Ava Grace had taken time off when Heirloom was open. Evans had invited her and Hyacinth for lunch before heading downtown to get Ava Grace's tattoo. After, they would come back here to watch the Yellowhammers game.

"It's only five after." Evans hung Ava Grace's jacket on the bronze coat rack.

She was late because they had been making a new meme and Jen had wanted to keep retaking the picture. This one showed Ava Grace seated behind a mid-century modern coffee table merchandised with baroque silver candlesticks, a bonsai tree, and a blue and white cloisonné bowl sitting on top of a stack of brightly colored modern art books. It said, *This is Ava Grace. Ava Grace isn't afraid to mix styles and periods. Ava Grace breaks the rules. Be like Ava Grace.*

"I know that's early for Ava Grace time, but I'm trying harder to be on time in real time. I'll bet Hyacinth has been here an hour."

Evans laughed. "Only half an hour. Be warned. She's already called dibs on driving."

"No!" Ava Grace said in mock horror. Hyacinth always called dibs on driving.

"She's pouring drinks." Evans led Ava Grace through the living room and down a hall to the breakfast nook off the kitchen.

"Thank you for taking off this afternoon, Hyacinth," Ava Grace said. "I need the moral support."

"No problem." Hyacinth set a glass of iced tea at each place setting. "Now that Brad's back, I deserve some time away from the shop after he ran off to Aspen and left Patty and me with it for two weeks."

"This looks so good," Ava Grace said as they all sat down.

"Chicken pot pie and hearts of palm salad," Evans said. "Coconut peppermint tarts for dessert." This would be a welcome meal. Ava Grace had mostly snacked since Luka had left. She'd gotten used to him feeding her. She could have gone to her mother's table anytime, but that felt a little too much like going from the dorm to the cafeteria like she'd done when she was at Belmont.

"Let's talk about this tattoo," Hyacinth said.

"What about it?" Ava Grace helped herself to the pie and passed it to Evans—just in time to see them exchange looks. She knew those looks, too. Hyacinth was chomping at the bit to have her say and Evans was warning her to dial it back.

"What kind of tattoo is it that you're thinking of getting?" Hyacinth asked.

"I'll show you, if you'll excuse me for bringing my phone out at the table." She reached into her pocket, found the picture of the laurel wreath, and passed it to Hyacinth.

"So not a full sleeve or a tramp stamp?"

Evans's eyes widened as she took the phone from Hyacinth. "Hyacinth!"

"I believe the preferred phrase is *lower back tattoo*," Ava Grace said.

"Sorry," Hyacinth said. "I didn't mean any offense. That's what I thought they were called. I don't know much about tattoos."

"In answer to your question, no." Ava Grace squeezed lemon into her tea. "I'm thinking something small—about the size of a quarter, on the inside of my wrist." She had considered Piper's suggestions, but what good was a tattoo that she couldn't see without a couple of mirrors and some complicated contortion moves, or being naked?

Hyacinth and Evans looked somewhat relieved—but only somewhat.

"At least the back of the wrist is one of the least painful places for a tattoo if you decide to go through with it," Hyacinth said.

"I thought you didn't know much about tattoos, and I've already decided to go through with it," Ava Grace said.

"I did some research when you came up with this wild notion."

Of course she had. Hyacinth was all about getting the facts. "So it's a wild notion?"

"You said yourself we were going to think you'd lost your mind," Hyacinth said.

That might be true, but it still didn't sit well. "I

thought y'all would be more supportive," Ava Grace said. "You've always teased me for being so conventional, so proper. Now, the minute I want to step outside the box, just a little, you say, 'Oh, no, no.'"

Evans finally spoke up. "Ava Grace, we do support you and we are not anti-tattoo snobs. But you have to admit this isn't like you. We only want to be sure you've thought this through."

"Research shows," Hyacinth chimed in, "that it's a bad move to make drastic changes to your life after a shock."

"Merry hell! I've moved on. What happened with Skip doesn't even seem like a shock anymore. And I'd hardly consider a small discreet tattoo as a drastic change to my life. In case y'all haven't noticed, there are more people who have tattoos these days than not."

"That's not true," Hyacinth said. "Thirty-six percent of the people in our age group have tattoos. More women than men regret tattoos."

Ava Grace put her hand to her head and closed her eyes. She should have gone by herself, or taken Piper. "Hyacinth, you're the prime example of someone who shouldn't be allowed to have access to the internet."

"I wouldn't be much of a friend if I didn't point these things out. And it's true about women regretting it. I had a bride last week who wanted a strapless dress, but could she have it? No. Because she didn't want her tattoos to show in the pictures."

"Are you saying every bride you have wants to cover her body art?"

"No. Of course not. But it was sad that she couldn't have the dress she wanted."

"Well, I don't see a wedding dress in my future. Even if I did, one little laurel wreath wouldn't matter." Ava Grace said it louder than she meant to.

Evans put her fork down. "Stop it—both of you. We are not going to have an argument. Ava Grace, best friends don't let each other do something out of character without asking questions."

Ava Grace caught her breath. They *were* best friends, weren't they? Time was, she'd thought of Hyacinth and Evans as best friends and herself as their sidekick. "That's fair."

"Was the tattoo your idea?" Evans asked. "Luka didn't suggest it, did he?"

"Luka? Of course not. Why would he?" Talk about veering off into the left lane.

Hyacinth shrugged. "A lot of men find tattoos sexy."

Ava Grace suspected Hyacinth knew what percentage.

"I don't know what Luka thinks of tattoos. I haven't discussed it with him. As for it being my idea, it wasn't initially. Piper suggested it and I dismissed it, but the more I thought about it, the more it appealed to me. Here's the thing." She didn't owe them—or anyone—an explanation, but she wanted them to understand. "I know getting a tattoo would have been unthinkable for the old me, but I'm changing, finding out new things about myself. I wouldn't get just anything, but the laurel wreath is not only about my home—it symbolizes strength and victory. I've had some victories lately and I could use something to remind me I'm strong."

Evans covered Ava Grace's hand with her own. "All

right. Are you sure you don't need to wait a little longer to be sure?"

"I'm sure. I'm tired of waiting for what I want. All I've ever done is wait."

"All right, then." Hyacinth pulled a folded piece of paper from under her plate and handed it to Ava Grace. "These are the top-rated tattoo shops in Birmingham." It was a spreadsheet with three names, addresses, and the estimated driving time to each. "It should take about an hour to get one that size done, if there's no waiting. So let's eat and get on the road. We want to be back in plenty of time for puck drop."

By the time Ava Grace found herself at Casablanca Ink an hour and a half later, she felt fully supported by her friends. Hyacinth admitted that she might consider getting a tattoo if Ava Grace's didn't hurt too much—maybe of a dress form. And Evans pronounced the laurel wreath design lovely, like you'd find on monogrammed stationery.

Ava Grace consulted with the artist, chose the perfect shade of green, and was waiting for him to set up.

"Just fill out this consent form," the receptionist said, handing her a clipboard and pen. "It shouldn't be more than a few minutes."

She briefly scanned the form. Yes, she'd been informed of the risks and advised on the aftercare for the procedure. Yes, she released Casablanca Ink from any liability associated with complications. Yes, she had been given ample opportunity to ask questions. No, she was not under the influence of alcohol or drugs. No, she did not take blood thinners, nor did she suffer from diabetes, hemophilia, or heart disease. No, she was not pregnant or nursing. No, she had not had an organ or bone marrow transplant. No, she had not…

Wait. Something wasn't right; something snagged on her thought process.

Her heart began to pound as she read back over the list.

No, she was not pregnant… Was she? She brought up a mental visual of a calendar and thought back. She was two weeks late, and she was never late. Why hadn't she noticed? Too busy eating Russian food, playing Scrabble, reinventing herself and—can't forget—doing what one did to get pregnant.

But it couldn't be. No. She was being paranoid. They'd used a condom every time, the most important of the condom rules and she knew all of them. Skip had schooled her on them when they first had sex. Make sure it isn't expired, inspect it for tears, have it fully in place before any genital contact, and all the rest of it.

But there was that one time and the one rule they hadn't followed. *For optimum protection, remove the condom immediately following ejaculation, when the penis is still erect, holding the condom firmly at the base of the penis.*

It was the night she'd tried to make chicken and dumplings and Luka had bathed her. After making love, she couldn't get him close enough and she'd begged him not to withdraw immediately. But it was only once, so how likely was it that she was pregnant? Lots of people tried for months—years—before conceiving.

She wasn't sure how long she stared off into space with the pen still poised over the clipboard.

"Ava Grace?" Evans said. "Everything all right?"

Ava Grace turned to look into their questioning faces.

"I can't do this after all." Not without knowing for sure. She'd have to get a test.

Evans and Hyacinth nodded simultaneously. "You don't have to," Hyacinth said.

"Of course not," Evans said. "You aren't the first and you won't be the last to decide you aren't ready."

They thought she was afraid—and no wonder. Her face had to be the very picture of fear, but for better reasons than a little encounter with a needle and some ink.

Hyacinth, woman of action that she was, stood up and took the clipboard. "I'll return this and tell them you've changed your mind." She knew how hard it was for Ava Grace to do the unexpected—and these tattoo people were expecting her to get a tattoo.

"Tell them I'm sorry to have wasted their time."

Evans took her hand. "Don't be embarrassed. We can always come back later when you're ready."

And how long would that be? Maybe a few days, if the test was negative. If not, she supposed it would be when she wasn't pregnant or nursing any longer. How long did nursing go on? She could get Hyacinth on that. She'd find out and have all the answers in no time.

Ava Grace should have gotten more answers before she embarked on what had turned out to be a fool's errand. Was it common knowledge that you shouldn't get a tattoo when pregnant? Or was she the only one who hadn't known? Of course, she'd not thought it was a concern—and it probably wasn't. Still, it was a scary thought. What would have happened if she hadn't read the form carefully or hadn't considered the possibility? And if she *was* pregnant, and had done it anyway? How bad were the repercussions? She didn't know why you couldn't get a tattoo while pregnant, but it didn't matter. It wasn't a good idea, or these people wouldn't say so. Maybe the world at large needed educating on this particular subject. She could help them out with that.

This is Ava Grace.

Ava Grace elected not to get a tattoo when she thought she could be pregnant.

Be like Ava Grace.

"All taken care of." Hyacinth returned and clapped her hands together. "What do you say we go back, settle in, and get ready for the game?"

"Sure," Ava Grace said.

Just another Saturday night, watching the father of her maybe-baby play hockey.

Chapter Twenty-Two

Luka was entering his hotel room in Winnipeg when his phone rang.

Ava Grace. Though she always answered for him, she had never called him before. She would text if there was a reason, but not to just say hello. His heart sped up and not in a good way. Maybe something bad had happened to her. They had spoken briefly last night after the second win over Toronto and she had seemed distracted, a bit distant. Maybe something bad was about to happen to *him.*

"Hello," he said with some trepidation.

"I hate to bother you on game day," she said.

Relieved, he kicked off his shoes and lay back on the bed. "I can assure you, you are never bother to me."

"Then I can call as soon as you make a goal? That wouldn't bother you?"

She was making jokes. This was good. "*Nyet.* Because I do not take phone on ice. But perhaps I like seeing that you have called later, yes?"

"You sound really happy—and you should be with the way you've played this weekend."

"*Da.* Has been a good weekend." Sounding happy

wasn't something that he was accused of very often, good game or not. The knowledge of the reason he sounded happy struck fear in his soul. It had nothing to do with how he'd played; it was because she had called.

"What are you doing?" she asked.

"Just returned from early skate and team meeting. I will take short nap before pregame meal. And you? No church this morning for the good church girl?"

"I taught my Sunday school class, but didn't go to worship." She hesitated. "I wanted to come home and call you. I hoped to catch you before you had to leave for the game."

"You caught me." The words were out of his mouth before he realized the double meaning.

"The thing is…"

"Yes?"

"The thing is—I have something to tell you."

All the joy he'd felt melted away like cotton candy on the tongue, but without leaving any of the sweetness behind. This was it. She was finished. It shouldn't have mattered; it was coming anyway. He'd hoped it would be later.

"Then please do." He fought to make sure his voice sounded the same.

"I…that is…"

"Yes, Ava Grace?"

She took a deep, audible breath. "I wanted to say you were wonderful this weekend. I'm proud of you. And I miss you."

Luka's world upended as her sweet words washed over him. So many emotions in so few minutes—that was a hard thing. But this was a good emotion.

"Thank you. Was a sweet thing to say. Perhaps I make goal today and bring you the puck?"

"I would like that."

"Plane will get in late, perhaps too late for you?"

"No. Not too late for me," she said.

"But I didn't say what time."

"It doesn't matter."

Wrecked, ruined, destroyed.

That was what he was. Did she know she had that power?

"I should go," she continued. "Take your nap. I'll be watching for my goal."

After ending the call, he stared at the phone for a full minute.

He'd get that goal, and God help the fool who got in his way.

After ending the call, Ava Grace stared at the phone for a full minute before the magnitude of what she'd almost done hit her.

What had she been thinking? You couldn't call up a man and say, *Guess what? You're going to be a father!* Aside from the lunacy of delivering news like that over the phone, Luka was a professional athlete with a game to play. Everyone knew an athlete, regardless of the level, had to have his head on right before a game. Even if she hadn't known that from her brother's high school football days, Evans and Hyacinth talked about it all the time.

She picked up the two pregnancy test sticks—both positive—and stuffed them in the sack with the box they had come in. Luka was coming over tonight and it wouldn't do to leave them lying around—that was an even worse way of delivering the news than the phone. She couldn't put them in the trash either, where he might see them. That was almost a cliché, considering the pregnancies that had been revealed via trash cans in books, movies, and television shows.

She took the bag to the bathroom and stuffed it deep in the back of the linen closet behind the towels. She'd take it to work tomorrow and throw it in the dumpster out back.

It wasn't that she planned to hide the pregnancy, but she didn't intend to let two sticks with pink plus signs deliver the news before she was ready to tell him. Though it really wasn't so much a question of when she was ready as when he was ready to hear it—and she had no idea when that would be. Not on a game day. She'd established that.

The Yellowhammers played this coming Tuesday and Thursday, then were off until Monday. So the ideal time—if there was such a thing in this situation—would be tonight or after the game on Thursday.

But which? She would put her energy into worrying about that instead of wondering how he would react. She could only control one of those things.

So tonight? It would be good to get it out of the way and let the chips fall. But, on the other hand, could she completely trust a home pregnancy test? Even two that immediately screamed, *Yes! Get the nursery ready!*

Sure. She could trust them but, still, it wasn't unreasonable to get confirmation from a health-care professional before blowing Luka's life up.

If this news was going to blow his life up. Who

knew? Maybe he'd send a check every month; maybe he wouldn't. Maybe he'd want to be part of the equation; maybe he wouldn't.

There was too much she didn't know.

She put her hand on her stomach. "He's a good guy, kid. I think you'll like him if it works out that you get to find out, but I need to warn you. It might be just you and me and, if that's so, we'll be fine."

Chapter Twenty-Three

One of the things Ava Grace loved most about Laurel Springs was that it was a tight-knit community where everyone knew everyone. But she did not love it today. No. It would have been better if her gynecologist wasn't her daddy's golf buddy, who always sat in the pew ahead of her in church—which meant that ninety-nine percent of the time they knelt side by side at the communion rail.

Yet, here she was, bright and early on Monday morning sitting on the examination table in a hospital gown. She'd briefly considered going to a walk-in clinic downtown, but what was the point? She was going to need care and she didn't want another doctor. Apparently she couldn't be pleased. She didn't want a doctor she didn't know, but she didn't want one who knew her. That was tricky—sort of like knowing when to tell the person you were having a fling with that he was going to be a father.

Luka had come in last night as happy as she'd ever seen him—and why not? The Yellowhammers had won three straight games and he'd been the first star for two of them. Also, he'd had a break from the godforsaken, football-loving South in real hockey cities. He hadn't said it, but he didn't have to. This wasn't news, so it wasn't fair that his zeal to get away from the Yellowhammers—and as a result from her—was getting under her skin.

But to her surprise, he complimented her on her recent successes, which he had learned about following Heirloom on social media. "I did not understand at first the reference to 'be like Ava Grace' on *The Face Off Grapevine*, but now I see." They'd been in bed and he'd wound one of her curls around his finger. "Everyone should be like Ava Grace."

That counted for something—maybe not enough, but something.

The door of the exam room swung open and Dr. Milton walked in.

"Ava Grace, what's going on with you?" He sat down at the computer and brought up her file. "You aren't due for your yearly exam for another seven months. Are you having a problem?"

She didn't see it coming, but she started to laugh. "Well, Dr. Milton, depends on how you look at it."

He swiveled his chair around to face her. "Oh?"

"I'm pretty sure I'm pregnant."

He nodded. "I see. Just pretty sure?"

"More than that, actually. I've missed a period and I took two home tests. They were both positive."

"Hmm. You know those things are pretty reliable."

"Just *pretty* reliable?" she retorted.

He let out something between a sigh and a laugh. "More than that, actually." They exchanged wry smiles. "What do you say we get some urine and do a pelvic instead of sitting here feeding our words back to each other?"

"That's what I'm here for."

Later, she was dressed and seated in his office down the hall from the exam room when Dr. Milton came in and sat in the leather chair behind his desk.

"You and your two tests were correct."

"I wanted to be sure." There was something about having the confirmations that caused a swirl of emotion—fear and distress, but she was excited, too. How could she not be when she was getting something she'd wanted her whole life?

"The good news is you're in excellent health and there's no reason you can't proceed in any way you see fit."

It took her a second to grasp what he meant. "You mean for an abortion?"

"Or carrying the baby to term. Whatever you choose."

She shook her head. "No. No abortion."

He reached behind him into a small refrigerator, brought out two bottles of water, opened them, and handed one to her. "All right. I wanted to mention it to make sure you knew I would support whatever you decide. This is a complicated situation."

He had no idea. "This moment isn't supposed to be complicated." Her eyes filled with tears. "It's supposed to be joyous." And she wasn't supposed to be here getting this news alone.

"I'm sorry." He handed her a tissue. "This hasn't been the best time for you. Does Skip know?"

She looked up, surprised. "This has nothing to do with Skip."

"I understand. You'll have to forgive me for being more frank with you than I would with most of my patients, but I've known you all your life."

She wiped her eyes. "I know. Golf with my daddy. Taking the body and blood together."

He smiled. "Exactly. Ava Grace, I'm old-fashioned, but I also know I'm right. Fathers have a right to know. If nothing else, children have the right to be supported by both their parents."

"I couldn't agree more," she said. "But it still has nothing to do with Skip."

It took a moment for that to sink in. "I see." He passed his hand over his face. "Lord. What a mess."

"It is that."

"But at the end, there will be a pretty nice dividend, don't you think?"

With his words, the excitement she was feeling morphed into joy. Maxwell Milton didn't beat around the bush, but he'd said the right thing.

"Just *pretty* nice?" she asked.

"More than that, actually," he repeated his words from earlier. "Tremendously so." He picked up his pad. "I'm going to give you a prescription for a multivitamin with folic acid." He handed it to her along with a printout. "Here's a list of things to avoid. You probably know most of them—alcohol, excessive caffeine, sushi—but there're other things that a lot of people don't realize, like blue cheese and undercooked eggs." She wondered if tattoos were on that list. "My guess is you're due around the end of September, but we'll get you back in here for a sonogram in a couple of weeks. That will give us a better idea."

"Thank you, Dr. Milton. I know I don't have to say this, but my daddy…"

"Absolutely not a word, Ava Grace. I like to think the day is done when doctors go behind women's backs for what they presume is for their own good—also, against the law."

She stood up. "Thank you. I guess I'll see you in church."

He winked. "Letting a little communion wine touch your lips won't harm your baby."

An image bloomed before her: standing at that altar holding her baby out for holy baptism. But who would be standing with them?

"Ava Grace?" Doctor Milton said as she turned to go.

"Yes?"

"If you have any questions or I can help you in any way, call me."

"Thank you. I will." *But I'm afraid you can't help me with what I need to do.*

She'd tell Luka Friday, or maybe Thursday night after the game. She only had to figure out how.

Luka was still fast asleep in Ava Grace's bed when the call came midmorning on Monday. He vaguely remembered her kissing him goodbye and telling him to sleep as long as he liked.

He knocked the bedside lamp over searching for his ringing phone.

"Fuck," he said instead of *hello*.

"And a hale and happy morning to you," Kurt said.

"Sorry," Luka said around a yawn and sat up against the headboard. "I did not mean to say that. I think I broke my girlfriend's lamp."

"I know it's early after such a long weekend, but I thought you'd want to know."

"Yes?"

"I've had a conversation with Toronto. To say they were impressed with you is an understatement."

His heart went into high gear—*Toronto*. Not only a great hockey city headed for the playoffs, but a great city in every way.

"You were smart to wait it out," Kurt said.

Luka caught sight of a long dark hair on Ava Grace's pillow and picked it up. "The wait was not much of an imposition."

Kurt laughed. "You could have fooled me. They want to get this sewn up as soon as possible so you have plenty of time to settle in before the playoffs."

"How soon?" It probably wouldn't be today, but who knew? The two organizations would have to speak and agree on the terms of the trade, but that often happened in minutes. Since Glaz knew Luka desired a trade, he and the owners had probably already decided what they would demand from every team in the league, as well as what they would be willing to accept. He shouldn't have cared; he had little to pack. Saying goodbye to Logan wasn't a concern. He would miss the daily interaction, but their goodbyes would always be more of a "See you soon."

Saying goodbye to Ava Grace was a different matter. It would be hard—and harder still if *she* did not find it hard.

"There's one other thing," Kurt said.

"Da?"

"They want you to come up and skate a couple of practices."

"What? A *tryout*?" Fuck, no. "I will not be treated like a junior hoping to rise in the division. I am a professional. They know my game. They will take me as I am or not at all." And so what?

"Then it will be not at all," Kurt said.

"Fine. I have team." The words came out of his mouth lightning fast, yet he didn't regret them. How dare they ask such a thing of him?

Kurt took a deep breath. "Luka, listen to me. It's not personal. They do this with every trade. This is the Toronto Coyotes, for crap's sake. You know what happened a few years back when they traded for Jasper Craig. They gave up two players and a first-round draft pick for him. Even at that, everyone thought it was the coup of the decade, but you know how it went. Craig didn't mesh with the new team. Not only did it hurt the Coyotes, it ruined Craig's career."

"I would mesh," he said stubbornly. "I mesh with anyone."

"Maybe so, but they don't know that. They haven't made a midseason trade since Craig where they didn't require this."

All this was true. He hesitated.

"Are you really going to let a little practice skate ruin your chances?"

"I don't know." He might. It wasn't an awful thought.

"Look, the Yellowhammers are off this weekend. There's a direct flight out from there Friday afternoon.

You can go up, do their early morning skate on Saturday, stay and watch the game. Let the brass buy you a meal. Skate early skate with them again Sunday. Then, fly back—or not, depending on how fast things move."

"I would want to come back here regardless—wrap things up." He owed it to Glaz, Able, Sparks, Scotty, and some of the others to look them in the eye and say it had been a pleasure.

If it has been such a pleasure, why must you do this? a voice whispered. He knew the answer: because a woman had destroyed him for all other women and he couldn't stand to be here when he had worn out his welcome. He tried to remember why he had ever cared that these Southern people were football crazy.

"What do you say, Luka?" Kurt cajoled. "Would a little trip be such a bad thing?"

Then, he had a thought. He hadn't worn out his welcome yet. Was it possible that Ava Grace truly cared for him? That he was more than a distraction? That thought led to an idea. *What if this didn't have to be the end with Ava Grace?* He tried to beat back the idea, but it took shape and ran wild. Maybe they could carry on. He wasn't fool enough to think she would drop everything and move to Toronto with him; he'd been that fool once and learned his lesson. But she could visit him. He would buy a beautiful house worthy of her. Even considering playoffs, the season would be over in a few months. They could take a trip together—anywhere she wanted to go. Maybe Russia. After that, he could return to Laurel Springs for the summer. And who knew? It was possible that by the time the season started again, she might be willing to move to Toronto—especially if he showed her what a great city it was.

"No. Not a bad thing. Make the arrangements with the Coyotes."

"I'll have them book you a flight and get you the particulars," Kurt said.

"*Nyet.* I will take care of my own ticket."

Kurt paused. "Okay. I don't see why, when we can have them pay for it, but you're the boss."

"I have my reasons." If the gods smiled on him, he would need two tickets.

"Are you ready?" Piper asked. She had attached her phone to a tripod that stood in front of Ava Grace. If these video blogs took off, she'd look into getting some equipment. Surely there was something out there better than a device you could get for free at a kiosk for signing a service contract.

"Just a second." She rearranged the mortars and pestles sitting on the counter in front of her. "I'm ready now."

"Okay," Piper said. "Jen, make sure you hold the cue cards where she can see them."

Ava Grace would have told them she didn't need cue cards, but why ruin their fun?

"Action!" Piper called out, and it was all Ava Grace could do not to laugh. She'd dreaded doing this, but it was turning out to be fun—and kept her from thinking about a certain conversation she was compelled to have.

"Hi," she said to the camera. "I'm Ava Grace Fairchild and I do things my way. Today, we're going to talk about clutter." She remembered to wrinkle her nose

like Jen had said she should do when they'd practiced.
"I don't like it. I don't know anyone who does, but it's
often a dilemma for me. I don't like to let the special
things in my life go and, often, they end up being clutter." She inclined her hand to the mortars and pestles.
"You see these mortars and pestles? My grandmother
collected them." She picked up a large brass one. "Her
grandfather was a pharmacist and this was the mortar
and pestle he had in his shop. My grandmother loved
him so much and loved spending time with him at work.
That's how she came to collect. Whenever she saw one,
it made her smile, so she picked them up when she trav-
eled—until she had twelve." She clapped her hands
together and laughed. "Twelve! I've heard it said that
three is a collection, but any more is a mess. That may
be so, but my family history is tied up in this mess
and I can't let it go. The only problem was they were
all sitting on my kitchen counter. I loved them for the
memories and stories attached to them, but I did not
love them for being in my way when I was trying to
prepare a meal. They became an annoyance. Believe
me, I considered packing them away or getting rid of
them altogether, but that's not the way of Ava Grace.
I found a solution." She brought out the white shadow
box she'd had built. "I took my mortars and pestles to
a cabinetmaker and had him make this custom cabinet
for them." She began putting them in the slots. "See?
Each one has its own place. Isn't that pretty? I'll hang
this on my kitchen wall where I can see them every
day, but they won't annoy me." She smiled brightly and
winked. "And if I need to crush a clove of garlic, they're
handy." She removed a wooden one and held it up. "I

think I'll use this olive wood one that my grandmother bought in Greece. I'm Ava Grace Fairchild. If you like my idea, take it and make it your own."

"Cut!" Piper yelled.

Ava Grace laughed. "Piper, I think it's the director who says *cut* so the camera person will stop filming. Since you're directing and running the camera, I think you can just turn off your phone."

"I like to add authenticity to a project," Piper said.

"You were amazing, Ava Grace," Jen said.

"I agree." Luka stepped forward and applauded. As he approached the counter, the girls melted away to other parts of the store.

"I didn't see you there," Ava Grace said. "When did you come in?"

"In plenty of time to hear you say how these things annoy you when you prepare a meal." He widened his eyes.

"Caught," she admitted. "So what if I fudged a little? It would have been a little cumbersome to say, 'It annoys me to see Luka try to prepare a meal with these in his way, while I sit on my lazy fanny and watch him.' I call it artistic license."

"Call it what you like." He leaned his forearms on the counter. "I am glad they are gone."

"Not gone," she said. "Hung. Or they will be if you can help me with that."

"Help you or do it while you sit on your lazy fanny and watch me?"

"That," she said. "Watching you isn't a bad way to pass the time of day. I'm surprised you're awake."

He yawned. "As am I." He stuck out his lower lip in

a mock pout. "I am sorry to say I broke a lamp—the one by my side of the bed. Was an accident. I will replace it." He looked around. "Is there one here in your shop you fancy?"

"That would be the blue ginger jar. I'll have to think about it. Maybe I'll replace it with something different."

"Whatever you wish. Perhaps you will give me good deal?"

"Perhaps. You really didn't need to get up to come tell me this. I know you were tired."

"Actually, there is another reason I am here. I have news and a question."

A sense of foreboding tap-danced on the edges of her nerves. "I'm listening."

"I must go to Toronto this weekend."

And just like that, her good day went bad. "You just got back from Toronto." Which had nothing to do with anything. It was something to say to give the truth time to settle in.

"Yes, but I must return. I am to skate with them."

"Congratulations." She gave him a bright smile that her heart didn't believe. "What about tomorrow night? How does that work? Will you still play the Yellowhammer game since you're leaving?" Would she see him play one last time? Would he sleep in her bed again? And how should this affect her plans for the great reveal?

He frowned. "Yes. I play tomorrow night. This is not done. They must see me at a practice skate. Is not an insult to me. They require that of all." Yet, he seemed insulted.

"I see." She moved the box at her feet to the counter

and started packing up the mortars and pestles. "I'm sure you'll do great and be in Toronto by this time next week. Will you live in a hotel there, too?"

He looked a little sad. "*Da*. At first. But I will find somewhere else. I have things in storage in Boston."

A whole life in Boston, soon to be his new life in Toronto, with only a stopgap in between that had no room for pieces of his real life.

Maybe she'd tell him about the baby right now. But, then, what if his head got the best of him and he played a terrible game tomorrow night? Would that hurt his chances for the trade he wanted so much? She rubbed the place between her eyes where a headache had set in. Merry hell. She didn't know enough about how this worked.

"Ava Grace?" Luka said. "Do you have headache? Should I go to pharmacy and purchase a painkiller for you?"

"No. I have some acetaminophen in my purse." She'd bought it when she'd filled her vitamin prescription, since other painkillers were frowned on during pregnancy.

He brightened a bit and she tried to do the same. "I said I have a question. Would you like to go to Toronto with me?"

Go with him? What did that mean? For the weekend? Permanently? Surely he didn't mean that, but she couldn't answer a question she didn't understand so she stood silent waiting for more information.

"We would leave Friday in the afternoon and come back Sunday." His mood picked up. "Have you been to Toronto?"

"No. I haven't."

"Then you must come. It is a great and beautiful city—almost as large as New York City. Is cold there, sure, but not nearly so cold as many Canadian cities. Also, unlike some areas, speaking French is not important. There is a mix of many cultures, including Russian. Perhaps we could go to a Russian restaurant, with fine dining. There is much to do. Many museums. I have little interest where that is concerned, but I would be happy to go with you. You could also explore on your own while I skate, though the practice would not last long."

"It sounds like an amazing place." Ava Grace fought to keep her voice steady. "But I'm afraid I can't."

"No?" His eyes dimmed. "Can I change your mind?"

"I've been invited to be on *Birmingham Today* at noon on Friday. It's a local show about things going on in the area." That was true, but it probably wasn't too late to change it. They'd only called an hour ago and she'd been given the choice of several dates. The real truth was she didn't want to go, didn't want a last hurrah, didn't want to see this amazing, beautiful, hockey and museum Mecca that was going to take Luka away from her and their child.

He nodded. "Ah. I see. I suppose this show will help people be more like Ava Grace?"

"Something like that."

"Then is good for you."

"Yes." She gave her hands a little clap. "So we'll both be doing things that are good for us on Friday."

He hesitated. "Would you like to go out to dinner tonight?"

"Sure."

"Or maybe I will cook for you. Since I have no practice today, I have extra time. I can make chicken crepes."

"That sounds good. And you'll have more room." She patted the box of mortars and pestles. "Since these are gone."

He nodded enthusiastically. "*Da.* Certainly an asset." He looked around and seemed to want to say something else. Finally he picked up the box of mortars and pestles. "Give me the little shelf and tell me where you would like it. I will install it."

"That would be amazing."

And wasn't every damn thing? Amazing day, amazing Toronto, amazing exit.

Chapter Twenty-Four

The last thing Ava Grace wanted was lunch—or any food. It would have been easy to blame her nausea on the pregnancy, but from what she'd read, it was probably too early for that. More likely, it was her nerves. Not that it mattered. Sick was sick and whether she wanted to or not, she was having lunch at the inn with Hyacinth and Evans. Hyacinth had called first thing this morning, beside herself with excitement. Robbie had proposed last night and the three friends were meeting for a mini celebration.

Ava Grace was happy for Hyacinth, but she was going to have to work hard to present much enthusiasm.

It had been a tough few days.

The Yellowhammers had lost Tuesday night, but Luka had played well, so she doubted if the loss had hurt his trade prospect.

Then the aftermath at Hammer Time. It had been like a surreal dream that wouldn't end. To begin with, the room was tense—maybe because of the loss. Maybe because word had gotten around about Luka's impending trip. Maybe because the special was fish tacos. Who the hell knew?

Then, of all things on the planet that she would have never imagined, Dietrich Wingo had waltzed in with none other than Piper on his arm. And if that wasn't enough, Piper was wearing one of the new T-shirts Ava Grace had allowed her to design and have printed with Ava Grace's picture, the words *Be Like Ava Grace* and Heirloom's web address. In that moment, if she could have turned back the clock, she would have nixed those shirts, no matter how well they were selling. Maybe that would have been a waste of a one-shot time machine trip, considering all the messes she'd made, but where did one start? It was a moot point anyway.

Then, despite the loss, another jersey had gone on the wall—Logan's. With that, the whole first line, except Luka, had been recognized. She supposed it didn't matter now. Tonight would likely be his last game with the Yellowhammers and tomorrow he was flying to Toronto to strut his stuff.

And strut it, no doubt, he would. All week, he'd acted like nothing was different. He'd gone right on cooking meals, setting up the Scrabble board, and taking her to bed. And she'd gone right on eating the food, beating him at Scrabble, and enjoying the bedding while she could.

And carrying her secret around.

It wasn't fair. She wanted to tell—wanted to tell her parents, her best friends, her brother, and the stray dogs she met on the street. Her desire to share the news was partly because she wanted assurance that she had support and everything would be fine and partly because she wanted to share happiness with those who loved her. She wasn't a fool. She knew they wouldn't rejoice immediately. They would have questions and concerns. She couldn't blame them; she had questions and concerns of her own. But in the end, they would rejoice with her.

But could she tell? Could she get what she needed? No, she could not. It wasn't right to tell anyone until Luka knew—and she couldn't tell him until he came back from Toronto. At least she shouldn't, not if she wanted him to go to this tryout with a clear, focused mind. If others knew how this was playing out, they might say she was procrastinating, but nothing could be further from the truth. She'd tell him right now, if she could. She'd go straight to that iceplex, have him pulled out of practice and tell him.

But it wasn't the right thing to do. However, Sunday was it—the deadline. She didn't care what happened— if things went well in Toronto, or if they didn't. If he got an offer to play in the Intergalactic Professional All-Star Hockey Championship on Mars, she wasn't carrying this around alone after Sunday. Until then, she'd keep it together. She'd go to the game tonight and to Hammer Time after. She'd make love to him tonight and kiss him goodbye tomorrow. And damn it all to hell, she'd be happy about it, too. Downright jolly.

At the inn, she bypassed Lila Cokesberry at the hostess desk with a wave. Miss Lila didn't like it when people did that, but too bad. There was a lot going on right now that Ava Grace didn't find exactly enchanting, so Miss Lila could deal.

Clearly she needed to bring her grievance journal out of retirement.

Hyacinth and Evans were already at their table by

the French doors. Of course they were. Hyacinth had probably been here since last night.

Evans waved. "Hurry, Ava Grace! She won't show the ring until we can see it at the same time."

The sweetness of that brought tears to Ava Grace's eyes. Or maybe that was the hormones.

She gave Hyacinth a one-armed hug and kissed her cheek. "I am so thrilled for y'all!" There. There was the Ava Grace everyone expected. She slipped into her chair. "Let's see it."

Hyacinth smiled a little Mona Lisa smile and pulled her hand from her lap and held it up. "Ta-da!"

Nothing could have prepared Ava Grace for the display on Hyacinth's hand. It was so large there was no flesh visible from her second knuckle to the base of her finger. Set in gold, the central stone of the ring was an oval emerald as large as a postage stamp surrounded by a wreath of diamonds and deep purple stones.

Hyacinth turned her hand palm out. "See the channel setting in the band?" Sure enough, there were alternating stones to match the wreath all the way around.

Evans spoke first. "It's lovely, Hyacinth." She took Hyacinth's hand to get a better look. "Are these hyacinths?" Evans ran her finger over the stones surrounding the emerald.

"Yes. And don't you dare refer to these purple gems as amethysts. Robbie will have you know they're orchid diamonds—very rare, but Neyland Beauford had a source. He's very proud of that."

Ava Grace took her hand, searching for some positive words. "What an artist Neyland Beauford is. Such perfect little hyacinths for our Hyacinth." Ava Grace saw Evans clandestinely glance at her own ring, to Hyacinth's, and back again. She was probably wondering how the same woman could have made both rings. Evans didn't have an engagement ring and the band she wore was very simple—thin, with small diamonds set in the band all the way around. The beauty of it was, she could take it off when making pies and snap it around the central stone in a diamond pendant Jake had also commissioned from Neyland Beauford. If Evans was comparing the two rings, she would not find her own wanting—quite the opposite. Ava Grace went on, "And that emerald. What a showstopper."

"Yes," Hyacinth said with a sigh, and gazed happily at the ring. "It looks a little like a Mardi Gras float, doesn't it?"

Unfortunately, Ava Grace had chosen that moment to take sip of water and much sputtering occurred.

"Are you all right?" Evans asked, alarmed.

Ava Grace waved a hand as she coughed into her napkin. "I'm fine. My water went down the wrong way. Hyacinth, did I hear you correctly?"

She held her hand up. "Well, it does—with the green, purple, and gold. And let's face it—a whole krewe, plus the queen, could ride on it."

Evans and Ava Grace exchanged looks, not sure of how to react.

"Are you saying," Evans said tentatively, "that you don't like it?"

Hyacinth's face morphed to shock. "Like it?" She laid her hand on her heart. "I *love* it. Sure, I know—it's too much, gaudy, even. And that color combination…

But how could I not love it? It's so Robbie. He designed it himself, you know."

"That much is obvious," Ava Grace said.

"I'm just trying to imagine Neyland Beauford trying to talk him down," Evans said.

"And I'm trying to imagine what it would have been like if she hadn't," Hyacinth said.

"I'm trying to imagine what he has in mind for a wedding band," Ava Grace said.

Everyone stopped.

"Mother of pearl," Hyacinth whispered. "I hadn't thought of that."

"I'm sure he'll come up with something special," Evans said.

Hyacinth closed her eyes and waved a hand. "I'll think about that later. I'm going to want you both for my honor attendants, of course."

Ava Grace's eyes filled—again. What was wrong with her? She would have thought she might be a bridesmaid, with Evans as the honor attendant. No one would ever know what this moment meant to her—or how much she needed it right now.

They all grasped hands. "There's no one else I'd rather stand up with," Evans said. "Except Ava Grace, of course, when her time comes."

"I'm afraid that ship has sailed," Ava Grace said. *But how do you feel about being a labor coach?*

"I don't know," Hyacinth said. "Luka seems pretty smitten."

A bride-to-be always thought everyone looked smitten. She ought to know; she'd been there, reading romance between unlikely couples around every corner.

But she had to admit, her friends had been uncharacteristically silent on the subject of her and Luka.

"Today is about you," Ava Grace said. "Have you
talked about a date?"

"Not a specific date yet, but soon—or relatively
soon. This summer. We need to see how long the playoffs last. Sometimes they go on into June. Even if the
Yellowhammers don't go the distance, Robbie will want
to invite every hockey player he's ever been on the ice
with."

Summer. She hoped Hyacinth would be all right with
an attendant in a maternity dress.

"Luckily, I think I might be able to come up with
a wedding dress," Hyacinth said. They all laughed together. "And, seeing that their home is a wedding venue,
Robbie's family can put together a wedding without
much lead time because—here's the best part!" She
rubbed her hands together. "We're getting married in
Scotland!"

"Fabulous!" Evans said. "I've never been to Scotland. I can't wait."

"Me either," Hyacinth said. "Ava Grace, have you
ever been to Scotland?"

"Yes, but never to the Highlands." Would she be allowed to fly then? Would Luka go to the wedding? That
could be awkward, depending on how he reacted to the
pregnancy and how they parted. Maybe he'd bring a
date—a potential stepmother for her child. She had to
stop. The nausea intensified. Deep breaths. She willed
herself back to the present. "I've always wanted to go
there and I can't think of a better reason." Might as

well be enthusiastic now and a party pooper later if she had to be.

The waitress appeared. "Do you ladies need some more time, or are you ready to hear about our specials?"

At the mention—however remote—of food, Ava Grace's stomach lurched.

"I think we're ready," Hyacinth said.

Please, God, let there be something I can get down.

"Today we have a Reuben sandwich with sweet potato fries." *No. Just no.* "And our soup is crab bisque." *And oh, hell, no.*

She couldn't bear to look at the menu. Besides, she knew it by heart and there was nothing there she could stand the thought of.

"And you, ma'am?"

Hyacinth and Evans were finished ordering already?

"Uh. I know it's not breakfast time, but I'd really like some grits. Is that possible?"

The girl never blinked. "Of course."

Sometimes if you asked for what you wanted, you got it—but only sometimes.

"Grits?" Evans said, once the waitress was gone. "That's all you're eating? You love crab bisque."

It was an involuntary response. Ava Grace put her napkin over her mouth and gagged.

"Sorry," she said, wiping her eyes. "I'm feeling a little sick."

Hyacinth grabbed her purse, opened it, and pulled out a large floral zippered pouch. "What do you need? I have Tums, Pepto-Bismol, Imodium…"

In spite of herself, Ava Grace laughed. "Hyacinth. Always prepared." She put her hand over her eyes. As if there was anything in Hyacinth's fix-it bag to help her, as if there was anything anywhere.

But there might be. It was she, herself, who had decided she shouldn't tell anyone she was pregnant until she told Luka. She could change her mind. It wasn't as if Evans and Hyacinth were random people who'd walked into Heirloom.

They were her sisterhood.

Hyacinth continued to rifle through her bag. "Let's see what else I have. Here!" She held up a tea bag. "Peppermint. Sometimes that helps."

"Got the equipment needed to deliver a baby in that bag?" She said it simply, without fanfare, without hysterics. "Because that's what I'm going to need come September."

Evans's and Hyacinth's faces were mirror images of what Ava Grace's had felt like that day in the tattoo studio and again when she took the tests. Neither said anything. Maybe they were waiting for Ava Grace to say April fool, but it wasn't April and wouldn't be for a long time.

"It's true," she said. "I realized it could be a possibility when I had to sign the form to get a tattoo. I took a home test, and I've seen the doctor. So, yes. I'm having a baby."

Then, in perfect unison, as if their moves had been designed by a Broadway musical choreographer, Hyacinth and Evans rose and knelt on either side of her.

"We're right here." Hyacinth gripped her arm, strong, steady, and sure.

"Whatever you need." Evans pushed her hair off her face.

"I just need to tell you," Ava Grace said.

And she did. When she said she already loved her baby, they rejoiced with her. When she said she didn't know what would happen with Luka, they assured her he was a good man, but she didn't need a man. When she said she hadn't told him—or anyone—yet, they swore it was a secret until she decided otherwise. And without prompting, they said they'd be there every step of the way. They promised baby showers, babysitting, and errand-running.

They said all the right things—and they meant them.

When the waitress approached with their food, Hyacinth called out to her, "Hey! Take that away and bring me the bill, please. Our friend is sick and doesn't need to look at food."

"Actually," Ava Grace said. "I'm feeling better. Could I get the bisque, after all?"

It was amazing what not feeling so alone could do for an upset stomach—and an upset soul.

Chapter Twenty-Five

Luka woke and turned to look at Ava Grace's sleeping face.

Toronto bound. Flight today. Tryout tomorrow—and that was what it was no matter how Kurt had tried to pretty up the words. *"Skate to see if you mesh with the team,"* his ass. It amounted to the same thing and it still didn't set right.

It was early, barely six o'clock. His plane didn't leave until 1:40, but Ava Grace would be up soon and he wanted to scramble her some eggs. She was a fussy breakfast-eater, but if he made something, she would usually eat it—and she needed to eat. She hadn't been eating much lately and hadn't seemed quite herself. Was it possible that she was out of sorts because Toronto was on the horizon? It was disappointing that she wasn't going with him, but he understood. She had her business to attend to and he had not let go of the notion that things didn't have to end between them. That's what airplanes and phones were for.

He considered waking her to make love, but thought better of it. She needed to sleep. They'd opted out of Hammer Time last night after the game and come straight here, where he'd immediately taken her to bed to obliterate his frustration.

And he had a right to be frustrated, though it was his own damn fault. The Yellowhammers had barely pulled out the win in overtime, and no thanks to him. He cringed at the memory of it all—missed shots, lost face-offs, and two trips to the box.

He checked his phone to make sure Kurt hadn't called to say Toronto was canceling. After all, what might have been an opportunity in Pittsburgh had evaporated after the bad game he'd had against the Sound. A sportscaster had once said that Luka didn't often have a bad game, but when he did it was spectacularly bad. This had angered him at the time, but he had to admit the truth of it.

So last night after the game, he'd hustled Ava Grace out the back door to avoid the press and the autograph hounds, something he didn't usually do. His avoidance would probably get a mention on *The Face Off Grapevine* tomorrow, but he didn't care.

He moved from the bed as quietly as he could and went into the bathroom. The shower felt good. After Ava Grace left for work, he'd go back to the inn and pack, though he wouldn't need much—toiletries, underwear, a couple of changes of clothes. No suit and tie, though. Kurt had mentioned the brass taking him out for a meal. That was fine, but he wasn't dressing up for them. He would try out on the ice, but not the dining room.

He stepped out of the shower and reached for the towel he'd used yesterday, but it was gone. Ava Grace didn't believe in using a towel more than once and she was given to putting perfectly acceptable towels into the dirty laundry bin. He opened the linen closet, grabbed the top towel, and brought the whole stack down.

Damn. When he bent to collect the towels, there was something else on the floor—a small bag that must have also fallen out of the closet. When he picked it up, the contents fell out. At first, he thought they were digital thermometers, but then he saw the box.

His heart skipped a beat, then went into overdrive. Pregnancy tests, both used, both positive.

What the fuck? But maybe they weren't Ava Grace's; she hadn't lived in this house long. Someone else could have left them here. He rifled through the bag, looking for evidence, and found the receipt—dated less than a week ago.

He sank into the floor and read the directions on the box, to be sure of what the symbol meant—though there was no need. He'd seen the television commercials.

This must be what it felt like to be dead—sitting around waiting for emotion to set in. Finally, it did. What he felt could have been worse. In some ways, it was a relief to have the universe take away his choices.

Perhaps this was a ticket to exactly what he wanted. But why hadn't she told him? A bit of anger moved in to join the relief—but what he felt was still mostly relief.

Besides, a *tryout*? Fuck that.

The sound of the shower woke Ava Grace. She looked at her phone. It was time to get up anyway. She put on her robe, stepped in front of the mirror, and twisted her hair into a chignon. She was going to be on television today. Should she wear it up or down? She let it fall around her shoulders. If she wore it down, she'd need to wash it, but not if she wore it up. She gathered it into the chignon again. Or maybe a messy bun at the nape of her neck. But what did it matter? Both styles looked about the same from the front and she doubted if the camera would see the back of her head.

She let her hair fall again. Who was she fooling? Her hairstyle was only a distraction, something that helped her avoid thinking about the weekend ahead. Two long days with nothing to keep her company except the anxiety over telling Luka about the baby.

The bathroom door opened and she caught sight of Luka in the mirror.

"Good morn…" That was all she got out before she noticed the expression on his face—and what he held in his hand.

Well, well, well. Looked like her Sunday just got freed up.

For reasons she couldn't fathom, words from an Alfred Lord Tennyson poem crashed through her head:

The mirror crack'd from side to side;
"The curse has come upon me," cried
The Lady of Shalott.

She was no Lady of Shalott, but this was going to be bad. She couldn't rule out the possibility of a broken mirror. He looked furious. Her stomach twisted into a knot.

"You were not going to tell me." There was no question in Luka's voice, or in his face. He'd tried and convicted her.

"That's not true. I intended to."

"When did that intention end?"

"It didn't. I was always going to tell you. It's been hard to find a time."

"*Nyet*. We are together much of the time."

"Not the *right* time. You had games that you needed to focus on. I was going to tell you last night, or today, but then the Toronto…opportunity came along."

"Call it what it is. Tryout."

"All right. Tryout. So I decided to tell you Sunday. I had settled on that. Believe it or don't, but that's the truth."

"What is this focus you speak of? I am a professional. When I go on ice I do not take my troubles."

It smarted a bit that he thought of this as trouble, but didn't she? Wasn't it?

She changed the subject. "In case you're wondering, I've seen a doctor."

He put the test sticks back in the bag and placed it on the dresser. "I was not. Now I am wondering why you did not invite me to this appointment. When Carol saw the doctor with Alexander, Logan went to all the appointments."

He'd wanted to go with her? Did that mean he had an interest, or that he didn't trust her to deliver the information?

"No. I didn't. I wanted to be sure," she said. "No point in turning the world upside down if the home tests were wrong."

They had been speaking to their reflections, but then he turned and met her eyes. "And this doctor? He concurred?"

"Yes. You can call him if you want."

He gave his head a dismissive toss. "You will marry me, of course."

Marry me, marry me, marry me.

For what seemed like an eternity, she couldn't make sense of the words; they were sounds without meaning, like the Russian phrases Luka muttered under his breath when he was frustrated or annoyed—but not like the ones he whispered in her ear when they were in bed. No, even if she didn't know the translations, she understood those very well. *Marry me.* Finally the meaning clicked into place. He was giving her the chance to hear those sweet whispered words for a lifetime.

She went hot and cold, all at the same time. She waited—there had to be more. Luka had to say something else. She didn't need a long flowery speech. She'd gotten that—or at least the beginning of it—from Skip, and look how that had turned out. But there had to be more than, *"You will marry me, of course."* There had to be some talk of love, if not for her, for the baby. Or if that was expecting too much too soon, at least some mention that he was feeling some degree of positive emotion about the baby. Or *some* assurance that things would turn out all right. That would do. Really, anything remotely optimistic would be a good start.

So she waited. Then she let her eyes bore into his and inclined her head to signal that he was to go on.

He mirrored her expression, apparently waiting for an answer.

A full minute passed. Finally, when she became convinced he wasn't going to, she gave in and spoke.

"Why?" she asked. Maybe with a little prompting he would say the right words, whatever they were.

"Why what?"

"Why do you say we should marry?"

He closed his eyes and spoke to himself in Russian—perhaps he was cursing; perhaps he was giving himself a pep talk. Maybe he was answering her and had forgotten she didn't speak Russian. Who knew?

"Speak English."

"Is obvious."

"Not to me it's not."

"You must marry me so I can take care of you and the baby."

She hadn't seen that coming, but she'd give him the benefit of the doubt.

"In what way?"

"In every way." He swung his arm around like a windmill.

"I don't need you to take care of me. I can take care of myself." *I need you to love me. I need you to want this baby. I need you to be happy.*

"You cannot. You cannot even feed yourself. How do you think to take care of a baby?"

And just like that, Ava Grace phased back to the woman she'd been. No. It wasn't the woman she'd been; it was the woman she was, her true self. She'd only been pretending with her memes, her interviews, and her video blog.

This is Ava Grace. Ava Grace can't do anything; she needs someone to take care of her. Don't be like Ava Grace.

"I can." Her voice was small, but she had to defend

herself, even if she didn't believe it. "I can take care of my baby."

"Have you ever changed a diaper?"

She thought back. "No. Not yet. Have you?"

"*Da!* Many times. I have niece and nephew. I sometimes take care of Alex. You need me. This is best."

Maybe she did need him—but was that the point? Shouldn't this be about what the baby needed? Maybe she should agree and hope things would turn out well. But he would expect her to go to Toronto, where she didn't know anyone, or even how to get to a grocery store—not that it mattered. As he had pointed out, she couldn't feed herself, so why buy food?

At that, something inside her rebelled. How dare he imply that she was incompetent? She could do what she needed to. She'd never needed to be able to cook. He probably didn't know how to lay the silverware for a formal dinner. That didn't make him an incompetent person.

He dropped the towel and began to dress. "I will go to your father now, speak with him man-to-man. I will ask for his blessing and assure him he has no more worries. I will take care of you now."

"What?" She had to run the words back through her mind to get the full impact of them. "You will not! My parents do not even know I'm pregnant."

"No matter." He zipped his pants and picked his dress shirt up off the floor, where he'd dropped it last night. "I will settle this. You speak with your mother. Make arrangements as you see fit. Please yourself in that matter. Small or a large party—or no party. It makes no difference to me. But it should be soon."

And then the anger moved in, and with it her momentarily lost backbone. She wasn't the woman she'd been. She might not be all she would be, but who was? She was *becoming*—and that meant something.

"Stop it, I tell you." She said it very quietly, but her tone must have been deadly because it got his attention. "I've not said I'll marry you."

He looked surprised. No wonder. He hadn't noticed, hadn't cared.

"What is to say? It is settled. You have baby. We make a home for him." Luka was now wearing half the dress clothes he'd worn from the rink last night—pants, but no belt. Wrinkled shirt, but no tie or jacket. "You will see. Is best for all. You are not to worry. I make arrangements. I will find the best doctor. I will hire nanny."

And there it was, what she'd been fighting, trying so hard not to see—he was telling her what she would do, making decisions for her own good, expecting her to sit back and let it all happen to her. It would have been easy; she was really good at letting life happen to her. But she was done with that.

"No. I will not marry you." Her heart didn't just break. It left her body and crashed at her feet. In that moment, she faced it—she was in love with him. She wanted to marry him, but not on these terms. Not at the cost of all she'd gained. She would not marry someone who saw her as useless. More than that, she wouldn't marry someone who didn't love her. Not five minutes ago anything positive would have been enough, but she'd been wrong five minutes ago. "I will never marry you," she added for emphasis.

He looked baffled. "But you must."

"No. This isn't 1955. I can make a life for my baby, regardless of your lack of faith in my abilities."

"Is my baby, as well. You would deny me the right to be a father?"

"No. I couldn't deny you that even if I wanted to, which I don't. I'm denying you the right to be my husband."

He looked panicked. "That cannot be."

"It can."

"What will you do? Move back in with your parents? Have your father hire a nanny and buy your food?"

"How is that any different from me moving to Canada with you, letting you hire a nanny, and having you buy my food?" Not that she was going to do either one. She'd find her own way. It would be hard, but hard didn't have to stop her.

He looked taken aback. "Is different."

"How?"

"Just is. That's all." He narrowed his eyes. "I will not go to Canada. I stay here and play for the Yellowhammers."

"Perfect. You'd like that, wouldn't you? Staying in a place you hate." *And having you resent this baby and me until we all hate each other.* "No, thank you. I don't relish creating a toxic atmosphere."

"I don't hate this place so much anymore. I tell you before. I like the grits and the barbecue. I like you, as well." He smiled, she supposed in what he thought was an attempt to be charming—not his strong suit under the best of circumstances.

"Well, thank you for that. It's good to be liked." She

hesitated. "For what it's worth, I do love you." If she felt it, she might as well own it. Besides, maybe there was a glimmer of a chance that her words might make a difference.

"Is worth everything. Certainly even more reason to marry me." But he didn't say the words she wanted to hear.

"No."

"I am not understanding you, Ava Grace."

"That's an understatement."

"You are overwrought. What can I do? Perhaps we will go shopping. I will let you choose your ring. I think Robbie made mistake with the ring he got for Hyacinth. It was…was…showy. Too much—and dangerous. Is the kind of ring someone would attack her to steal. I would have you safe and I want to please you."

"I'd hate to think how this would be going if you *didn't* want to please me."

"This is a better idea. It is better that you have a ring when I speak with your father. Perhaps you lie down for a bit longer while I make you some eggs. Then we will go shopping."

Merry, merry, merry hell and all the local environs. *Get some rest, have some food, buy something pretty.* Exactly what she needed: Buck 2.0.

"Have you not heard a word I've said? You are not going to speak with my father or anyone else. You are not going to buy me a ring. I am not going to marry you."

"You must. And you say you love me."

She clasped her hands to either side of her head and

squeezed her eyes closed. "I feel like I am in some kind of time warp loop."

"*Time warp loop?* I do not understand this phrase."

She took a deep breath. "We keep going around and around in circles and saying the same thing over and over—except you aren't hearing me, and are still living with the delusion that I am going to marry you, when I'm not."

"Is the only way. I do not mind staying here. Is best. You can continue to keep your shop and do your little things if you like. Or you don't have to. I have money— I have earned much and have many good investments. I get money for saying I like to fly on JetNow airplanes and drink Arctic Fox vodka. You will have no money worries. You may choose what you do." His accent was getting thicker by the second.

"I can choose? You're going to *allow* me to choose?"

"You are taking wrong what I say. I am only saying you have freedom. I can take care of things."

For someone who'd lived her life trying to please everyone and be a ray of sunshine, she was mustering up a pretty good dose of rage.

"You can, can you? You—living in a hotel room?"

"You forget who I am. I can buy a house tomorrow— today. Five houses if I choose."

"No doubt. How about your plans for life after hockey? How's that going?"

A bit of hurt crept into his eyes. "I do not need plans for after hockey. I tell you before. I have money enough."

She regretted what she'd said about his future. It was a cheap shot. She well understood how he worried about life after he retired from the game he loved, and that it had never been about money; it was about being productive and content, having passion for an endeavor. Still, she was too angry to apologize.

"Perhaps I do not need future career," he went on. "Perhaps I will be modern husband and take care of children while you teach people to be like Ava Grace."

"Perhaps you will," she said evenly. "Let me know when you find this wife who will have these children you will take care of because it's not going to be me!"

He spoke Russian under his breath. She was reasonably sure he was saying the worst words he knew.

"You will see reason, perhaps tomorrow. I will call Kurt and cancel trip. We will shop for ring then. Perhaps we look online now, so you may consider what you like."

She was a volcano. Red-hot lava boiled in her stomach, coursed through her veins, and finally spewed out her mouth.

"Really?" She might have been boiling inside, but her voice could have frozen hell. "You said I forget who you are. Well, you forget who I am, if you ever knew." She lifted her chin. "I am Ava Grace Fairchild, lately of Fairvale, and child of Laurel Springs Village. My mother is the mayor and my daddy doesn't take any shit. I've got a brother with a temper and a trust fund all my own. I know exactly who I am and what I can do. Nobody around here crosses me or mine. So, go get on your plane. Maybe somewhere along the way you'll find out who you are."

His face emptied of emotion. "Yes. I see," he said quietly. "Was always going to be like this. I forget that for a moment. I thought the baby changed things. Was incorrect."

He left without looking back.

When she heard the door shut, the lava that had erupted cooled and hardened. What had happened? What did he mean that it was always going to be like this? If it meant anything. Regardless of her haughty little speech, she had no idea what to do next.

Then it came to her. Since she had barely written in it this year, it took a few minutes to remember where she'd hidden her grievance journal but, at last, she located it in her chest of drawers under a pile of sweaters.

She wrote:

People who try to boss me around.

People who say I can't feed myself.

People who don't love me back.

She could have written more, but her heart wouldn't take it. When she went to return the book to the dresser drawer, she caught sight of the puck Luka had brought her from the Canada road trip. She picked it up and hurled it at her refection.

And the mirror did, indeed, crack from side to side.

Then she threw herself on the bed and cried.

Chapter Twenty-Six

Back in his suite at the inn, Luka placed his duffel bag on the bed—the bed that he often napped in, but rarely greeted the morning in. He and Ava Grace had slept here a few times, but mostly stayed at her house, which had suited him. He liked the coziness there and having a kitchen to cook in. But that was over.

He threw socks and underwear into his bag. He would insist on having a magnificent, state-of-the-art kitchen in Toronto. He would not miss Ava Grace's unreliable oven and too-small refrigerator.

He supposed, in time, he wouldn't miss her either. He sat down on the bed. There was nothing of her in this room—not surprising since they'd stayed here so seldom. His things were scattered all over her house—clothes, shoes, ice packs, protein powder, phone and laptop chargers. He supposed he'd have to get all that at some point. And there were other things to discuss. He'd need a nursery in Toronto. And a nanny. But how soon would he be allowed to bring the baby there? Would it need a passport? Would she allow him to take it to Moscow to meet the family? Could she stop him?

Maybe she would go, too. Not for him, but for the baby. Wouldn't she have to feed it?

That last thought brought him up short. He'd been grasping at straws all morning—maybe ever since their first encounter—but no more. There was no Luka and Ava Grace. He'd known that from the beginning. He was a fool to think this changed anything. As she'd said, she was *"Ava Grace Fairchild, lately of Fairvale."*

He got up, collected some sweatpants, hoodies and T-shirts, and put them in the duffel. He went to the bathroom for toiletries, but thought better of it. He wanted to take another shower, wanted to wash away everything that had happened him. He'd finish packing these clothes, shower, dress for the plane, and, last, pack the toiletries. Then he'd go downstairs for some breakfast. He didn't feel like eating, but nutrition was important. He couldn't fail at this tryout.

He threw in some snow boots, a phone charger, and a partial box of protein bars. What else? Ah, things he hadn't needed many times in Alabama—a warm hat, gloves, and scarf. When he opened the bottom dresser drawer to retrieve the seldom used items, the air froze in his lungs.

There was something of Ava Grace here after all. There, shoved to the back of the drawer, a bit of silvery blue fabric peeped out. He removed the remnants of the dress she'd bought to wear for another man and brought it to his nose. It still smelled like her. He hadn't been able to throw it away. She hadn't asked about it. Why would she? It was in tatters. She'd torn it in order to run away. He'd finished destroying it on the way to something that would end up destroying him.

Fuck it. He threw what had once been a dress in the trash and bolted out the door, his plans for a shower and fresh clothes forgotten.

Luka intended to go into the dining room, but found himself in the bar instead.

The bartender looked up from the pitcher of Bloody Marys he was mixing, surprised. He probably didn't get a lot of people bellying up to the bar this early.

"Good morning, Mr. Zadorov." He handed the pitcher off to the waiting server. "Bloody Mary? Mimosa?"

Ha! Morning drinking was morning drinking, no matter the delivery. He would not pretty it up with what society deemed acceptable. The body didn't care.

"Is your Stolichnaya in freezer?" There was no other place to keep vodka, but not all Americans knew that.

"Of course."

"A shot." It wouldn't be his last, but he would order them one at a time. He wanted it as cold as possible to match the coldness in his heart. Though it really wasn't early for him. It was afternoon in Moscow. Who came up with the five-o'clock rule anyway? Ava Grace would know. She knew all the rules.

The bartender set the shot in front of him. He knocked it back and said, "Another."

He knocked that one back too, but declined a third. He'd let that settle in first.

"Would you like some breakfast, Mr. Zadorov?" the bartender asked. "I can put in an order for you."

"Nyet!" He said it with more vehemence than he meant, but not as much as he felt. The bartender faded into the background. Smart man.

Playing back the scene with Ava Grace in his mind, he picked through his mistakes, but he didn't know what he should have said instead—that he loved her and he would be glad to stay in this football country if he could be with her? Sure, she'd said she loved him, but he didn't believe her. She'd made it up to cause him pain. That was obvious from the other spiteful things she'd said to him.

So it was good he hadn't admitted his love for her. That would have only made her pity him and he'd take anger over pity any time. Maybe the anger was good. It had made her say what he had always known—that she was a princess, comfortable with her life and that she didn't need or want him. It had made her sneer at him for having no house and no life plan.

The disappointment had stuck a hard blow, because he had begun to let himself believe there was a future for them, even before learning about the baby—but the baby sealed the deal. He had thought Ava Grace would have no choice but to make a family with him. He'd hoped that, given time, she would adjust to being with him permanently, maybe even like it.

But women like Ava Grace always had choices and didn't have to adjust to anything.

What a fool he'd been. He had learned with Tatiana that class couldn't be bought and money would never be the great equalizer—especially to a woman like Ava Grace who had her own trust fund. He had forgotten it for a bit. She didn't want him, didn't want him for herself, and probably not for the baby. Maybe the best thing he could do was to leave them alone—send support if she would have it, make a trust fund if she wouldn't. Let her find someone from her world.

He wanted to slap himself. Those were the thoughts of someone who allowed self-pity to creep in, and that could not be him. He would know his child; he would be the best father he could, considering the distance, but he would not complicate Ava Grace's life or try to be part of it.

He was considering asking for another shot when a hell morning that couldn't possibly get worse got worse anyway.

"If it's not the defector." The voice came from behind him.

Luka growled, cursed under this breath, and laid his head on the bar. Anything but this.

"Want me to get you a pillow, Zov?"

"What do you want, Wingo?"

"Many things, but nothing from you. I didn't expect to see you." He slid onto the stool beside Luka. "Tomato juice," he said to the bartender. "And give him another of whatever he's been indulging in."

"If you didn't expect to see me, why did you come to my residence?"

"This is a residence?" Wingo was wearing a navy blue blazer and khaki pants. The white turtleneck he wore instead of a blue button down shirt was all that saved him from being a Skip clone.

"You are dressed like you are going for job interview."

"You're not." Wingo sipped the juice the bartender set in front of him. "Ironic, since you're the one with the 'interview.'" He sounded bitter.

Luka pushed his shot away. He would drink when he decided, *if* he decided.

"I'm dressed like this because I'm meeting someone for breakfast who I feel like upping my game for. Why are you dressed like you picked up your clothes off the floor?"

"Is not your business, college boy," Luka said.

"No." Wingo sighed. "It's not. Nothing about you is anybody's business, is it? That's why you have to go look for something else. You won't find it there either. And you know why? You're selfish. You're not a team player."

Anger—the kind that made his hands shake and his breath short—washed over Luka.

"Not a team player?" He made sure his voice was low, but deadly. "Check the stats. I have more assists than goals. I have assists on goals where I could have probably made the score, but *probably* wasn't good enough. When it is only probably, I put the puck in the hands of my teammate with the sure thing."

"I'm well aware of that," Wings said. "I'm the goalie, remember? I see everything and I always know where the puck is. None of that matters. Everything you do, you do for yourself. You can be selfish without being a puck hog. Everyone hates a puck hog. Hell, we learned that before we were eight years old. If you were a puck hog, Toronto wouldn't be looking at you. Neither would anyone else. Nickolai Glazov damn sure wouldn't give you the time of day."

There was some truth to what the boy said about being a puck hog, but Luka was surprised he knew it.

"What would you have me do, Wings? It's no good to be a puck hog, but according to you, it's no good not to be."

He slammed his hand on the bar. "I'd have you stay here and be part of this team. I'd have you think about something more than yourself for once."

Luka laughed a mean little laugh. "Says you? The Emperor of Self-Love?"

Wings nodded. "You're right. I do have a big ego. I do run my mouth too much. And I love myself more than I can say—but I don't love myself more than I love my team."

Luka hated having to defend himself against this asinine man-child, but he did it anyway. Besides, what was a little more self-hate at this point?

"Easy for you to say, Wings. You have landed in a place you like. If you were traded today, how soon would your embrace your new team, since you say you love the Yellowhammers so much?"

"Just like that." Wings snapped his fingers. "I've been playing hockey since I was five years old. I've been on a lot of teams. I learned early on that you *have* to embrace your new team. Hell. It's not even your *new* team. It's just your team. You move on."

Luka looked at the shot Wings had ordered for him. He was tempted but resisted.

"Did you know the Sound drafted me, first round?" Wings asked.

"Nyet." Sparks probably knew it and not only because the Sound was his former team. He made it his business to know the background of every man on the team. Luka had never seen the need.

"They did. That's when Pickens Davenport—the

owner—was also acting as GM. He paid— Never
mind. These Southern women say it's tacky to talk
about money, so I won't, but the signing bonus alone…
Well. I was pretty pumped. They'd won the cup a couple
of times—and it was Nashville. I thought it would be
a cool place to live and play. My sister and I had flown
out twice to look at places for me to live. Had a great
time. There's lots of nightlife, fine dining, and pretty
women with a guitar and a half-written song looking
for a good time. Anyway. Not long after, Thor Eastrom
took over as GM. The first thing he did was trade me
to the Yellowhammers—for Kenny Gillette and three
third-round draft picks, spread out over three years."

"Fuck." Luka hadn't meant to say that, but he'd never
heard of a player going so cheap—at least not one as
good as Wings. He didn't know who Kenny Gillette
was. That was a huge insult, no matter how annoying
Wings was. "Were you very angry?"

"No." He shook his head. "That's hockey. That's
how it works." Luka knew that, but it was easier to take
when it was somebody else. "Thor called me. He was
blunt. He didn't want me, thought Davenport had made
a mistake. He said it was no good for me either—that
Emile Giroux was the Sound's starting goalie and that
wasn't changing. I appreciated his honesty." He took
another drink of his juice. "So in the blink of an eye, I
was a Yellowhammer. I didn't expect to start here either. But then they traded Dustin Carmichael for you,
so it worked out for me. It's working out for the team,
too. It would be working out for you, if you'd let it."

"I give my all."

Wings nodded. "You do when it's going your way,

though I question your motivation for giving your all. You do the right thing for the wrong reason, until you don't. When you have a shit game like you did last night and against the Sound a while back, you give up. If you had any pride in this team, if you gave your all with as little as one thought for anybody but yourself, you wouldn't have those kinds of games."

"Everybody has a shit game. Even you."

Wings downed the rest of his juice. "Not that shitty. After you've made yourself look bad once, you just go ahead and stink up the whole rink, the team be damned. Like I said, you quit trying."

"Is not true." But was it? Did he give up the second something didn't go like he envisioned? Is that what he'd done with Ava Grace this morning?

What if she *did* love him? At what point in the argument had she said it? Was it before or after she'd said those terrible things? Why couldn't he remember? Maybe it was the vodka. More likely, he'd been concentrating so hard on his sales pitch, he hadn't stopped to take it in.

"I see it all, Luka." Wings rose and laid a twenty on the bar. "There's my girl." He smiled and waved across the way. "Good luck in Toronto."

Luka looked where Wings was looking. The girl smiled and waved to Luka like she knew him.

Wait. Maybe she did. Wasn't that…? Yes. Piper. It clicked into place. She'd been with Wings at Hammer Time Tuesday night. Luka hadn't paid any attention to her beyond noticing that she wore one of those Ava Grace shirts. He hadn't recognized her because she'd changed the blue stripes in her hair to pink.

"Wings?" Luka said, as Wings walked toward Piper. "That girl works for Ava Grace. Do not mistreat her." He could at least watch out for Ava Grace in this way, perhaps spare her an unhappy employee who might cause discord in her shop.

Wings turned and looked him square in the eye, his face open and honest. "Have you ever seen me mistreat anybody? Even once? Tell me that, Zov."

"Nyet," Luka was forced to admit. "I have not." After all, annoying the shit out of everyone wasn't mistreatment.

"And, Luka? You'd do well to love yourself a little more. You might even be able to get what you want."

"How do you know what I want?"

"I don't. But I know you don't have it now."

He watched Wings loop an arm around Piper's shoulders and usher her to the dining room.

He downed the lukewarm shot, laid a twenty to match Wingo's on the bar, and stood to go upstairs. He had to finish packing—and do his best not to think.

Chapter Twenty-Seven

Claire ushered Ava Grace, Evans, and Hyacinth into her dining room. "I'm so glad it worked for us to get together tonight. I wouldn't have thought of asking it of you on one of the few weekends the boys have off, but when I heard from Coach Glazov that Robbie and Jake were going up to Nashville for the Sound game, I took a chance. Sorry the invitation was last-minute."

It was Friday night. Hard to believe it was only this morning that The Great Confrontation had occurred. It seemed to Ava Grace that she'd lived three lifetimes since then, none of them good. She hadn't had a chance to tell Hyacinth and Evans about the latest development. She would, though, when she'd had a little more time to digest it.

"This is great," Hyacinth said. "I would have probably eaten popcorn for dinner. Jake and Robbie wanted to see some of their old teammates, but no way was I going to go sit in that cold arena. Seeing Robbie play is one thing, but a random game is another."

"I needed a little less testosterone and little more estrogen tonight," Evans said.

Got you covered, my friend. It was hard to fathom

relationships that were so secure and healthy that the couples relished a night apart. She'd had her last night with Luka and hadn't even seen it coming.

"I have our plates ready," Claire said. "Hyacinth, will you help me bring them in? Evans, there's a bottle of white Bordeaux breathing on the sideboard. Will you pour that?"

Ava Grace looked around for something she could do to be helpful, but saw nothing. There were already goblets of ice water at each place setting and the rolls and butter were on the table. Maybe Claire didn't trust her with a chore. Ava Grace had switched off and on all day between feeling empowered and inadequate. Apparently, it was inadequate's turn.

She took her seat. At least she wouldn't be in the way.

After Claire and Hyacinth left the room, Evans began to pour the wine. Oh, hell. Claire would notice that she wasn't drinking and wonder why. Another person might not, but Claire noticed everything and worked every angle. What to do, what to do? Pretend to sip? Say she didn't want any? But Claire knew she loved white Bordeaux.

Since Luka knew, there was nothing standing in the way of her telling Claire she was pregnant, but she wasn't ready for that. She really ought to tell her parents first. Though, who knew? She might change her mind and blurt it out before the meal was over like she had with Hyacinth and Evans. If she did, that was her business, but she didn't want to be outed by a glass of wine, or lack thereof. Why was everything so hard?

But after filling the other wineglasses, Evans

glanced over her shoulder toward the kitchen and retrieved the water pitcher from the sideboard.

"You'd have to look close to tell the difference," Evans whispered as she filled Ava Grace's wineglass with water. "I don't think even Claire will notice."

Relief and a feeling of foolishness washed over her in equal parts. Such a simple solution, yet she'd needed Evans to think of it for her.

"Thank you." She wasn't alone.

Evans took her seat as the others swept back into the room.

"So Luka left today," Claire said, as she placed a plate in front of Ava Grace.

Merry hell. Not now, please. It would be preferable to never discuss Luka, but failing that, please, God, not now. But good girls replied when spoken to.

"Yes." She placed her linen napkin in her lap. "His flight was this afternoon." He should be there by now, though she hadn't heard from him, nor was she likely to.

"We hate to see him go, but I suppose it's for the best if he isn't happy here." Claire put her own plate down and took her seat.

Maybe if you'd put his jersey on the wall, he would have been happy here and stayed. Ava Grace longed to say that, though she knew it wasn't true, wasn't fair.

And it was just as well she didn't say the words. With any luck the Luka talk was over. Claire walked a fine line where their personal lives were concerned and Ava Grace knew her well enough to know she'd come as close as she was likely to.

"This looks delicious," Evans said. "What are we having?"

Ava Grace shot her a grateful look before peering down at her food. Oh, no. There was something encased in puff pastry—likely beef Wellington. It would be rare, which meant she shouldn't eat it. And didn't beef Wellington have pâté? No organ meat either.

"Chicken and artichokes *en croûte*," Claire said.

Right. The wine was white. Claire wouldn't serve white wine with beef. Was this how it was going to be for the next nine months? Analyzing every single thing that went into her mouth? Maybe it would have been easier to have given Luka the no-no list and said, *Here! Feed me. I can't do it myself.* But that ship had sailed or, more accurately, that plane had taken off.

"Maybe Luka won't make that team," Hyacinth said bluntly. Great. She hadn't gotten the memo that the subject had been changed. "Then he'll have to stay here."

Ava Grace took a ragged breath. Hyacinth was trying to be supportive, show she was on the Ava Grace team, and Ava Grace loved her for it, but why couldn't she have let it go?

"I'm sure he'll do fine." Ava Grace took a sip of her fake wine.

"I know you were seeing him." Claire had made a declarative statement, but that didn't mean she had to give an answer.

"We're good Scrabble buddies. I'll miss him. But he's never made any secret that he wanted a trade. It's no big deal." Because going through a pregnancy, giving birth, and raising a child alone was hardly worth mentioning.

You turned him down, an inner voice reminded her. But what was she supposed to do? She'd been over it in her mind a hundred times and if there was another answer hiding there, she couldn't find it.

"Is this risotto?" Evans held up her forkful of what was clearly risotto.

"Mushroom risotto," Claire confirmed. "There are also roasted carrots, and asparagus in brown butter sauce. It might be too much, but I was hungry when I ordered it." She probably thought she ought to go ahead and recite the menu before Evans asked more questions.

"It looks wonderful," Ava Grace said. "Exactly right for a cold night."

"Better than popcorn," Hyacinth said. "That's for sure."

"Save room for dessert. Evans brought us the most beautiful individual brandied cherry pies in the shape of envelopes." Never had they talked so much about food, though it was probably a good thing since she needed to know what she was eating. The tarts should be safe, since the alcohol would have cooked out of the brandy.

"Something I was trying out for Valentine's Day," Evans said.

Valentine's Day—now, that was something to look forward to. She supposed there would be no roses from Skip this year—unless he had a standing order that he had forgotten to cancel. Not that she wanted them.

"Before we move on to business talk," Claire said, "let's catch up. First, let's celebrate our big news of the week."

Ava Grace's mouth went dry. Claire seemed to know everything before anyone else but, since Evans and Hyacinth wouldn't have told her, how could she possibly know this? Spy at the pharmacy where she'd bought the test? Hacked into Dr. Milton's computer? Or had she simply read Ava Grace's mind?

Claire raised her glass. "To Hyacinth and Robbie. Much happiness and many blessings."

Right. There were other people in the world, some of them at this table.

They clinked glasses and sipped.

"I hope you'll be able to come to the wedding, Claire," Hyacinth said.

"I would be there if you were having it in the Sahara Desert on the hottest day of the year, but a trip to Scotland doubles the pleasure. Are you working on your dress yet?"

"I've made some sketches, but nothing beyond that. Robbie keeps wanting me to try on different styles so he can give his very expert opinion, but I told him to forget it. He gets no input into my dress. The cake is his domain."

"He'll think whatever you wear will be perfect," Evans said.

"Don't be too sure. Remember, he thinks he knows everything about weddings that's worth knowing."

"Make arrangements as you see fit. Please yourself in that matter," Luka had said. And she had—by saying no. So why didn't she feel pleased? Not that she would be pleased if she had acquiesced to his demands.

"You should wear a tiara," Evans said dryly. "Task him with designing it and getting it made. That ought to keep him busy."

"Ohhh." Hyacinth pointed at Evans and shook her head. "Don't you dare put that idea in his head. Anyway, that's enough about me. Ava Grace almost got a tattoo."

"Thanks, Hyacinth," Ava Grace said. "Tell the world."

"Well, we're catching up. And it's true." Hyacinth cut into her chicken.

"Ava Grace, you shouldn't be afraid," Claire said. "It really isn't as painful as some would have you think."

They all stopped, forks and glasses in midair.

Claire had a tattoo?

Claire seemed not to notice anything except the piece of asparagus she was putting in her mouth. Evans and Ava Grace looked at Hyacinth—the one among them mostly likely to verbalize what everyone else was thinking. But she didn't seem to be willing to ask what the tattoo was or its location.

"Anything new with you, Evans?" Claire asked.

"Nothing personal, but I do have some Crust news."

Ava Grace breathed a sigh of relief. They were on to business talk. For once, she was more comfortable with that than what was happening in her private life.

Evans went on. "I've hired a new baker." She set her wineglass down and smiled. "Because I've contracted to provide Sideboard with ten pies a day."

"Evans, that's marvelous!" Claire said. They all gave her a little round of applause. "I knew supplying restaurants was a goal, but I didn't realize you were actually working on it. And Sideboard… What an accomplishment."

Sideboard was a downtown fixture that always made the lists of best places to eat in the Southeast.

"It just happened," Evans said. "The farm where

I get my dairy products also supplies Sideboard. The owner mentioned in passing that the pastry chef had lost her assistant and was having a hard time keeping up. So I called. I offered a discount if they would put on the menu that the pies were from Crust and they agreed. The contract is for six months. I thought any shorter wouldn't give either of us time to work out the kinks and I didn't want longer in case it isn't working out for me."

"Smart," Claire said. "Exactly what I would have done."

"We all have to go one night and have pie—only pie," Hyacinth said. "We won't have anything else."

"I don't know about you," Evans said, "but Ava Grace and I won't step foot in Sideboard without having the lamb."

"True," Ava Grace said—except lamb was only good if it was medium rare. That was all right. The chef could probably do amazing things with plain white rice and salt—but salt only if her blood pressure remained normal.

"Well done," Claire said. "Hyacinth, what do you have to share?"

Hyacinth rubbed her hands together. "Aubrey Jamison has commissioned me to make her wedding dress—and she has approved the design. I didn't want to tell until she gave me the go-ahead."

"That's so great, Hyacinth," Ava Grace said. "I'm so excited for you." Hyacinth's goal was to design and make dresses, and this was huge for her.

"She's lucky to be getting a dress from you," Evans

said. "I don't care how big of a country music star she is."

"I agree on all counts," Claire said. "See? I told you to be patient and your time would come."

Hyacinth took a drink of her wine. "We all know how patient I am."

"Patience isn't easy for anyone, I think." Luka had said that once. Did every word everyone spoke have to remind her of something he'd said or done? In time, she would forget—but that thought made her sad. Maybe she'd repurpose her grievance journal, call it *The Wit and Wisdom of Luka Zadorov.* But really, if she was going to be honest, there wasn't enough wit in Luka to write about. Seems she didn't need to laugh as much as she needed to be loved, but he wasn't providing that either.

"There's something else," Hyacinth said hesitatingly. "I'm not sure about this. I've always wanted a real workroom. I thought that one day I would be able to build onto Trousseau where the courtyard is. But Robbie is urging me to renovate the attic instead—and to do it now since I'll be making my own dress and Aubrey's."

"You don't seem sold," Claire said.

"It would be great to get out of that small dark space I'm using now. I'd love to put in some skylights and have real cutting tables…" Hyacinth's voice trailed off.

"But?" Evans said.

"It's a risk. What if I go to the expense and never get another commission? The thing is, Robbie wants to pay for it—invest in the business, he says. That's hard for me. You know how independent I am. But on the other hand, things have changed. It's not just me any-more. He's going to be my husband. It wouldn't be like I was accepting a handout from a stranger, but I can't let him do something foolhardy."

"Robbie and I have talked pretty extensively about our various financial interests," Claire said. "I can assure you he's no fool about how he invests his money."

"That may be true, but he's a fool about me." She held up her hand with the engagement ring as evidence.

Everyone laughed, but Ava Grace felt hollow. What did it feel like to have someone love you beyond all reason? Skip certainly hadn't been a fool for her, but she hadn't missed it; she missed it now.

"You have a point," Evans said.

"I'm not going to let him pay for this just because he wants me to have it," Hyacinth said. "I'm willing to do it, if it's a good investment. So, Claire, could you sit down with us and discuss the feasibility of it?"

"Sure. I suggest you get some estimates about what it will all cost—renovation and equipment. Increase in utilities and insurance. We'll hash it out."

"Thank you," Hyacinth said. "Believe it or not, that's all I have."

They all laughed.

"What?" Evans said in mock horror. "You must have been too tired from hauling that ring around to get a spreadsheet together." Usually at these meetings Hyacinth went into excruciating detail about everything she'd bought for the shop, what she'd sold, and how she hated herself for what she hadn't sold.

"That's wonderful news from both of you," Claire said. "You've worked hard and earned these successes.

But I think we all agree the star of the show tonight is Ava Grace."

Ava Grace's head popped up. What?

"Yes," Hyacinth said. "Hear, hear."

"Absolutely," Evans said. "We're so proud of you. I know I want to be like Ava Grace."

The accolades felt good, but they were making too much of it. "Thank you," she said, "but really. A couple of memes and video blogs hardly compares to a deal with the best restaurant in the state and making the wedding dress for someone who's a household word."

"No," Claire said. "It's bigger. You've found a niche. You've struck a chord. Encouraging people to dig down deep and really think about how they want their surroundings to look—and make them feel—instead of following one style or the latest trend is inspired. I know it's made me think. I love my grandmother's things and I love mid-century modern, but I have been considering that I'm too married to it. I'd like to make some changes—keep the style, but insert some surprises. Mix it up a little. I'm going to think about it some more, and then I'm going to come to you for help."

Ava Grace caught her breath. Claire *got* it and she wouldn't have said those things if she didn't mean them. But could Ava Grace live up to it?

"And you're showing them how to do it," Evans said. "The video blog with the mortars and pestles— what a cute idea. And people could do that with anything—vases, teapots. My grandmother is wild for, of all things, cream pitchers. And you were born to do that kind of thing—so charming. The camera loves you."

"You were great on TV today," Hyacinth said. "I especially liked the part where you put that snotty hostess in her place."

"What are you talking about? She wasn't snotty and I didn't put anyone in their place."

"I knew you'd think that. You're too nice." Hyacinth pulled a folded piece of paper out of her pocket. "I wrote it down."

Everyone burst out laughing.

"You would," Claire said. "I saw it, but let's hear it."

Hyacinth unfolded the paper. "She said, 'I think some people have misunderstood the Be Like Ava Grace concept. They would say you aren't telling them to find their own way at all, that you're telling them to do what you tell them to do. What would you say to these people?'"

"That?" Ava Grace said. "She wasn't being snotty. She was giving me a chance to clear something up that people didn't understand."

"Yeah?" Hyacinth said. "Who are *these people*? Did she say? Have you heard from *these people*? No. And I'll tell you why. There are no people. She made it up to be a bitch and make you blunder and flounder around."

"That can't be true." Ava Grace looked from Evans to Claire, who nodded.

"She was snotty," Evans said.

"And a bitch," Claire said. "You'd have thought she was interviewing a human trafficker on network news instead of doing a noontime local human-interest show."

"But did our Ava Grace take the bait?" Hyacinth asked. "No, she did not. This is what she said: 'Well, now, Tiffany, I don't think anyone really thinks I want people to be like me. That's only a little catchphrase. I only want them to be like me in that they decide what they like. I am hoping to help people find a way to make the things they love work together and make their surroundings meaningful.' Brilliant."

Evans and Claire chimed in with their agreement.

"Look," Ava Grace said, "y'all are very kind and I appreciate it, but I don't think you get that I stumbled into this. I didn't plan it at all. A customer annoyed me, and I made that meme. Then it took off, with a lot of help from Jen and Piper."

"You have no idea," Claire said, "how often a moment of unplanned serendipity leads to something wonderful."

"I do believe that," she said with conviction.

After all, what could be more serendipitous than a woman ripping her dress to the waist to crawl on the back of a hockey player's Harley-Davidson? There might be some heartache mixed in, but her baby would be wonderful.

"What are you doing for your next video blog?" Claire asked.

Ava Grace hesitated. "It sounds kind of dull, but it's important."

"Don't worry about that," Evans said. "It won't be dull. I told you. The camera loves you."

"All right. It's about silver flatware. You know how silver seems to be going out of vogue? This generation doesn't want it. Not only are brides not registering for it, they're refusing to take their family silver. I've wondered why, so I've done some reading and asked people who come into Heirloom. I thought it was the expense that was holding them back, though that doesn't make sense. Family heirlooms and wedding gifts are free.

"I have figured out people are afraid of silver. Most think it's pretty, but they're already so overwhelmed with work and life in general that the thought of having to polish silver is inconceivable. Most don't know that properly cared for and stored silver almost never needs more than a little buff with a polishing cloth. So I thought I'd emphasize the need to use it often, show some silver cloth storage products, and demonstrate how to clean small tarnish spots. And I'm also thinking of showing how to do a full-out polish job since people may have silver that's been sitting around unprotected—show how, with the right polish, it's not that hard."

"I had no idea these young girls didn't know these things." Claire picked up her dessert fork—Silver Sculpture by Reed & Barton. "My chest is lined with silver cloth and it keeps it shiny. But it's smart to show how to do a deep polish job. Sometimes you have to clean something up before you can move on to preserving it."

If only there was a way to so easily keep life shiny.

Chapter Twenty-Eight

When Noel Glazov walked into Heirloom, Ava Grace was clearing away the things she'd used for her video blog—the silver cloth bags, lined silver chest, and cleaning products. Ava Grace was a little star struck, but not because Noel was Nickolai Glazov's wife. Noel was an artisan quilter, a superstar in the textile arts world. She had a shop in Beauford, Tennessee, and was in the process of opening a second one down the street from Heirloom.

They had met casually a few times, but did not really know each other.

Ava Grace came from around the counter. "Hello, Noel. Welcome to Heirloom."

Noel looked around. "What a beautiful shop. I've been meaning to stop in, but what with bouncing back and forth between here and Beauford, trying to get the new shop open, and dealing with a toddler and being pregnant, I haven't made it until now." She laid her hand on her barely there baby bump. "And it *is* hockey season."

"When are you due?" A month ago she wouldn't have thought to ask that.

"July," Noel said. "Thank goodness it'll be in the off season."

Ava Grace tried to think what would be going on with the Yellowhammers at the end of September. Maybe preseason games. But what did that matter? Even if Luka had an interest in the baby, he wouldn't be here.

"I just saw your video blog," Noel said.

"You did?" Her blogs got lots of traffic, but it was hard to imagine someone who had been featured in *Garden & Gun* and made baby quilts for celebrities watching.

"Yes. I was down the street at Piece by Piece II." She looked at the ceiling and shook her head. "Or what will be Piece by Piece II if the renovations ever get done. Anyway, I saw your blog and came down on a whim. I had no idea silver didn't have to be high-maintenance."

Ava Grace nodded. "It doesn't. Silver cloth really is your best friend—after you shine it up, that is."

"My mother never made silver cloth's acquaintance, let alone befriended it, but she never was one to embrace what she called newfangled notions. I'm surprised she allowed electricity in the house."

"Eccentric?"

They laughed together. "A bit." Noel held up her hand and spaced her thumb and index finger an inch apart. "I grew up in a Victorian house with a family long on history and short on money. My mother was the guardian against the newfangled and the worshiper of the original to the house. I can't tell you the hours I spent polishing the family silver—silver that I thought should have been sold to replace the antiquated plumbing. I swore I'd never have any in my house—and I haven't." She smiled and shrugged like a woman who was about to eat her words.

"But you're having second thoughts?"

"Maybe… I really liked the pattern you used in your demonstration. And I loved that you said you don't have to wait to bring out the fine china to use it. I don't even have fine china."

"You don't have to in order to enjoy silver. Using it keeps it shiny, and I love an unexpected table. They have some great whimsical disposable products out these days. I'd put silver and crystal with some pretty paper plates for a birthday or holiday."

"Really?" Noel asked. "I would have thought you'd be against paper plates."

Ava Grace laughed. "I don't relish filling the landfill, but for a special occasion, they can be fun. Mixing the old with the new keeps people on their toes."

Noel paused for a moment. "This set of silver you showed? Is that something that's for sale? Is there a whole set?"

Ava Grace's heart sped up. Selling that Tiffany silver would make a huge difference in her month-end report.

"There is." Ava Grace led Noel to the case and took out the cherrywood chest. "It's vintage English King by Tiffany, first made in 1885. This is an eighty-five-piece service for twelve, including a full suite of serving pieces." She handed Noel a dinner fork.

Déjà vu. She'd spoken almost the same words before—but to a woman who didn't see the value of the silver and would have mangled it.

"I love the weight of it." Noel held the fork as if to eat.

"Tiffany is still making it. You can get all kinds of fun pieces like crumbers and sugar tongs. And this set has some wonderful obscure pieces like this tomato server, jelly spoon, and oyster ladle."

Noel picked up the oyster ladle and laughed with delight. "I can't see serving oysters, but sometimes you want something just because it's fun to have."

"Exactly. I'd love you to have this, but silver is an important purchase." There was no question, of course, of Noel being able to afford it. Even if her husband had not been a retired pro hockey player and a well-paid coach, her quilts sold for a king's ransom and she had a mile-long waiting list. "This is the only complete set I have, but it's more important that you have *your* silver than that I make a sale. If this isn't the set for you, I'll be happy to help you research patterns."

Noel turned, met her eyes, and was quiet for a moment. "My philosophy exactly." She looked at the ladle she held. "No. This is my silver. I want this." She smiled. "Now give me the bad news."

Ava Grace reached into the case for the price tag and handed it to her. Noel wouldn't be surprised; she knew the sale of a set of sterling would bring enough to replace plumbing.

"Ouch!" Noel said, but she laughed and reached into her bag and brought out her credit card.

"But the good news is the chest is lined with silver cloth."

"That looks heavy," Noel said as she signed the receipt. "Can I leave it here until Nickolai can come pick it up?"

"Of course." Ava Grace stored the chest back in the case and locked it. "It'll be right here waiting for you."

Noel nodded. "Ava Grace. What would you say to doing a video blog together?"

Ava Grace almost dropped her keys. "Pardon?"

"I used to do video blogs all the time, and I have some great equipment. But lately I haven't had time. Maybe we could do something on different ways to use quilts in the home? And mix them with different styles? I'd love to do it with you—if you wouldn't think I'd be riding your coattails."

Ava Grace laughed out loud. "*You* riding *my* coattails?"

"You're doing really well."

"Still. You're Noel Glazov. It would be more like my riding yours."

"Then why don't we say nobody is riding anybody's coattails? We're just two artisans trying to bring some beauty into people's lives."

Two artisans. Noel had called her an artisan. Maybe she was on her way, after all—even if she was on her way alone.

When she looked at Noel's signed receipt for the silver, the impact of the sale hit her.

This was pure profit. The silver had belonged to her, not Heirloom. Sure, it was almost the same thing, but not quite. It would go a long way toward a down payment on a condo or small house for her and the baby. She could get out of her parents' guesthouse and truly be on her own. She couldn't do it right now, of course—not without going into her trust fund, and she wasn't going to do that. While she had never invaded the principal, she hadn't had any qualms about spending the dividends on whatever she wanted.

That had to stop. She had more to think about than herself. Beyond the basic needs, there would be braces, dance classes, sports equipment, and who knew what else? Later, a car, college, wedding—it was overwhelming.

And she still didn't know where Luka stood. She could make him pay child support, of course, but did she want anything for her child that he didn't want to give freely? That was a hard question to answer—and one she didn't have to think about today.

She took deep breaths. Today she would only think about how to decorate with quilts.

After all, he was in Toronto. She'd sort it out the best she could when he got back.

Chapter Twenty-Nine

Luka met Glaz's wife coming out of Heirloom as he was preparing to go in.

"Hello, Luka." She didn't look surprised to see him. Either Glaz had told her of his changed plans or she had never known he was supposed to be gone.

"Hello, Noel. Lovely day today." He had no idea why he'd said that; it wasn't lovely. It was overcast and cold in a way he had not experienced before coming to the South—not so low in temperature, but a humid cold that leaked into the bones. He must be getting soft, acclimating to this Southern weather and these Southern ways.

Noel looked at the sky. "I suppose there's something lovely in every day if you look for it." Spoken like a woman who loved and was loved. "See you on the ice."

Yes, she would, but Ava Grace didn't know that. He'd given some thought to what Wings had said to him about giving up. He was staying, and had made a plan to show Ava Grace he would try to be worthy of her. And if she still wouldn't have him, well—the plan was still made. He had a baby to raise.

He opened the door and Ava Grace looked up. Her mouth dropped open. Noel may not have been surprised to see him in town, but the same could not be said for Ava Grace.

"Luka?"

He advanced to the counter where she stood. "*Da.* Is me. The same. I have no twin."

"You're back."

"*Nyet.* I never left."

She shook her head. "I don't understand."

"Nothing to understand. I did not go. Can you come away with me for a bit? I have something to show you."

"But why didn't you go?"

"I will explain in good time, but first I want you to come with me. Will you?"

She looked hesitant. "That depends. Are you going to start issuing orders to me? Assume you know what's best for me and that I can't think for myself?"

He shook his head. "I promise I will not. I was wrong to do such things. I was…overwrought. And surprised." *And trying to have you for myself any way I could.*

She sighed and ran her hand through her hair. "I can understand that. For what it's worth, I would not have had you find out that way. And I was going to tell you. I wanted you to go to Canada with a clear head."

Did that mean she wanted him to perform at his best to be rid of him, or so that he could leave, like he'd insisted he wanted to do? He'd know soon.

"The towels came tumbling down. There it was. But is over. Will you come with me?" This was three times he'd asked; he'd ask another hundred if necessary.

"Where? What do you need to show me?"

"Come with me. Is not far." She looked torn. "Please. My car is outside."

She nodded. "So is mine. I'll follow you."

Not what he wanted, but he'd take it. "All right. I won't lose you."

He meant those words in more ways than one.

Merry hell. Ava Grace didn't know what to think. Had Luka canceled on Toronto or had they canceled on him?

After telling Piper and Jen she was leaving, Ava Grace went out the back door and got in her car. By the time she turned on to Main Street, Luka was in his car with the engine running. She stopped to let him pull out in front of her.

She hadn't refused to ride with him because she thought he would kidnap her or do her bodily harm, but she needed to be in charge of her own comings and goings. She might never ride with anyone again.

At first, when Luka drove to the edge of town and turned on to the winding road that led to the old stately houses, she thought they were going to Fairvale.

He had a key to the windmill house. Despite her best intentions, a little wave of excitement—and longing— went through her. What if he had done something really romantic, like fill the house with vases of roses, or brought her favorite mocha praline fudge ice cream from the Double Scoop? It was the wrong time of day for a meal, but he could have made the blini with strawberries she liked so much.

Maybe he was going tell her that he still wanted to marry her—not because she needed taking care of, but because he loved her.

If he did, what would she do? Her heart knew the answer, even if her mind didn't. She'd been lonely for

him last night. Sure, they'd spent nights apart when he
was on the road, but last night had been different. Before, he'd always been coming back.

They were almost to the turnoff that would take them
to Fairvale. But he kept driving, past the Landrys, the
Hamptons, the Masons, and other houses Ava Grace
had been in and out of all her life. Luka drove on and
on, over the little hilly, two-lane blacktop through
the trees, bare of their leaves, where new houses had
popped up—houses her mother referred to as McMan-
sions.

Finally, Luka turned down a twisty gravel road unfa-
miliar to Ava Grace. She picked up her phone and was
about to call him and ask where the hell he was taking
her when it came into view.

Merry hell.

She'd heard about the house but, unlike many, she'd
never had enough interest to venture out to take a look.
The story was a couple who'd won the Georgia Power-
ball had starting building it, but had run out of money.

People had dubbed it the Lottery House.

If the newer houses they had just passed were Mc-
Mansions, this was a McCastle, complete with towers,
crenulations, and balconies. She'd heard someone say
the exterior was marble, but she could see, even from
a distance, that wasn't true. It was a combination of
limestone and granite. It was pretty—in an awful sort
of way.

The question was, what were they doing here?

Luka was out of his SUV and ready to open her car
door by the time she parked.

"What do you think?" he asked. "The driveway must

be paved, the grounds were left unfinished, but the house is done, except for a few small things—some chandeliers, electronics, and a bit of painting in some of the rooms. It's entirely livable."

Merry, merry hell.

"There were plans for a wall around the property and a gatehouse. I am not sure that is necessary. Is safe enough with state-of-the-art security system."

Ava Grace took a deep breath. "Luka, are you thinking of buying this house?"

He smiled, like he was exceedingly pleased with himself. "I already have."

Ava Grace came as close to fainting as she ever had. Thankfully, Luka didn't notice.

He took her arm. "Let's go inside."

Steady on her feet again, she entered into a dreamlike state, though she couldn't have said if it was a nightmare or only alarmingly surreal. Luka led her through his new acquisition: great rooms, parlors, libraries, bedrooms, and chambers she—a trained, licensed interior designer—could not put a name to. It was easy to see why there was no marble on the exterior. They'd bought it all up for the inside. There was plenty of stone, tile, and carved wood, too. While the house was clearly meant to have an old-world, European look, there was a media room, and the kitchen could have been plucked from a multimillion-dollar modern New York penthouse.

"I could cook some amazing meals in here, yes?" Luka ran his hand over the eight burner Aga range.

"Yes, but—"

"Come. We are not done." He took her hand and led

her up a grand staircase, then down a hall that ended at the foot of a spiral staircase. Once at the top, he opened a door that led to a balcony. "There." He pointed to a large half-built structure. "That is my future. After hockey."

"That? You're going to finish building it? What is it?"

"*Nyet.* I am no builder. They were building gymnasium. I will have built a rink for my hockey school."

Her head was spinning. He had a hockey school now? "Luka, I feel like I've tuned into a movie in the middle. You were headed to Toronto, only you didn't go—and I don't know why. Now you're here talking about a hockey school. And this house…"

"Sorry. Let's go back inside where it's warm. Is not good for you to be here in the cold."

"No. I'm fine. And I'm not waiting another second to hear why you didn't go to Toronto. I don't even know if it was your decision or theirs."

His face went serious. "Was mine. I canceled. I had much thinking to do. I will stay with the Yellowhammers and be a real part of the team. You said I had no home. Now I do. You said I had no plans for after hockey. I thought of something Glaz said. Hockey will never be loved as much as football here, but it can be loved. There needs to be better training for children. I will build the rink and organize the school. The Yellowhammers and Glaz will help with the training and financing. I will have purpose—a passion. All will be welcome—those who can pay and those who cannot. We will change lives."

There was no doubt he'd found the thing he could

be passionate about. She could see it in his eyes. "I'm glad for you, Luka. Truly. What a wonderful thing." And what a wonderful thing for her baby. It would be his baby, too, beyond biology.

"And I am passionate about you. I have a home now. I hope it will be yours too, that you will be my wife." Her heart went into high gear. "But if you don't want that, I accept it. I will stay regardless. I will be a Yellowhammer and a father to my child."

She wanted to say yes, that she would marry him and live in this house with him—despite its grandiose flamboyance. It wasn't lost on Ava Grace that Luka had been so judgmental about the ostentatious ring Robbie had given Hyacinth, yet he had bought this monstrosity. It was awful. No denying that, but she could make it work, showcase what was beautiful, downplay what was too damn much—throw in the unexpected. She could make it her own—if he would only say the right words to make her his own.

He got a faraway look in his eyes. "There was a girl in Moscow—a long time ago. Tatiana. She was of noble birth. I thought that didn't matter, but it did. She would not have me. I was too lowborn. I am still that." He met her eyes. "There is no formal nobility in America, but it exists all the same. You are the best of it. I know that. You are princess, far above me."

"What? No." Where did he get such an idea?

"Is true. When I was young, I thought money was an equalizer. I know that is not true now. Money will never make me equal to you, but it bought this great house and it bought me a future after hockey that will be a noble cause. That's all the nobility I can offer you, but it's yours if you'll take it."

Her heart sank. He had not said the words. She felt like she was a million years old.

"None of that's true, Luka," she said wearily. "You aren't beneath me. I've never done one thing to make you think that's true. You're making me pay for how this Tatiana treated you." He opened his mouth to speak, but she silenced him with a wave of her hand. "I didn't refuse to marry you because you didn't have a home or a plan for the future. I said those things in the heat of the moment, just like you said things in the heat of the moment, ordering me around like I didn't have good sense or the ability to take care of myself. I told myself that was the reason I refused you, and that's partly true. But the main reason I said no was because you don't love me—and I deserve to be loved, even if I can't cook a meal, even if I have been slow to learn a lot things I should have already. I deserve that; everyone does."

His eyes widened with surprise. "Not love you? Of course I love you. What man wouldn't?"

"Plenty don't."

"Then they are fools. What have I done that could make you think I don't love you?"

"You didn't say it until I asked for it, which means it counts for nothing."

"But the baby..." he stammered.

"The baby will be very lucky indeed, that you've decided to stay. I'm glad. I think you'll be a great father. For your sake, I hope you learn to like it here, but I won't be the reason you stay, because I won't marry you. We'll be parents together but, in every other way, we're done."

The walk down the staircases, over the black and white checked floors, past three fireplaces that were large enough to roast a hog, was the longest journey of her life.

Chapter Thirty

"That bastard! I'll kill him with my bare hands!"

It was Sunday afternoon. The Yellowhammers had practice and Evans, Ava Grace, and Hyacinth were in the Crust kitchen, where Evans was rolling out pie dough. Ava Grace put her face in her hands. What Hyacinth lacked in tolerance she made up for with passion.

"What exactly are your reasons for wanting to kill Luka?" Ava Grace asked. She'd told them the whole thing—how Luka had found out about the baby, his demand that she marry him, the purchase of the McCastle. All of it.

Hyacinth looked momentarily flustered. "For not being what you need him to be."

"That's hardly fair, Hyacinth." Evans fitted a crust into a pan and began to crimp the edges. "He bought a house, canceled his plans to leave town, and asked her to marry him. What else did you want him to do?"

If Ava Grace didn't like Hyacinth's reaction, she liked this less.

"Are you defending him?" Hyacinth demanded.

"Of course not. I'm only repeating back what Ava

Grace told us." She washed her hands and reached for another disc of dough.

Evans had a point. "A loveless marriage isn't good for anyone," Ava Grace said. "Least of all the baby."

"Are you sure it would be loveless?" Evans asked. "I had hoped when Jake told me Luka was staying that the two of you would work things out."

"We have worked things out," Ava Grace said. "He's staying. We'll parent our child."

"You know what I meant…"

"Not everyone has to be all coupled up," Ava Grace said. "You said yourself I didn't need a man."

"You don't," Hyacinth said. "It's just that…" Her voice trailed off.

"What?" Ava Grace said.

Evans picked up where Hyacinth had left off, probably because they had discussed it. "It's just that you seemed so happy with Luka—happier than we'd ever seen you."

Yeah. But that was when she thought he could still fall in love with her, when they hadn't had to fast-forward.

"That ship has sailed," Ava Grace said. And there was no life preserver.

"I don't want to try to tell you what to do," Evans said.

"I do," Hyacinth said.

"Hyacinth!" Evans burst out. "Stop it. We're going to support Ava Grace."

"Giving guidance *is* support," Hyacinth said.

"Maybe the guidance needs to come *from* Ava

Grace, not crammed down her throat." Evans turned to Ava Grace. "Tell us what you want."

"First off, don't kill him."

"I wasn't literally going to kill him," Hyacinth said.

"And be nice to him. We're all going to be in each other's lives for a long time." She didn't want to think about the stepmother he would one day bring to the dynamic. "And he has done the best he can." That was true. You couldn't help who you loved and who you didn't—and he'd tried to pretend he did when that was what she needed.

"We can do that," Evans said.

Hyacinth nodded—maybe not as fast as Ava Grace would have liked, but a nod from Hyacinth was a promise.

"And also, could I have some chocolate pie?"

As substitutes for love went, chocolate wasn't a bad one.

It had been almost a week since Luka had seen Ava Grace, though he'd heard from her twice.

He'd gotten his hopes up when her text had come in shortly after she'd left him standing on the balcony of the house he'd hoped they would live in together. He'd thought she had realized the lunacy of thinking he didn't love her, but no. Her text was only to say she had not told her parents about the baby yet, so to keep her pregnancy to himself until she told him otherwise.

He'd been right to not be so optimistic when the second text came three days ago. This text had informed him of the time and place of her doctor's appointment and to say he was welcome to meet her there if he wished. When he'd offered to pick her up, she'd turned him down.

No marriage, no ride. It seemed she wanted nothing from him. He'd tried to think of a way to convince her that she was wrong, that he did love her, but she had been so decisive. And truly, what else could he do? If there was anything, it eluded him.

Perhaps, regardless of what she claimed, Ava Grace had other reasons for not wanting him, reasons she didn't want to give and he wouldn't want to hear. There was a difference between giving up too soon and facing reality, and it was time to face reality.

He had considered contacting her to make sure she understood she was to call him if she needed anything, but had decided against that, too. He didn't want to upset her with unwanted attention. Besides, she knew he'd do anything for her. How could she not know something that was so true? Yet she claimed not to believe he loved her. The whole thing made his head spin.

No one had noticed her absence from his life. Likely, Logan was the only one who would have, and he was busy with Alex and, now, Molly. At least things were going well for them.

He might have been tempted to confide in Logan, but he had promised Ava Grace he wouldn't tell anyone about the baby until she gave him the go-ahead after telling her family. Besides, if he told about the baby, he'd have to admit there was no chance for him and Ava Grace, and he wasn't ready to speak those words out loud.

Luka was still living at the inn, though he'd hired contractors to finish up the small things inside the house. He'd hoped to have help from Ava Grace in choosing the paint and other things, but since that hadn't been possible, he'd done the best he could to Be Like Ava Grace when he made the selections.

Her latest video blog had been no help. It was with Noel Glazov and it was all about how to use quilts to decorate the home in places other than beds. He didn't have any quilts.

Though he dreaded it, he supposed he'd sleep in the house tonight. The things that had been in storage in Boston had arrived yesterday so there was no reason not to. Besides, he was resolute in his desire to make a home for his child, but it would be hard living where he'd thought the three of them would be a family. Lonely. Maybe he'd get a cat. He liked cats.

But for now, the lights were strobing, the music playing, and the broadcaster announcing the Yellowhammers first line. Thoughts of Ava Grace and the cat that was meant to replace her had to be left behind.

He had to take the ice and face off with Cory Reed, one of the best centers in the league. The Colorado Mavericks were favored over the Yellowhammers, but Luka tried not to let those predictions bother him. They generally came from people who had never put a hockey stick on ice.

What did bother him was that he bungled the face-off and lost the puck. Killjoy went to the boards with two Mavericks, came up with the puck, and sent it back to Luka. He had two choices—go for the shot or send it to Robbie. Such times were more about instinct than decision; decisions took time and there was no time.

He took the shot—and it was intercepted by Maverick forward Gil Patterson, who got a breakaway and sent the puck into the Yellowhammer net. Wingo was alone down there and never had a chance. The score was 1-0, after less than a minute of play.

Glaz called a timeout. Wings caught up with Luka on the way to the bench.

"Zov. Listen to me. Suck it up. Shake it off. It happens. There's fifty-nine minutes of play left. Make them count. Don't fuck this up."

And, somehow, Luka found a way to do that. In the end, it was Yellowhammers 3, Mavericks 2—and Luka had made one of those goals.

Maybe that ridiculous man-child college boy could give him some love advice. He couldn't do any worse.

Luka entered Hammer Time. He wouldn't have come except for the atonement he owed for his initial refusal to fully embrace the team as his own. He was a Yellowhammer now and he would act like it, so long as no one expected him to actually wear a bird suit. He owed these guys.

It wasn't personal that he didn't want to be here with them tonight.

People had become accustomed to seeing Ava Grace here with him and were bound to wonder where she was. He hated questions—especially the ones he didn't like the answer for. Also, it felt wrong to be here without her.

She had not been at the game. The seats that belonged to Ava Grace, Evans, and Hyacinth had remained empty, with Evans and Hyacinth having moved to the wives and girlfriends suite—a place Ava Grace had made perfectly clear she would never sit. Would she come once the baby was born? Bring him—or her—to see him play? Carol had taken Alex to see Logan play when Alex was a babe in arms, though that was probably more about Carol wanting to go than Alex being there. Would he—Luka—last long enough for his child to remember seeing him play?

So, so many questions, and no answers.

"No Ava Grace?" Logan asked when Luka slipped into the seat beside him. So here it was.

"No little Viking?" Maybe that would deflect the question.

It worked. Logan smiled and put an arm around Molly. "Sitter. We thought it might be nice to have a meal without being interrupted for a diaper change."

"It won't be long," Molly said. "He's doing pretty well with potty training."

Luka's ears perked up. "*Da?* When does that happen?" And how did it happen? Would he be expected to participate?

"Depends," Logan said. "Alex is a little later than average, but you don't want to try to make them until they're interested. That'll only make it take longer."

"How do you know this?" As far as Luka knew, Logan had no previous experience with children. His brother and sister were younger, but not enough that he would have learned anything useful about childrearing.

"My mom. And the internet." He sipped his beer. "Mostly the internet since she's not here. Why the sudden interest?"

"You mistake curiosity for interest," Luka said.

He would have to look some of these things up—

though, first, he'd have to figure out what to look up. Maybe there was a list that advised what a father should do every month for twenty-one years.

"Good game tonight, guys," Able said. He pulled out the chair across from Logan for Ariel and seated himself across from Luka. It was the captain's job to tend to morale.

"Rough start," Luka said.

Able grinned. "That's why I didn't say, 'Great game,' but it's all good."

"Luka! I'm so glad you decided to stay." Fuck. It was Evans and she came in for a hug. She was a hugger. And now she was sitting in the chair beside him, with Sparks on the other side. Robbie and Hyacinth wouldn't be far behind. No. There they were, going around the long table in order to sit across from Evans and Sparks.

He was going to be surrounded. At least Wings and Piper were at the other end of the table. Considering recent developments, Luka didn't know how to deal with him anymore and there was too much marching around inside him to try to figure it out tonight. Besides, Wings was still annoying.

Robbie and Hyacinth took their seats.

Hail, hail, the gang's all here—only not quite.

"I hear you bought the Lottery House," Hyacinth said. Her tone was terse, which made him wonder if Ava Grace had told her friends what happened—including buying the house. On the other hand, Evans had been so friendly and his purchase of the house was not a secret. He'd told his teammates himself because he wanted them to know he was serious about staying.

That traffic light ring flashed as Hyacinth turned the pages of the menu. "Congratulations."

"Thank you. It has nice kitchen."

"Hyacinth!" Evans said. "Don't call it that. It's Luka's house now." She turned to him. "Jake told me about your plans for a hockey school. I think it's wonderful."

"That is my hope. It will take a while. The rink must be finished, plans made."

"Hey," Jake said. "Maybe Ava Grace can do a meme in hockey gear. 'This is Ava Grace. Ava Grace is learning to play hockey. Be like Ava Grace.'"

Hell. He was in utter hell. He pulled at his collar. Hyacinth and Evans exchanged a look. *Da*. They knew—probably the whole story—but their men did not. He supposed the not telling rule applied only to him. But she was the one who was pregnant, so he would respect her wishes.

"She could do it," Hyacinth said. "At least she can ice-skate. I'd be flat on my ass."

Ava Grace could skate? He'd never asked and it had never come up. Most of the people who lived here had never been on skates and he'd assumed she hadn't either. What else didn't he know? What else had he assumed—apart from thinking she understood that he loved her?

Where was the server? He needed something to drink. He grabbed Logan's beer and drained it.

"Hey!" Logan said.

"Sorry. Was thirsty. I will get you another."

He looked around for someone—anyone—who worked here. He needed some water, needed some food, needed to get the meal behind him so he could get out of here.

Finally, finally there was someone who worked here—only it wasn't good news. And she didn't so much work here as rule it with an iron hand. She marched in like she owned the place—which she did—with that kid called Soup behind her, carrying one of those giant shadow boxes. Another jersey was going on the wall.

"Congratulations on the win, gentlemen." Claire never had to raise her voice to get everyone's attention. "I know you're all hungry, but before you order, let's take care of a little business. Able, Dietrich, Jake, Robbie, Logan, join me please."

They went to stand under their framed jerseys. Now, if she would get on with it. It wouldn't be him—especially after the first play of the game—and he didn't care. He wanted to put in the rest of his time here tonight and leave.

"Luka, this wall of excellence can't continue to be excellent without you," Claire said, and motioned for Soup to turn the jersey around. "I think I speak for everyone when I say we're delighted you're still here with us."

So that was it. She hadn't ever planned to put up his jersey as long as he had one foot out the door, no matter how many goals he scored or face-offs he won. Funny that. Ava Grace only wanted him as long as he had one foot out the door.

The applause and cheers interrupted his thoughts. He'd told himself this was stupid, that no other team he'd ever played for did such a hokey, meaningless thing. But tradition was important to hockey, important to him. Traditions had to begin somewhere, and this wasn't a bad one to be on the ground floor of. The wall was more than goals scored and games won. It was the heart of a team. Though he'd never have the love of his life, he had this. And he'd have his child.

The catcalls continued.

He knew the drill. He ought to; he'd seen it five times. Hugs, pictures, the rest of it.

When he came back to his seat, Evans said, "I got some pictures. I'll text them to you." She paused and looked sad. "Ava Grace will be happy to hear this. She really wanted this for you."

Don't be too sure, Evans. Ava Grace doesn't care.

Chapter Thirty-One

Regardless of T.S. Eliot's take on the Gregorian calendar, April was not the cruelest month; that was February, hands down. At least this February.

Yet, here was Ava Grace in Powells Department Store shopping for—of all things—valentine gifts.

The irony wasn't lost on her that she, the sad, single pregnant woman, was buying gifts on the day meant to celebrate lovers, but Piper and Jen had been so good that she wanted to buy them something. She wasn't sure exactly what, but it needed to be pretty and fun—nothing over-the-top; just a small gift to show her appreciation. Maybe some silver bracelets or quilted cosmetic bags in festive prints.

The smell of Powells—the mix of perfume, new fabric, and silk—had always reminded Ava Grace of back-to-school shopping, dance dresses, and Easter shoes.

Today, it made her want to throw up—so much so that she considered leaving. The holiday was still a week and a half away so she had time, but what was the use of leaving? These days, everything made her want to throw up, so she might as well be here as anywhere. Maybe it was the pregnancy, maybe it was because she hadn't told her parents yet, maybe it was because she hadn't seen Luka and she missed him.

Or maybe it was because she would see him tomorrow for her doctor's appointment and that was going to make her miss him more. She'd wanted to call him every day. She'd almost done it the night Evans had sent her the pictures of him getting his jersey on Hammer Time's wall. He'd looked happy and she was happy for him. She'd known it mattered to him, though he'd insisted it didn't.

But why call him? Talking wouldn't change anything.

Besides, she had other things on her mind—like telling her family she was pregnant, coupled with the news that she wasn't seeing the father of her child anymore. And she should tell Brad. She'd never kept anything this important from him before, but he was even more outspoken than Hyacinth and she was in no mood for it.

Though she had to wonder, what exactly was holding her back? Was she waiting for them to just magically know? What had happened to the woman who had been so eager to share her news?

She'd tell for sure after she saw Dr. Milton tomorrow, when she had a firm due date. The more concrete facts she had, the less likely they were to talk about her emotional state.

She flipped through some silk scarves. Jen would like several of these, but Ava Grace had never seen Piper wear a scarf. The leather gloves were nice but, again, Jen would love them and Piper couldn't be bothered with gloves. She ran into the same problem at the jewelry counter and with the cosmetic bags. Why did Piper have to be so hard to please?

Then it dawned on her. Piper wasn't hard to please. If anything, she was incredibly easy to please. She just didn't like the same things Ava Grace and Jen did.

Imagine that—people liking different things, having different styles, expressing themselves differently. Wasn't that what the whole Be Like Ava Grace premise was based on?

Feeling like an idiot, she selected a silver bangle bracelet for Jen. Simple and classic. She'd love it. Now, to get Piper some brightly colored socks in wild patterns and headbands with pom-poms and hearts—preferably pink to match the new streaks in her hair.

She paid for the bracelet and turned down the offer of gift wrapping. She could do that herself. On the way to the accessories department, Ava Grace stopped abruptly. She'd been in this store hundreds—maybe thousands—of times and had never given the baby department a second glance. Why would she?

For a few minutes she looked at the tiny clothes, stuffed animals, and blankets from afar. With so much bearing down on her, it had not occurred to her to look at baby things, even online. She would need everything. She didn't enter the department at first, but stood on the outside looking in. She almost carried on to get the socks and headbands, but why not take a closer look? She certainly wasn't going to buy anything today, but she was here. Might as well see what they had.

So many tiny, pretty things—smocked dresses for little girls, overalls with appliqués for little boys. And what tiny shoes! It was hard to believe a foot could be that small. For the first time she wondered if she'd need the dresses or the overalls.

Then she caught sight of the furniture. No doubt Emma Frances still had the crib she and Emerson had slept in. Probably strollers, car seats, and high chairs, too. Emma Frances never got rid of anything. She had it hauled up to the attic. But didn't baby equipment become obsolete, get declared unsafe?

She paused to look at a white wicker bassinet with a skirt made of yellow and blue toile with bunnies. Immediately, a nursery took shape in her mind—a mixture of white wicker and wood furniture with a fluffy rug and soft-colored fabrics in coordinating, but not strictly matching, patterns. Maybe wallpaper, maybe paint with a mural.

Of course, there was no place for all that in the windmill house. There was only one bedroom. Would she be able to find somewhere, move, and decorate before the baby came? The very idea exhausted her. Maybe Luka had been right—that she'd have to move back into her parents' house. But would that be so bad?

Yes; the answer was yes, even for a little while. It was losing ground. And if she moved in, she might never leave. She rested her hand on the bassinet and closed her eyes, imagining her baby turning two, four, and eight in the house she grew up in—the sixteenth birthday party, the leaving for college. A lifetime with no forward motion.

She'd felt a myriad of emotions since becoming pregnant—not the least of them her undeniable love for the father of the child—but this was the first time she'd felt fear.

She was probably a fool not to have felt it until now.

It would be easy to convince herself to believe what Luka had said when he had nonchalantly tossed out that he loved her, but it couldn't be true. Love wasn't blasé and couldn't be delivered as if it was a given. Love wasn't an *of course, what did you think?* kind of thing.

But she'd be fine—so much better off than many. She was smart. She had resources. She had a career she'd learned to be passionate about. Most important, she already had an unshakable support system in Evans and Hyacinth and that support would be stronger once she told her family and the other people in her life.

Just not the kind of support she wanted from the right person.

She might have stood there until the store closed if she hadn't heard her name called.

"Ava Grace?"

She turned. "Skip. Hello." She wasn't surprised to see him. Their world was small. It did surprise her that she didn't feel inclined to run from him. "What are you up to?"

"Picking up a suit I had altered. You?"

"Not much. Buying some little gifts for the girls who work with me. They've been fantastic."

Such a bland exchange, considering what they'd been through. But was it really? Bland? Or was it just normal conversation, people who knew each other exchanging information? Yes. And, in that moment, that was what she wanted. Finally, she didn't want to be angry with Skip anymore. There was no time for anger, no time for humiliation. She wanted it done and she wanted her friend back.

"*You're* doing fantastic," he went on. "I love your video blogs. And those memes—hilarious."

"Be like Ava Grace!" She shook a hand in the air like a cheerleader with a pom-pom.

Skip looked at the bassinet where her other hand still rested and brought his eyes back to hers, sad. "I'll never be able to say I'm sorry enough, but I have to try again. I know how much you wanted to start a family—to have a baby."

For reasons she couldn't explain, she began to laugh, partly from hysterical fear and partly because this situation was so damn sitcom-worthy.

And she divulged her secret. Maybe that was the best way to go forward, to share with him. "Well, I'm going to have one."

The sadness, along with the color, drained from Skip's face and was replaced with shock. "Do what? What did you say?"

"You heard me." She placed a hand on her still-flat abdomen. "I'm going to have a baby, Skip. I'm pregnant."

He closed his eyes and froze. He didn't seem to be breathing.

"Aren't you going to congratulate me?" she asked. "For getting what I've always wanted?"

He opened his eyes and put his hands on her shoulders. "You're sure? You've seen a doctor?"

"Merry hell, Skip. Of course I'm sure. Do you think I would have said so if I wasn't? Yes. I've seen Dr. Milton. First sonogram tomorrow."

He took a deep breath. "We'll get through this. Of course, I'm right here. I'll be by your side through it all. You aren't in this alone. I will be there, Ava Grace. You don't have to worry."

"Skip, that's sweet, but—" Then it slapped her in the face. "Wait. Did you think I meant the baby is *yours*?"

She didn't think his eyes could have gotten wider or wilder, but they did. "Isn't it?"

"No." She shook her head until her brains probably rattled. "Sorry. I didn't think. But no."

"But at Thanksgiving…" His voice trailed off. "Condoms can fail."

Believe me, buster, you don't need to tell me that.

"Yes," she said. "At Thanksgiving, we were together, but not after. Not when you first came home for the gala and, then, well. After…"

"Yeah. So you're sure?"

"Very, very sure, Skip. I promise there is no chance."

"All right." The relief was clear on his face. "I suppose it's that hockey player?"

"I love you, Skip, but this is not a conversation we're going to have."

He nodded. "I understand. But, Ava Grace? I'm still right here for you—and your baby. I always will be, if you'll have me. Whatever you need." She read the truth of that in his eyes.

This was the moment. "I'll have you," she said quietly. "I've got this—at least I think I will most days. On the days that I don't, I won't forget that you're there."

He held his arms out to her and she went into them. "You have no idea how good it is to hear those words."

"I think I do. I know how good it feels to say them. It's time we found our footing with each other in this new reality."

She felt better now. She'd had a moment of panic and it probably wouldn't be her last, not if she had any sense, but it would be all right.

But as she chose the silly little things that Piper would love, the conversation with Skip niggled at her. There was something there, like a grain of sand in her shoe—so small that it wasn't worth stopping and removing, but still *there*, refusing to let her disregard it. And she couldn't quite find it.

She sat in her car for fifteen minutes playing the conversation over and over in her mind. Then she took out the gifts she'd bought for the girls and inspected them. So different, such different approaches to life—neither wrong, but often misunderstood by the other.

Finally, it all came together. She sat, thinking, for another ten minutes until she grew cold.

She went into action. She found a recipe, stopped at the Piggly Wiggly, and went home. There, she cooked chicken in broth with celery and onion. When the chicken was done, she stripped the meat and put the skin and bones back in the broth to simmer while she mixed flour, shortening, and milk.

This time, she did not need a rolling pin. Instead, she dropped spoonfuls of dough into the rich broth to make fat, pillowy dumplings. Maybe she'd master the art of the rolling pin sometime in the future. Or maybe not. Maybe this was her way. It looked pretty good.

She filled a bowl, poured a glass of milk, and went to sit at the kitchen table.

There, she'd fed herself.

She'd never be a gourmet cook—maybe not even a solidly adequate one—but she could feed herself. And that was a victory.

Chapter Thirty-Two

The long, gravel driveway—the one that Ava Grace had mistaken for a road before—leading to the McCastle was pitch-black. Luka must have seen her headlights long before she arrived, because he was standing on the porch wearing a puzzled expression when she got out of her car.

"Ava Grace, this is surprise." He was barefoot, in shorts and a thin T-shirt, as if it wasn't winter. "Is all well?"

She didn't answer his question; she didn't know yet.

Instead, she handed him the covered Pyrex dish she carried. "Here. I brought you some chicken and dumplings. I made them myself—by myself."

"Thank you?" Since when was *thank you* a question?

"I wanted you to know I can feed myself—and you, too, if you'll eat that."

He lifted the dish. "I will eat. Will you come in?"

He led her through the vast foyer and turned into the first huge chamber on the right. There was a fire blazing high in the oversize fireplace. No wonder he was wearing shorts. She unbuttoned her coat.

"Here. Let me." Luka set the dish on a table to take her coat.

That's when she noticed the room had furniture—and what a mix it was. There was a huge leather sectional sofa—the kind with cup holders and recliners—in front of a big flat-screen television that didn't look like it had been hooked up yet. There were a couple of upholstered chairs against one wall and a futon against another. And there, in the far corner, was a king-size bed with night tables on either side. It looked like he planned to live in this one room. Maybe he was going for the open concept, New York loft look.

He must have seen her assessing the furnishings. "I know." He rubbed the back of his neck. "Is a large place to furnish. These are my things that were in storage. I was unsure what to do. Would you like to sit down? Yesterday I could not have made that offer."

She ignored it all—how he could have arranged his furniture and the offer of a seat.

"I have a question for you." She went to stand in front of him.

He nodded. "You have only to ask. I will answer."

"Why didn't you ask me if the baby was yours?"

He narrowed his eyes, confused, and wrinkled his forehead. "I did not need to. You are a forthright, honest woman. You would have told me if it was otherwise."

"Yes, yes, I know. After we got into a conversation, I certainly would have. I'm talking about before, *at first.* When you first found the tests and came out of the bathroom, it would have been reasonable to ask if the baby was yours. After all, I'd been in a long-term relationship up to the very *hour* I slept with you the first time. It wasn't as if Skip and I never had sex. You and I talked about it that first night together at the inn. So why didn't you ask?"

After all, Dr. Milton and Skip had both immediately assumed the baby was Skip's. Hyacinth and Evans might have if she hadn't led with it. Luka should have at least considered it. She wasn't sure why this was important, but her gut said it was.

Confused, Luka's mouth formed an O and he closed his eyes. When he opened his eyes again, it was clear he had the answer.

"I did not ask because it did not matter."

"What?" Of all the things he could have said, she would have never expected that. "It didn't matter? How could it not?"

He shook his head. "*Nyet.* Just didn't. Doesn't. Sure, I have big ego, bigger than I knew short time ago. I like idea that I put a baby in your body—that he or she has my DNA and perhaps the look of me and will be good on skates. But that is small. In the end, what difference does it make? It is *baby.* It is *you.* How could I fail to want your baby?"

The magnitude of it all hit her—what she'd been waiting for.

She stepped closer and leaned her forehead against his chest. "Luka, I have been very, very wrong."

And he put his arms around her. It was the best feeling in the world.

Luka would never understand this woman, but she was letting him hold her and that was good.

"Come. Sit." He took her hand and led her to the

couch where he'd been sitting when he saw the headlights approach the house. He pushed his laptop aside
to clear a space. "Tell me, *dorogaya*. What are you
wrong about?"

"You *do* love me."

"*Da.* Of course. I said as much."

"But you said it in such an offhand manner—like
you'd say to an aunt who said she loved you and you
answer her back to be polite."

She made no sense. "I am not polite person. You
have seen me speak to Wingo. What is the difference
of the delivery, if is true? I would not have said so if it
wasn't true, not to aunt, not to you."

She nodded. "I know that now." She looked to the
ceiling. At first he thought she was thinking, then it
went on so long he wondered if she was admiring the
new chandelier he had selected that had the look of a
wagon wheel and antlers.

"Do you like it? The light?" he asked.

She met his eyes. "That's a conversation for another
day." She took a deep breath. "I'm sorry I didn't believe
you. But people approach life differently. It's like I'm
the bangle bracelet and you're the pink headband with
pom-poms and hearts."

He scratched his head. "Ava Grace, is good we are
seeing doctor tomorrow. I have read is normal for pregnancy to rob a woman of her thoughts. But we will discuss it with him to be sure."

"There's nothing wrong with me. I'm trying to explain. A bangle bracelet is classic, predictable, expected. A headband with pom-poms and hearts is not
so expected, at least not what a bangle bracelet would

expect a headband to be. A bangle bracelet would expect a headband to be tortoiseshell or grosgrain ribbon. But the wonky headband still gets the job done, holds the hair in place."

"I understand," he lied. Perhaps a call to the doctor tonight was in order.

"You don't understand, do you?"

"No."

"Let me try again. I'm more like Jen. You're more like Piper."

This he did understand, but would not accept. "I can assure you I am not the girlfriend of Dietrich Wingo."

"Hear me out. Jen and Piper approach everything they do differently but, in the end, they are successful with whatever project they're working on together. They just get there in a different way. It's the same with you and me, in how we express ourselves. Let's just say that I've learned there's more than one way to express love."

Ah, *love*. Perhaps she would make sense soon. Perhaps this would end in a good place. It felt right, but things had always felt right with Ava Grace and had gone very wrong.

"I'm about huge declarations; you are quieter in your delivery," Ava Grace said. "Asked and answered. It's not necessary to revisit it." She looked at him and bit her lip. "You don't understand a thing I'm saying, do you?"

He wanted to make her happy and tell her he did, but he'd already lied about it once. "No. Nothing." He brightened. "But you're here and I'm glad. Does that count?"

She briefly covered her face with her hand. "That counts, but let me try again. I see now that you didn't get all flowery about loving me, because you saw it as obvious. By the same token, I didn't take any time assuring you that it was a stupid notion for you to believe that I thought you were beneath me—because it was obvious that wasn't true."

Finally, something resonated—and it was balm for his heart.

"Asked and answered," he repeated her words back to her. "It's not necessary to revisit it."

"But there is something I would like to revisit."

"I hope it is a good visit." He had a feeling it would be.

"Our marriage. If you're still open…"

That he understood *very* well—and he told her so with his mouth on hers.

Later, much later, after they'd kissed and laughed and made love, she whispered in his ear, "Luka? Just because I *can* feed myself, doesn't mean I want to. Is that all right?"

"*Da.* Is perfect."

Epilogue

The people of Laurel Springs Village could never remember a wedding being held on a Wednesday night before.

Some said it was because Ava Grace Fairchild wanted to get married on Valentine's Day; others said it was because she wanted to draw attention to her "brand" of being different, doing things her way.

Those close to the couple insisted the reason was more practical. There was a hockey schedule to work around and the wedding needed to happen before the rapidly approaching Lent Season since the Episcopal Church frowned on weddings during that time. So there hadn't been a lot of options.

Amazingly, the date had been the biggest problem.

The venue was a given. If you had a house with the look of a castle, why not use it?

No one was surprised that Ava Grace's best friends would be her maid and matron of honor and it was very sweet that she'd asked the young girls who worked for her to be bridesmaids—but Ava Grace was sweet. She always had been.

As for the groom's attendants—no one had ever

heard of twenty-one groomsmen before. Add in the best man, Logan Jensen, and the groom himself, and that was the whole team. It was rumored they would wear their hockey jerseys since there was no way to get formal attire for so many in such a short time. Marvell Crenshaw swore she'd overhead the groom saying something about a Viking being the ring bearer. Nobody knew what that meant.

Some thought Luka was slighting his family by not having them in the wedding party, but their hands were full. It seemed they had flown in with a trunkful of recipes and special cooking equipment they would need to make the wedding food—though they weren't making all of it.

Robbie McTavish was making the cake and Evans Pemberton Champagne was providing individual heart-shaped cherry pies.

No one knew how Claire Watkins had procured so many roses for the one day of the year when every rose in America was spoken for. (They should have put her in charge of the tuxedos, because, jerseys? Really?) Perhaps she knew an underground rose grower. Perhaps she had ambushed floral employees on the way to make their deliveries. Or maybe she'd simply conjured the flowers up in a cauldron in her basement. All they knew was the whole venue was covered in enough roses to put the New Year's Day rose parade to shame.

The people of Laurel Springs knew this because they had all come. There had been no time for formal invitations, of course. There had been phone calls, emails, text messages, and Ava Grace had posted a video blog to the Laurel Springs Village Facebook page, assuring everyone she hoped they would come.

And they had come. Despite the short notice, despite the cold rain, despite that it was Wednesday night and everyone had work, school, and all the other daily demands coming on Thursday morning, they had come. Churches that normally held Wednesday evening services canceled because the pews would have been empty.

Some came to get a look at the Lottery House, others because they wanted to see if Skip would really turn up and he and Brad would serve the cake. A few were curious about the Russian feast that would be served. But most came to celebrate Laurel Springs's favorite daughter and, though they didn't know it then, the man who would, before he retired in a few years, be instrumental in their hometown hockey team winning the cup. After that, he would teach their children to play hockey and be one of the men credited for bringing the love of hockey to Alabama—though it would never be quite as beloved as football.

All agreed the wedding really was lovely, regardless of the unorthodox touches. After all, Ava Grace did things her way, and that was never a bad way.

But one had to wonder—what did Emma Frances Fairchild think of all this?

It had turned out to be a good Valentine's Day, after all.

The ceremony had been everything Ava Grace had wanted—and much more. After speaking his vows, Luka had leaned in and whispered in her ear, "And I promise to tell you I love you every day, *dorogaya*—with words. I understand is important."

As soon as they had exited the great hall, Ava Grace had escaped upstairs to her newly furnished bedroom to use the restroom and catch her breath before the reception. She sat down at the dressing table to refresh her lipstick.

There was a knock at the door and Emma Frances glided in, ever tasteful in pale pink beaded silk.

"Hello, Madam Mayor." Ava Grace stood up and turned toward her mother.

"I'm not the mayor tonight. I'm just a mother and a grandmother-to-be celebrating her daughter's marriage—and her happiness."

"You're always the mayor—and a good one."

Emma Frances smiled and ran her hand over Ava Grace's hip. "I don't know when I have ever seen you look so beautiful. What a perfect fit. Hyacinth is a wonder."

"She is," Ava Grace said. "There was no time for her to make my dress, but she has worked nonstop to make the changes I wanted to this one."

"It couldn't be more perfect for you."

"Are you sure you want to hang my portrait in the library with the other Fairchild brides?" Ava Grace teased. "Since I'm not wearing the ancient and honorable gown?"

When Ava Grace had admitted to her parents she didn't want to wear the heirloom gown, her father had seemed puzzled and not overly interested; Emma Frances had said Ava Grace should wear what she wanted. Ava Grace suspected that by the time the wedding attire came up, Emma Frances was so relieved that Ava Grace was in love with the father of her baby and that they would be married, that she would have been agreeable had Ava Grace wanted to wear a Baby Yoda Halloween costume.

"Oh, I think there's room for some change. My very smart and successful daughter taught me something. It's more important for Ava Grace to be like Ava Grace than to uphold a tradition."

"Seriously, Mama, thank you for understanding."

"I think it's time we retired that dress anyway. It's looking pretty sad in places. I've had a thought…" Her voice trailed off.

"What, Mama?"

"I got out the Fairchild christening gown to have it cleaned for Emerson and Sharon's baby. I'd forgotten how small it is. Babies get bigger every year. I'd already had it let out so it would fit Emerson and you, but even Hyacinth couldn't enlarge it any more. What would you think of a new baptism dress made from an old wedding dress?"

Chills went over Ava Grace and her eyes filled.

Ava Grace threw her arms around her mother. "Oh, Mama. What a perfect idea—something new, while honoring the past. I know Hyacinth will make it for us. And we can frame the old christening dress in a shadow box."

"You might get a video blog out of it." Emma Frances wiped her eyes. "Let's not cry. We'll ruin our makeup."

"Nothing could ruin this day." And that was true.

The door opened. *"Dorogya?"* Luka stuck his head in. "I came to see if all is well."

"Ah, my new son," Emma Frances said. "I'll leave you two." She squeezed Ava Grace's hand and kissed Luka's cheek on the way out.

"You were taking long time." Luka slipped an arm around her and placed a hand on her stomach. "You are sure is not too much for you?"

"I'm fine. I was having a moment with my mother. Maybe you and I can have a moment before we go down to the party?"

"I'd like more than a moment." He kissed her neck.

She laughed. "It would take much more than a moment."

"I wish there could be honeymoon," Luka said.

"You have to play hockey." She straightened his tie. "We'll have a nice trip when we go to Scotland." Doctor Milton had said he saw no reason she couldn't fly this summer. "Besides, our whole life is a honeymoon." She took his hand. "Come with me." She led him down the hall and up the winding staircase to the balcony where she'd left him standing the day she'd thought she was leaving him for good.

The rain came down and the wind blew, but it was a beautiful night. She pointed in the direction of the gym/rink. "It's coming along."

"What? You cannot see. We need to get lights out here." He was right about not being able to see right now, but the work had begun.

"Just imagine. We'll skate there as a family. You'll change lives." She kissed him. "I am so proud of you—and proud to be your wife."

"Oh, *dorogaya*." He wound a curl around his finger. "You destroy me."

"Destroy you?" Merry hell. What did that mean?

"But only in a good way."

"I don't understand."

He laughed. "I know how you feel. The not understanding. Believe me. Is good."

"If you say so." She supposed they had a lifetime ahead of them of not understanding everything. That's how bangle bracelets and pom-pom headbands got on. But she believed him. It was good.

"We must go to our party." He took her hand. "Little Viking was eyeing cake. He is entirely able to destroy it—and *not* in a good way."

They only stopped to kiss three times—or was it four?—on the way to their party.

* * * * *

Acknowledgments

Thanks to:

Nomad Tony and John and Paula Alderman, who coached me on how a passenger would mount and dismount a motorcycle.

Lynn Raye Harris, who helped when I hit a wall and is always a great cheerleader.

About the Author

USA TODAY bestsellers Stephanie Jones and Jean Hovey write together as Alicia Hunter Pace. Stephanie lives in Tuscaloosa, AL, where she teaches school. She is a native Alabamian who likes football, American history, and people who follow the rules. She is happy to provide a list of said rules to anyone who needs them. Jean, a former public librarian, lives in Decatur, AL, with her husband in a hundred-year-old house that always wants something from her. She likes to cook but has discovered the joy of Mrs. Paul's fish fillets since becoming a writer. Stephanie and Jean are both active members in the romance writing community. They write contemporary romance. You can find them at:

AliciaHunterPace.com
Facebook.com/AliciaHunterPace
Twitter.com/AliciaHPace
aliciahunterpace@gmail.com

Missed Jake and Evans's story?
Keep reading to find out how it all began...

Chapter One

Five months later

Evans Pemberton considered the dough on the marble slab in front of her.

What was wrong with pie in this country was the crust. No one made quality crusts anymore or thought about which kind of crust went best with what pie. Butter crusts were wonderful with fruit pies, but too rich for pecan pies. Savory pies needed a sturdy crust, but it was important to get the right balance so as not to produce a soggy mess. A bit of bacon grease gave crusts for meat pies a smoky taste, and Evans liked to add a pinch of sage for chicken pot pies. Crumb crusts had their place, too.

As did Jake Champagne, she thought, as she gave the ball in front of her a vicious knead. And his place was now apparently *here*. He was going to land in town any day, any hour.

He hadn't spoken to her in almost three years. Sure, back in March, he had texted to thank her for the funeral flowers she'd sent when his uncle died and apologized for not making more of an effort to keep in touch.

According to her business manager, Neva, he'd also stopped by the shop a month later when he'd come to Laurel Springs to sign a lease on a condo, but Evans had been in New York taking a mini puff pastry course.

She didn't know why she was thinking about him anyway. Who knew if he would even try to contact her again? He had abandoned her once after a lifetime of friendship. There was no reason to think, despite the text and drop-in, that anything would change.

"You're looking at that dough like you don't like it," said a woman behind her.

"I don't." She turned and handed her friend, Ava Grace Fairchild, an apron and chef's hat. Ava Grace was no chef, but Evans had given up on trying to keep her out of the pie shop kitchen, so she'd settled on doing what she could to make Ava Grace acceptable should the health inspector make a surprise visit to Crust. "Though I suppose it's not so much that I don't like it. I don't *know* it."

"I thought you knew every dough." Ava Grace tied the apron over her linen dress and perched the hat on the back of her head so as not to disturb her loose chestnut curls. She looked like a queen dressed as a chef for Halloween.

"I don't know this one." Evans placed her hand on the dough. Normally, she wouldn't think of putting her warm hand on pastry dough, but this was a hot water pastry so it was warm to begin with.

Ava Grace slid onto a stool and crossed her long, perfect legs. "What makes this one different?"

"It's for a handheld meat pie with rutabagas, potato, and onions. The crust has to be sturdy but not tough. That's tricky." She gave the dough another vicious slap. "They're called Upper Peninsula pasties, from Michigan."

"Never heard of them," Ava Grace said.

"Claire has, and she wants to feed them to the new hockey team on their first day of training camp tomorrow."

Ava Grace's mouth twisted into a grin. "For a silent partner, Claire isn't very quiet, is she?"

Evans laughed. Ava Grace would know. Claire was her "silent" partner, too. "Well, she never promised to be quiet."

"That's a promise she couldn't have kept. Why is she so set on these little pies?"

"You know as well as I do that Claire doesn't have to have a reason, but she says most of the team is from up North, so we should give them some Northern comfort food."

Evans had not pointed out to Claire that not all hockey players would associate these pasties with home. She knew of one in particular who would need barbecue pork, hot tamales, and Mississippi mud pie to make him think of home. Claire wasn't an easy woman to say no to, even if Evans had been willing. Saying no had never been Evans's strong suit, which was why she was catering this lunch when she just wanted to make pies.

Evans had thought it would be years before she could fulfill her dream of having her own shop, until Claire had taken her under her wing. Now Crust was thriving.

The old-money heiress had excelled in business, and successfully played the stock market rather than living off her inheritance. A few years ago she had decided to help young women start their own new businesses. Evans and Ava Grace were two of Claire's girls, along with Hyacinth Dawson, who owned a local bridal shop.

"Claire must really like hockey," Ava Grace said.

"I don't think it's that, so much as she likes a project and loves the chase." Claire was one of several locals who owned a small part of the Yellowhammers. Her uncle and nephew had been the ones to bring the team here, but Claire had quickly formulated a plan to turn Laurel Springs into Yellowhammers Central. "She knows a bunch of rich hockey players are going to live and spend their money somewhere and she wants it to be here." She had convinced the owners to build a state-of-the-art practice rink and workout facility in Laurel Springs, renovated the old mill into upscale condos, lobbied for more fine dining and chic shops, and turned the old Speake Department Store building into a sports bar and named it Hammer Time—all to welcome the new team.

"It looks like she's getting her way," Ava Grace said. "Everywhere you look there's a gang of Lululemon-wearing men in Yellowhammer ball caps."

"We should be thankful for them," Evans said. "Sponsoring our businesses was part of her master plan to make the area appealing to the team. Had to be."

Ava Grace pulled at one of her curls. "I'm sure she knows what she's doing. I've lived here all my life, and I've never known Claire to fail," she said wryly. "At least not yet." Of the three businesses Claire had backed, Ava Grace's antique and gift shop was the only one losing money. Claire insisted that was to be expected in the beginning, but it was still a sore subject.

"Anyway." Ava Grace clapped her hands together like she always did when she wanted to change the subject. "Hockey in Birmingham. Hockey people here in our little corner of the world. I've never even been to a hockey game. Have you?"

And here it was. She'd never mentioned Jake to anyone in Laurel Springs, not even Ava Grace and Hyacinth, who were her best friends. And she was loath to do it now. What if he ignored her as he had the last few years?

"I have. A guy I've known all my life is a hockey player." She wasn't about to mention that he'd been the best-looking thing in Cottonwood, Mississippi—plus he had that hockey-mystique thing going for him in a world where most of the other boys played football and baseball. "His parents and mine are best friends, so we went to a lot of his games when I was growing up. After college, he went on to play for the Nashville Sound, but he's going to play for the Yellowhammers now."

Ava Grace widened her eyes. "Really? He's coming here?"

"If nothing has changed since the last time I talked to my mother. I haven't talked to him in a while." Technically not a lie—condolence texts didn't count as talking.

"Is he married?"

"Not anymore." She slammed her fist into the ball of dough.

Ava Grace's eyes lit up and Evans knew what was coming. Ava Grace was all but engaged and was always looking for romance for everyone else. "Is this an old boyfriend?"

"No! Of course not." She hadn't meant to sound so vehement.

Ava Grace narrowed her eyes. "You never went out with him a single time?"

"No. Never entered my mind." If she'd been Pinocchio, her nose would be out the front door. There had been this one time at a holiday party—for just a fraction of a minute—when Evans had thought he'd looked at her differently, when she'd been sure that Jake was finally going to ask her for a date. But they'd been interrupted, and the moment had passed. To this day, she never saw a sprig of holly or heard a Christmas bell without the memory of the humiliating disappointment slamming against her rib cage, driving the breath out of her.

"It's a new day," Ava Grace said. "I grew up with Skip, and look where we are. It could happen for you, too."

"Not likely." Evans floured her rolling pin. "A couple years back, my cousin Channing married and divorced him in the space of about seven months in the messiest way possible."

"Wow." Ava Grace raised her eyebrows. "Your cousin just up and stole your man, easy as you please? Why, you must've been madder than a wet hen!"

Evans shrugged. "He wasn't mine." She clenched her fist and the dough shot up between her fingers. "I doubt he would be open to romance with another Pemberton woman. Not that I would—be open to it, I mean."

The words had barely made their way out of her mouth when one of her assistant bakers ducked into the kitchen.

"Evans, there's a guy here to see you."

She stilled her rolling pin.

"I think I conjured up a man for you." Ava Grace laughed and removed her cap and apron. "See you tonight at Claire's house."

"Right." It was mentor dinner night with Claire, something they did every few weeks where Evans, Ava Grace, and Hyacinth gave reports and swapped advice.

Ava Grace nodded. "I'll just slip out the back."

"Who is it, Ariel?" Please, God, not the rep from Hollingsworth Foods—a regional company that provided frozen foods to grocery stores. According to Claire, they were interested in mass-producing her maple pecan and peanut butter chocolate pies. So far, the rep had only tried to contact her by phone and it had been easy enough to elude his calls, allowing her to tell Claire that she hadn't heard from them.

Ariel shook her head and played with the crystal that hung around her neck. "I don't know."

Evans sighed. Of course she wouldn't have thought to ask. The female hadn't been born who was more suited to her name than Ariel—ethereal, dreamy, not of this world. But she could make a lemon curd that would make you cry.

"All right." Evans reached for a towel and wiped her hands. As tempting as it was to follow Ava Grace out the back door, she supposed it was time to deal with it. "Will you cover these and put them in the refrigerator?" She gestured to the sheet pans of oven-ready meat pies.

Ariel nodded. "I'll just get the plastic wrap." And she floated to the storeroom.

Evans still had a few meat pies, then peach cobblers

to make for the Yellowhammer lunch tomorrow, so the quicker she sent him away, the better.

She hurried through the swinging door that led from the kitchen to the storefront—and looked right into the eyes of Jake Champagne.

Eyes.

He had eyes all night long and possibly into the next day. Big, cobalt blue eyes with Bambi eyelashes. They weren't eyes a woman was likely to forget even if he turned out to be a man she had to walk away from. Still, Evans had thought the day was done when those eyes would make her forget her own name. *Evans. Evans Blair Pemberton*, she reminded herself.

Jake widened those eyes. That was a willful act. She was sure of it because she'd spent years studying him— so she knew what it meant when Jake Champagne went all wide-eyed on someone. He understood the value of those eyes and the effect they had on people. When he widened them, he was either surprised or angling to get his way. This time he was surprised. If he'd been trying to get his way, he would have cocked his head to the side and smiled. If he wanted his way really bad, and it wasn't going well, he'd bite his bottom lip.

Speaking of what he wanted—what in the ever- loving hell was he doing here? She was pretty sure he had not gone to work for Hollingsworth Foods.

"You look great, Evie." She was suddenly sorry she'd studied him. Knowing he was surprised that she looked great wasn't the best for the ego.

Besides, she didn't look great. Her hair was in a messy ponytail, she was wearing an apron covered in flour, and any makeup she'd applied this morning was a memory. She only looked great compared to the last time he'd seen her—at the Pemberton family Thanksgiving two years ago, when she'd been coming off a bad haircut and sporting a moon crater of a cold sore. That had been five months after his wedding and two months before his divorce. Now, three years later, he could still send her on a one-way trip back to sixteen.

"Hotty Toddy, Jake!" Why had she said that—the Ole Miss football battle cry? Neither of them had gone to Ole Miss, though most of their families had. They were fans, of course, but she didn't normally go around saying *Hotty Toddy*.

"Hotty Toddy, Evie. That's good to hear in Roll Tide country."

She stepped from behind the counter and the awkward hug they shared was softened by his laughter. Though she didn't say so, he really did look great—however, in his plaid shorts and pink polo, he looked more like a fraternity boy on spring break than a professional hockey player. Jake's eyes might be his best feature, but he was gorgeous from head to toe. His caramel blond hair was a little shaggy and his tan face clean-shaven.

They came out of the hug and she looked up at him—way up. He was over six feet tall to her barely five feet four.

"It's good to see you, Evie."

Evie, rhymed with *levy.* He'd christened her that—probably because it was easier for a toddler to say than Evans. "Only people from home call me Evie now," she babbled.

He raised one eyebrow and his mouth curved into

a half smile. She'd forgotten about that half smile. "I *am* from home."

He had a point.

"Would you like some pie? I have Mississippi mud." His favorite. The meringue pie with a chocolate pastry crust and layers of dense brownie and chocolate custard was one of her most popular. She glanced around to see if one of the round marble tables was available. Though it was after one o'clock, a few people were still lingering over lunch, but there was a vacant table by the window.

"No, I don't think—" He stopped abruptly and narrowed his eyes. "Yes. I would. Can you sit with me? For just a bit?"

Of course she could. She was queen of this castle. She could do whatever she wanted. But did she want to? Ha! What a stupid question, even to herself.

"Sure." She might still be making cobblers at midnight, but that was nobody else's business. "Joy?" She turned to the girl behind the counter. "I'm going to take a break. Can you bring a slice of Mississippi mud and a glass of milk? And a black coffee for me." She met his eyes. "Unless you've started drinking coffee."

He looked a little pained and she wondered why. "No. I still don't."

He held her chair before sitting himself down in the iron ice cream parlor chair opposite her. What had she been thinking when she'd bought these chairs? Apparently, not that hockey players—let alone this hockey player—would be settling in for pie. He looked like a man at a child's tea party. She laughed a little.

And in that instant, with the sun shining in the window turning his caramel hair golden, Jake came across with a smile that lit up the world. Good thing she'd packed up all those old feelings, right and tight, when he'd gotten involved with her cousin. Her stomach turned over—a muscle memory, no doubt.

"What's funny?" he asked.

"I was thinking I didn't choose these chairs with men in mind."

"You don't think it suits me?" He leaned back a bit. "Maybe you could trade them for some La-Z-Boys."

"Not quite the look I was going for."

He looked around. "So this is your shop? All yours?"

"I have an investor, but yes. It's mine."

She loved the wood floors, the happy fruit-stenciled yellow walls, the gleaming glass cases filled with pies, and the huge wreath on the back wall made of antique pie tins of varying sizes. Five minutes ago, she'd loved the ice cream parlor chairs. She probably would again.

"I knew you had a shop." He looked around. "But I had no idea it was like *this*. So nice."

You might have, if you'd bothered to call me once in a while. Evans bit her tongue as if she'd actually spoken the words and wanted to call them back. Instead, she packed them up and shoved them to the back of her brain. Jake was here. She was glad to see him. That was all.

"I've had some good luck," she said.

His eyes settled on the table next to them. "You serve lunch, too?"

"Nothing elaborate. A choice of two savory pies with a simple green or fruit salad on the side. I would offer you some, but we sold out of the bacon and goat cheese tart and you wouldn't eat the spanakopita."

He frowned. "Spana-who?"

"Spanakopita. Spinach pie."

He shuddered. "No. Not for me, but I'm meeting my teammate Robbie soon for a late lunch anyway." She knew who Robbie was from *The Face Off Grapevine*, a pro hockey gossip blog she sometimes checked. They called him and Jake the Wild-Ass Twins, though they looked nothing alike. For whatever reason, this Robbie was coming to play for the Yellowhammers, too. Jake went on, "He's been in Scotland since the season ended and just got in this morning. We're going to a place down the street."

So I'm only a pit stop. "Hammer Time. Brand-new sports bar for a brand-new team."

He nodded. "I hope Hammer Time is half as nice as your shop. You obviously work really hard."

"I do. But I don't have to do it on skates." She held up her chef clog-clad foot. Why had she said that? Belittled herself?

He laughed like it was the best joke he'd ever heard. Ah, that was why. She'd do anything to make him laugh. She'd forgotten that about herself.

"Here you go, Evans." Joy set down the pie, milk, and a thick, retro mug decorated with cherries like the ones on the wall.

"No pie for you?" Jake picked up his fork.

She sipped her coffee. "No. I taste all day long. The last thing I want is a plateful of pie. Are you sure you want that? Aren't you about to eat lunch?"

"I want this more than I've wanted anything for a

long time." He took a bite and closed his eyes. "Other people only think they've had pie."

If she never got another compliment about another thing, this one would do her until death. "Mississippi mud is a hit in Alabama."

"Don't tell her, but this is so much better than the one from your mother's bakery."

No kidding. Anna-Blair Pemberton was all about a shortcut. "If she'd had her way, I'd be back in Cottonwood, making cookies from mixes and icing cakes with buttercream from a five-gallon tub."

Jake laughed a little under his breath. "My mother might have mentioned that a time or six."

"No doubt." Christine Champagne and Evans's mother were best friends. When Evans had deserted her mother's bakery after graduating from the New Orleans Culinary Institute, it must have given them fodder for months.

"I, for one, am glad you're making pie here." Jake took another bite. "There's something about this… something different. And familiar." He wrinkled his brow. "But I can't place it."

Evans knew exactly what he meant, and it pleased her more than it should have that he'd noticed.

"Do you remember the Mississippi mud bars we used to get when we went to Fat Joe's for tamales?"

"Yes! That's it." He took another bite of pie. "We ate a ton of those things, sitting at that old picnic table outside. Didn't Joe's wife make them?"

"She did. I got her secret and her permission to use it. She used milk and dark chocolate, and she added a little instant coffee to the batter."

He stopped with his fork in midair. "Coffee? There's coffee in here?"

Evans laughed. "You've been eating Lola's for years without knowing." She reached for his plate. "But if you don't want it…"

"Leave my pie alone, woman." He pretended to stab at her with his fork. "Those were good times."

"They were. We did a lot of homework at that picnic table."

He grimaced. "Well, it wasn't the homework I was thinking about. I'd have never passed a math class without you."

"Oh, I don't know about that."

"*I* do." He shook his head and let his eyes wander to the ceiling like he always did when he wanted to change the subject. "What about the beach this summer. How was it?"

The question took Evans aback. Jake hadn't been on the annual Champagne-Pemberton beach trip since Channing came on the scene. She was surprised he even thought about them anymore.

"Sandy. Wet. Salty," she quipped. "Like always."

He grinned. "Must have been a little *too* sandy, wet, and salty for you. I hear you only stayed two days."

"Lots to do around here." She gestured to the shop.

He let his eyes go to a squint and his grin relaxed into that crooked smile. "Too much sorority talk?"

"I swear, it never stops." She slapped her palm against the table. All the women in that beach house—Evans's mother and two older sisters and Jake's mother and younger sister—were proud alumnae of Ole Miss and Omega Beta Gamma, the most revered and exclusive sorority on campus. Addison, Jake's sister, had recently made the ultimate commitment to her Omega sisters by taking a job at the sorority's national headquarters.

Jake took a sip of his milk and chuckled. "I hear you. Especially with rush coming up."

"It's like being in a room full of teachers who won't talk about anything except test scores and discipline problems. You just get tired of it." But it was more than that. Legacy or not, Evans would have never made the Omega cut had she gone to Ole Miss instead of culinary school. She wasn't tall, blond, and sparkly enough. She loved those women—every one of them—but she had always been a little out of step with them. Plus, living with all that sparkle could be hard on the nerves.

Jake laughed. "Well, they have to do their part to keep Omega on top, where it belongs."

"Sorority blood runs deep and thick in Mississippi," Evans said. "Sisters for life."

Jake went from amused to grim. "I don't think Mama and Addison feel very sisterly toward Channing anymore."

Channing had, of course, been the poster child for Omega. "For what it's worth, my mother and sisters don't either." *And I don't feel very cousinly toward her. Not that I ever did.*

He shrugged. "I've moved on—not quite as fast as she did, of course. Miss Mississippi, hockey wife, music producer wife, all in the space of eight months. I suppose you've heard she's pregnant?"

"Yes." The baby would probably have mud-colored

eyes like Mr. Music Producer, when it could have had the bluest eyes in the world. Baffling.

"But I'm better off," Jake went on.

She studied his face and decided he meant it. "I'm glad you know it. You're better than that, Jake. You deserve better."

Jake looked at his pie, and back at her again. "You remembered my favorite pie and that I'm not a coffee drinker?"

Thank goodness for the change of subject. "How could I not remember? You always asked for Mississippi mud pie when you came into the bakery at home."

He took a deep breath. "I'm glad to see you, Evie."

"I'm glad to see *you*," she echoed. And she was. But something was niggling deep in her gut. It seemed Glad and Mad were running around inside her, neither one able to get complete control. She beat back Mad and embraced Glad. It was impossible to control most emotions, but mad wasn't one of them. She had always believed that if you didn't want to be mad, you didn't have to be. So what if he'd only come to see her because Crust was near his lunch spot? They had history. That was what was important. And he'd been through a lot: divorce, Blake's death, a new town and team, and—well, she didn't know what else, but wasn't that enough?

"I probably don't deserve for you to be glad to see me, but I appreciate it." Oh, hell. He was going to try to get negative now, just when she'd talked herself into a good place. She would not allow it. The only thing she was better at than turning out a perfect puff pastry was turning a situation around.

"Why wouldn't I be glad to see you?" She smiled like she meant it, and she did. Everybody always said you had to clear the air before you could move on. As far as she was concerned, that was way overrated. Sometimes it was better to just let it go. Saying yes when others might say no sometimes made life go smoother.

"Let's not pretend I don't owe you an apology." He cocked his head to the side and widened his eyes. What was the point of that? She'd already forgiven him.

"Jake, there is no need for all of this."

"There is. I haven't been the friend to you I should have been. I guess when I met Channing, I didn't think about anything except her and hockey. I know I texted that to you a few months ago, but I wanted to say it in person." He lifted one corner of his mouth. "I did come by before I took Olivia and the kids to Europe, but you weren't here."

"I was in New York."

"I know. Please say you forgive me."

It would have been easier to downplay the whole thing and say it didn't matter. But no one was going to believe that, so she did the next best thing. "It's in the past. Our friendship goes back far and deep. It can withstand a storm or two." The truth of that lightened her heart.

Jake looked relieved, happy even. Maybe she did matter to him. "I shouldn't have let our friendship slip away—let you slip away."

The hair on the back of her neck stood up. *Slip away?* With that, Mad slammed a boxing glove into Glad's face and a foot on to its fallen body.

Why had he had to go and say that? She hadn't
slipped away. She had gone kicking and screaming.
It was true that she hadn't contacted him for a month
after *that Christmas*—the Christmas of Channing—but
wasn't she entitled to that, considering how things went
down? And he damn sure hadn't bothered with her.

Evans had been home from culinary school for the
holidays, and Jake from the University of North Dakota.
They hadn't seen each other since summer, so they'd
filled their plates with Anna-Blair's fancy canapés and
found a corner to catch up—though catching up wasn't
really necessary, because back then they talked and
messaged each other at least three times a week. But
they laughed and talked and she thought she'd finally
seen the spark she'd felt for twenty years reflected in
his eyes. He almost confirmed it when he said, "You
know, Evie, my fraternity spring formal is going to be
in New Orleans, and I was thinking that—"

But she'd never know for absolute certain what he
had been thinking. Maybe he wasn't going to invite her.
Maybe he was only going to ask her for a ride from the
airport or advice about where to get the best gumbo.

Channing's family seldom made the trip from Mem-
phis to Cottonwood and never for Christmas—but they
had that year. And Channing chose that precise moment
to sail in, looking like Vogue and smelling like Chanel.
Or maybe it was Joy. Who the hell knew? It damned
sure wasn't vanilla extract. Whatever it was, Evans
had gotten a good whiff when Channing swooped in
and hugged her—something Evans could never re-
call happening before. Of course, Channing had never
walked in on Evans in conversation with someone who

looked like Jake before either. "Well, cousin, who do you have here?" Channing had asked. Evans had introduced them, and then it was all over but the crying.

And Evans had cried—for a month. But what purpose would it serve to go into all that with Jake? It was over. It didn't matter—except it did. Strange that it only occurred to her now that if Jake had been planning to ask her to the dance, maybe it was because she was going to school in New Orleans anyway—convenient.

"You know, Jake, I didn't slip away." She took down her ponytail and put it back up again. "I didn't go easily." After that month had passed, she'd batted back the humiliation and put on her big girl panties. Still, no matter how many times she'd called or texted, he never had time for her. Even if he answered, he was somewhere else. The next time she'd seen him had been in New Orleans the morning after that dance, when she'd met him and Channing at Brennan's for breakfast. Channing had brought the nosegay of white roses and succulents that Jake had bought her for the dance and held hands with him under the table. Evans had cursed herself for saying yes to that breakfast invitation, when she should have said no. It wasn't the first time, and it wouldn't be the last. "I fought for our friendship."

The moment the words cleared her mouth, she was sorry. He'd apologized. What more did she want? Jake's face went white and he put his fork down. Understandable. He probably didn't want to eat any more of her pie after what she'd said. Why hadn't she just left it alone?

"I'm sorry. I shouldn't have said that," she said hurriedly.

"Why? It's true." There was real hurt on his face.

"Nonetheless. You apologized, and I wasn't gracious about it. And after all you've been through. It's behind us. Let's move forward."

He looked skeptical, but nodded. "That's all I want. And you've been gracious to forgive me at all." Eyes wide. Head cocked. Lip bite. "I'll make it up to you."

He had never, as far as she could remember, had to get to the lip biting with her before. "There's nothing to make up."

He picked up his fork again. "I disagree, though it may not be possible. But I will say this: for a while there, I forgot what was important. After the divorce, I forgot my raising. But after Blake… It made me stop and think. I won't forget again. I'm going to be a better man—a better friend."

He covered her hand with his, and her heart dropped like a fallen star.

"We're good." What was wrong with being convenient anyway?

Then he nodded and smiled like he was pleased. Pleasing Jake Champagne had once been her life's work.

She supposed she was glad she had finally accomplished it.

Don't miss Sweet as Pie, *available now*
from USA TODAY *bestselling author*
Alicia Hunter Pace.

www.CarinaPress.com